The Experts Praise

THE GOOD SPY
By Jeffrey Layton

"The excitement never stops in *The Good Spy* by Jeffrey Layton. Richly detailed and bristling with fascinating political intrigue, the story sweeps between the United States and Moscow as the danger intensifies. This is high adventure at its very best."
—**Gayle Lynds,** *New York Times* bestselling author of *The Assassins*

"An explosive high-stakes thriller that keeps you guessing."
—**Leo J. Maloney,** author of the Dan Morgan thrillers

"Layton spins an international thriller while never taking his eye off the people at the center of the tale. A page-turner with as much heart as brains."
—**Dana Haynes,** author of *Crashers, Breaking Point, Ice Cold Kill,* and *Gun Metal Heart*

"Breathless entertainment—a spy story with heart."
—**Tim Tigner,** bestselling author of *Coercion, Betrayal,* and *Flash*

"A fast-paced adventure that will challenge readers' expectations and take them on a thrilling journey—even to the bottom of the sea. Written with authority, *The Good Spy* is a visceral yet thoughtful read about an unusual pair of adversaries who join forces in an impossible mission."
—**Diana Chambers,** *author of Stinger*

THE FAITHFUL SPY

"An exciting novel launching readers into political and military intrigue... *The Faithful Spy* is the perfect novel for military enthusiasts who enjoy the technicalities of submarine espionage and warfare, and for those who love an unlikely hero. Modern warfare fans will be captivated with the ultra-high-tech military nautical weapons and reconnaissance equipment at the center of the story—from crawler bots, acoustic sensors, nuclear submersibles, and autonomous underwater vehicles, to mini aerial drones that fire nine-millimeter hollow-point bullets..."

—*The Big Thrill*

Books by Jeffrey Layton

The Faithful Spy
The Forever Spy
The Good Spy
Vortex One
Warhead
Blowout

*Published by Kensington Publishing Corporation

The Vigilant Spy

A Yuri Kirov Thriller

Jeffrey Layton

LYRICAL PRESS
Kensington Publishing Corp.
www.kensingtonbooks.com

LYRICAL UNDERGROUND BOOKS are published by

Kensington Publishing Corp.
119 West 40th Street
New York, NY 10018

All Kensington titles, imprints, and distributed lines are available at special quantity discounts for bulk purchases for sales promotion, premiums, fund-raising, educational, or institutional use.

Special book excerpts or customized printings can also be created to fit specific needs. For details, write or phone the office of the Kensington Sales Manager: Kensington Publishing Corp., 119 West 40th Street, New York, NY 10018. Attn. Sales Department. Phone: 1-800-221-2647.

Lyrical Underground and Lyrical Underground logo Reg. U.S. Pat. & TM Off.

First Electronic Edition: May 2020
ISBN-13: 978-1-5161-0559-5 (ebook)
ISBN-10: 1-5161-0559 1 (ebook)

First Print Edition: May 2020
ISBN-13: 978-1-5161-0561-8
ISBN-10: 1-5161-0561-3

Printed in the United States of America

For Cody and Tyler

Chapter 1

The city of nine million woke as first light oozed heavenward from the Yellow Sea. A leaden stratum of vapor rich clouds hovered over the coastal metropolis of Qingdao. Drizzle smeared the windshield as the boat puttered along the one half-mile-long waterway. Its diesel exhaust lingered over the still waters of the harbor.

Along the north flank of the waterway, an immense industrial wharf protruded westward into the embayment. Workboats, barges and fishing vessels occupied assorted floating piers that connected to the dogleg-shaped wharf. At the western terminus of the waterway, an offshore breakwater split the channel, providing north and south navigational passageways to and from the adjacent bay.

Elegant, slender buildings jutted skyward twenty to thirty stories along the channel's southern shore. Lights blinked on as hundreds of the tower residents rose to the new day.

Two men were inside the cabin of the 35-foot workboat as it approached the midpoint of the waterway known as *Zhong Gang*—Middle Harbour. They had patrolled the eastern half of the channel for over an hour, running back and forth, broadcasting the recall signal. The hydrophone hung three feet below the aluminum hull, suspended by a cable secured to a starboard guardrail located amidships.

"It should have surfaced by now," said the slightly built man standing on the starboard side of the cabin. In his early thirties, he wore gray coveralls and work boots. A mop of dense black hair hung over his ears. A cigarette dangled from his left hand.

"Something's wrong," replied the man standing at the helm station. Like his companion, the workboat's captain was of Central Asian lineage. He was several years older, half a head shorter, and thirty pounds heavier than his cohort. A ball cap concealed his balding scalp; a navy blue windbreaker encased his chunky torso.

The observer took another drag from the Furongwang and turned to face his collaborator. "Maybe we should boost the signal. The recorder might be buried deeper in the mud than planned."

"Good idea. Go ahead and turn it to max."

Both men were fluent in Mandarin, but when alone they spoke in their native tongue—an offshoot of Turkic.

The observer relocated to the nearby chart table. A laptop rested on the surface. Yusup Tunyaz fingered the keyboard. "It's now at maximum strength," he reported.

"Okay, I'll make another run." Ismail Sabir spun the steering wheel, turning the boat about.

Ten minutes went by. The boat drifted near the eastern end of the channel.

Ismail peered at the instrument panel display. "GPS says we're over the coordinates that Talgat provided. You see anything?"

"No."

"It should be in this area."

"The recorder must have malfunctioned."

"Maybe."

Yusup crushed the spent butt in an ashtray. "What do you want to do now?"

Ismail's brow wrinkled as he peered through the windshield. The bow pointed westward. The twin wipers were set to cycle at minimum speed. He was about to comment when he noticed a skiff speeding from the bay into the channel's north entrance. Powered by an outboard, it carried five men, all wearing raingear, hardhats, and flotation vests. "We've got visitors."

Using binoculars, Ismail watched as the skiff tied up to an enormous crane barge moored on the north side of the waterway, about two thousand feet away. The crewmen scurried up a ladder and boarded the barge. Within two minutes, a cloud of black soot spewed as a diesel generator powered up.

"Wonder where they're going?" Yusup commented. Both men had noticed the moored marine construction equipment earlier.

"Probably some place for the port. It has all kinds of work going on around here."

"Yeah, that's it."

One of the construction crew boarded a small tugboat tied up to the far side of the crane barge. After starting the engine, the operator engaged the tug's propeller. The tug, still lashed to the barge, began to pull the crane barge away from the pier. Secured to the crane barge on the opposite side was a second steel barge. It was about the same size but with an extra four feet of freeboard.

The tug and double barge combination moved to the center of the channel near the mouth of the Middle Harbour's northern entrance. Instead of heading westward into Jiaozhou Bay, the floating equipment stopped moving. Mammoth steel pylons—spuds—towering fifty feet high on each side of the crane barge were lowered, anchoring the barge to the bottom.

Yusup squinted. "Now what're they doing?"

"I don't know." Ismail set his binocs aside and advanced the throttle, seeking a closer look.

From a hundred yards away, Yusup and Ismail observed the colossal steel truss boom on the crane barge rotate seaward from the deck. A steel bucket the size of a Ford pickup truck, its clamshell jaws wide open, hung over the water suspended by four steel cables that passed through a block at the peak of the towering derrick. The bucket plunged into the water and sank to the bottom. The generator aboard the barge blasted out a fresh exhaust plume as the crane struggled to lift the payload.

"Dammit," muttered Ismail as the revelation registered.

The bucket rose above the water's surface, its jaws clamped tight. The crane operator swung the boom across the deck until the bucket hovered over the companion barge. The jaws opened and twenty-four tons of bottom muck plopped into the dump barge.

"They're dredging the harbor," Yusup said.

"They dug it up. That's why we can't find it."

"There was nothing about this in our orders."

"I know."

"What do we do now?"

"Let me think."

After a five minute search on his smartphone, Ismail found the article. The port authority advertised the project on its website. The Middle Harbour was being dredged to increase water depth for deeper draft vessels to match the newly deepened Jiaozhou Bay navigation channel. That was not an unusual activity for such a sprawling enterprise as the Port of Qingdao.

However, what did not follow the norm for China's state-owned port and harbor facility—one of the busiest in the world—was the disposal of the dredged materials from the commercial waterway. Instead of dumping the spoils offshore in deep water or reusing the sediments as fill to create new dry land, the 150,000 cubic yards of bottom mud from the Middle Harbour was allocated for an environmental mitigation project.

Mimicking projects sponsored by public ports in the United States and Western Europe, China's Ministry of Environmental Protection funded the Port of Qingdao's 'Project Seagrass.' Dredged material from the Middle Harbour formed the core of a new intertidal island located in nearby Jiaozhou Bay. When filling operations ended with a cap of clean sand, the artificial atoll would cover the area of fifteen soccer fields. Later in the year, the mound was scheduled to be planted with patches of eelgrass—*Zostera marina*—transplanted from donor sites. Over several years, project scientists expected the seagrass to propagate, eventually covering most shallow sections of the knoll. By providing protection for fin fish and shellfish and offering a host of nutrients and microorganisms, the underwater eelgrass forest would offer an oasis for marine life within the otherwise degraded industrial harbor.

After digesting the web article, the two men considered their options.

"It's gone," Yusup said as he sucked on another cigarette. "We should just go back to the marina."

"My orders were explicit—recover the recording device at all costs." Ismail remained at the helm.

"Talgat should have known about the dredging project."

"I agree. But still it's my—our problem."

Yusup took a deep drag on the fresh Furongwang. His religion frowned on smoking, but the habit provided good cover for his work. "So," he said, "what do you want to do?"

Ismail stepped to the navigation table. He pushed the laptop aside to view the nautical chart of Jiaozhou Bay. "The website said the disposal site is in this area." He pointed with a finger.

Yusup said, "You think we might be able to recover it at the dump site?"

"Unlikely. That dredge bucket probably destroyed the recorder. But at least we can make a couple of runs with the hydrophone broadcasting the recall signal." Ismail faced his companion. "By checking the dump site, Talgat won't be able to blame us for not completing the mission."

"Good plan. Let's go."

* * * *

After a thirty minute run across the bay, the workboat slowed to a crawl. Hundreds of rice paddies lined the muddy shore to the north. Southward, a sleek modern bridge dominated the skyline. One of the world's longest bridges over open water, the Jiaozhou Bay Bridge spanned a distance greater than the width of the English Channel between Dover and Calais. Ismail and Yusup watched the depth sounder. Built into the instrument panel, the device displayed a profile of the bottom depth.

"This must be the right area," Ismail said. "It's definitely shallower here, just a meter and a half deep."

"Probably exposed at low tides."

"Drop the hydrophone overboard and let's see if we get a response."

"Okay."

After passing over the shallow zone, the workboat idled; it drifted westward with the quarter knot current. Both men scanned the water around the boat, each hoping the lost recorder would magically pop up to the surface.

"I don't see anything," Yusup announced.

"Neither do I."

"Are we done?"

"Let's make one more run then we'll go."

"All right."

It was a fateful decision. Had the two men from China's Xinjiang Uyghur Autonomous Region started their return trip after the initial pass, they would have survived. But their lifespan was now limited to seconds.

The object the boat crew searched for was buried in bottom sediments about fifty yards away. The Uyghur dissidents believed they were searching for an acoustic recording device used to spy on the Qingdao Naval Base, located just north of the Port of Qingdao's Middle Harbour. It was a lie fed to them by their Russian handler, cover name Talgat. Unknown to Ismail and Yusup, their hydrophone was actually signaling a bomb.

Designed to resist hydrostatic seawater pressure to a depth of over three thousand feet and endure subzero freezing conditions as well as function in temperatures exceeding the boiling point of water, the weapon survived dredging. It lay in wait at the bottom of the bay.

Entombed within the excavated sediment, the audio receiver inside the warhead compartment listened for the command signal. The three feet of mud over the cylindrical steel casing degraded reception significantly. But as the workboat approached, the digital signal from the hydrophone penetrated the muck. Recognizing the acoustic command, the bomb's electrical firing circuit triggered the detonators embedded in the concentric lenses of plastic explosive that surrounded the core. The semtex charges exploded, compressing the tennis ball sized hollow sphere of uranium-235 to the size of a grape. A microsecond later, the nuclear weapon detonated.

Chapter 2

Day 1—Wednesday

It was great to be home. Absent for over six weeks, Yuri Kirov relaxed alone on the spacious deck. Perched at the crest of the suburban hillside east of Seattle, the 5,000 square foot contemporary had a fabulous view of Lake Sammamish. Water skiers towed by high-powered runabouts blazed across the azure lake waters as the sun retreated.

Yuri took a long pull from the chilled bottle of Redhook Big Ballard IPA, his second of the afternoon. After arriving home an hour earlier, he had changed into a tank top and a pair of cargo shorts. Ray-Bans covered his slate-gray eyes and sandals encased his feet. A strapping six-footer with jet-black hair and a rugged square-jawed face, 31-year-old Yuri Ivanovich Kirov was a fine-looking man.

As Yuri reclined on the lounge chair, he luxuriated in the warmth of the sun. It was the end of August and it wouldn't be long before the dreary rainy season returned. He tolerated the damp. Compared to the bleak winters of frozen Russia, the Puget Sound region's wet, temperate climate was a blessing.

Yuri took a final swallow of the beer and set the bottle on the deck beside the other empty. He settled into the lounge chair's back cushion. Utterly exhausted, all he wanted for the time being was a nap.

* * * *

"Yuri...Yuri, wake up!"

Yuri had been asleep for nearly an hour when awakened. "Hi, sweetie," he said, addressing his lover and best friend who stood at the foot of the chair. He never tired of looking at Laura Newman.

The professional pantsuit and sheer silk blouse that Laura wore flattered her sleek five foot eight frame. A striking blend of Scandinavia and Africa, she had inherited her Swedish mother's high cheekbones, full ripe lips, azure eyes, and russet hair. Her father's tall willowy frame and cocoa skin, all linked to his distant Bantu ancestors, complemented Laura's birth mother's genes.

"How was work today?" Yuri asked.

"You haven't heard, have you?" Laura cast a stern, anxious look. She was two years older than Yuri. Adopted as an infant, she was raised by a Caucasian couple in northern California.

"What's going on?"

"Something's happened in China. I heard about it on my car radio when driving home." Laura glowered. "An explosion. Very large."

"In Qingdao?!"

"Yes."

"Govnó!"—shit, muttered Yuri.

"Let's go inside. I already turned on the TV. It's on just about every news channel."

Yuri and Laura scrutinized the kitchen television. Tuned to a network news channel, the wall-mounted screen displayed the image of a male correspondent. He provided an update:

"We have just confirmed with a source at the Pentagon that the explosion in Qingdao, China was from a nuclear device. The detonation occurred about an hour ago. It's Thursday morning in China at this time.

"No damage reports have been issued yet but thousands could have been killed and wounded."

The television screen flashed to a Google Earth image that displayed a bird's eye view of Qingdao. The correspondent continued his report. "Qingdao is a seaport city, one of the busiest in China. It was the host city for sailboat racing during the 2008 Summer Olympics.

"The location of the detonation is unknown at this time and our efforts to contact the Chinese government for comment have been fruitless. China has issued a state of emergency, shutting down all internet activity and curtailing international communications. The government also closed all Chinese stock exchanges.

"Our calls to the White House regarding the U.S. defense posture have not yet been returned. However, we have some indication of what might be happening at the Pentagon right now."

The television switched back to a split screen with the correspondent and another individual. The retired U.S. Air Force four-star general was introduced. The news anchor said, "General, please provide our viewers with your thoughts on the dire events in China."

"Well, it's really too early to know what happened other than some type of nuclear device was detonated in Qingdao. The yield of the weapon . . ."

Yuri muted the television. He massaged his brow while leaning against the kitchen counter.

"This is horrible," Laura said. "Do you think it had anything to do with the mission you were on?"

"I'm sure it did. The device planted in Qingdao was similar to what was left behind at Pearl Harbor."

Laura looked down at the hardwood flooring. "The FBI must not have believed you."

"I'm afraid so."

For five days, Yuri was grilled around the clock by a squad of U.S. government representatives from the FBI, CIA and the Department of Defense. During the interrogations, Yuri warned that Russian commandos might have left a nuclear bomb in China.

Yuri walked to the refrigerator and opened the freezer compartment. He removed the bottle of Stolichnaya. After locating a shot glass in a cupboard, he poured the chilled vodka into the glass. He downed the alcohol in a single gulp.

Laura was on instant alert. *Oh, no!* Yuri rarely touched hard liquor, preferring beer and usually just a couple per week. She opened a cabinet and grabbed a package of crackers. She slid the container across the counter.

"Thanks," Yuri said as he opened the packet and munched on a saltine.

Laura was familiar with the Russian ritual.

Yuri poured a second shot. He hammered it back and chewed another cracker. He made no offer for Laura to join him, knowing she did not care for vodka.

"When will Maddy and Amanda be home?" Yuri asked.

Laura glanced at her wristwatch. "Soon."

Laura's one-year-old daughter and her twenty-six-year-old nanny spent the afternoon at a children's animal farm in nearby Redmond. Discreetly following the pair was a two person FBI security detail.

"Good," Yuri said. He poured a third shot, gulped it and consumed another cracker. He returned the bottle to the refrigerator.

Laura did not comment on Yuri's uncharacteristic action, praying it was nothing more than a consequence of stress. She recognized all of the warning signs—her ex was an abusive alcoholic.

Yuri picked up the TV remote and clicked to another channel. He turned up the volume. The comely female reporter in New York City said, "We just received cell phone video of the explosion."

The screen switched to a fuzzy image of a classic nuclear mushroom cloud, a broiling brownish-black mass rising into the overcast sky. Shot from miles away overlooking a vast cityscape, it was not possible to determine the extent of damage.

"Oh, dear Lord," Laura whispered.

Yuri's stomach flip-flopped, aided by the sizzling Stoli. He managed to suppress the urge to vomit but a veil of guilt engulfed his well-being. *Thousands may have been killed—and I was part of it!*

Chapter 3

While Yuri returned to the same lounge chair on the deck, Laura tended to the kitchen stove. The string beans in the steam pot were almost ready. Thick salmon filets from Costco broiled inside the right-hand oven of the professional grade stainless steel gas range.

As Laura retrieved the internal container from the steamer, she heard the front door open. Amanda Graham strolled into the kitchen with Maddy riding her right hip.

"Hi, Laura," Amanda said. A cute brunette with bangs, she was slightly overweight for her five foot four height.

Laura turned. "How was the farm?"

"Great. We had fun, didn't we Maddy?"

Laura's daughter beamed, her trademark dimpled cheeks in full bloom. Madelyn Grace Newman had ash blond hair, sapphire eyes and fair skin. Laura's ex-husband was the child's biological father, but Yuri treated Madelyn as his own—a blessing Laura cherished.

Amanda lowered Madelyn Grace to the floor where she rushed to her mother. Laura reached down and scooped up her daughter. "Hi sweetie pie. What animals did you see today?" Laura asked as she stroked Maddy's angel soft hair.

"Goats and piggies."

Articulate for just over a year old, Maddy already had an impressive vocabulary.

As Laura and Madelyn conversed, Amanda spotted the muted TV. A pair of talking heads jabbered silently while a looped video of the mushroom cloud played in the background.

"What happened?" Amanda asked.

"Nuclear explosion in China."

"Oh my God!" Amanda took in the images. "Do they know how it happened?"

Laura reached for the remote and restored the sound. Amanda stepped closer to the television to hear the latest news.

Laura had just taken the salmon out of the oven when a cell phone announced its presence in the adjacent living room. The tone was distinctive—a shrill, high-pitched tone. It was the special phone the FBI gave Yuri.

Laura picked up the phone and answered. "Hello."

"Who am I speaking to?" asked the female caller.

"You know who this is. Now who are you?"

"Ms. Newman, this is Special Agent Michaela Taylor. We met on Sunday. Please give this phone to Mr. Kirkwood. We know he's home." John Kirkwood was Yuri's cover name.

"Just a minute."

Laura stepped onto the deck; she carried the cell but had muted the caller function. Yuri was again stretched out on the lounge chair. "Yuri, there's a call for you—on the special phone."

"Who is it?"

"Taylor."

"Hmmm."

"She must be calling about China."

"No doubt."

Laura unmuted the phone and handed it to Yuri.

Holding the phone next to an ear, he said, "Hello, agent Taylor."

Laura listened to the one-sided call.

"Yes, it's all over the news.

"Tonight?

"All right. I'll be ready."

Yuri switched off the phone and inserted it into a pocket of his shorts.

"What does she want?"

"They want to meet with me about Qingdao. They're sending a driver to pick me up in forty-five minutes." Yuri stood. "I need to shower and change clothes."

"Okay, but I have dinner ready for you now. You should eat before meeting with them."

"Sounds good."

Laura followed Yuri back into the house. He was steady on his feet but she could tell the alcohol had taken its toll. Dog-tired when he was finally released yesterday, Yuri was spent. The FBI had promised they would let him relax for the rest of the week before resuming the debrief.

Laura's worry quotient spiked knowing Yuri's delicate liaison with the American government, as well as her own predicament with the U.S. Justice Department, remained hanging in the balance.

I better make him a pot of coffee, too!

Chapter 4

The conference room was spacious, at least three times larger than the interview room Yuri Kirov occupied earlier in the week. The mahogany table could seat twenty but this evening it was just Yuri and three others. FBI Special Agent Michaela Taylor sat on his right side. In her late thirties, Taylor's jet-black hair brushed her shoulders. The Ann Taylor pantsuit with matching jacket she wore flattered her shapely figure.

Michaela was part of a four-person team that had interrogated Yuri for nearly twenty-six hours, spread over three days. During the debrief, he was confined to a holding cell at the FBI's field office in downtown Seattle. Prior to the Seattle questioning, the Navy had grilled him for two days at Joint Base Pearl Harbor-Hickman.

Two additional members of the interrogation team sat on the opposite side of the table. U.S. Navy Captain Robert Clark and CIA Counterintelligence officer Steve Osberg.

Clark was in his late forties. A bit stocky for his five-foot eight height, he was not in uniform. He wore tan slacks and a short sleeved polo shirt. His straight nose, high cheekbones and round firm chin personified his image as a distinguished senior military officer, marred only by the receding hairline of his salt and pepper mane.

Osberg was the oldest in the room at fifty-six. His lush, slightly grayed blond hair, Nordic facial features, and sleek, tall frame suggested a younger man. He wore designer blue jeans with a navy-blue blazer.

Michaela checked her wristwatch: 7:09 P.M. "The conference will commence in about a minute," she announced.

All in attendance turned toward the wall-mounted home theater sized screen at the far end of the conference table. The FBI logo filled the screen.

When the logo disappeared, the view of another conference room appeared. A dozen were seated around the table in the FBI Headquarters Building in Washington, D.C. Nearest to the video camera was Supervisory Special Agent Ava Diesen—the fourth member of Yuri's original interrogation team. In her mid-forties, the mother of three had sandy blond hair. Diesen retained her youthful form by regular jogging and, when her scheduled allowed, attending Jazzercize at a mall outlet near her Fairfax home. She had returned to the east coast the previous evening.

"Good evening," Diesen said, addressing the Seattle contingent. She spent the next minute introducing the FBI Headquarters participants, which included the assistant FBI director and the executive assistant directors for the National Security Branch, Intelligence Branch, Science and Technology Branch, Information Technology Branch, and the Criminal, Cyber, Response and Services Branch.

Michaela Taylor made the Seattle introductions.

With the preliminaries concluded, Ava Diesen kicked off the meeting, directing her comments to the Seattle audience. "As you all know by now, a nuclear weapon detonated in China today at the city of Qingdao. It exploded about three hours ago. The director will be meeting with the president and the National Security Council later this evening. The purpose of our meeting is to provide the director with our assessment of the event." SSA Diesen peered directly into the video camera. "Because of Mr. Kirov's association with the similar event that occurred in Honolulu last week, we believe there is a direct connection to what happened at Qingdao."

Ava turned to a nearby aide and issued a request. The video screen in Seattle changed to a color aerial photograph. Yuri recognized the image. Less than a month earlier, he had conducted an underwater espionage mission for the Russian Navy at China's Qingdao Naval Base.

Ava continued, "This is a satellite image of Qingdao recorded yesterday. The city has a population of just over nine million and is one of the world's busiest ports. It also has..."

Yuri squirmed in his seat. *I warned these people that this could happen. They didn't believe me.*

* * * *

Five thousand four hundred miles across the Pacific from Seattle and fifteen time zones ahead, the Central Military Commission of the People's Republic of China met in a secure underground facility northeast of

Beijing. It was 10:18 A.M. The CMC was responsible for the command and control of the People's Liberation Army. The PLA was China's armed forces, which consisted of five branches: Ground (Army) Force, Air Force, Navy, Rocket Force and Strategic Support Force.

Several hours earlier, the Commission's assembly of military officers and government officials were whisked from their Beijing offices and residences to the bunker by a caravan of vehicles—armored Mercedes Benz sedans and Range Rover SUVs. The entire sixty-mile route from city center to the CMC's emergency operations center was underground. For the past twenty years, the PLA constructed a 5,000-mile-long military tunnel system across the vast nation. The network allowed the PLA to transfer troops, weapons and equipment to key areas within China undetected by spy satellites and without notice by its citizens. The maze of passages and caverns, bored through rock hundreds of feet below the surface also housed most of China's land based nuclear forces. Mobile launchers with nuclear tipped ICBMs could race to the surface launch sites in tunnels at up to sixty miles an hour.

The Commission had been in session for thirty minutes. Configured to duplicate the layout of the CMC's war room at the Ministry of Defense headquarters building in Beijing, twenty-one individuals occupied a U-shaped table within the subterranean chamber. All but four attendees wore uniforms. A mammoth flat panel screen was mounted on a wall opposite the open end of the table. A satellite image of the northeastern coast of China filled the display.

The CMC Vice Chairman Admiral Soo Xiao stood at the lectern next to the screen. He also served as Chief of Staff of the People's Liberation Army-Navy. At fifty-eight, Soo was the eldest in the room. He maintained a trim build that reflected regular exercise, healthy eating habits, moderate drinking and complete disdain for cigarette smoke.

Admiral Soo clicked the remote he held and a new image materialized on the screen. He turned toward the occupant at the center of the table. "Comrade President, this is a series of photos of the event. They were recorded by one of our weather satellites. The images are high altitude and wide range." He turned back to the screen. "This photograph was recorded about ten minutes before the blast." Soo used the laser pointer on the remote to highlight a metropolitan area along the coast of the Yellow Sea. "Qingdao is right here." He advanced to the next image. "This one is less than a minute from the event."

The third image appeared on the screen. A brilliant flash dominated the upper center quadrant of the photo. Gasps and mumblings erupted from the audience.

Soo said, "Obviously, this was the instant of detonation." He moved to the next slide. The new image revealed a circular brownish black smudge near the shoreline. "This shows the debris cloud rising into the atmosphere from Jiaozhou Bay. Preliminary analysis of the blast indicates the weapon had an explosive yield of around eight kilotons of TNT—about half of the power of the Hiroshima bomb."

Soo presented the final slide in the sequence. "Here, you can see that the wind is pushing the plume toward the southeast across the bay, toward the ocean."

"Is it still heading out to sea?" asked China's president. Fifty-six-year-old Chen Shen also served as Chairman of the Central Military Commission, General Secretary of the Communist Party and was the first ranked member of the Politburo Standing Committee. An inch over six feet with a husky build, Chen was the tallest in the room. He wore his profuse, jet-black hair long, hanging over his ears and brushing the collar of his suit jacket.

"Yes, sir. The breeze continues to flow toward the southeast."

"Damage estimate?"

"That's still underway but it appears minimal." Admiral Soo clicked on a new slide, an oblique aerial view of Qingdao centering on Jiaozhou Bay. "This photo was recorded forty minutes ago by one of our naval reconnaissance aircraft. The bomb exploded in the water, not on shore." He lased a portion of the bay halfway between the shoreline and the Jiaozhou Bay Bridge. "The bridge is the only nearby structure, about three kilometers away. It's intact and appears to have only suffered minor thermal damage from the blast, mainly peeled paint."

"What about casualties?" asked President Chen

"No fatalities so far. A couple of trucks were knocked over on the bridge and numerous automobile wrecks. Some of the accident victims also have retinal damage from the nuclear flash. The bridge was busy when it detonated but would have been packed within an hour."

Another slide appeared. "This is a closeup of the blast zone. The crater is visible just beneath the water surface here." He circled the brownish-white blemish of the emerald green waters with the laser pointer. "It's about 160 meters in diameter. We don't know the depth yet but expect it's twenty to thirty meters deep."

"What about radiation?" asked a PLA general sitting to the left of the president.

"Teams are currently taking measurements throughout the city, especially downwind from the blast. I'll know more in an hour. However, measurements taken on the bridge by first responders reported whole-body radiation exposure readings of fifty to one hundred rem."

"That's high," the same general said. "What about the residential areas in the fallout zone?" The PLA general's parents lived in an apartment in the Badaxia Residential District of Qingdao. The home had a delightful view of the Yellow Sea.

"The entire area in the fallout zone is being evacuated. Everyone should be out by noon."

"Good, thank you."

Admiral Soo answered several additional questions and was about to sum up his presentation when President Chen pushed his chair away from the table a couple of inches. He reached into a jacket pocket and pulled out a pack of Marlboros. His minions waited in silence as he lit up, accustomed to Chen's addiction to nicotine. After taking a deep drag he said, "Well, Admiral, who the hell did this to us?"

* * * *

The Seattle-D.C. video conference ended five minutes earlier. Yuri was still seated at the conference table in the FBI Seattle field office along with the other three participants. Yuri was drained. Most of the questions from headquarters were directed to him.

Michaela Taylor took a swig from her water bottle and looked Yuri's way. "I don't know if it would have made much difference if we had been able to warn Beijing like you recommended. Other than radiation and water wave damage, the blast damage appears minimal, almost like it was a warning."

"I don't buy that," Yuri said. "Somehow the weapon was moved. The *Spetsnaz* divers would not have had time to go to that location from where we locked out from the minisub."

U.S. Navy Captain Bob Clark responded. "I agree with Yuri. Something's off. We know the nuke at Pearl Harbor targeted the *Roosevelt*. And with the Chinese blaming us for what happened to their Yulin base, our reaction to the Pearl Harbor attack could have easily resulted in a tit for tat response, like nuking the Qingdao Naval Base." Clark glanced at the navigation chart of Jiaozhou Bay laid out on the table. "From what Yuri told us, we know the Russians were behind the Yulin e-bomb attack and the attempt on Pearl Harbor. They also conducted espionage operations in Jiaozhou Bay, including the Qingdao Naval Base." Clark pointed to the chart. "The bomb detonating in mudflats just doesn't compute for me."

CIA officer Steve Osberg commented next. "Maybe the Russians got cold feet after Yuri foiled the Pearl Harbor op. Decided to move the weapon out of harm's way as a limited response. Something they think we might do for trying to take out Pearl—a very big warning shot across the PRC's bow."

"That does kind of make sense to me," Michaela Taylor said. "The bomb planted in Hawaii did explode, but in deep water with minimal impact." She smiled at Yuri. "The Chinese might take it as a warning like Steve suggested."

Yuri suppressed a yawn, exhausted—the alcohol he'd consumed earlier didn't help either. "I'm Russian. None of you are. What happened in Qingdao today was half-assed. That's the term I think you use. The Kremlin does not operate like that. Either the Qingdao Naval Base would have been incinerated or the weapon would have been removed."

"So, what happened?" Captain Clark asked.

"I don't know...but something's not right."

Michaela took over, addressing Osberg. "Sounds like the CIA needs to do some research on what's been going on in Qingdao. Maybe your analysts can figure out how the bomb was moved." She placed a finger on the chart. "Yuri estimated the divers placed the device in this area of the base." Michaela wavered as the new thought snapped into focus. "Hey, what about this—someone found the bomb, recognized what it was, and then transported it from the base so it would explode in the water. Like what Yuri did at Pearl Harbor."

Before Yuri could respond, Captain Clark reacted. "If that were the case Michaela, they would have taken the bomb offshore into deep water, away from the city." He used a pencil to trace the route on the nav chart. "The ocean is closer to the base than where it went off in the bay."

"Damn," muttered Michaela.

* * * *

Yuri Kirov was in the passenger seat of the Subaru Outback. FBI Special Agent Michaela Taylor was behind the wheel of her personal vehicle. They were eastbound on the I-90 floating bridge crossing Lake Washington.

When the briefing concluded, Michaela offered to drive Yuri to his home in Sammamish; she lived in nearby Issaquah. It was 9:57 P.M.

Irritated, Yuri said. "I still don't understand why Washington didn't warn Beijing about the bomb threat."

Michaela said, "The State Department was in the process of arranging a meeting with the Chinese ambassador when the Qingdao bomb went off."

"All they had to do was make a phone call."

"I know but certain protocols had to be followed for this situation."

Yuri stared out the window in silence. The lights of Mercer Island were approaching.

After another mile, Michaela reengaged Yuri. "I know this has been a tough process for you and Laura, but I want you to know that we're all truly grateful for what you did in Hawaii. You saved thousands." She turned briefly toward Yuri. "I just wish you could be publicly honored."

"Thanks, but I don't need it. All Laura and I want is to be left alone."

"I understand," Michaela said as the Outback traveled eastward. She decided not to pursue the topic further. Yuri's request for political asylum was in fast-track mode at the State Department. An order granting Laura Newman broad immunity for her actions involving Yuri's espionage activities in the United States was also ready for the U.S. Attorney General's signature. However, both matters were contingent on Yuri's agreement to assist the American intelligence community for the next three years. He had not yet consented.

The Outback crossed into Bellevue, still on I-90. Yuri broached a new subject. "When will you be removing the equipment from inside our home?"

"The techs are scheduled to come out on Friday."

"Good. What time? I want to observe."

"I'll get that time for you."

"Okay."

While Yuri was on his special mission in East Asia—serving as an intelligence officer for the Russian Navy, the FBI had secretly installed video and audio devices inside the Sammamish home owned by Laura Newman. The surveillance was authorized by a federal court as part of an effort to trap Yuri. When he finally returned home, Laura told him about her run in with the FBI and her suspicions about cameras. Yuri had located three devices but suspected more were hidden inside the residence.

Yuri changed subjects. "How long have you been with the FBI?"

"Twelve years. Before that I was a detective with the Minneapolis PD. Investigated ID theft, ransomware stuff, bank hacks, digital forensics."

"Computer crimes?"

"Yes, I have a degree in computer science—cyber security. I really enjoyed the work and that's what helped me get into the FBI."

Michaela made a lane change, preparing to exit the freeway in Issaquah to drive north to Sammamish. After revealing a smidgen of her history, she decided to probe further into Yuri's background. "Does your dad still live in Moscow?"

"Yes, but we haven't talked for a while."

Special Agent Taylor had read Yuri's CIA file on numerous occasions. Retired Russian Army Colonel Ivan Kirov resided in Moscow. An alcoholic, the senior Kirov lived alone in a one bedroom apartment on the southwest outskirts of the Russian capital. He and Yuri were not close. Yuri's mother died when he was twelve years old. Colonel Kirov had avoided home, preferring a field assignment during the awful six months it took Irina to succumb to ovarian cancer.

Michaela said, "If you don't mind me asking, how did you happen to join the navy?"

"My grandfather, my mother's father, was in the Navy. After Mom died, I spent several summers with him in Saint Petersburg. We'd spend a lot of time at the naval facilities in the area. Early in his career he was a submarine officer. I loved to listen to his stories about the missions he went on."

Unknown to Yuri, the CIA file had a section on his maternal grandfather Semyon Nikolayevich Fedorov who rose to the rank of Vice Admiral. Thanks to Fedorov's position and Yuri's aptitude, Yuri attended the Nakhimov secondary school in Saint Petersburg. He next entered the Higher Naval Submarine School located on the Saint Petersburg Naval Base campus for five years of officer training. Admiral Fedorov died during Yuri's fourth year at the academy.

"I understand Saint Petersburg is quite beautiful," Michaela said.

"It is. And much friendlier than Moscow."

Twelve minutes later, Special Agent Taylor drove down the private drive and stopped in the parking court next to the Newman residence.

As Yuri opened the passenger door, he said, "Thanks for taking me home. I enjoyed our conversation."

"My pleasure. Try to get some rest."

"I plan to. Good night."

"Good night."

Michaela followed the driveway back to the public street. She admired Yuri Kirov but worried about his welfare. Headquarters pressed Michaela to bring him aboard. During the drive she'd been tempted to remind Yuri that he needed to make a decision. In the end, she decided to wait. He really had no choice in the matter. One way or other, Yuri Kirov was destined to spy for the U.S. government.

Chapter 5

Yuri Kirov sat at his office desk. None of the other two dozen employees at Northwest Subsea Dynamics had yet showed up for work. He slept poorly and woke early—residual stress from the previous evening's meeting with the FBI. He left the house a few minutes after six o'clock. NSD was a fifteen minute drive away, situated in an office park in the city of Redmond.

The company designed and manufactured cutting edge autonomous underwater vehicles—AUVs. NSD employed the underwater robots to map the ocean depths, conduct geophysical surveys and monitor environmental conditions.

Yuri made a brief appearance at the office the day before, spending an hour with the staff during the afternoon. He'd been absent for a month and a half. Everyone at NSD knew he had been in Denmark, attending to his cancer plagued sister. It was a lie that he concocted and Laura perpetuated.

Using the alias of John Kirkwood, Yuri served as the general manager. Laura purchased controlling interest of the company as an investment. But she really acquired NSD for Yuri, knowing he could use his underwater engineering skills to help turn around the struggling business.

Yuri had just reviewed a company profit and loss report on his PC when he heard a door open in the hallway outside his office. Footsteps resonated on the tile flooring. Yuri recognized the gait.

A short and rotund individual entered the open doorway of Yuri's office. He held a paper cup with a Starbucks logo. "Morning," Bill Winters said. "Have a seat."

Winters settled into a chair fronting Yuri's desk. He was forty-eight, the senior NSD employee. Winters was a co-founder of the company. The four original partners, all former NOAA engineers and scientists, created remarkable underwater robotic machines. But like so many startups, NSD burned through its cash reserves. After exhausting personal savings and repeatedly striking out with angel investors, NSD was about to fold when rescued.

Bill Winters kept his 25 percent interest while his partners cashed out. Laura appointed Yuri as general manager; Winters retained his chief engineer position.

Winters took a taste of his café mocha and said, "I'm sure glad you're back. It's been like a three-ring circus since you left. We've got a huge backlog of work."

"I'm indebted to you for taking over for me." Yuri gestured to the Dell monitor on his desk. "I've been reviewing the latest P and L report. It's terrific, best ever. Laura is thrilled."

Winters beamed while running a hand through his shaggy mop of graying blond hair. "Thanks. I really appreciate hearing that."

They discussed company finances for ten minutes before moving on to Alaska.

"So," Yuri said, "I gather it's still a difficult situation in the Chukchi."

"It is but there's been some improvement since you left. It appears that most of the contaminated pack ice has melted, allowing recovery operations to proceed full throttle."

NSD was under contract with the U.S. Coast Guard to monitor a mammoth oil spill in the Chukchi Sea offshore of Barrow, Alaska. An oil well blowout in nearby Russian territorial waters during the winter had contaminated large swaths of the Arctic with crude oil. For the past several months NSD's autonomous underwater vehicles had kept track of the oil laden ice that reached Alaskan waters.

"That's encouraging," Yuri said. "Can they get it cleaned up before the freeze starts?"

"I doubt it. A lot of the oil has washed up on beaches. Hundreds of miles of shoreline are contaminated from Barrow to Kotzebue Sound. I don't think enough time is left to clean it up. After the fall freeze up, the whole mess could start over again next spring."

Yuri and Winters transitioned to NSD's other Alaska operation.

"*Deep Guardian* is doing a bang-up job for the Aurora tract," Winters reported. "It's just as reliable as *Deep Explorer*, maybe even a little better."

Deep Guardian and *Deep Explorer* were autonomous underwater vehicles. *Deep Explorer* was NSD's flagship machine. It was the principal AUV assigned to monitor the Russian oil spill in the Chukchi Sea.

"That's good to hear," Yuri said. "If *Deep Guardian* works out for Aurora, I think the Canadians and Norwegians will be interested."

Deep Guardian was NSD's latest autonomous underwater vehicle. It was currently surveying a huge bottom tract of the Chukchi Ridge north of Barrow. Still covered by pack ice, the 20,000-acre tract was leased from the U.S. government by a Houston based company. Preliminary geophysical surveys hinted that the Chukchi Plateau, located in deep waters near the limit of the United States' Arctic Ocean continental shelf claim, held enormous hydrocarbon reserves. *Deep Guardian's* innovative sonar and photographic systems coupled with its new geophysical testing equipment and extended under ice endurance capability were all well suited for surveying the site.

"I agree with you," Winters said. "I've already had an inquiry from Equinor. Apparently, they've been following the Aurora work."

"Wow, that's encouraging."

"It is and I've been thinking about our future a lot. The company does well with our survey work and we should focus on it." Winters shifted in his chair. "But maybe we should consider branching out now."

Yuri cocked his head, curious.

Bill Winters said, "I think we should create a manufacturing division and start selling individual units adapted for specific purposes: hydrographic, geophysical and environmental monitoring...plus, one other."

"Military?" Yuri guessed.

"Yes, that alone has huge potential." Winters grinned, clearly pumped. "I've run some preliminary numbers and . . ."

Yuri spent half an hour with Bill going over the expansion plan. What Winters recommended made logical business sense. The potential for exponential growth was legitimate, especially in the defense sector. But that aspect troubled Yuri.

How could he run a company that sells cutting-edge high-tech underwater equipment to the U.S. Department of Defense and function as a spy for the FBI and CIA at the same time?

Chapter 6

Day 3—Friday

It was early evening in the Kremlin. The three men met in a conference room adjacent to the president's office, sitting around an oak table once used by Czar Nicholas I. Tea was just served and the steward dismissed. Meeting with the president were the directors of two of the Russian Federation's key intelligence agencies—the FSB and the SVR.

"What happened in China?" asked President Pyotr Lebedev. The Russian leader was fifty-six. Shorter than most heads of state, he compensated with a robust build, maintained by a regimen of vigorous daily exercise including weightlifting. His russet hair was thick with hints of gray.

"Somehow the weapon was moved from where the divers placed it." General Ivan Golitsin directed the Federal Security Service—*Federal'naya Sluzhba Bezopasnosti*. The FSB was Russia's FBI—and then some. Sixty years old with thinning hair, sagging jowls and a stocky frame, Golitsin wore a business suit today rather than his uniform.

"How could that have happened?" asked Lebedev.

Golitsin raised his hands. "We don't know. The agents sent to activate the device were not under the rein of the FSB." He faced the man sitting on the opposite side of the table. "They were run by Borya's people."

Borya Smirnov expected the deflected question. "The two Uyghur operatives were run by one of our deep cover agents in Tianjin. He directed the Uyghurs to recall the weapon using the coordinates provided by the divers—Ivan's people. Obviously, the Uyghur's deviated from their orders." In his early fifties, Smirnov wore a custom tailor-made summer ensemble that complemented his lanky frame. With stylish blond hair, azure eyes and a chiseled face, he was the best looking of the trio—by a long measure.

Smirnov served as the director of the *Sluzhba Vneshney Razvedki*. The SVR was the successor to the former First Chief Directorate of the KGB. Responsible for foreign intelligence operations, the SVR functioned as Russia's CIA.

Agitated by the dueling intelligence chiefs, President Lebedev said, "Why would they have transferred the bomb from the harbor into the bay? That makes no sense to me."

General Golitsin responded, "Sir, they were never supposed to even touch the device. Once the recall signal was transmitted by the hydrophone, the bomb should have detonated instantly."

"So, what happened to them?" Lebedev directed his question to the SVR director.

"At this point, we suspect that they may have been taken out by the bomb...as was originally intended."

"But at the wrong location."

Smirnov nodded.

"What about your agent?" Lebedev asked referring to Talgat.

"No contact from him. He was obviously spooked by the bomb going off."

"He didn't know?"

"No sir."

The president rubbed his neck, obviously frustrated. "I can't believe how screwed up this whole operation has turned out. The bomb in Hawaii exploded offshore in the ocean followed by the fiasco in Qingdao. The plan you two hatched has turned to shit." Lebedev focused on Golitsin. "What have you learned about the Hawaii situation?"

The FSB General sank into his chair, expecting the rebuke. The two operators sent by spy sub to both Qingdao and Honolulu were his people. To conceal the real purpose of their mission from the submarine's crew, the men masqueraded as *Spetsnaz* operators—naval commandos. They were charged with installing underwater espionage gear at Chinese and American naval bases. In reality, the men were part of an elite unit designated OSNAZ, an abbreviation for *osobovo naznacheniya*—special purpose detachment. The OSNAZ team was part of a *Delfin* or Dolphin combat diver unit operating from St. Petersburg. Although designated military units, OSNAZ *Delfins* bypassed the normal Ministry of Defense chain of command. They reported to the FSB director who in turn, had a direct line to the president of the Russian Federation.

General Golitsin said, "Mr. President, our source at the Pearl Harbor base has confirmed that a submerged sensor detected our divers, probably when they made their exit. Apparently, some type of underwater drone was deployed by the Americans. It followed the trails left by the divers' transport machines, small furrows in the bottom created by propeller wash, to where the bomb was placed."

"That should never have happened, General."

"I know. We expect the Americans added additional sensors in the area around the aircraft carrier prior to the team's arrival. Otherwise, our divers would have avoided it."

"How was the bomb disposed of?"

"Apparently, U.S. Navy divers recovered the weapon and a patrol boat rushed it to the ocean as far as it could before the timer on the detonator ran out. About ten kilometers or so offshore. Our agent reports that the crew barely had time to dump the weapon overboard before it exploded."

The president kneaded his forehead, now facing the SVR director. "Why are the American's silent about the explosion? It's still not hit the press."

"The bomb exploded deep down, around six hundred meters. At that depth, water pressure prevented the blast from reaching the surface."

"Unlike what happened at Qingdao?"

"Exactly. The bomb in Hawaii detonated on the bottom, which produced minimal disturbance on the surface, just some churning water that dissipated rapidly."

"What about radiation?"

"Nothing has been reported about surface contamination but there will certainly be substantial radioactivity on the bottom and in the water column." Smirnov took a quick taste from his tea cup. "Although the bomb's blast effects were suppressed, the underwater noise and seismic energy it released cannot be masked. Our sensors in Petropavlovsk-Kamchatskiy picked up the blast. I'm sure the Japanese, Koreans and Chinese heard it along with others that ring the Pacific."

"So, it's eventually going to get out."

"Absolutely. Like you said, I'm amazed that the story hasn't surfaced yet."

"What about the diversion plan?" Lebedev asked.

"As directed, our asset passed the story on to her MSS handler. Beijing knows by now." Simonov referenced a female Russian mole planted years earlier in the U.S. State Department. Unaware of her true allegiance, a Ministry of State Security officer operating in Washington, D.C. recruited the SVR plant to spy on America for China.

"Well, at least that part of your plan appears to be working," President Lebedev commented. While sipping tea, he recalled another enigma. Setting his cup aside he reengaged the FSB director. "What happened to the GRU officer?"

General Golitsin said, "The captain of the *Novosibirsk* reported that Captain-Lieutenant Kirov locked out of the minisub at the Pearl Harbor base but never returned. Somehow, he discovered the OSNAZ's team's real mission and tried to stop them."

"Could he have been responsible for what happened to the weapon?"

"Unlikely, sir. Our intel on what happened is solid. The Americans found it on their own. Personally, I think Kirov used the opportunity as a way to return to the States."

"What?"

SVR director Smirnov joined in. "Mr. President, Kirov was promised by the Pacific Fleet commander that if he completed his mission in China, he would be permitted to retire from the Navy and return to his lover in the United States. After finishing the China assignment, the *Novosibirsk's* side trip to Hawaii provided him that opportunity...early retirement."

"So, he's back in the States?"

"Yes, he was spotted yesterday at his office and home in the Seattle area."

"Could the American authorities have picked him up?"

"We have no indication of that."

President Lebedev intertwined his fingers. "All right gentlemen, the Chinese and the Americans will soon be pointing their fingers at us so just how do we extract ourselves from this catastrophe?"

Chapter 7

Ten time zones behind Moscow, Yuri Kirov was at home. It was half past ten in the morning. Laura left several hours earlier. She worked in nearby Bellevue at Cognition Consultants. As one of the three owners of the 2,000-plus-employee IT firm, Laura served as Senior VP of Operations.

At Yuri's request, Amanda and Madelyn visited a nearby park. Yuri had informed Maddy's nanny that the alarm company would be servicing the home's security system this morning, which would require minor construction. He didn't want Maddy exposed to the work. It wasn't a complete fabrication.

With Yuri in tow, the two FBI technicians methodically shuttled from room to room, removing the dozen wireless audio-video devices inside the three-level home. The techs had been at it for over an hour.

"You're certain that's the last one?" Yuri asked.

"Yes sir. We have them all now," the senior technician said.

"How many will stay outside?"

"The six existing cameras."

A detail from the Seattle field office assigned to provide security of the Newman residence was currently in a home three doors away. Two person teams monitored the cameras around the clock. The FBI had leased the house while it monitored Laura during its pursuit of Yuri. After Yuri surrendered, the FBI decided to maintain surveillance of Laura's residence due to potential threats from China and Russia, or so Yuri was told. Although the threats were real, Yuri also suspected that the FBI wanted to keep track of his activities.

After the technicians left, Yuri called Amanda's cell and let her know the work was complete and it was okay to return home.

Yuri climbed into his Highlander and exited the garage. As he drove northward toward Redmond, he had mixed thoughts regarding surveillance. Both he and Laura were desperate to get rid of the interior spy hardware. But would the exterior cameras be enough? After one kidnapping and two subsequent close calls, Yuri worried that his family home was still vulnerable.

Chapter 8

The President of the United States and his national security advisor were alone in the Oval Office. It was midafternoon. They sat in chairs facing each other near the fireplace.

Both men were in their late fifties. President Tyler Magnuson's belly had expanded a couple of inches since taking office, but he'd managed to keep his chestnut hair. His roguish face and tall frame helped retain his youthful appearance—a blessing for any politician.

National Security Advisor Peter Brindle went bald years earlier, and his face had leathered from three decades of smoking that finally ceased after a heart attack scare.

Magnuson and Brindle were veterans. The president served as an Army infantry platoon leader after graduating from Texas A&M with a degree in political science and a commission as a second lieutenant earned during his four years in ROTC. After three years of active duty, he left the Army to pursue a career in law and politics.

Brindle was a graduate of the Naval Academy. He spent thirty-two years as a surface warfare officer before retiring as a four-star admiral.

Today, the subject of their meeting was Russia and China. U.S. relations with both countries were in a tailspin.

"How much time do we have?" President Magnuson asked.

NSA Brindle clasped his hands. "A couple of days at best. The ship's crew are not the problem. It's the scientists that were aboard. Other than grant funding, NOAA has no leverage with them." The previous day, a National Oceanic and Atmospheric Administration research ship berthed in Hawaii conducted a routine biological survey offshore of Oahu's southern coast.

"What do they know?" asked the President.

"When the trawl net was hauled aboard, most of the captured marine life was sent to the ship's laboratory for analysis and storage. That's where the trouble started. Apparently, one of the fish snagged in the net was highly irradiated—from byproducts of the nuclear detonation. One of the scientists had decided to run a radiation background check."

"Why would they do that?"

"As I understand, it was to establish background conditions to compare against fallout from the Qingdao explosion. The winds will eventually carry radioactive debris to Hawaii and beyond."

POTUS nodded. "Have our people been able to identify the source of the Pearl Harbor bomb?"

"Both Livermore and Los Alamos are working on it. So far, they've determined the fissile material was plutonium. They're trying to link it to Russian reactors but haven't found a match yet."

"But those scientists in Hawaii don't know what really happened, correct?"

"Yes, plus the press remains in the dark about the detonation offshore of Honolulu. But plenty of rumors have surfaced on the internet about 'something' that happened last week." Brindle extracted a photograph from a folder he held. He handed the photo to the president. "You've seen this before, sir."

Magnuson examined the color print. It was an enlargement from a NOAA weather satellite that monitored the central Pacific Ocean. A marble sized gray-white blemish, surrounded by deep turquoise water, was visible offshore of Honolulu's coastline.

Brindle continued the accounting. "Even though the bomb detonated about two thousand feet deep, light from the nuclear flash reached the surface. It was visible for just an instant. A couple of airline pilots called in the sighting as well as one private aircraft that was in the area." Brindle recalled another factor. "The blast was also picked up by our earthquake sensors and underwater sound recorders. So, you can expect the same for the UN monitoring system as well as other foreign nuclear event monitoring facilities."

"I get it, Pete. Someone's going to put all this together." He placed the photo on the coffee table fronting his chair.

"I'm afraid so. That's why I believe we need to be proactive."

The president pressed his lips tight, working overtime to contain his fury.

"Sir, I recommend that you address the nation tomorrow evening or at the very latest the next day. The people need to know what happened."

"Not the weekend. We have the state visit and dinner for the Indian Prime Minister."

"Right. I'll set it up for Monday."

"How am I going to explain this, Pete, this impossible mess that we're in that's no fault of our own?" Magnuson shifted position, his lumbar spine the focus of the mounting stress that assaulted his well-being. "The people will be terrified. Congress will be all over me. And the damn Russians will deny everything."

"I'll help script your speech but I don't recommend pointing the finger at Russia, at least not yet."

"For God's sake, Pete, those idiots in the Kremlin detonated a nuclear weapon inside the United States. I've got to respond to that without starting World War III."

"I understand. But it's not just Russia."

"What do you mean?"

Brindle cleared his throat. "We suspect the event in China is tied directly to what happened at Pearl. Until we fully understand that linkage, I recommend holding off on retaliation against Russia."

"How long?"

"The FBI and CIA are working the issue around the clock. They need about a week."

"Too damn long. Tell 'em to step on it. I want options ASAP."

"Will do, sir."

Chapter 9

It was mid-afternoon at the Qingdao Bureau of the Ministry of Public Security. The MPS serves as China's domestic police authority. Every cubicle on the second floor of the government building was occupied. The eighteen data analysts toiled away under a mandatory overtime directive issued from Beijing.

Photo imaging specialist Yu Ling queued up a new video on her desktop computer. The petite twenty-five-year-old had shoulder length glossy black hair. The thin wireframe spectacles she wore hardly detracted from her charming face.

The video Yu scrutinized was recorded on Thursday, like the other two dozen she had already reviewed as part of the MPS investigation of the nuclear bomb attack. The Port of Qingdao's surveillance cameras monitored every quay, pier and wharf that the port operated along the shores of Jiaozhou Bay.

A quarter of the way through the current footage, Yu paused the video. "What's this?" she muttered. She had just watched the accelerated image of a small boat make a series of east to west and west to east sprints along a commercial waterway. Yu checked the file name of the recording: Zhong Gang—Middle Harbour. She recognized the images. An ex-boyfriend lived in a high-rise apartment near the waterway. Located along the eastern shore of the Jiaozhou Bay, the Port's Middle Harbour bordered Qingdao's thriving Shibei District on the south and east and the PLA Navy's Qingdao

Naval Base on the north. A new cruise ship terminal was located just north of the waterway near the base.

Yu Ling also had access to surveillance videos on the Jiaozhou Bay Bridge. One of the cameras on the span captured the detonation. Just prior to the explosion, the image of a nearby small boat was captured. Her supervisor along with other higher ups in the MPS suspected the boat might have been involved with the bomb. Yu was tasked with identifying the mystery boat.

Yu Ling resumed the video, viewing at normal speed. She watched as the boat departed the waterway and entered Jiaozhou Bay. She checked the time stamps on the video. *It fits. That's got to be the boat!*

Chapter 10

Day 5—Sunday

Yuri and Laura enjoyed breakfast at the deck table of their hillside home. Madelyn Grace was in her nearby playpen, busy lining up her collection of toy horses. Yuri drank coffee; Laura sipped orange juice. They had just finished the meal—scrambled eggs, toast and fruit prepared by Yuri. The temperature hovered in the mid seventy degrees Fahrenheit. In the distance, the sapphire waters of Lake Sammamish shimmered.

"Where'd Amanda go?" Yuri asked. Maddy's nanny left half an hour earlier.

"To meet her boyfriend and some friends. They're all going hiking today, somewhere near the pass."

"Have you met the guy?" Yuri crossed his ankles. He wore sandals, Bermuda shorts and a T-shirt.

"Once. He came by to pick her up. Nice guy. Courteous. Didn't say much." Laura wore a sleeveless blouse, a pair of blue jeans and tennis shoes.

Yuri took another sip. "She seems a good match for Maddy."

"She is. I'm very pleased so far."

"Good."

Fretting all weekend, Laura decided it was the right time to bring up a delicate subject. "I had a visitor at the office Friday…a detective assigned to the Sarah Compton case."

"What did he want?"

"The detective was a she. Sarah's family is pressing hard. They want a court hearing to investigate her disappearance. Both of us will be called to testify."

Yuri let out a deep sigh. Six months earlier, he'd hired the security company to provide around the clock protection for Laura and Maddy. Sarah Compton was on duty at Laura's home when the kidnappers invaded. Laura and Madelyn were snatched; Sarah vanished.

Yuri said, "If the local cops start checking up on me, everything will unravel."

"I know. Maybe Tim Reveley can delay the hearing." Laura referred to her personal attorney.

"It's probably worth trying." Yuri drained the coffee mug and set it on the table. The consequences of his actions regarding Sarah's disappearance simmered. "I'm convinced those bastards killed her and disposed of her body—she'll never be found."

"It's not your fault, Yuri. She must have confronted them; she was doing her job."

"She never had a chance. They were military." Yuri grimaced, recalling the Chinese operatives that abducted Laura and Maddy as a ploy to force him into cooperating. Sarah Compton was collateral damage.

"Stop beating yourself up. They used us to get to you."

"I should have never involved you with the *Neva*. You would be fine and Sarah would be alive. It would have been better if I'd never escaped."

"Honey, what you did was miraculous. Russia left the *Neva's* survivors to rot but you rescued them. I'm so proud of what you did."

"But look what's happened. I've endangered you from my actions. Kwan and his PLAN operators kidnapped you and Maddy. And then an MSS hit team targeted you—twice!" Yuri raised his arms. "And the U.S. Justice Department is still threatening you because of me. I'm ashamed to have caused you so much grief."

Laura reached across the table and took hold of Yuri's hand. "You're an honorable man, Yuri Ivanovich Kirov. You have nothing to be ashamed of."

* * * *

Fifteen time zones ahead, Ministry of Public Security technical specialist Yu Ling was in her cubicle at the Qingdao bureau. It was late evening;

most of the others left hours earlier—burned out from the compulsory extra work over the weekend. Yu and just one other staffer slogged away.

The day was long and boring for Yu as she fast-forwarded through dozens of surveillance videos of the City of Qingdao's bay and coastal shoreline. She attempted to track down the mysterious workboat that was sighted near the Jiaozhou Bay Bridge just before the nuclear bomb detonated. The previous day she discovered that the same vessel had operated in Qingdao's Middle Harbour waterway an hour before the blast.

Yu queued up the next video, downloaded from a master file in the bureau's mainframe computer. A recent decree from Beijing required all commercial and public entities operating in China's principal cities to provide live video feeds of their security cameras to the MPS. Patterned after the City of London's video camera surveillance system, the Qingdao system collected hundreds of terabytes of digital images each hour.

The video Yu currently viewed was recorded at 5:12 A.M. the day the bomb exploded. The camera was located at the entrance channel of a small boat moorage facility located in eastern Qingdao near Maidao Island. The HD video captured the image of a workboat as it navigated through the marina entrance.

"That's the boat!" Yu muttered.

The yacht club that operated the moorage facility had installed the high-end surveillance system after several yachts moored in the harbor were burglarized. The black and white image Yu viewed was exceptionally detailed due to the camera's FLIR night vision system. The forward-looking infrared optics revealed that the 10.5-meter-long workboat was of modern construction with clean lines. As the boat's stern passed by the camera, it captured the vessel name. Yu Ling froze the image and magnified the name. Although the Mandarin script was blurry, the name was legible: *YI JIE.*

Happy and Pure was the English translation for *Yi Jie.*

Yu Ling stretched out her arms, suddenly weary from the taxing day but pleased. She now had a name and a location to resume the search.

Yu gathered her personal items from the desk and placed them in her handbag. As she made her way to the door, she embraced the thrill of the hunt. She sensed that she was on to something important. It would consume her thoughts for the rest of the evening, following to her dreams.

* * * *

Laura Newman was asleep in the master bedroom; Maddy slept in her own room. Yuri wasn't ready to retire yet. He was alone in the living room with the lights off. A few minutes earlier, he heard Amanda's Honda Civic when she returned home. Maddy's nanny lived in the apartment over the attached three car garage.

Amanda had no idea that her comings and goings at the Sammamish residence were videoed and manually recorded in an official log book by the FBI.

The presence of the nearby federal agents provided Yuri with a measure of relief. Should Laura again be targeted by foreign intelligence services to get to him, she would be protected. But how long would that last? The FBI would eventually retrieve their outdoor cameras and shut down the surveillance op. What then?

Yuri broached that subject with Laura earlier this evening. He suggested that for the next six months they rent a condominium in a building that was just a couple of blocks away from Cognition's headquarters. Security in the Bellevue luxury high-rise was top notch, which was one of its main selling points. Laura said she would think about it.

Yuri would push for temporary relocation. It would help mitigate his angst. He recognized that once again he would likely not be around to protect Laura and Maddy.

In the coming morning, Yuri had another meeting scheduled with the FBI in Seattle. During the course of the debriefing, Special Agent Michaela Taylor would undoubtedly pressure Yuri to make a decision on the Department of Justice's offer to drop espionage charges against him and—Laura—in return for his full cooperation with the U.S. Intelligence Services for the next three years.

Yuri was now ready to make that commitment, knowing that he would forever be turning his back on his birth country—and his colleagues and friends in the Russian Navy.

Chapter 11

Yu Ling was pumped. It was mid-afternoon in Qingdao. She had returned to her office half an hour earlier after sitting in on the interview. The manager of the yacht club cooperated without hesitation when Yu and two officers from the People's Armed Police—the muscle of China's domestic police force—demanded access to the club's customer files. The workboat *Yi Jie* was owned by a Shanghai based company that conducted marine environmental surveys. Yu had just contacted the Shanghai bureau of the Ministry of Public Security, requesting all information on the company and the workboat. The data dump would be emailed by five o'clock.

During the interview, the manager revealed that the club had a camera on the marina's entry gate. Every person that inserted an electronic key into the gate lock was photographed. Since it recorded photos instead of videos, the camera was not linked to the MPS's video surveillance system for Qingdao. The manager accessed the camera's cloud storage file and downloaded the entire contents to a flash drive. It contained six months of photos, each one time stamped.

Yu Ling inserted the drive into a port on her PC and called up a specific date file. The digital image was recorded at 4:47 A.M. The man was in his mid-thirties and had a husky frame. He wore a ball cap and windbreaker. *Who are you?* Yu wondered. *And what were you doing with that boat in the Middle Harbour, and then in the bay where the bomb went off?*

While at the yacht club office, Yu had requested the manager retrieve all photos during the early hours of the date in question. Only one photo was recorded—the same one Yu currently viewed. When questioned by Yu the club manager indicated she did not recognize the individual. The keycard ID data used to gain access to the marina was registered to the survey company only.

Yu Ling copied the image and loaded the digital photograph into the Ministry of Public Security's Residence Identity Card database. The MPS issued the cards to Chinese residents over sixteen years old. Besides basic ID data—name, sex, citizenship status, race, birthdate, and address, the card contained a color photograph of the bearer.

Yu commenced the search. China obtained the best facial recognition software it could acquire or hijack. The latest version running in the MPS's master mainframe in Beijing was emailed three months earlier by a twenty-eight-year-old H1B visa holder from Tianjin. He worked for a Seattle startup that won a $20 million contract with the U.S. Transportation Security Administration to help speed up airport passenger screening.

The search took just a minute. She stared at the digital copy of the ID card. *That's him!*

Yu scanned the info that accompanied the photograph and instantly went on alert. The individual was red-flagged. *He's a Uyghur!*

Yu Ling downloaded the data file and printed it out. After collecting the hardcopy, she headed for her boss's office.

* * * *

As instructed, Yuri drove his Highlander to the bottom level of the parking garage in a high-rise tower in downtown Seattle. The office building housed the law firm that represented Cognition Consultants and Laura Newman. He was ten minutes early. The morning commute had mitigated by the time he drove west across Lake Washington, allowing unencumbered access to Seattle's financial district.

Eight minutes after Yuri pulled into an empty stall, a late model black Chevrolet Suburban arrived. Yuri was ushered into the backseat. Although every window in the SUV was tinted black, concealing the occupants from outside viewers, the driver instructed Yuri to keep his head down. After a brief drive, the Chevy delivered Yuri to the secure subterranean parking garage of the FBI's Seattle field office.

Yuri currently drank from a coffee mug in a conference room. It was the same room he visited the previous week—just after the Qingdao bomb detonated.

Yuri's mug was half full when Special Agent Michaela Taylor arrived at 10:32 A.M. "Good morning," she said with a warm smile. She wore a knee length pleated skirt with a white blouse and a pair of three-inch heels. Her hair was in a ponytail today.

"Good morning," Yuri replied. He sported a pair of designer jeans and a navy-blue windbreaker with a Northwest Subsea Dynamics logo over the right breast—his typical business apparel.

Michaela took a chair opposite Yuri. "Sorry for the cloak and dagger stuff to get you here but we don't want to take any chances on you being spotted."

"No problem."

Michaela opened a multi-page document from one of the folders she carried. As she started to scan the file, a telephone at her side on the conference table rang. She picked up the handset. "Taylor," she announced. "Yes, he's here and we're ready...okay, I'll connect now."

Agent Taylor returned the phone to its cradle and glanced Yuri's way. "They're set in D.C. so I'm going to join on the conference. It'll be like what we did before."

"Okay."

Michaela activated the secure videoconference hardware. The wall-mounted home theater sized screen at the far end of the room blinked on. FBI supervisory special agent Ava Diesen stared back. She wore a ruffled silk blouse with a flared skirt. Sitting next to her was a male in his early fifties. He was garbed in a custom cut dark suit with a white shirt and red tie—standard G-man attire.

"Good day," Ava announced.

Michaela and Yuri responded in kind.

Ava gestured to her right side. "Mr. Kirov, this is John Markley. He's the Bureau's Assistant Director for Counterintelligence."

"Good to finally meet you," Markley said.

Yuri returned the greeting.

Ava said, "I asked John to sit in on our discussion today. He oversees all FBI matters related to foreign intelligence operations and espionage."

Yuri instantly assessed that his fate was in Markley's hands.

SSA Diesen said, "We understand that you have reached a decision on the offer that the Bureau has made for your services."

Yuri stiffened, knowing he had reached the point of no return. He cleared his voice. "Yes, I accept what has been proposed."

"Excellent," Ava announced.

Markley nodded his approval.
Michaela smiled at Yuri.
Yuri slumped. *Dear God, please help me.*

Chapter 12

The *Novosibirsk* arrived in Vladivostok late morning, tying up to its berth in Uliss Bay. Tucked away in sheltered waters just inside the Bosfor Vostochnyy Bridge, the submarine base was one of Russia's larger naval facilities.

Prior to surfacing and sailing under the bridge that spanned the Eastern Bosfor Strait, the *Novosibirsk* released the minisub that it had transported half way across the Pacific Ocean and back. The one-hundred-foot-long *P-815* with its four-man crew would stay submerged. It would loiter offshore of the strait until late evening before cruising under the bridge submerged. About a mile north of Uliss Bay, the *P-815* would surface and power to a floating dry dock located near the entrance to Diomid Bay. Moored to the shoreside of the dry dock was a covered boat shed. The aluminum roof would hide the minisub from American and Chinese spy satellites.

Captain Leonid Petrovich served as the *Novosibirsk's* commanding officer. After docking his ship, the forty-four-year-old submariner was escorted by a lieutenant to the Pacific Fleet Headquarters Building in downtown Vladivostok. He was just granted entrance into Admiral Oleg Belofsky's office.

The admiral looked up from his desk, peering over the top frame of the reading glasses parked on his nose. "Welcome back, Captain," Belofsky said. Pushing sixty, Belofsky was bald and heavyset. His leathery, wrinkled facial skin telegraphed heavy smoking. Three gold stars were displayed on the epaulettes of his uniform jacket.

"Thank you, Admiral."

Belofsky gestured for Petrovich to take a seat.

Captain Petrovich parked his five foot ten frame into the chair. The summer uniform he wore revealed his solid, muscular build. His graying auburn hair was close cut—almost a buzz. Petrovich's wife, Alena, and their children—daughters Katerina, fourteen; Kira, eleven; and son Anton, eight—were just a forty-minute drive away. Their sprawling home—a renovated farmhouse, overlooked Amur Bay. At sea for weeks, Petrovich yearned to reunite with his family. But first, he had unpleasant business to take care of.

Admiral Belofsky reached for the teapot on his desk. An orderly delivered the fresh pot just before Petrovich was escorted into the office by a secretary. He poured two mugs, passing one to the sub commander.

After taking a taste, Admiral Belofsky said, "I've read the after action reports you radioed in. Sounds like you and your crew had quite the adventure."

Petrovich fidgeted in his chair, unsure where the admiral was heading. "It was like nothing I've done before, Admiral." He took a quick swallow from his mug. "The *Spetsnaz* operators that were aboard, they lied to me about their mission parameters."

"Tell me about it."

Petrovich let everything out, his anger bubbling to the surface during a couple of accounts. He expressed his bitterness about being left out of the big picture. Admiral Belofsky took it all in. Even he was in the dark regarding several of the *Novosibirsk*'s mission parameters. They had been issued straight from Moscow, bypassing Pacific Fleet Command.

Belofsky swiveled in his chair, digesting the mission details while staring out of his office windows. His penthouse office overlooked Vladivostok's Golden Horn Bay, a natural inlet that extended about four miles inland from the open waters of Amur Bay. Just east of Fleet Headquarters was the Golden Horn Bridge. The majestic cable-stayed structure spanned the waterway, providing a shortcut to the southern half of the city. Warships lined the quays fronting the headquarters building. Commercial craft were moored alongside the wharves and piers on adjacent shorelines.

Admiral Belofsky turned back to his subordinate. "Tell me, Captain, what do you think really happened to Captain-Lieutenant Kirov?"

* * * *

Yuri spoon fed Madelyn at the kitchen table. She was in her highchair. It was 5:57 P.M. Maddy's nanny left an hour earlier. Amanda Graham and her Microsoft beau had tickets to a Mariners ballgame in downtown Seattle.

"Come on sweetie, these are good for you."

After the first bite, Maddy ejected the veggies. The puree dribbled down her chin. Yuri placed the recharged plastic spoon next to her mouth. Maddy turned away, her lips sealed.

Yuri was at a loss on how to proceed when the door from the garage opened and Laura sauntered in. "I'm glad you're home," Yuri said. "I'm having no luck feeding Maddy."

Laura chuckled. "She's picky lately. Have you tried fruit?"

"No."

"I'll take care of it." Laura stooped beside the highchair. "Hi sweet pea!" Maddy exploded into her trademark dimpled smile. Laura used a napkin from the table to clean her daughter's face. "Would you like some apple sauce?"

"Peasse!"

"How'd it go with the FBI today?" Laura asked while opening the refrigerator door.

"Good," Yuri said.

Laura grabbed a container of organic sugar-free apple sauce. "What about the asylum process?"

"They tell me it's on track."

"Great. I'll call Tim Reveley tomorrow for an update."

Yuri did not volunteer that he'd parked in the law firm's parking garage as part of the FBI's evasion tactics to thwart potential tails. After the meeting, Yuri almost took the elevator to Reveley's office to seek advice. But he decided against it. He was now under Uncle Sam's thumb.

Yuri picked up the TV remote and turned on the nearby Sony. It was tuned to a network news channel. Expecting the six o'clock news, two newsreaders sat side by side at a counter. The female said, "The president will be addressing the nation within the next few minutes and at that time we will switch to a live feed from the Oval Office in the White House."

The male joined in. "The subject of the president's address is listed as a national security matter but no details have been provided."

"That's odd," the female said.

"It is. We've reached out to our contacts at the Pentagon. A source who requested anonymity indicated it concerns some type of event that occurred in Hawaii."

"*Govnó,*" Yuri muttered.

Laura turned away from Maddy. "Oh my God—it's going to be about you."

While Laura fed Maddy, Yuri watched the television screen. The President of the United States stared back.

"Good evening my fellow Americans," the president said peering into the camera while reading the carefully crafted script from the camera's built-in teleprompter.

"Tonight, I need to inform you of a serious event that occurred a week and a half ago in the State of Hawaii.

"At that time, our military forces at Pearl Harbor discovered a . . ."

* * * *

"What a bunch of BS," Laura said.

"I'm not surprised," Yuri replied.

The president just concluded his address to the nation. Yuri and Laura were seated at the kitchen table. Maddy sat in a highchair playing with her food, diced chicken with a side dish of sliced strawberries. The television screen displayed the same two network talking heads that had preceded the White House speech but Yuri muted the sound. Laura poured herself a glass of 14 Hands merlot. Yuri had already cracked open a bottle of Redhook.

"You saved Pearl Harbor, not some Navy security detail." Laura took her first taste of wine.

"It's part of the cover story to protect me—us. Don't fret about it."

On orders from the Secretary of Defense, the U.S. Navy perpetuated the fabricated story that Pearl Harbor security forces discovered the bomb, which resulted in saving the naval base and the USS *Roosevelt*.

"Still, it's not fair—you're the hero." Laura sulked, not done yet. "And he blamed it on terrorists. Russia was not mentioned once. That's not right."

"He couldn't tell the truth, at least not for now." Yuri took a swig of beer. "He was careful with his words, 'suspected terrorists' is what he called them. That covers a wide spectrum and is probably believable by most people."

Still troubled, Laura said, "He said the bomb in China was not related to what happened in Hawaii. Just coincidence. More BS."

"I'm sure it all has to do with national security. If he accused Russia of planting the bombs, especially the one at Pearl Harbor, that would be considered an act of war and would require immediate retaliation."

"But they did it and they're going to get away with it!"

Yuri took another taste of beer as he contemplated how best to calm Laura. "The president is in an impossible position right now, partially because of me."

That statement captured Laura's instant attention. "What do you mean?"

"During the debriefings, I told them my suspicions about China being the instigator of the trouble in Alaska. Russia's oil well blowout, sinking of the tanker...sabotage of the pipeline."

"What about that submarine from Hood Canal?"

"Yes, they know about that too...from both of us."

Laura nodded, acknowledging her own interrogations by the FBI.

Yuri rubbed his chin. "At first I don't think they believed me. But based on what I told them, I expect it won't be long before they verify that both China and Russia have been scheming against the United States but for different reasons. China was the original initiator but Russia is now just as complicit. And that's the problem."

Laura squinted, not yet making the connection.

Yuri carried on, "If the president outright accused both China and Russia of attacking the United States, the pressure for retaliation would be enormous. Economic sanctions won't cut it—especially with the Russian nuke in Hawaii and China's attempt to sink the American sub here. Russia and/or China might not wait for an expected U.S. military strike."

Laura set her wine glass down. "World War III."

"Exactly."

"So, what do you think is going to happen?"

"Behind the scenes diplomatic negotiations to defuse the current hair-trigger climate." Yuri had another meeting scheduled with the FBI and Navy tomorrow where he suspected the latest turn of events would be on the agenda. He decided to delay telling Laura until the morning. He did not want to cause her further anxiety tonight.

Laura processed the news. "They're going to bury it."

"Probably."

Chapter 13

Day 7—Tuesday

Guo Wing entered the spacious office, escorted by a PLA staff officer. "Good morning, sir," Guo said, addressing the President of the People's Republic of China. It was 11:10 A.M. in Beijing.

Chen Shen was seated behind his desk in an elegant building located in the heart of China's government—the Zhongnanhai. He gestured for Guo to take a seat. President Chen had returned to Beijing three days earlier from his exile at the Central Military Commission's emergency underground operations center in northeast China.

Guo settled into the chair, facing his boss across the spacious black marble desk. Guo's squat thick frame, double chin, corn-kernel teeth and balding scalp contrasted sharply with the president's trim six foot plus height, sparkling veneered smile and luxuriously thick mane. Guo was fifty-two and looked it. Although the president was several years older and smoked like a chimney, his face retained its youthful look. Guo had long suspected that Chen relied on dentures and cosmetic surgery but he could never verify it.

"What's going on?" asked President Chen, annoyed at the request for the unscheduled meeting.

"I have new information on the Qingdao event." Guo Wing served as the deputy minister of operations for China's Ministry of State Security. The MSS was responsible for foreign intelligence, counterintelligence and domestic political security. It functioned similar to a merger of the FBI and CIA.

Guo reached into the file folder he carried and took out a photograph. "There's a remote possibility that internal dissidents were responsible for the bomb."

The news hit President Chen with the impact of a tsunami. "What—how's that possible?"

Guo slid the color print across the desk. Chen picked up the blowup of the resident ID card. Guo recited the data listed on the card. "His name is Ismail Sabir. Thirty-six years old. He's a Uyghur. Born and raised in Xinjiang. Migrated to Qingdao about ten years ago. Employed as a technician at a boat manufacturing and repair company in Qingdao."

"Muslim?"

"Yes."

"So how did he get on your radar?"

"The MPS made the initial discovery. One of the surveillance cameras on the Jiaozhou Bay Bridge picked up a small boat in the vicinity of the detonation. It was traced back to a yacht club marina in Qingdao, which led to this guy being eventually ID'd. That's when we took control of the investigation from the MPS. Sabir has an older brother in Ürümqi. He was easy to locate; he was already interned in a reeducation facility."

Guo made reference to China's network of camps that detained over a million residents of the Xinjiang Uyghur Autonomous Region—most of whom were Muslim. Beijing propaganda touted the camps as providing job training to escape the poverty of the region and to mitigate radical Islamic enticements. In reality, the camps functioned as a cheap labor source.

Guo said, "The brother owned a restaurant but our local people believe he's tied in with one of the local troublemaker groups." Guo removed a second photo and gave it to the president.

Chen compared the photos, the likeness between the two men was obvious. "So, what are you doing about this?"

"Ismail Sabir is likely dead. We believe he was aboard the boat when the bomb exploded. The brother is currently under interrogation. Up to now, he maintains his innocence and claims he has nothing to do with Ismail since he left Xinjiang."

"Dragon shit."

"I agree, sir. I expect we'll know more soon."

President Chen set the photos on his desk. He reached into a drawer for his pack of cigarettes. After lighting up a Marlboro, he glanced at Guo and said, "If the Uyghurs are responsible for Qingdao, where did they get the device?"

"That remains a puzzle. One possibility we're exploring is that some fissile materials could have been left behind from past testing at Lop Nor." China's nuclear testing program took place in the Lop Nor salt flats of Xinjiang Uyghur Autonomous Region from the 1960s to the 1990s. Dozens of nuclear weapons were detonated above and below ground.

"That's hard to believe, Guo."

"I understand, but we still need to check." Guo collected the photos of Sabir and his brother from the desk and returned them to his file. "The other possibility is that the Uyghurs were supplied with a weapon."

"By whom?"

Guo raised his hands. "We're exploring that now. Maybe the Indians. But that doesn't really fit with the way they operate, which makes me believe the Uyghur angle, if it's real, is a clever ploy concocted by the Americans to deceive us."

That comment recharged Chen. "Did you listen to the speech by that dog Magnuson?" Prior to leaving his residence this morning, Chen listened to President Magnuson's live broadcast."

"I did."

"And?"

"He's lying to buy time to intimidate us. Blaming the Hawaii attack on Middle East terrorists is an easy out. The American public will buy it, another 9/11 but this time stopped just in time."

"But what does that accomplish for them?" Chen asked.

"We know from our Washington source that the U.S. government suspects we were behind the Pearl Harbor attack as revenge for sabotaging the Yulin base. Blowing up a similar weapon in Qingdao is their payback."

The source Guo mentioned was a high-level employee in the U.S. State Department compromised by the MSS. Unknown to President Chen and spymaster Guo, the Foggy Bottom employee was a deep cover mole planted two decades earlier by the Kremlin.

Confused, Chen cast a frown and said, "So what happened in Hawaii—who the devil lit off that bomb?"

"There could have been a terrorist attack like Magnuson claimed but I think the Americans did it themselves. Detonated a small nuke in deep water. No one hurt. No shore side damage." Guo locked eyes with his boss. "The *Heilong* actually picked up the detonation. Classified it as a nuclear depth charge."

Still not sold, President Chen said, "They detonate two nukes…to what end?"

"To intimidate us from responding to the Yulin attack should we be able to prove their involvement...but more importantly, retaliation for what happened in Alaska." Guo referred to China's sabotage of crude oil facilities in the forty-ninth state. "We know a U.S. submarine was in the Qingdao harbor last month. It could have easily planted the bomb at that time."

"You continue to believe the Americans took out Yulin to defuse Operation Sea Dragon?" Chen asked. Sea Dragon was the invasion of Taiwan. With the Yulin fleet disabled, the attack on the rebel province could not proceed.

"I do, Comrade President."

"But how would they have known about Sea Dragon, and our Alaska operations?"

"We're still investigating."

"Kwan?"

"Yes. It's possible he was compromised before his death. If he talked, that would explain much."

President Chen had befriended the Hong Kong billionaire, having vacationed aboard Kwan Chi's megayacht, the *Yangzi*. Kwan Chi had worked for the Ministry of State Security, reporting directly to Guo. Ten days earlier, Kwan was murdered in his Kowloon high-rise penthouse. The MSS suspected the CIA.

President Chen rolled his chair away from the desk, the half spent Marlboro hanging from his right hand. "I'm still having a hard time believing the Americans would do such a thing, even as retaliation for what happened in Hawaii or Alaska. That's not how they work." Chen spent six years in the United States, earning a BA from Cornell and an MBA from Stanford University. Chen took another drag. "What about the Russians?"

Guo stroked his balding scalp. "Nothing to report. Our relations are strong."

"My gut tells me the Russians are somehow behind all of this. The Uyghur thing is a smokescreen." Chen glanced out a window. The smog was especially dense today. "Besides, where the bomb went off still makes no sense to me."

"As I mentioned, it could have been done to intimidate us with future demands from the Americans to come."

"Where are the demands?"

"It's still early, sir. We need to—"

"You're missing something, Guo," Chen interrupted. "Continue with the Uyghur connection but I want you to go back to the source and look again. Blowing up that weapon in a mudflat bothers me—something's wrong."

"Understood, sir. I'll personally look into the matter to see if something was missed. In the meantime, should we continue the preparations with the PLA for our response?"

"Yes, by all means." The president crushed out the butt in an ashtray. "One way or the other, whoever did this to us is going to pay."

* * * *

Nicolai Orlov was alone in the secure room of the Consulate-General of Russia in Houston, Texas. Located on the thirteenth floor of a polished high-rise near the downtown business district, the windowless interior room was about twenty feet square. To defeat electronic snooping by the FBI and other U.S. intelligence units, the room's perimeter walls, ceiling, and floor were lined with special copper wiring.

Tall and trim with fashionable dark hair and a wolfishly attractive face, Nick Orlov was a few months shy of forty. His appealing looks were coveted by women and begrudged by men.

Recruited by the SVR after he completed his university studies in Moscow, Orlov rarely spent time in Russia. He served in several foreign posts before he was assigned to the Main Enemy. His last duty assignment had been at the San Francisco Consulate until Washington forced its closure as part of an ongoing diplomatic dispute between the Russian Federation and the United States. He transferred to Houston, where he was promoted to SVR *rezident* of the consulate. Single with no strong family ties to the homeland, Nick found that his nomadic lifestyle suited him.

Nick focused on the monitor positioned at the end of the conference table. It was a few minutes past midnight in Houston. His boss was eight time zones ahead. The encrypted video teleconference was prearranged.

SVR chief Borya Smirnov was alone in his office at Russia's foreign intelligence headquarters in Moscow. "So, what do you make of Magnuson's speech?" Smirnov asked. He had watched a rerun of presidential address from his home before his security detail transported him to his office.

"Very strange, sir." Nick said. "Why would terrorists try to knock out a highly secure military installation like the Pearl Harbor base when they could have put the damn bomb in the trunk of a car, driven to downtown Honolulu and let it rip?"

"I had the same reaction."

Nick planted his elbows on the conference table. "And this business about what happened in China. Two nukes going off in metropolitan areas half a world apart within a week of each other and with virtually no casualties, in my mind that is not a coincidence. They're related somehow."

"I share your conclusion. Something's off. Anyway, Washington Station is investigating. Any feedback from your China sources would also be welcome." As part of Nick's duties at the San Francisco Consulate he had developed contacts with Chinese nationals working in Silicon Valley.

"I can make a few calls but doubt that I'll get anything meaningful."

"Understand." The SVR director moved on to the primary purpose of the call. "There's something else I need your assistance with."

"Yes, sir."

"I want you to contact your asset in Seattle."

"Kirov's back?"

"Yes, our people in Seattle spotted him at his place of work."

Nearly two months earlier, Nick had helped launch Yuri's return to Russia. Nick was also privy to Yuri's mission: spying on China's naval installations.

"How long has he been home?" Nick asked.

"A couple of days. We need to know what he's doing back in Seattle."

"I thought he was going to be permitted to retire from the Navy and return to the States when he completed the China mission."

"He's AWOL—again. He returned to the U.S. without permission from the Navy and without providing a mission debrief. There also are questions about the status of the intelligence data that he was supposed to generate from the China op."

Oh shit, Nick thought.

Chapter 14

Yuri Kirov arrived at the naval base at half past ten in the morning. The helicopter flight from Paine Field to Bangor took fifteen minutes. FBI Special Agent Michaela Taylor accompanied Yuri on the cross-sound flight. The pilots were U.S. Navy officers but both wore civilian clothing. The helicopter was a rental.

After landing, another officer assigned to Naval Base Kitsap-Bangor escorted Yuri and Michaela to the meeting locale—a conference room inside a massive building located on a forested hillside above Hood Canal. The building served as the command headquarters for the submarine base. Stretching along two nautical miles of waterfront, the 7,000 acre facility and its collection of piers and wharves served as the homeport for eight Ohio class ballistic missiles submarines, two guided missiles subs, and a Seawolf class attack submarine. The base also contained a modern-day underground storage complex that stored 1,300 nuclear warheads. Downtown Seattle was just 20 miles away.

Yuri and Michaela were currently alone sitting at a conference table. Both enjoyed coffee provided by an aide.

"This must seem a bit odd for you," Michaela said.

"That's for sure. Never in my wildest thoughts did I imagine I'd set foot in this place."

Michaela grinned. "I expect the folks you'll be meeting will have a similar reaction to your presence."

"That's what I'm worried about."

"Don't be. They're the ones that requested the meeting."

"Hmmm," Yuri muttered, not convinced.

The conference room door opened and two U.S. Navy officers in service khaki uniforms entered.

"Good morning," greeted the older officer. Early forties, heavyset, ruddy complexion. The insignia pin on his shirt collar identified his rank as a captain. "I'm the base CO." He gestured to his companion. "The commander here is my deputy."

The three striper was half a head taller than his boss, rail thin and prematurely gray.

Yuri and Michaela exchanged greetings with the officers. Yuri used his cover name: John Kirkwood.

After taking a seat, the captain turned toward Yuri and said, "Mr. Kirkwood, I expect you are wondering why we requested this meeting."

Yuri nodded.

"I was briefed by Captain Bob Clark, who I understand both of you know."

"That's correct," Michaela said. Clark had served on the team that interrogated Yuri.

The base commander addressed Yuri. "First, I wanted to thank you for what you did at Pearl. I have countless friends at the base and aboard the *Roosevelt*. Thank you."

Stunned at the senior officer's appreciativeness, Yuri again tilted his head forward.

The captain cleared his throat. "Now, what we'd like to talk to you about today is your past excursions into our waters…here in the Pacific Northwest."

"I assume you're referring to my activities aboard the Russian attack submarine *Neva*."

"Yes—how the heck did you manage to evade our sonar sensors in the Strait of Juan de Fuca?"

Yuri clutched his hands, distraught by the secrets he was about to give up. "We followed a pre-surveyed path that was designated Backdoor. The underwater route . . ."

* * * *

Nineteen hundred miles east of the Puget Sound region, SVR *resident* Nicolai Orlov walked into the office of the Consulate-General of Russia. It was late afternoon in Houston.

"You wanted to see me, sir," Nick said.

The late fifties diplomat with thinning gray hair and a plump belly sat behind his desk. He gestured for Nick to sit. Nick picked the guest chair on the right.

"I've got bad news," announced the CG. Nick crossed his arms, unsure what was to come. "I just spoke with the Ambassador. The Americans have ordered us to close the consulate."

"Dammit," Nick mumbled.

"We have forty-eight hours to shut down operations and vacate the premises."

"Everything?"

"Yes, everything here, my residence plus the guest quarters in Piney Point."

"Why now, what's changed?"

"The State Department said Magnuson ordered the closure because of the oil spill in the Arctic—our refusal to participate in the clean-up of the oil that reached Alaska."

"Magnuson didn't mention that in his speech last night."

"I know. The State Department told the Ambassador the closure is not related to Hawaii...just a coincidence of timing."

Nick reflected on the news. "What about our staff?"

The CG scowled. "Everyone here has been designated *persona non grata*. We have to be out of the States in forty-eight hours."

"We can't even relocate to the Washington embassy?"

"No, besides me and my deputy, you were named personally for expulsion."

Nick sank into his chair. "This screws up everything I have going."

"I get it, Orlov. I know this is the second American consulate you've had to vacate."

Nick said, "I just received a priority assignment from Moscow that must be completed before leaving, but it means that I need to travel to Seattle to take care of it."

"That's going to be problematic. The State Department order absolutely prohibits any staff travel outside of the consulate. We are only permitted to return to our personal residences but that's it. The Ambassador said we should expect extreme surveillance by the FBI and the State Department's Diplomatic Security Service."

"He's probably right," Nick said.

Nick dreaded the ramifications of the Ambassador's warning. He was already surveilled twenty-four seven by the FBI. His plan to take a charter flight to Seattle was predicated on his ability to shake the followers. But with the expected increased scrutiny, it was unlikely he would be able to evade the Americans.

Dammit, how am I going to reach Yuri?

Nick had already tried to contact his friend and colleague by digital means but failed. Yuri did not answer or respond to the voicemail messages Nick left on the burner phone he'd provided Yuri. And neither Yuri or Laura responded to the draft email message he left in the anonymous Gmail account that all three shared.

Something's happened to them—I'm certain of it. But what?

"So how are we supposed to leave?" Nick asked.

"The embassy is arranging for a charter flight to take everyone back to Moscow—all staff and family members."

"How about me, I'd like to go to Mexico City and work out of the consulate."

"Sorry Orlov, the State Department orders require everyone to board the flight. No exceptions."

"Govnó!"

* * * *

It was a date night for Yuri and Laura. They were seated at a table in a quiet corner of the downtown Bellevue restaurant. It was half past seven. Amanda was at home with Madelyn.

Tonight, Yuri relinquished his usual beer and instead shared a bottle of a Columbia Valley merlot with Laura. They were served a few minutes earlier. Yuri worked on a sizzling filet mignon; Laura enjoyed prime rib.

Laura just finished briefing Yuri on her workday. Laura and her partners were currently in preliminary discussions with a Silicon Valley IT giant regarding the acquisition of Cognition Consultants. Cognition was a software company specializing in the analysis of 'Big Data' by employing Artificial Intelligence. Cognition's innovative work already led the pack with huge potential ahead.

"That's an unbelievable payout for you and your partners," Yuri said. If the sale occurred, Laura's share would be nine hundred million dollars and change.

Laura smiled. "It's what every startup hopes for…build up the value of the business and cash out while still on top."

"But?" Yuri said.

"I don't know if I'm ready." Laura was still in her early thirties; her partners were knocking on the door of fifty.

"How long would you have to stay with the company after the acquisition?"

"Just a year."

"That's not bad."

"No, but each of us would have to sign a noncompete agreement that would run for five years after that."

"Not surprising, plus you wouldn't need to work."

"Yuri, you know me. I'd be bored stiff."

He beamed. "I know what you should do!"

"Let me guess, set up a foundation and run that?"

"No. You should take over management of NSD. With your business skills and Bill Winters engineering innovations, you could really help grow the company." Yuri continued his pitch, reciting Northwest Subsea Dynamics' chief engineer's plan to pursue the lucrative market of developing underwater craft and subsea systems for military applications.

Yuri and Laura discussed the idea for the rest of the meal. She was lukewarm. Yuri was happy that she didn't outright reject it.

Over dessert, caramel covered vanilla ice cream—Laura's favorite—and decaf coffee, Yuri recounted his trip to Naval Base Kitsap-Bangor earlier in the day.

"That must have been quite an experience for you," Laura commented.

"It was. I can still hardly believe it." He swallowed a spoonful of ice cream. "That base is impressive, much more sophisticated than anything Russia has. They even showed me their training facilities. Incredible stuff."

"Did you get to see any of the submarines?"

"I did. They drove us out to a quay. Delta Pier. One of the Trident subs was moored to it." Yuri sighed. "I spent much of my career trying to find those behemoths. To see it in person, up close, was overwhelming."

"Did they take you aboard?"

"No. I think that might have been pushing things."

Laura sipped her coffee while considering Yuri's story. "Was it the one we were involved with?"

"The one I saw was called the *Louisiana*. I didn't ask about the *Kentucky*."

"So, they didn't bring that up?"

"No, I'm not sure they knew about it and Michaela didn't mention it. Our discussions centered on the *Neva's* activities."

Laura wiped her lips with a napkin. "Sounds like it was a courtesy visit. The U.S. Navy has plans for you."

"I think you're right."

* * * *

After leaving the restaurant, Yuri and Laura drove home in Yuri's Highlander, like they did most weekdays. This morning he had delivered Laura to her office at 7:45 A.M. and then drove to Everett to catch the helicopter flight to Bangor.

The Toyota's radio was on. The news summary just aired, leaving both Yuri and Laura astounded. The announcement from the State Department ordering the closure of the Houston Consulate was released in the late afternoon. Neither Yuri or Laura had heard about it until the radio broadcast.

"What's Nick going to do?" Laura said.

"The report said they're expelling the staff so he's probably going back to Moscow."

"Why now?"

"The news said it was about the oil spill in the Chukchi Sea but I suspect there's more to it than that—a lot more."

"Pearl Harbor?"

"Yep."

"Hmmm," Laura mumbled. "I wonder what Nick will do next?"

"He'll be fine. He's one of the SVR's stars."

Still, Yuri worried about the well-being of his colleague and friend. Once Russia determined that Yuri had defected to the United States, Nick Orlov might be tainted by their relationship.

Yuri was forced to break off all unauthorized communications with Russia as part of his agreement with the U.S. government, which meant he could no longer contact Nick. He disposed of the burner phone that Nick had provided him and avoided accessing the common Gmail account he shared with Nick.

As Yuri and Laura drove east on SR-520, heading downhill from the Microsoft campus into the Sammamish River valley, they each contemplated Nick's welfare.

Laura prayed. *Lord, please watch over and protect Nick.*

Yuri thought of his friend. *Nick's going to be in trouble because of me. How can I help him?*

Chapter 15

Yu Ling spent the previous day and most of the current morning going over her case file in detail—three times! Nothing new, no new leads.

Why are they pushing so hard? I located the workboat and I identified the man who operated it. What else do they need?

When Yu had arrived for work on Tuesday, her supervisor took her aside. He showed her the directive from Beijing. The Ministry of State Security ordered the Qingdao bureau of the MPS to conduct a top to bottom review of its work regarding the nuclear detonation. No explanation was provided with the directive but Yu's supervisor took it as a rebuke.

Yu Ling had expected praise for her work on the case; instead, her boss ordered her to check everything and start over fresh. His tone was not friendly.

Yu massaged her temple. The headache was in its infancy. She stared at the PC monitor on her desk. The Windows folder contained everything she had assembled on the case. As she started to review each individual digital file for the fourth time, she muttered to herself, "What did I miss?"

The revelation materialized a couple of minutes later. She had just clicked on a file that contained video images of the workboat *Yi Jie* in Qingdao's Middle Harbour. *The boat—I never followed up on why it was in the harbor before the blast.*

She observed the video on fast forward as the workboat repeatedly patrolled up and down the waterway. The last segment of the surveillance camera video showed the *Yi Jie* as it cruised past construction equipment. *What's this?*

Yu Ling played back the video at normal speed and clicked on 'pause' just as the workboat passed the crane barge. She studied the image. *That's a dredge!*

She checked another file, verifying that the *Yi Jie* was owned by a company that conducted marine surveys.

Maybe I had all of this wrong!

Yu now suspected that the *Yi Jie* was somehow associated with the dredging project in the Middle Harbour.

What if it was conducting a dredging survey for the port?

Yu's stomach flip-flopped as her theory that Uyghur dissidents were involved with the bomb began to unravel.

But why did it speed off to the north part of the bay?

Maybe they saw something and went over to investigate.

Yes, that's got to be it!

Yu Ling called up a digital telephone directory for the Port of Qingdao. After finding the number for the Port's maintenance division, she picked up her desk phone and placed the call.

Chapter 16

The People's Liberation Army-Navy building on Hainan Island in southern China was located five miles southeast of the resort city of Sanya. Notched into the hillside above the shoreline, the 65,000 square foot three story structure had commanding views of the South China Sea. Construction of the building was completed four months earlier.

Just west of the building was a massive reinforced concrete pier. With a width of 400 feet, the wharf jutted into the harbor for nearly half a mile. Three offshore artificial breakwaters provided shelter for the pier. Designed to moor China's largest military vessels, the pier was part of the naval base. It served as the homeport for the South Sea Fleet's aircraft carrier.

Immediately south of the building and the pier was a recreational complex for Navy personnel. It consisted of basketball courts, a track and field complex with a four hundred meter track and a regulation size soccer field.

The sign at the entrance to the PLAN building identified it as the Shendao Fleet Logistics and Support Center. The building included a warehouse on the ground floor, training facilities on the second level and offices and meeting rooms on the top floor. A partial basement was located at the building's southern end. The twenty-foot square subterranean chamber provided access to a tunnel.

The three hundred and thirty-foot-long tunnel stretched into the adjacent hillside where it connected with an auxiliary complex. Constructed within a cavern carved from rock, the two level 30,000 square foot facility housed one of the PLAN's most secret installations: South Sea Sound Surveillance System, aka S5.

S5 served as the hub for China's vast network of underwater listening posts in the South China Sea. For the past three years, China covertly installed the system, utilizing an armada of non-military vessels ranging from innocuous fishing boats to research ships operated by the Chinese Academy of Sciences. In all cases, the vessels involved in the installation work were staffed with PLAN crews who wore civilian clothing.

Ships installed tsunami and weather monitoring buoy stations, workboats lowered research instruments into the water column for biological sampling and water quality testing, and fishing boats deployed deep-sea lines and nets in search of anything that swam. Working as civilian craft, the secret operation was designed to dupe satellite reconnaissance and to avoid raising "red flags" to the multitudes of foreign ships that sailed across the 1.35 million square mile sea.

The parabolic antennae nested on the roof of the Shendao Fleet Logistics and Support Center building intercepted a constant stream of encrypted acoustic data from PLA satellites linked to the underwater monitoring system. Fiberoptic cables transmitted the raw data to supercomputers housed on the lower level of S5. Programmed with China's latest artificial intelligence algorithms, the computers searched for manmade sounds; U.S. submarines in particular.

PLAN officers and enlisted techs on S5's upper level analyzed the flood of data generated by the computers. Hamstrung with flaws in AI coding, manual interpretation of the computed results was still needed. The ocean depths were filled with a smorgasbord of natural acoustic energy, ranging from the songs of humpback whales and the clatter of mating shrimp to plate tectonics and subsea volcanic eruptions. Attempting to decipher the suppressed sound prints of submarines, especially those of the U.S. Navy, was a daunting and frustrating process for the S5 staff.

The S5 computer system routinely pegged errant subsea sounds as hostile underwater craft. But when investigated, the probable contacts turned into false alarms. The AI technology was part of the problem but the inexperience of the S5 staff also contributed to questionable performance of the overall surveillance system.

High on the PLAN's list of needs was improved submarine detection technology. The MSS and the PLA's Second Bureau were authorized to entice potential foreign turncoats with offers of mountains of cash. The hackers in the PLA's Unit 61398 in Shanghai were offered cash bonuses including luxury apartments if they could digitally steal subsea secrets from the U.S. Navy and its legions of private contractors.

This afternoon, a PLA naval officer and a civilian scientist from the University of Science and Technology of China (USTC) met in a second floor conference room of S5. Captain Zhou Jun was the commander of the South Sea Sound Surveillance System. An inch under six feet, his tailored summer uniform revealed a sinewy frame. His full black mane, honed to military length, was freckled with specks of gray. He wore a pair of wire rim glasses that complimented his handsome, distinguished face.

Facing Zhou across the conference table was Dr. Meng Park. In her mid-thirties, Meng was exceptionally attractive. Tall with a svelte frame and mid-back length jet-black hair, she frequently turned heads. Today she wore a plain cotton dress that flattered her subtle curves and displayed her shapely legs. Meng earned her Ph.D. in electrical engineering from MIT. After completing a postdoc fellowship at the University of California Berkeley and working a year at a Silicon Valley tech firm, she returned to China where she accepted an Associate Professorship with USTC. Her specialty was robotics.

Dr. Meng just arrived at S5. She and Zhou had met numerous times before.

"Thank you for coming on such short notice," Captain Zhou said.

Meng Park cast a friendly smile. "I'm always happy to come to Sanya. Hefei is awful right now. Scorching and no wind. Here, it is delightful." The City of Hefei was located about two hundred and fifty miles west of Shanghai. With a population of nearly eight million, it was the capital and the largest city in China's Anhui Province.

Zhou returned the smile. "No doubt, Sanya is the best duty assignment I've had. It is wonderful here alright." Forty-four years old, Captain Zhou had served aboard a warship early in his career and later was posted to a half a dozen naval bases scattered between China's three fleet commands. Because of his exceptional technical aptitude and keen management abilities, he was selected for fast-track advancement. A benefit of the career program that Zhou was assigned to was advanced education, which resulted in Zhou earning a Ph.D. in Information Science and Technology from China's prestigious Tsinghua University.

Captain Zhou dropped the bombshell. "Fleet has ordered S5 to accelerate the deployment of Serpent."

Caught off guard, Meng Park said, "How soon?"

"Immediately."

Dr. Meng glowered. "But we're not ready. We've barely started field testing."

"I understand. Nevertheless, Beijing has ordered the immediate deployment of your system." Zhou grabbed a water bottle on the table and took a swig. "Park, we had a serious intrusion at Yulin several weeks ago."

"By an AUV?"

"No, divers. Launched from a minisub offshore of the base."

"Did they get inside the harbor?" she asked, taken aback. Meng had helped design the underwater defense system for the Yulin Naval Base, which was located about ten miles east of Sanya.

"They did, and they inflicted serious damage to the base."

"Americans?"

"We believe so but have no hard evidence yet."

Dr. Meng processed the news. "None of the sensors detected the intrusion?"

"Nothing on the divers but a hydrophone did pick up the minisub about half a kilometer off the harbor's southern entrance. Drone patrol boats investigated but were not successful in targeting the intruder."

Meng grabbed the water bottle on her side of the table. After removing the cap, she took a long sip. "What about the ships at Yulin? Were they damaged?"

Captain Zhou pined. "Park, they're all dead in the water."

"What? How can that be?"

"The divers set off an EMP device. The microwave burst fried the electronics in just about everything aboard the ships and the base's shore facilities."

The color of Meng's face faded as the news registered. "I've heard nothing about this."

"Beijing does not want to alarm the people, especially after what happened in Qingdao." Captain Zhou sugarcoated Beijing's herculean efforts to suppress the dreadful news about the Yulin attack. Until the PLA could confirm for certain who sabotaged the base, the news blackout would continue. Only when the culprit was identified would China seek revenge.

"Park, I'm letting you know what happened because of the gravity of the situation. However, you must not repeat anything I tell you about Yulin."

"Of course, I understand." Meng crossed her legs. "What is being done to repair the damage?"

"Fleet is currently trying to restore power to both carriers but it's a tough process. The computers controlling the power plants are burned out. Replacing them is a nightmare."

Dr. Meng grimaced, aghast at the destruction.

"It's not all bad," Zhou offered. "None of the missile subs moored inside the mountain were affected." The subterranean chamber was hollowed out of rock inside a hillside along the eastern shoreline of the Yulin base. A tunnel connected the sub pens to the harbor.

"That's fortunate," Meng said.

"Propulsion has also been restored to half a dozen frigates and destroyers. A couple have departed Yulin and are now at their homeports for additional repairs." Zhou gripped his hands. "Even though we've had success in restoring propulsion power, almost all comms, radars and other sensors on the ships at Yulin are non-repairable. They will need to be completely replaced."

"That's awful."

"Indeed."

Meng took another drink of water. "Why was the *Shandong* at Yulin?" During her last visit to Hainan Island, the aircraft carrier was moored to its Shendao homeport pier just across the road from S5.

"The computers controlling the fuel system on the carrier pier malfunctioned. After *Shandong* returned from an exercise, it diverted to Yulin to fuel. Same for the *Liaoning.*"

"How convenient."

"The carrier pier's fuel system was hacked."

Dr. Meng suppressed a curse, her fury nearly erupting. "It must be the Americans behind all of this. They have the means and the motivation."

"Probably."

"Immediate deployment of Serpent will be my highest priority."

"Excellent," Zhou said, pleased that Meng was now obviously motivated.

* * * *

Captain Zhou stayed in his office; Dr. Meng Park departed half an hour earlier, returning to her hotel room in Sanya. He had dinner reservations for 8 P.M. at one of their favorite restaurants in Sanya's Jiyang District. It overlooked Dadonghai Bay and the South China Sea beyond. Both single, yet married to their careers, the Navy captain and the robotics professor hooked up frequently.

Zhou studied his orders from South Sea Fleet headquarters in Zhanjiang.

Park's right! We're not ready for deployment.

But he had no choice. Captain Zhou's career now depended on Dr. Meng Park and her evolutionary machines.

She can do it—Serpent is the key to stopping the Americans!

Chapter 17

President Chen Shen leaned against the balcony railing of his official residence. He enjoyed his final Marlboro of the day while gazing at the illuminated grounds of the Zhongnanhai. Located adjacent to the Forbidden City, the Beijing enclave housing China's national government consisted of over a dozen buildings—palaces, temples, halls and offices—scattered over 250 elegantly landscaped acres that included two lakes. Chen's home was just a short walk from his office complex. It was a few minutes before ten o'clock. His wife had already retired to their bedroom.

Chen took one last drag. He had just snuffed out the butt in an ashtray when a guard stepped onto the balcony from the living room. "My apologies, Mr. President, but there's an urgent phone call for you."

"Who is it?"

"Deputy Minister Guo."

President Chen relocated to an alcove off the home's grand entryway. The amber light on the cradle of the encrypted phone sitting on Chen's desk blinked. He picked up the handset. "What is it, Guo?" he said, his tone broadcasting annoyance.

"Sorry for the late hour," Comrade President." The MPS spymaster's voice was dull, a washed-out monotone that resulted from the encryption software. "I just received an update on Qingdao. I thought you would want to know."

Chen sensed bad news. "Go ahead."

"You were correct, sir…about the Qingdao situation. We now believe the bomb was initially located at another position before it was moved to the actual detonation site."

"Why would they do that?"

"It was not an intentional move," Guo said. "We believe the bomb was supposed to have detonated in a Port of Qingdao waterway called the Middle Harbour. It's located just south of the Qingdao Naval Base. The base may have been the actual target. We think the bomb was placed on the bottom but it was dug up accidentally by a dredge and disposed of in the mudflats north of the bay bridge."

Dumbfounded by the news, President Chen asked, "How did you come up with this scenario?"

"The Qingdao MPS bureau did the legwork. They discovered that the port has had a harbor deepening project in the waterway for the past month or so. The dredged material from the channel was hauled away by barges to the mudflats where it was dumped. It was part of the Port's plan to construct an artificial island in the bay to be used for marine habitat improvement."

"That's where the bomb blew up?"

"Correct, near the center of the fill site."

Chen mulled over the latest developments. "What about the Uyghurs… how are they connected?"

"We have video of the boat they used running back and forth in the Port's waterway, as if searching for something on the bottom."

"Were they working for the Port?"

"No, and they weren't working for the dredging contractor either. We now think they were searching for the bomb. Not finding it, they figured out it was dredged up. The boat crossed the bay to the mudflat area where it was obliterated when the bomb exploded."

"Why would they blow themselves up?"

Guo said, "Our current theory is the bomb's firing circuit was damaged when dug up by the dredge. We think the Uyghurs were trying to recover it at the mudflats when it accidentally detonated."

President Chen cursed.

Guo continued, "We believe the Uyghurs' plan was to return the bomb to the Middle Harbour."

"If the naval base was the target, why use the waterway?"

"The bottom of the base and its entrance channel are regularly swept for mines. The Port's commercial waterways are not."

Chen pieced the puzzle parts together, alarmed more than ever. "Then it was just luck that we didn't lose the base."

"Correct, sir. The Qingdao Naval Base plus the Port's cruise terminal and the residential towers on the south side of the waterway would have all been destroyed. A very conservative estimate of the death toll is fifteen thousand."

"This does not sound like the Americans to me."

"I concur. We are continuing to follow the Uyghur angle."

"I think they're just being used as a scapegoat."

"Sir?" Guo said, unsure of President Chen's comment.

"It's the Russians—they're on to us."

Chapter 18

Day 9—Thursday

The *Heilong* surfaced at 1:20 A.M. Commander Yang Yu clambered up the tunnel ladder inside the submarine's sail, opened the topside hatch and climbed onto the bridge deck where he stood upright. The bulky sea coat he wore swathed his lean, athletic frame. His gleaming teeth, wrinkle free skin and perfect facial symmetry all contributed to his attractiveness. His coal black hair, ruffled by the sea breeze, brushed his ears and hovered over his shirt collar. He needed a trim.

A couple of months away from forty, Yang had served as a line officer in the People's Liberation Army-Navy for seventeen years. He was captain of the *Heilong*—one of China's most advanced hunter-killer subs.

Yang wore a headset with microphone. He opened a watertight compartment in the sail's bridge station and plugged the wire lead from the headset into a receptacle. "This is the captain," he said, addressing the ship's officer of the watch two decks below in the attack center. "I have the conn. Send up the watch standers."

The watch officer acknowledged the order.

Two sailors followed Yang, taking up watch stations in the bridge well behind him. It was a moonless night in the Yellow Sea. Swells rolled in from the southeast, washing over the aft deck of the 377-foot-long warship. After tangling with U.S. subs near Hawaii, the Type 095 nuclear powered attack submarine took extreme care to ensure it was not followed home by the Americans.

The *Heilong* was three miles offshore of the Jianggezhuang Submarine Base. Located in Shandong Province, China's oldest sub base was fifteen miles east of the Qingdao Naval Base. North Sea Fleet headquarters ordered Yang to bypass its temporary berth at Qingdao and return to its homeport at Jianggezhuang.

Commander Yang surveyed the distant shore with binoculars. Lights from buildings outlined the perimeter of the artificial harbor. Penetrating the upland light pollution was a single flashing red light. The beacon was a navigation aid. It marked the south breakwater of the base.

Yang retrieved a compact tablet from an inside pocket of his sea coat. He consulted the digital navigation chart. "Conn, bridge," he said, activating his lip mic.

"Bridge, conn," replied the watch officer.

"I have the outer marker of the breakwater in sight. Proceed on a heading of zero two eight. Make turns for eight knots."

The WO repeated the order.

Yang turned about to address the observers. "Stay alert, men. We don't have far to go but fishing boats work around here. They're typically low to the water and many avoid using navigation lights to hide from the authorities."

The sailors acknowledged the order while scanning the waters with binoculars. Overhead, an orbiting radar antenna also searched the sea surface.

Heilong's captain savored the fresh air. The ship's high tech oxygen generator and ventilation system produced clean air but it was sterile. Yang tasted the salt in his mouth; his nose captured a hint of earthiness.

Captain Yang Yu and his crew had been at sea for a month. He hoped the crew could enjoy shore leave but was uncertain how long they would stay in port.

Instead of mooring at its usual floating pier at Jianggezhuang, North Fleet Headquarters ordered the submarine to berth inside the coastal rise on the eastern shore of the base. Jianggezhuang had its own subterranean sub pens for housing boomers—similar to the Sanya-Yulin base. A tunnel connected the harbor to the hollowed out chamber inside the hillside.

This would be Yang's and the *Heilong's* first venture inside the underground seaport. A PLA Navy pilot would board the *Heilong* after it sailed into the harbor to guide the attack sub through the tunnel.

The concealed harbor was reserved exclusively for PLAN ballistic missile submarines. Jianggezhuang's cavern included facilities for the loading and servicing of nuclear tipped ICBMs as well as providing all other needs of the subs. By berthing China's waterborne strategic weapon systems under several hundred feet of rock, military satellites from the USA, Russia and India were thwarted from spying on the missile boats.

Fleet provided Captain Yang with no explanation for deviating from the *Heilong's* normal mooring arrangement, which piqued his curiosity. *They must have something important planned for us—but what?*

Anxious to find out what Fleet had in store for the *Heilong*, Yang Yu's thoughts focused on another pressing matter. During the homeward voyage, Yang had been apprised of the nuclear detonation. Yang and most of his crew lived in Qingdao.

Although Yang's apartment was not in the A-bomb's fallout zone, his lover's residence was. Sun Tao's luxurious penthouse apartment in Qingdao's Badaxia neighborhood had a sprawling view of the Yellow Sea. Married and the father of a fourteen-year-old daughter, Tao owned a booming restaurant in the financial district of Qingdao. Commander Yang and Tao had a longstanding relationship. They connected regularly when Yang was in port.

Captain Yang pictured his lover's rugged face and brawny build.

Soon, Tao, soon!

* * * *

President Tyler Magnuson and National Security Advisor Peter Brindle were alone in the President's private dining room near the Oval Office. It was a working lunch. After munching on health friendly tossed green salads and delicious halibut sandwiches—a specialty of the White House Chef—the two men enjoyed coffee while discussing pressing matters.

"When do you expect we'll have the evidence to go after Moscow?" asked Magnuson. Russia's scheme to incinerate Pearl Harbor with a nuclear weapon haunted the president.

"It's complicated, sir. We know they're behind it but we have scant physical evidence to definitively pin it on them. We've had no luck in identifying the source of plutonium, which we were expecting to have originated from a Russian or Soviet reactor."

"What about that Russian naval officer...the one who dumped the bomb offshore? Can't he testify about what happened?"

"Kirov can and we may need to eventually do that, but for now we believe he's much more valuable to us as an intelligence asset. His knowledge of the Russian Navy and his recent experience with China are golden. We've never had an asset like that before."

"Hmmm," Magnuson muttered. "Does Moscow know he's working for us?"

"We don't think so. They may have suspicions but he's returned to his job and maintains a low profile."

The president bit his lower lip, recalling a critical item. "Are you certain he was not involved with the attempt on Pearl?"

"I am. I've now read the transcripts of Kirov's interrogations and spoke with key personnel from the FBI, CIA and Navy who questioned him. His actions were truly heroic." Brindle collected his thoughts, knowing what he was about to reveal would infuriate his boss. "Something else has come up regarding Kirov that you need to know about."

Curious, the president said, "Go on."

"It's about China."

For the next ten minutes NSA Brindle laid out the facts. President Magnuson's demeanor slowly evolved as the story unfolded, from suspicion to astonishment and finally fury.

"Sabotaging the Russian oil well and attacking our facilities in Alaska and then targeting one of our subs," POTUS said, his voice almost a shout. "Beijing has been playing us the entire time!"

"It appears so."

"Just how confident are you with all of this?"

"It fits. Kirov filled in the missing pieces. The DNI briefed me this morning after he finished his review of the interagency analysis. A detailed summary will be in your daily briefing tomorrow morning."

"No wonder Lebedev has been such an ass about the oil spill. He was screwed just as much as we were."

"Without a doubt."

President Magnuson stroked an ear while processing the National Security Advisor's info dump. "How solid is the business about the Trident sub?"

"Kirov's story is credible. The physical evidence that was collected along with the mission profile of the *Kentucky* suggest that what he claimed could have actually occurred." Brindle mentioned the failed effort to sink an *Ohio*-class ballistic missile submarine as it departed Puget Sound, bound for the Pacific. The U.S. Navy was not aware of the attempt.

Reagitated, President Magnuson lashed out at Beijing's treachery. "The bastards! We almost went to war with the Russians because of them."

"They played us both, and nearly succeeded."

"But why would they do such a thing? It makes no sense."

Brindle cupped his hands. "We think it was about Taiwan. China's ready to forcibly return the rebel province to the fold, but only one obstacle stands in the way."

"We're the obstacle," POTUS said. "They incite a war between us and Russia and we end up seriously depleting our forces."

"Correct, sir. We'd prevail with a conflict with the Kremlin but we'd need months to recover. That would be the time for Beijing to make its move."

"Sun Tzu tactics," offered Magnuson." He referred to the *Art of War,* a definitive work on military strategy written over two millenniums earlier by Chinese General Sun Tzu.

"'All war is deception'," Brindle said, quoting Sun Tzu.

"But it all turned to crap for them."

"So it seems. Yet they almost succeeded."

President Magnuson's brow crumpled. "If China had taken out the *Kentucky*, we—I would have assumed it was Russia. That would have sparked the war for sure, just as Beijing planned."

"We were incredibly lucky that Kirov intervened."

"Definitely."

NSA Brindle summed up his position. "The Kremlin figured out Beijing's scheme and decided to turn the table on them."

"And us, too."

"Yes. The Russians took out the Yulin base on Hainan Island but left evidence that would convince Beijing we were behind the raid." Brindle pinched the bridge of his nose. "Moscow then dispatched a sub to Hawaii where a *spetsnaz* unit planted the nuke at Pearl Harbor."

President Magnuson completed the rundown. "And we would have taken the bait, believing China took out Pearl as revenge for the Yulin attack."

"That's right."

POTUS said, "Pete, this nightmare is right out of the old KGB's playbook for the sixties."

"It is…an updated replay of *K-129*."

Brindle referred to a 1968 scheme hatched by rogue elements in the USSR to launch a nuclear-tipped ballistic missile from Soviet submarine *K-129*. The target was Honolulu. The KGB left a trail of evidence that pointed to Red China as the attacker. The nuclear strike failed when the missile exploded in its launch tube north of the Hawaiian Islands. The event precipitated the CIA's most complex Cold War espionage operation— Project Azorian. Employing Howard Hughes's deep ocean mining ship, the *Glomar Explorer*, the CIA secretly raised a portion of *K-129's* hull from the seafloor three miles deep.

President Magnuson folded his arms and uttered a curse, his rage scarcely in check. "I want options on the table ASAP for dealing with both China and Russia."

"Diplomatic…economic sanctions?"

"No—military. We're way beyond sanctions now."

Chapter 19

Day 11—Saturday

The ship was 345 kilometers—187 nautical miles—southeast of Hainan Island. With still air and temperatures in the low nineties Fahrenheit, the South China Sea was a millpond this afternoon. The ninety-four meter research ship hailed from its homeport of Sanya. Less than a year old, the *Lian*—the Graceful Willow—bristled with the latest navigation, communication and underwater sensing electronics. Diesel powered, the ship had a maximum speed of eighteen knots. Accommodations for the scientists that staffed the ship's laboratories were luxurious.

The Chinese Academy of Sciences was the principal operator of the *Lian* but the People's Liberation Army-Navy owned the vessel. For its current voyage, the ship's normal complement of Academy staff was replaced with PLAN officers and sailors, all garbed in civilian clothing.

Dr. Meng Park was the only non-military aboard. Wearing coveralls, hardhat and an automatic/manual inflatable life vest, she was on the equipment deployment bay near the stern. She stood on the top level of an aluminum scaffold next to a collection of stainless steel canisters that had the appearance of oversized oil barrels. The lids for all barrels had been detached. She peered down into the nearest canister. The drum was nearly eight feet tall with a diameter of about five feet. Captain Zhou Jun observed from Meng's right side.

A metallic tube roughly a foot in diameter and eighty-two feet long—twenty-five meters—was coiled inside the circumference of the canister. Meng bent forward and reached inside the drum where she manipulated a control panel built into the end of the tube. She turned toward Zhou. "All systems are nominal, permission to arm it?"

"Yes, go ahead."

Meng completed the same procedure for the other five barrels. Each canister contained her latest creation, codename VIPERINA. Named after *Thalassophina viperina,* the venomous sea snake was indigenous to the waters of the South China Sea.

The half dozen barrels were secured to a steel cradle in two equal rows. A few inches of open space separated the drums. Clamps built into the cradle anchored the base of each barrel, preventing movement. A one-inch diameter coil of electrical cable was lashed to the cradle's deck.

After inspecting the arrangement, Dr. Meng addressed Captain Zhou. "I think we're set now."

"Good. Let's proceed with deployment."

Meng and Zhou repositioned forward twenty feet. Zhou turned around and raised his right arm. He rotated his wrist, signaling the sailor inside a cab beside the A-frame hoist. The heavy steel assembly straddled the ship's stern deck.

The hoist operator engaged the winch. A steel cable linked to a harness that connected to the four corners of the barrel cradle pulled taut. Once clear of the deck, the A-frame hoist rotated aft until the cradle was suspended over the sea, ten feet away from the hull.

The hoist operator made eye contact with Captain Zhou. Zhou issued a new signal, directing the sailor to lower the package. Within seconds, the prototype of the VIPERINA antisubmarine warfare (ASW) system disappeared from view.

* * * *

The package was delivered to the seabed 1,660 feet beneath the ship's keel. While the winch cable was reeled back aboard the *Lian,* Captain Zhou and Dr. Meng transferred to the sensor control room in the interior of the ship near midships.

Overhead red lighting in the compartment created a cave like environment. Four wide-screen displays covered the forward bulkhead. Although air-conditioned, the odor of hot electronics permeated the control room.

Meng was in a chair next to the sensor operator. The PLAN lieutenant had over two thousand hours of mission time piloting ROVs—remotely operated vehicles. The ROV named *Ming Ue*—Bright Moon—hovered ten feet above the mud bottom. A pencil thick neutrally buoyant tether connected the underwater robot to its garage, which was about fifty feet away.

The ROV's garage consisted of a steel frame assembly. It was supported by a cable that connected to a topside winch mounted to a retractable side door platform currently cantilevered six feet seaward from the portside hull aft of the control room. Integrated into the cable were a steel wire rope for support, an insulated cable supplying electrical power, and multiple fiberoptic strands for communications and control.

A reel built into the subsea garage housed the *Ming Ue's* umbilical cord. The tether supplied power and comms to the free-swimming robot.

Ming Ue was about the size of a household washing machine. The main body of the ROV contained ballast tanks, a collection of thrusters, an onboard computer and multiple sonars for navigation and targeting. Mounted to *Ming Ue's* forward section were three cameras, two video and a still. An overhead rack of floodlights provided illumination for the cameras and also for the ROV operator. Two mechanical arms were located below the cameras. The four-foot-long articulated devices included handlike appendages. The left robotic arm's vice grip was capable of exerting enormous clamping pressures on underwater hardware, powered by the ROV's onboard high-pressure hydraulic pump system. The steel fingers on the right arm were capable of retrieving delicate *in situ* biological samples and placing them inside collection containers.

The HD screen centered in front of the ROV pilot displayed a real time color image of the seabed package. The cradle containing the VIPERINA canisters had landed within two meters of the intended coordinates.

Dr. Meng said, "Let's check the power hub before we do anything else."

"Yes, ma'am." The pilot worked the joystick control on the left armrest of his chair. *Ming Ue's* four thrusters worked in unison, propelling the craft twenty feet to the north.

The power hub consisted of a canary yellow steel box about the size of a medium size pickup truck. Standing six feet high, all four sides of the hub sloped downward to the seafloor. The one atmosphere pressure chamber housed inside the protective outer steel shell contained a compact nuclear reactor and an electrical power generating system. The hub was installed a month earlier.

Meng studied the image of the subsea installation, looking for anomalies. Satisfied she said, "Looks good. Go ahead and connect the cable."

"Aye, aye, ma'am."

The pilot maneuvered *Ming Ue* back to the package where he recovered the coil of black cable stored on the cradle. He next carefully paid out the cable while guiding the ROV back to the hub. *Ming Ue* currently hovered beside the power center with the end of the cable secured by the starboard mechanical arm. The port robotic arm was clamped to a steel bracket protruding from the hub; it anchored the ROV.

"Permission to make the connection?" asked the pilot.

"Yes, proceed."

The pilot rotated his right wrist, which was encased by a sensor laden glove. The glove converted the pilot's manipulations into electrical pulses that were transmitted through the tether to the robotic right arm.

The male end of the power cable entered the power hub's female receptacle. With an additional twist of the pilot's wrist, the cable was locked in place.

"We've got a positive connection," announced the pilot.

"Excellent work, Lieutenant."

"Thank you, ma'am."

Dr. Meng swiveled her chair. In the shadows, Captain Zhou stood next to a bulkhead. "Captain, before we do anything else, I'd like to run a complete set of diagnostics on the power transfer system to verify it is operational. Are you okay with that?"

"Yes, that's fine."

* * * *

Dr. Meng completed the testing program and was ready to proceed with deployment. She faced Zhou. He manned a control panel that connected to the ship's sonar unit. "Captain," Meng said, "We're all set now."

"Very well. I'll proceed with the launch." Zhou triggered a toggle switch on the panel, which activated a thru-hull transducer located near the *Lian's* bow. The narrow beam acoustic pulse sped downward at 5,100 feet per second.

The apparatus coiled inside canister one recognized the unique sound signal from the ship. Within a heartbeat, the autonomous machine transformed from hibernation mode to search. The terminal end of the coiled tube disconnected from the power connection at the base of the cannister.

Dr. Meng fixated on the screen displaying the ROV's video transmission. Months of work and hundreds of millions of yuan were invested in her brainchild. *Come on! I know you can do it!*

Viperina One's head rose from the canister as it slowly uncoiled. Within a minute, the tail cleared the container.

"Stay on it, Lieutenant!" Zhou ordered.

"Aye, aye, Captain." The pilot maneuvered the ROV's thrusters, maintaining video lock on the target.

Dr. Meng smiled as she observed her creation maneuver. Stretched out to twenty-five meters, it snaked through the abyss. Its body oscillated horizontally several meters, propelling itself forward at four knots.

The test program called for the unit to orbit the subsea base, centering on the power hub.

"How does it look?" Captain Zhou asked.

"Perfect," she said, turning his way and flashing a warm smile. "Better than I expected."

"Outstanding. What's next?"

"I'd like to observe for the next hour or so, slowly extending range."

Zhou faced the ROV pilot. "How far away can we let it roam and still observe by video?"

"Water clarity's good, but I'd limit it to no more than fifty meters from *Ming Ue's* camera.

"Can you keep up with it at that range?"

"Yes, at its current speed. We have plenty of reserve tether and the currents are minimal."

"Very well. Let's proceed."

* * * *

Testing continued through the afternoon. Sunset was a half hour away but no one inside the ship's sensor control room noticed. Dr. Meng and Captain Zhou observed Viperina 1 as it successfully completed each test exercise. It was currently in listening mode.

Configured into a horizontal string, Viperina 1 hovered next to the ROV, several hundred feet above the bottom. Embedded inside the length of its snakelike body were tiny omnidirectional hydrophones. The eighty sensors listened for manmade sounds.

The *Lian* had deployed the target three hours earlier. The twenty-foot-long by two-and-a-half-foot diameter autonomous underwater vehicle had proceeded southward just below the surface at six knots. After running for an hour, it descended sixteen hundred feet and commenced its return voyage toward the ship.

Now heading northward at five knots, the AUV's electric motor was in effect silent. The only sound the robotic craft generated came from its propeller, which produced a faint acoustic signal.

The *Lian's* sonar sensors could not hear the AUV, nor could the ROV, which was still deployed over the clandestine subsea base. However, Viperina 1's integrated sound surveillance array detected the AUV's propeller as it closed on the base. Programmed to ignore the ROV's acoustic output and thruster wash from the *Lian's* dynamic positioning system, Viperina 1 transferred from surveillance to pre-attack mode. Switching from a linear array to a vertical circular arrangement, the machine's brain head linked with its tail. All eighty hydrophones tracked the target, each one sending data to the miniature AI computer in Viperina 1's head.

Dr. Meng's heart beat at Mach speed. She watched the ROV's video output. "It's in pre-attack mode now," she announced.

"The AUV must be getting close," Captain Zhou said.

Meng turned to the ROV pilot. "Be ready to track it. It could—"

Before Meng could complete the warning, Viperina 1 decoupled and it raced southward. Now stretched to its full length, it slithered through the deep at an accelerated clip.

The pilot uttered a curse as he attempted to keep the camera trained on Dr. Meng's machine.

Viperina 1 focused on the advancing AUV, calculating the optimum angle of approach. And then it attacked.

V-1 wrapped itself around the AUV starting a couple of feet aft of the bow and continuing to the propeller and rudder assembly. Half-inch-long metallic spikes embedded along the length of Viperina 1 gripped the AUV's steel casing. Like a python coiled around its prey, V-1 overwhelmed the target vehicle in just seconds.

Astounded, the ROV pilot expressed another expletive.

"Incredible," Captain Zhou said.

Thank the gods, thought Meng Park.

Chapter 21

Day 14—Tuesday

"I think I like this place," Yuri said as he placed his empty coffee mug in the kitchen sink.

"It's nice, and a lot quieter than I expected." Laura checked email on her iPhone.

"Quality construction...the soundproofing seems to work well."

"It does."

Yuri and family spent their second night in the apartment. Because of Yuri's resolve, Laura leased the 24th floor unit in the downtown Bellevue condominium tower for six months. The owner, a Microsoft executive, was on a temporary assignment in Europe.

Yuri and Laura were about to leave for work. Maddy was buckled to her highchair. Her nanny, Amanda Graham, waited by the Keurig as it brewed her coffee.

Laura slipped the phone into her purse. She kissed Maddy on the forehead. "You have a wonderful day sweetie!"

Madelyn Grace giggled her response.

Laura addressed Amanda. "We'll be home at the usual time tonight."

"Okay, great." Amanda slept in the apartment's guest bedroom.

The new plan called for dual living arrangements. Yuri, Laura and Maddy would spend their weekends at the Sammamish residence. But from Sunday evening to Friday afternoon, they would reside in the luxury apartment located just a couple of blocks away from Cognition Consultants.

Chapter 20

Day 12—Sunday

The robot woke up. Thirty days—720 hours—had elapsed since Yuri Kirov deployed the crawlerbot on the harbor bottom of the PRC's Sanya-Yulin Naval Base.

After completing its spy mission inside the Hainan Island subterranean cavern that housed ballistic missile submarines, the autonomous amphibian had returned to its launch coordinates. It promptly buried itself a foot deep in the harbor's silty bottom soil. The robot had waited patiently for the recovery signal or until the thirty-day default time expired.

About the size of a laptop computer and shaped similar to the shell of a leatherback sea turtle, the crawlerbot extracted itself from its temporary grave by activating dual sets of articulated legs. After digging its way out, the crawlerbot expelled seawater from its internal ballast chamber with a squirt of compressed air.

It took a couple of minutes for buoyancy to carry the robot to the surface. As it floated in the protected waters of the Chinese naval base in the early morning darkness, it deployed a wire antenna and commenced transmission. Within five minutes, its encrypted and compressed data package was uploaded to one of the low orbit Russian military satellites that provided continuous coverage of the South China Sea. A U.S. based commercial telecom satellite also uploaded the data.

With its mission completed, the crawlerbot returned to the seafloor and reburied itself, burrowing nearly three feet into the sediment.

Fully furnished, the 3,200 square foot flat had a view of Lake Washington's Meydenbauer Bay and the Seattle skyline beyond. Security in the building was state of the art, which won Yuri's approval. The building's security center was staffed twenty-four seven, which included video monitoring of the lobby, every exit, stairway and elevator, and the entire parking garage. Staff knew every resident by eyesight; unaccompanied visitors or service personnel required pre-approval by the unit's occupants.

* * * *

Laura and Yuri strolled side by side on the sidewalk. The walkways and streets buzzed with fervent energy as commuters converged on downtown Bellevue's financial core. Cognition's tower was five minutes away.

"You know you don't have to do this every day," Laura said.

"You don't like my company?" Yuri replied, his voice purposely sheepish.

"I love that you do this for me but it's a pain for you. I can walk the couple of blocks alone in safety." She stopped and raised her hands. "Look, honey, people and cars everywhere. No one's going to do anything to me here."

They'd had this discussion before. "Don't worry about me. It's my honor to escort you."

"Okay."

After dropping off Laura by the elevator that would carry her to her office, Yuri returned to the condominium's garage. He opened the front door to his Toyota Highlander. Before climbing in, he removed the compact .45 caliber semiauto pistol and its clip-on holster from the small of his back. He slipped the weapon into the coat pocket of his jacket.

FBI agent Michaela Taylor arranged for the federally issued permit that allowed Yuri to carry a concealed weapon virtually anywhere inside the United States. It was a trivial concession on the part of the FBI, knowing the risks ahead for Yuri and his family. Laura and Madelyn had been kidnapped together. And later, two attempts on Laura's life were made, both thwarted by the FBI.

Yuri drove out of the garage and headed east. He would arrive at his Redmond office in fifteen minutes.

Three cars behind, the man who had been surveilling Yuri Kirov this morning kept a close eye on the Highlander.

* * * *

It was late morning at Northwest Subsea Dynamics. Yuri and NSD's chief engineer met in Yuri's office. Spread across the desk was a poster sized schematic drawing of a new submersible—Bill Winters' brainchild. With the working title of 'Sea Lance', the autonomous underwater vehicle represented a radical departure from previous craft constructed by NSD. Sea Lance was a weapon, designed to intercept and kill other AUVs.

"Okay, Bill, I like the concept and the budget seems reasonable to me. I'll talk to Laura about it to make sure she's on board."

"Great, I really think it's a path the company should pursue. The Navy spends a bundle each year on subsea weapons systems. Sea Lance could fit right in with their plans."

"I agree."

"Thanks boss."

After Winters returned to his office, Yuri spent another minute looking over the conceptual drawing, admiring Bill's innovative design. He was about to fold up the drawing when the intercom on his desk phone buzzed. He picked up the handset. "Yes," he said addressing NSD's receptionist.

"John, you have a visitor." She recited the name and his company but neither clicked for Yuri. "You met in Vancouver earlier this year. He was visiting nearby and wondered if you might have time for lunch."

"I'll be right out," Yuri said, suspicious.

When Yuri entered the lobby, Nick Orlov rose from the chair and with his right arm extended, he approached Yuri. "John," he said, "sorry to barge in on you unannounced."

Startled, Yuri hesitated for an instant before grasping the extended hand. "Nice to see you again."

Yuri steered the SVR officer into the conference room and closed the door. The two men embraced, Russian style.

"How are you, my friend?" Orlov asked in Russian.

"Please, English only here."

"Of course."

Yuri and Nick took seats by the conference table. Still reeling from the surprise encounter, Yuri said, "I thought you were expelled when the Houston consulate was shut down."

"I was. Booted back to Moscow with all of the staff."

"How'd you get back?"

"I flew into Vancouver for meetings at the trade mission." He referred to the Russian Trade Mission in downtown Vancouver. The Russian Federation's Ministry of Industry and Trade established the office to promote trade between western Canada and eastern Russia.

"And you decided to make a quick side trip down here."

Nick winked. "I did."

"How'd you manage the border?"

"Same passport I used last time, like yours."

Orlov mentioned the Canadian passports both he and Yuri had used. Manufactured by a special unit in the SVR's Illegals Directorate, the passport booklets were authentic. Two hundred blanks were purchased from an agent recruited at a Canadian government office in Ottawa. Canada Customs and Immigration remained in the dark regarding the theft.

"You're down here without diplomatic immunity. That's risky for you."

"Won't be here long."

Antsy, Yuri couldn't delay any longer. "Nick, what are you doing here?"

"SVR Director Smirnov sent me to check up on you."

Govnó!

* * * *

Dinner was over. Yuri and Laura were in the living room of the Bellevue high rise rental, sitting in a pair of sofas by the windows. Laura held Madelyn in her lap.

"Looks like our summer's going away," Yuri said peering out the windows. A new Pacific front had rolled in during the afternoon bringing unwelcome rain. The thick overcast and receding sun created a gloomy pall that engulfed the entire Puget Sound region.

Laura said, "Soggy and chilly days are on the way. But I don't mind, I'm used to it."

Yuri did mind but left it alone. Besides, the Pacific Northwest's climate was tropical compared to Moscow's bleak and frozen late fall and winter seasons.

Laura glanced down at Maddy. It was near her daughter's bedtime; she was almost asleep, her eyes barely open. "Time for bed, sweetie," Laura said.

Laura carried Maddy to her bedroom.

Yuri stared at the window wall but the view no longer registered. Instead, his thoughts raced. The unexpected visit from Nick Orlov in the morning was heavy on his mind. *What should I do?*

He had not yet told Laura about Nick and debated throughout the day as to whether he should. When Laura returned, he made up his mind.

Laura reclaimed her position on the sofa.

"You get her down okay?" he asked.

"Yes, she's worn out." Amanda and Madelyn had spent the afternoon at the Woodland Park Zoo in Seattle. Amanda already left; she frequently spent her evenings with her Microsoft boyfriend in his Redmond apartment.

Yuri cleared his voice. "I need to tell you something…Nick Orlov visited me at the office this morning."

Laura's right hand skyrocketed to her mouth. "No!"

"We ended up having lunch together."

"What did he want?"

"He was sent to check on me."

Yuri spent the next few minutes providing highlights of the encounter.

Laura settled back into the couch, relieved but still perplexed. "How did he react when you told him about the bomb in Pearl Harbor?"

"I didn't tell him."

"Why not? He should know what kind of people he's working for."

"Nick doesn't need that kind of problem."

Yuri made no mention of the Pearl Harbor mission or the bomb when they met. That was a closely held secret privy to just a handful of elites in the Kremlin and the two special operators that planted the nuke. Yuri had sensed it was best for Nick if he were not included in that loop.

Laura said, "He doesn't know what you did?"

"No."

"So, Russia doesn't know about the FBI?"

"Nick didn't seem to know or didn't want to know. I just told him that all I want is to be left alone. I stressed that I completed my assignment and that I was promised I could retire."

"What about asylum?"

"I told him that you had attorneys working with the State Department to allow me to stay in the States. I mentioned that I might have to request political asylum to make that happen."

"How'd he take that?"

"He said he understood."

"That's all he said?"

"I could tell he didn't want to hear about any of the details. Asylum is not going to be received well back in Moscow."

"What's he going to do?"

"I'm sure he's in Vancouver by now. He'll send in a report from the trade mission and probably fly back to Moscow." Yuri slumped into the couch. "He took a huge risk coming down here after being expelled; if he were picked up or ID'd at the border crossing, he'd end up in prison."

"I hope he'll be okay." Yuri and Laura were indebted to Nicolai Orlov. He had saved both of their lives nearly two years earlier.

Yuri said, "I tried to isolate him from what went down at Pearl Harbor but if it gets out, he'll be tainted because of me."

"Because of both of us."

"Right."

Yuri could not reveal that he had sabotaged Moscow's effort to ignite a war between the United States and China by dumping the Pearl Harbor nuke in the ocean. And if the SVR knew he was now working for the Americans, he'd be a marked man.

"Are you going to tell the FBI about the meeting with Nick?"

"I don't know. That might put Nick in additional jeopardy." Yuri stretched out his arms. "I might just keep it to myself...and you."

"That's risky. You should tell them."

"I'll think about it."

Yuri didn't reveal everything to Laura about his meeting with Nick.

Late the previous evening Yuri had checked the FTP site. The 30 days were up. Yuri was astonished to find the encrypted data file in his personal Northwest Subsea Dynamics folder, which was accessible only by him.

Yuri had programmed the Yulin crawlerbot to execute two data transmissions. First to a Russian military satellite, as planned. Second to a private global satellite communications network used by NSD for data collection from the company's fleet of autonomous underwater vehicles. It was Yuri's insurance policy.

After typing in the passcode, Yuri had spent an hour reviewing the videos. He was flabbergasted at the content. The autonomous amphibian carried out its mission flawlessly.

And today, while lunching with Nick Orlov in a Redmond restaurant, Yuri had decided to plant the seed. The opportunity was far sooner than he had dreamed possible.

Knowing Nick would have to report their meeting to Moscow, Yuri asked him to convey a cryptic message to the director of the SVR. The communiqué would not be received well by Borya Smirnov.

The barter was part of Yuri's strategy to make a permanent break with the homeland, allowing him and his adopted American family to finally live in peace—he hoped.

Chapter 22

The USS *Tucson* cruised northwestward at a stealthy twelve knots. It was 600 feet beneath the South China Sea, 147 nautical miles east of Sanya. SSN 770 was on a reconnaissance mission. One of China's state-run oil companies was drilling a new natural gas well in a deepwater field located northeast of Hainan Island.

Tucson was charged with taking closeup photos of the floating semisubmersible drill rig, both above and below the waterline. Its mission also called for acoustic monitoring of the rig's underwater drilling activity. The vessel was the first of its class, designed and built entirely in China. The CIA and the U.S. Navy jointly needed to verify that the drill rig was being used solely for petroleum exploration purposes.

Commander Scott Arnold was in *Tucson's* control room. Six foot two with broad shoulders and a barrel chest, his physique conveyed athlete. Towheaded, his receding hairline was barely noticeable but a harbinger of future annoyances to come.

Arnold was one of the younger sub skippers in the Pacific Fleet at thirty-six. It was his first command, having served as executive officer aboard another attack sub for two years. His wife of ten years and their two sons resided in a hillside home that overlooked Honolulu and the Pacific beyond.

Tucson was an Improved-Los Angeles class attack submarine. With its four torpedo tubes and twelve vertical launch missile tubes, it packed a mighty offensive punch.

Arnold turned to address the ship's executive officer who hovered over a nearby plotting table. "XO, what's our ETA?" he asked.

Lieutenant Commander Hal Russell looked up. "We should be on station in about an hour." Unlike the captain, Russell was average height with a gangling build. His nut-brown hair was thick with no signs of balding. Two years junior to Arnold, he served as *Tucson's* second in command. A bachelor, Russell rented an apartment near Pearl Harbor.

"What about the sun?" asked Arnold.

"It's setting now so we should have plenty of dark for night ops."

"Excellent. Nice job bringing her in."

"Thanks skipper."

Russell was tasked with making the approach. Arnold had just reclaimed the conn.

Standing near the twin periscopes, Commander Arnold paged through various digital documents on the tablet he held. As *Tucson's* CO, he received continuous status reports from key department heads. He had just completed reviewing a report from Engineering when an overhead intercom speaker broadcast.

"Conn, sonar. Unknown contact bearing two one seven. Range four hundred and forty yards. Depth nine five five feet and ascending. Closing on our position at fourteen knots." The tech sounded the alarm from his console in the sonar room, located forward of the control room.

Arnold grabbed an intercom microphone from an overhead rack. "Sonar, Captain. What is it?"

"Captain, I don't know. It's not propeller driven. Very quiet, mainly picking up flow disturbances. I've never heard anything like it before."

"Biologic?"

"There's nothing like it in the computer. Plus its speed is up there for a biologic."

"Designate contact as Master Four Nine and standby."

"Master Four Nine, aye."

The sonar contact was considered potentially hostile and earned a "Master" designation.

Captain Arnold looked forward at the officer of the deck. The lieutenant stood just behind the helmsman and the planes operator. "Mr. Johnson, come right to course zero eight five. Make turns for twenty-five knots. Do not cavitate. Make your depth nine hundred feet."

The OOD repeated the orders and *Tucson* began racing away from the mystery contact. To minimize sound generation from cavitation, power to the ship's screw was increased carefully to prevent the spinning propeller blades from leaving a noisy knuckle of churning water behind.

Arnold joined *Tucson's* XO at the plotting table. A digital chart of the northern half of the South China Sea was displayed. *Tucson's* position was marked with a blue submarine icon. A red X marked Master Four Nine.

"What do you think, Hal?" asked Arnold.

"Very odd, skipper, coming up from the deep like that."

Arnold started to comment when the intercom speaker blared out a new report. "Conn, sonar, Master Four Nine has accelerated to thirty knots and is definitely tracking us. Range three hundred eighty yards and closing."

Arnold muttered an expletive and keyed his mic. "Sonar, conn, standby." He addressed the OOD next. "Steady as she goes, all ahead flank. Make your depth one thousand two-hundred feet."

* * * *

Viperina Six—V-6—continued its pursuit of the target. The autonomous underwater sentry was in attack mode. Slinking upward from the deep, the robotic serpent accelerated. Its eighty-two-foot-long neutrally buoyant sinuous body undulated up to twenty feet from side to side. Propelled by internal servomechanisms that mimicked muscle power, the mechanical serpent was capable of reaching burst speeds of nearly forty knots.

V-6 was not alone. Its hunting partner, V-5 maneuvered to the east, preparing to set the trap.

Hunting in pairs, the AUVs patrolled offshore of Hainan Island, ranging up to a hundred miles from seabed Viper HUB Station 1. When within a hundred meters of each other, the vipers communicated with lasers. Beyond the optical limit, they used sonar.

Both units were low on battery power and were scheduled to return to their home base for recharging soon. However, twenty minutes earlier while suspended vertically in the water column fifteen hundred feet below the surface, both Viperinas detected the American submarine as it approached from the southeast.

While in monitoring mode, the vipers had communicated optically, devising the attack plan. Battery power was critical but enough juice was left to prosecute the attack. As V-6 advanced on the target, V-5 slinked eastward, anticipating in advance how their prey would react.

* * * *

"Conn, sonar. Master Four Nine is now running at thirty-three knots and accelerating. Range three hundred yards."

Captain Arnold didn't have time to answer sonar's latest warning. Instead, he issued new orders to the OOD. "Launch countermeasures. Come right to new course of one three zero."

Within a couple of heartbeats, two canisters were ejected from the hull. The cylinders began discharging compressed air. The deluge of expanding air bubbles flooded the water column with a deafening roar. The noisemakers helped mask the *Tucson's* high-speed retreat.

* * * *

V-6 swam into the bubble cloud. Overwhelmed by the racket, its sonar sensors lost contact with the target. V-6's computer cut power to propulsion. Still engulfed by the bubbles, it attempted to reacquire sonar lock on the target but failed.

V-5 detected the underwater storm as it slithered into position. Based on the prey's maneuvers, V-5's CPU, programmed with China's latest AI algorithms, refined the attack plan.

* * * *

The USS *Tucson* raced through the depths. Tension inside the control room was electric. Captain Arnold and his crew worked together flawlessly, the years of training and endless drills coalescing into textbook evasion procedures.

Captain Arnold keyed his handheld mike. "Sonar, conn. Contact update."

"Conn, sonar. Noisemakers at eighty-three percent. Master Four Nine has dropped off the screen."

"Very well. If Four Nine shows up again, I want to know immediately."

"Sonar, aye."

Arnold stood next to the plot table with his executive officer. "Skipper, what the hell was that thing?"

"I don't know. Let's just hope we outran it because—"

The overhead speaker interrupted Arnold. "Conn, sonar. Reacquired Master Four Nine. Range increasing to six hundred sixty yards. Speed decreasing to twenty knots."

"Sonar, conn. Keep on Four Nine. I want to know ASAP if it increases speed."

"Sonar, aye."

Lieutenant Commander Russell said, "Looks like whatever it is doesn't have long legs."

Arnold remained miffed. "I don't know what the Chinese are doing but they're up to something. Anyway, will continue at flank for another—"

Again, Commander Arnold was interrupted. "Conn, sonar. New contact. Similar acoustic output as Master Four Nine. Rising from depth. Bearing zero seven two—oh my God, range is just a hundred yards."

Sensing imminent disaster, Arnold engaged the 1MC and activated the ship wide intercom system. "This is the captain. Rig the boat for collision."

Seconds later an an enormous clang reverberated throughout the control room, bursting eardrums and knocking those standing to the deck.

Chapter 23

Commander Arnold struggled to pick himself up from the deck. His ears rang, the coppery bite of blood flooded his mouth and his head ached. He grasped a handhold on a control panel to steady himself. His right temple grazed the edge of a console on his way down. After catching his breath, Arnold made a quick survey of the control room. The other dozen men were in various stages of recovery; some had already remanned their stations.

Arnold located the officer of the deck. Standing beside the twin periscopes, the lieutenant took damage reports. The OOD wore a headset, which allowed him access to every department on the boat. "Status report, Mr. Johnson," Arnold said.

"Captain, the ship continues on a heading of one three zero at twenty-eight knots. Our depth is one thousand one hundred seventy-two feet. No reported flooding."

Arnold was astonished that his command was still underway. He'd expected that the collision would have triggered an automatic shutdown of the reactor.

"Damage reports?" Arnold asked.

"All compartments and sections report nominal shock damage. No leaks. No equipment problems as yet. Minor crew injuries."

The fog of confusion in Arnold's brain persisted. Finally, he remembered. "The bogeys… where are they?"

"Sonar reports no contact with either Master Four Nine or the undesignated contact." The OOD rubbed the back of his right wrist. He sprained it when thrown to the deck. "Sonar also reported a significant change to self-generated noise—it's off the charts. We have exterior hull damage, which is also slowing us down."

"Where on the hull?" Arnold demanded, the inflection of his voice conveying alarm.

"It's the sail, sir. Sonar reports that MIDAS is offline. Plus, they're picking up massive hydraulic drag racket in that area, which is consistent with exterior hull damage." MIDAS was an acronym for Mine Detection and Avoidance Sonar.

"Reduce to ten knots, maintain depth."

The OOD repeated the order.

Eight minutes went by. Commander Arnold wore a headset with a voice activated microphone, which allowed him to have a private conversation with the sonar supervisor in the sonar room. "Any thoughts on what might be responsible for the fairwater racket," Arnold asked. Fairwater was another name for the sail.

"It's possible we lost fairing covers on one or more of the masts. That might be part of the problem but I still think we have more damage than that."

"Elaborate."

"I believe we have major damage to the sail itself. Whatever struck us targeted the sail."

Arnold processed the news. "Any idea what we were up against?"

"Negative sir. We're still in the dark but this much I know…it was not a conventional torpedo, not even close. No propeller cavitation, no active search sonar, just a faint but creepy swishing signature."

"Very well. Make a copy of all recordings. When we return to base, I want the raw data forwarded to Fleet for further analysis."

"Aye, aye, Captain."

Arnold took off the headset, careful to avoid the throbbing welt in his scalp. The tip of his tongue also pulsed. His teeth clipped it when he was tossed to the deck.

The executive officer approached Arnold. "What did sonar report?" Lieutenant Commander Russell asked.

"Still don't know what it was. Damage appears to be limited to the fairwater."

"Should we take a look? Plenty of dark topside."

"Yes, but bring her up slowly. I want sonar to have a good listen before we surface. Who knows what else is around here?"

Russell acknowledged Arnold's directive and issued new orders.

Twelve minutes later, *Tucson* was sixty-five feet below the surface heading east at five knots; sonar had just completed a sweep for nearby traffic. The ship was alone in this section of the South China Sea.

Arnold stood beside the Type 18 search periscope. He wanted to make a quick three sixty scan with the scope's night vision optics before surfacing. "Up scope," he said addressing the quartermaster of the watch.

The chief petty officer repeated the order and triggered the switch controlling the hydraulic mechanism that raised and lowered the search periscope.

The tube did not rise. "Chief?" Arnold said.

"It's not engaging, Captain. I don't know what's wrong. Should I try the attack scope?"

"Yes."

The CPO repeated the same procedure with the Type 2 attack scope to no avail.

"They must have been damaged, Captain," the chief reported.

Arnold nodded, a new squadron of butterflies taking flight in his belly. He turned to his executive officer. "XO, surface the boat, slow and easy."

* * * *

Commander Arnold was the first to ascend through the sail's tunnel. After opening the top hatch and climbing onto the bridge—what remained of it—he gawked at the damage. The port, starboard and forward sides of the bridge cockpit were missing, leaving the bridge deck exposed. While grasping a metal bracket from a remnant of the cockpit he used a flashlight to survey the sail. "My god," he muttered as he took stock of the carnage.

The forward one third of the sail from just above the tunnel hatch was peeled back like the lid of a half open tin of sardines. The torn and bent steel covered most of the sail's topside. The wreckage blocked the radio and sensor masts and the twin side by side periscopes, preventing their deployment.

Commander Arnold leaned outboard and trained the flashlight beam on the starboard section of the sail, looking aft for additional structural damage. The rear section of the sail appeared intact except for a horizontal blemish across the aft side wall at the bridge deck level. The steel plate under the anechoic coating was gouged, as if something sharp had gripped the metal. *What's this?* he wondered.

Arnold knelt on the bridge deck and peered down the sail's access tunnel into the pressure hull. The *Tucson's* executive officer was a couple of stories below. "Come on up," Arnold shouted.

Russell clambered up the tunnel ladder. "What the hell happened?" he said after joining Arnold.

"I'm not sure but we now know why we can't raise any of the masts or scopes."

"No kidding." Russell directed the beam from his flashlight onto the debris. "And with all that crap hanging around here, no wonder we're so noisy. Even the Chicoms can track us now."

"Yes, and they may be back again."

"What do we do, Skipper? We've got no scopes, comms or radar."

Arnold reached into his jacket pocket and pulled out a compact commercial portable Satphone. "We'll have to use this to call home."

"Wow, that's going to be a first."

"While I make the call, you go below and organize a damage control party. Let's see if we can use a torch to cut back the debris to free up the masts and at least one scope."

"Aye, Skipper."

"And Hal, get the ship's photographer up here. I want a complete photographic record of the fairwater damage before we start cutting out the debris."

"You got it."

Chapter 24

Day 16—Thursday

Nicolai Orlov avoided SVR headquarters whenever possible. But the director himself ordered that he return for a face to face. Nick arrived the previous evening. He departed Vancouver International on a direct flight to London where he boarded a connecting shuttle to the homeland. This morning he walked the five blocks from his hotel to Russia's foreign intelligence HQ, located in the Yasenevo District of Moscow.

Nick was in the SVR director's office, sitting at a conference table with Borya Smirnov. Tea had been served; both men sipped from Russian crystal hot tea glasses with antique Podstakannik metal holders.

The preliminaries were over. Smirnov commenced the debriefing. "What's your opinion about Kirov?"

"My first reaction was that he appeared worn out, tired." Nick set his half full tea glass onto the desk.

"And?"

"He said he's done with Russia and that he has no intention of returning." Smirnov took a swallow of tea. "Go on…what else?"

"He didn't provide me with any details other than he said he'd completed his mission in China and as far as he was concerned, his obligation to the Navy has been satisfied."

"How did he return to Seattle?"

"I asked. He said it was classified."

"What about his post-China mission?"

Nick squinted. "What do you mean, sir?"

"He was also involved in a U.S. operation. Did he mention that?"

"No, in fact, he wouldn't say anything about his China mission, only that he completed what was required."

"What do you know about his China mission?"

Nick suppressed a jet-lagged yawn. "Only what Captain Zhilkin revealed when we met with Yuri in Houston. Yuri was tasked with assisting the Navy to spy on several PLA naval bases. That's all I know."

"You said he told you that he's not coming back. So, what are his plans?"

Nick's body stiffened, uncomfortable with what he was about to reveal. "The American he lives with, Laura Newman, is wealthy and because of her position she has considerable influence."

"Influence with whom?"

"The American government."

Director Smirnov glared.

Nick said, "Yuri told me that Newman and her attorneys are working with the U.S. State Department to grant him political amnesty."

"He's defecting?!" Smirnov said, his voice elevated.

"He said no. According to Yuri, in order for him to stay in the United States, political amnesty is the only avenue open to him."

Smirnov tugged on an ear, obviously concerned with Nick's report. "Kirov is an officer in the Russian Navy—an intelligence officer with the GRU. Don't think for a minute that he won't be grilled for his secrets."

"I said the same to him but he just waved me off."

Smirnov's bearing hardened.

Nick said, "He asked me to convey to you something that I found perplexing."

"And what is that?"

"Yuri wants nothing more to do with Russia. He said he's ashamed at what happened and has evidence to prove it."

"Prove what?"

"He didn't say and wouldn't elaborate when I questioned him."

"He threatened us?"

"Not in a direct context. It was more of a bargaining chip." Nick leaned forward. "Sir, he repeated several times that all he wants is to live in peace with his American family."

* * * *

Nick was on his way back to the hotel. He needed a nap, his internal clock knocked out of kilter from multiple time zone changes. He was scheduled to return to headquarters in the afternoon to attend a senior staff level briefing from the chief of the SVR's China Desk. Once again, strife brewed in the Far East.

The meeting with Smirnov left Nick anxious. Nick's report that Yuri had requested political asylum with the U.S. had dismayed the SVR director.

Smirnov was noncommittal regarding how the SVR might respond to Yuri's denunciation of his homeland. Still, Nick sensed peril for his friend. Betrayal, for whatever reason, was not tolerated within Russian intelligence services.

Just what the hell was Yuri involved with in China? Nick wondered.

Yuri reported that he completed his mission but offered no details.

And what is he holding over Smirnov's head?

Nick had picked up on his boss's unconscious body signals—stiffened spine, flush face and gritted teeth—just after Nick repeated Yuri's warning of having "evidence."

Something else is going on between those two but what?

Nick returned to the hotel. As a high-speed elevator car carried him skyward, another nagging thought tugged at his fatigued brain.

Why Hong Kong—especially now?

Director Smirnov informed Nick that he was being temporarily reassigned to Russia's Consulate in Hong Kong. He was tasked with reviewing the diplomatic outpost's security measures—and cleaning up lingering issues from a recent SVR 'wet' project.

Under ordinary circumstances, Nick would have welcomed the opportunity. But he suspected the MSS might have a target on his back.

Smirnov is using me as bait—bait for what?

* * * *

Yuri Kirov thought about Nick Orlov from a booth in the downtown Redmond café. It was 9:04 A.M. The breakfast rush was over; he was alone in a back corner nursing a cup of coffee. He'd taken extra care to make sure he was not followed. Yuri worried that he might have compromised Nick with his exit plan. Nevertheless, Yuri was committed—and he was about to move to the next level.

Yuri spotted his contact standing in the lobby. He signaled with his right arm.

"Good morning," FBI Special Agent Michaela Taylor said as she slid into the bench seat opposite Yuri.

"Thanks for meeting me."

A waitress approached the table with a coffee pot.

"Just coffee for me," Michaela said, sliding a mug toward the server.

Yuri declined a refill.

After the waitress left, Michaela said, "So, what's up?"

Yuri reached into a pocket of his windbreaker and extracted a thumb drive. "I have some intelligence data here that I'd like to get to Captain Clark and Steve Osberg as soon as possible. It's raw video footage from my mission at the Yulin Naval Base on Hainan Island. I just received the data files."

Michaela's eyes ballooned.

Yuri smiled. "Please consider this a goodwill measure on my part."

Chapter 25

Day 20—Monday

Ministry of Public Security technical specialist Yu Ling monitored the grilling of the Uyghur suspect remotely. An HD video camera in the interrogation cell transmitted images and audio via cable to a wall-mounted monitor in the observation room. The image of a thirty-five-year-old woman sitting rigid in a metal chair filled the LCD screen. Pixie faced with a button nose and auburn hair hanging below her shoulders, she was pretty. The prison jumpsuit concealed her lissome five-foot four frame. Her right wrist was handcuffed to an armrest. Sleep deprived, famished and scared out of her wits, Meryem Ahmet stared at the tile floor, avoiding eye contact with her tormentor.

The female People's Armed Police officer conducting the interview was eighteen years older than Meryem. The cop's prune face and gray hair, butchered to a bob, contrasted sharply with the captive. Major Huang Genji was a practiced interrogator with decades of experience dealing with dissidents from Tibet and the Xinjiang Uyghur Autonomous Region. After Yu Ling managed to track down Meryem in a suburb of Qingdao, Huang was flown in from PAP headquarters in Beijing to conduct the interview. About the same height as the prisoner, Huang was forty pounds heavier.

"We know you were sleeping with Ismail Sabir," Huang said. "Who else did he associate with besides Yusup Tunyaz?"

"Yusup is the only one I know. Ismail worked with others but I don't know them."

"Tell me about the company Sabir worked for…what was his position?"

"He installs electrical equipment. The company builds and repairs boats and ships."

"What kind of equipment?"

"Radios, navigation systems. That's what Ismail told me."

Huang switched gears. "When is the last time you went home?"

Meryem looked up. "To Ürümqi?"

"Yes."

"Last summer to visit my mother. She was very ill."

Huang consulted a tablet she held. "I see that she was hospitalized for lung cancer. You went to visit her after the surgery. Correct?"

"Yes," Meryem said, perplexed that Huang had researched her family.

"Did Sabir go with you?"

"No, he had to work."

"Doesn't your faith frown upon having sexual relations outside of marriage?"

Meryem again studied the tile floor.

Not expecting a response, Major Huang said, "Why did you meet with Sabir's brother when you were in Ürümqi last year?"

How could she know that? Meryem pondered. But then she remembered; a couple of months earlier the Armed Police picked up Ehmet. He was still confined to a reeducation camp. "Ismail asked Ehmet to check on me to see if I needed anything."

"So, you had dinner with him?"

"He owns a small restaurant and invited me."

"He's not married. Correct?"

"Yes."

"Did you sleep with him, too?"

Her ire peaked, Meryem managed to restrain her voice. "Of course not. I'm not like that."

Yu Ling continued to watch the interrogation. Major Huang's questions were relentless and at times petty. Designed to wear down the interviewee's defenses, Yu admired the senior officer's skills.

So far, Meryem Ahmet had not revealed any useful information that the MPS and the MSS had not already discovered. Major Huang was thorough in her questioning and appeared to be wrapping up the interview. That's when Huang hit the bonanza.

While Huang consulted her tablet, Meryem asked, "What happened to Ismail and Yusup?"

"We don't know. As I said before, we're trying to track them down. The boat they were working on is missing."

"You think they stole it?"

"The company that owns the boat contacted us. They reported it stolen. Ismail and Yusup were the last ones that had access to it—doing some kind of repair work on it. We're interviewing anyone that knows them." Huang fabricated the theft story to pump Meryem.

"They're not thieves."

"I tend to agree with you. They appear to be hard workers with clean records but then again—"

"The boat must have sunk," interrupted Meryem.

"There have been no reports about that." Huang decided to explore a new angle. "Could they have been someplace else with the boat other than in Qingdao?"

"I don't know. Ismail said they had some repair work to do at the port."

"Could they have been working for someone else, without the company knowing?"

"Ismail never said anything like . . ." Meryem's voice trailed off as a new thought developed. "He did get a call from someone I'd never heard of the night before he left for work."

That statement captured Huang's attention. "And who was the caller?"

"His name was Talgat."

"His full name, please."

"I don't know, just Talgat."

"Did you meet him?"

"I spoke to him on the phone once."

"He called you?"

"No, it was Sabir's cell phone. He was asleep. I thought it was about work so I answered."

"Go on."

As Meryem continued the rundown on the Talgat contact, Yu Ling accessed her laptop computer and submitted a name check inquiry for "Talgat" to the Ministry of State Security's ethnic Muslim citizen database. She started with the Xinjiang Uyghur Autonomous Region and got the phone book. She refined her search to the coast from Shanghai Municipality to Liaoning Province. The list decreased to several hundred. When she added the keywords "boat repair" and "boat electronics" to the search, just one name was left, Talgat Ramazan.

The forty-four-year-old was born in Yining, Xinjiang near the border with Kazakhstan. After receiving a mechanical engineering degree, he moved to China's east coast. He was currently employed by an engineering company based in Tianjin. The business specialized in the design and renovation of commercial workboats, fishing boats and small ships. The file reported Ramazan was single with both parents deceased and no siblings.

As Yu Ling stared at the digital photo of Talgat Ramazan, she whispered to herself, "Gotcha."

Chapter 26

Day 21—Tuesday

The USS *Tucson* was berthed alongside a wharf at a U.S. Navy base in the western Pacific Ocean. The attack submarine slinked into Guam's Apra Harbor the previous evening. A prefabricated cover composed of heavy-duty aluminum struts and Kevlar reinforced nylon fabric spanned SSN 770's sail. The awning concealed the damage to the submarine's superstructure from spying satellites and aircraft.

A collection of senior American naval officers and civilian employees hovered under the awning this afternoon. They were atop portable aluminum scaffolding that surrounded the entire sail. Most in attendance had arrived late morning aboard a U.S. Air Force C-17 transport from Joint Base Pearl Harbor-Hickam.

Standing beside the jagged remains of the bridge station, *Tucson's* commanding officer, Commander Scott Arnold, continued with the rundown. "As you can see, the device latched onto the leading edge of the fairwater in this area and—"

"What did it sound like," interrupted one of the onlookers, "when it attached itself?"

Arnold glanced at the Navy captain. "I don't recall hearing anything other than the detonation. We were running at flank and had launched decoys so it was noisy inside the control room."

"Got it, thanks."

Arnold pointed to the sail's damaged leading edge. "The explosive used in the device appeared to be some form of a linear shaped charge. Note the severed surface where it detonated."

"It looks like a line charge alright," commented one of the civilians. "What's the overall length of the detonation pattern?"

Commander Arnold shifted his stance while turning to address the visitor. "At least sixteen feet."

"That's incredible…what kind of weapon could do that?"

"Something quite radical, that's for certain."

Arnold took a couple of steps aft on the scaffold deck, beyond the remnants of the peeled back cowling that had covered the sensor masts and periscopes. Prior to heading to Guam, part of the damage had been cut away with a torch to free the radio mast and the search scope. The torched fragments lay on the aluminum deck.

Commander Arnold pointed to the marks that ran along the aft section of the sail. "Gentlemen, you can see the indentations of the coating in this area. Identical marks are on the port side."

The navy Captain who had commented earlier ran a hand across the abrasion. "Looks like something cut right into the steel, like a clamp or some kind of a grapple device."

"Yes, sir. It's right in line with the line charge area, which makes me believe they are connected."

"Misfire?"

"That's my thinking at this time."

"What's the circumference of the fairwater?" asked another officer.

Arnold was ready for the expected question. "About sixty feet."

It took several seconds for the revelation to sink in. The captain connected the dots first. "How the devil could something that long chase down and wrap itself around a six eighty-eight running at flank?"

"I don't know, Captain. At least two of those damn things attacked us. If just one of 'em had managed to attach itself to the pressure casing rather than the sail, we would not be having this conversation."

* * * *

Two thousand nautical miles northwest of Guam, Dr. Meng Park and Captain Zhou Jun met in Zhou's office at the South Sea Sound Surveillance System. Meng had arrived half an hour earlier at S5, taking a commercial flight from Hefei to Sanya. It was late afternoon. Like the Americans who also caucused in Guam, Meng and Zhou conducted their own post-mission debrief.

The pair had just finished listening to an acoustic recording of the undersea battle that took place offshore of Hainan Island the previous week. The soundtrack was an amalgam of data collected by subsea hydrophones spread across the South China Sea and a mini acoustic recorder left aboard Viperina Six. The digital device housed in V-6's computer compartment had been used to collect test data after it returned to its seabed base—Viper Hub Station 1. Captain Zhou was awestruck with the results revealed by the recording; Dr. Meng less so.

"Something failed," Meng said. "The Americans escaped." She wore a silk blouse and a pleated skirt cut an inch above her knees. A pair of three inch heels completed the assembly.

Captain Zhou wore his summer whites. He countered Meng's doubt. "The submarine was obviously damaged. For the first strike of the system, that is most impressive." Over the objections of Dr. Meng, Fleet had ordered S5 to activate the first Viper station.

Meng's eyebrows arched, hardly marring her lovely face. "The recording clearly revealed that V-5 detonated. I just don't understand why it didn't sink the submarine."

V-5 and V-6 hunted as a pair. V-6 broke off the pursuit when its battery reserves reached the mandatory minimum. It had just enough juice to return to the hub. V-5 had not yet reached its minimum and prosecuted the attack.

"It's impossible to tell from the recording just where V-5 attached itself to the hull." Zhou rubbed his chin. "It may have latched itself to a non-critical part of the casing…the bow cap covering the spherical sonar array, the rudder assembly, diving planes. Maybe even the fin. The weapon detonates but does not breach the hull."

Meng said, "Perhaps I should refine the attack parameters to prioritize specific target areas."

"That would be helpful."

"But I'd still like to find out exactly what went wrong with Viper Five."

"Other than analyzing the recording data, I don't know what else can be done."

"What about using a submersible?" Meng offered.

"To do what?"

"Search the bottom below the attack area for possible remnants of V-5. We have the coordinates from V-6."

Captain Zhou considered the request. "We could try that but you know it's unlikely we'll find anything."

"I know but we should still try—before the American's do the same."

The specter of the U.S. Navy returning to investigate the attack galvanized Zhou. "I'll set it up for tomorrow."

"Thank you." Meng peered at the tile floor, another frown broadcasting her disappointment. "I just don't understand what went wrong."

"Park, you have much to be proud of. What you have developed is a true game changer. When Serpent is fully deployed, the Americans will no longer be able to intimidate us with their submarines."

Meng looked up. "Thanks, I really do appreciate your support."

"You're welcome." Zhou checked his wristwatch. "Let's wrap this up. I have a table reserved at the Red Sun."

Dr. Meng beamed her approval.

Meng Park had anticipated the pending rendezvous, even fantasizing while aboard the Airbus during the southbound flight. Although Zhou Jun was ten years her senior she longed for his company. With legions of younger men available for sex back at the university, Park preferred the navy captain. Jun was the consummate lover, focusing first and foremost on her pleasure.

Chapter 27

Day 22—Wednesday

It had been over two weeks since Yuri last visited the FBI's Seattle office. This morning he was alone in a conference room deep inside the warren of offices and cubicles. He nursed a cup of coffee, offered by his escort. The FBI logo filled one side of the ceramic mug.

Yuri employed the usual countermeasures to ensure he was not tracked. He parked in an underground garage at Union Square where he was picked up by an FBI agent and driven to the garage of the nearby Seattle field office. After a security guard collected Yuri's cell phone and the Colt, placing both in a secure locker and providing Yuri the key, the driver-agent escorted Yuri to the conference room.

Yuri's mug was empty when Special Agent Michaela Taylor entered the conference room. She carried a manila file folder. "Good morning," she announced. "Nice to see you again."

Yuri returned the greeting.

As Michaela settled in, she said, "Thanks for coming in today."

"No problem."

"Just so you know, Captain Clark and Steve Osberg have the data you provided me last week. They both asked me to thank you personally."

Yuri flashed a smile.

Michaela opened the folder and briefly studied the contents before glancing Yuri's way. "The reason I asked to see you this morning concerns the issue with Ms. Newman's missing bodyguard, Sara Compton."

Yuri's spine stiffened.

"As you know," Michaela said, "Compton's family has been pursuing the issue regarding her fate. The Sammamish police are also investigating and reached out to our office for assistance."

"Is this about the hearing?" Yuri asked.

"Yes, the family's attorney has been pressing hard for a court hearing to declare Ms. Compton dead."

"And they want Laura and me to testify."

"Yes. Since Laura was the last person to see Ms. Compton before Laura and her daughter were kidnapped, the family wants to make the case that their abduction led directly to Compton's own abduction and eventual death."

Yuri said, "This would be a public hearing where the press could have access?"

"Unfortunately, yes."

Yuri massaged his forehead. Laura's attorneys had managed to keep the kidnapping out of the news because the police were not involved, but a public hearing would put a spotlight on Laura. "The local reporters will be all over it because of Laura's wealth. And then someone might get interested in me."

"I agree, and so does the Attorney General."

Taken aback, Yuri cast a questioning gaze.

Michaela said, "In order to keep you off the radar, we have quietly squashed the hearing process."

"How?"

"The Department of Justice informed King County and the City of Sammamish that neither you or Laura can participate in the hearing due to an ongoing national security investigation related to Laura's kidnapping."

"That will stop the hearing?"

"Yes, since neither of you will be available to testify, they don't have a case."

"What happens if they go directly to the press?"

"They could, but I don't believe they'll do that. DOJ left a juicy carrot for the family."

Yuri puckered his brow, not sure of Taylor's idiom.

"Ms. Compton was in the Army reserves and the company she worked for has security contracts with the U.S. military. At the request of Justice, the Department of Defense indicated it would invoke federal statutes to declare Compton dead. That would take just a fraction of the typical time if left up to the state. With an official declaration of death from the federal government, the family would be eligible for death benefits from Compton's employer, which are significant—five million dollars in life insurance. It will also offer some form of closure for them." Agent Taylor recalled another item. "The family may also be entitled to DoD death benefits; a couple hundred thousand."

Yuri signaled his confusion. "How's that possible?"

"It's all under the national security umbrella."

"You mean me."

"Yep."

Yuri exhaled an audible breath.

Michaela smiled, "This should come as a relief to both you and Laura."

"It does...thank you."

* * * *

It was Dr. Meng Park's first dive in a submersible. The *Xiu Shan* cruised twenty feet above the mud bottom. The three person submarine was 5,550 feet below the surface, heading northward at three knots. Floodlights illuminated the seabed and surrounding water column in the otherwise perpetual darkness of the deep.

"This is just unbelievable," Meng muttered as she took in the 3-D bubble view.

"Indeed," Captain Zhou said.

Meng was in the starboard seat of the cockpit. Captain Zhou claimed the port station. The pilot manned the aft control console behind the passengers. All three wore blue jumpsuits. A transparent acrylic sphere, just over six feet in diameter, encapsulated the trio. Located behind the pilot's station were the submersible's electronics and life support systems. A top opening hatch placed at the peak of the orb above the pilot's seat allowed crew ingress and egress. Two articulated robotic arms were appended to the forward end of the steel frame that supported the pressure sphere.

Attached to the aft end of the plastic bubble was a tapered, hydraulic slick fiberglass fairing that extended ten feet in length. The service module housed the minisub's ballast chambers, compressed air and oxygen tanks, and battery compartment. At the base of the module was a compartment containing two hundred kilos of lead shot. In an emergency, the ballast could be jettisoned, allowing the sub to ascend without the need for expelling seawater from ballast tanks.

Launched six months earlier, the *Xiu Shan*—Elegant Coral—was China's latest class of deep diving research vessels. Rated for 2,000 meters—about 6,500 feet, the *Xiu Shan's* hull had a sleeker profile than its predecessors.

Sacrificing extreme deep diving capability for endurance, the *Xiu Shan* could cruise at four knots continuously for twenty-four hours.

"Captain, the search sonar has just picked up something," reported the pilot. The twenty-six-year-old was a lieutenant in the PLAN. He was one of two dozen young officers handpicked by senior staff to command China's growing fleet of manned submersibles.

"What's the range?"

"Sixty meters. Should be coming into view soon."

The *Xiu Shan* had descended eighty minutes earlier after it launched from the support ship *Lian*. The bottom search commenced from the coordinates of the attack on the American submarine—roughly 154 nautical miles east of Sanya. The submersible made two tracks along the planned survey route before the *Xiu Shan's* sonar registered return echo's from its ranging pulses.

"Target in sight!" announced the pilot.

Meng Park shifted forward in her bucket seat. "I see it!"

The *Xiu Shan* hovered over the eighteen-foot length of *Viperina Five*. The remnant of the one-foot diameter weapon was strung out along the sea floor; it had the appearance of a utility pipe.

"Could the charges still be primed?" asked Captain Zhou.

A two-kilogram shaped charge was positioned about every foot and a half along the length of the *Viperinas*. Designed to blast through high tensile steel pressure hulls of U.S. subs, the shockwave from a detonation now could crack *Xiu Shan's* synthetic polymer sphere like an egg shell.

"No, it should be safe," Dr. Meng answered. "The charges were designed to detonate simultaneously. This is the tail end of the unit. The trigger signal would have been issued from the CPU. A fault in the wiring may have caused the misfire."

"So, it's okay if we recover it?" Zhou asked.

"Absolutely. This is exactly what I was hoping for. I can run diagnostics on it to determine what happened."

Captain Zhou addressed the pilot. "Lieutenant, go ahead and retrieve the unit."

"Aye aye, Captain.

It took the *Xiu Shan* almost two hours to ascend. When it broke through the sea surface, the remains of Viper Five were wrapped around the submersible's starboard articulated mechanical arm.

Chapter 28

Yuri and Laura lunched at the conference table in Laura's office. Yuri stopped at a nearby deli before taking the elevator to the 25th floor of Cognition Consultants. It was an impromptu encounter. After meeting with Special Agent Michaela Taylor, Yuri called Laura to tell her he was bringing sandwiches.

"Ummm, this is delicious," Laura said after taking another bite from the club sandwich.

Yuri grinned. "I thought you might like it." He munched on the same. If he were alone, however, he would have picked up a juicy, fully decked out cheeseburger at Red Robin.

Laura dabbed her lips with a paper napkin, wiping away a smear of mayonnaise. "So, how did your meeting with the FBI go?"

Yuri took a swig from one of the flavored water bottles he brought. "That's what I want to talk to you about."

Laura's heart rate soared. She sensed trouble. "Are they hassling you again?"

"No, actually it's good news—for both of us." He took another gulp of water. "I think the issues regarding Sarah Compton are going away."

Astounded, Laura said, "How?"

Yuri spent the next five minutes summarizing the legal maneuvers.

"That's terrific news," Laura said, visibly relieved. "I've been worrying about having to testify at a hearing."

"You can stop worrying." Laura smiled but Yuri noticed her furrowed brow. "What's wrong?" he asked.

"I still can't get over what they did to Sarah…because of me."

Yuri reached across the table and clasped Laura's right hand. "It was not your fault. The men that abducted you and Maddy and took Sarah were military—a special ops team operating inside the U.S. under the control of Kwan Chi. That's what the FBI finally concluded. We could never have stopped them on our own. Sarah was nothing to them."

"I should have left town like you asked me."

"Please stop beating yourself up about what happened. We know who was responsible."

"I know, thank you."

Yuri released Laura's hand. "It's going to be okay."

Laura reached for her water bottle and took a swallow. "I am relieved that the FBI is following through like they said they would. That's a comforting sign to me that maybe this nightmare is coming to an end."

"I agree."

After another bite from her sandwich she asked, "What else did Taylor have to say?"

Yuri had fretted about what was to come next. "They want me to visit Pearl Harbor again."

"When?"

"I have to fly out tomorrow morning."

Clearly agitated, Laura planted her elbows on the table and grasped her hands. "What do they want from you?"

"Attend a meeting. I'm being brought in as a technical consultant. They're even going to pay me through NSD!"

"What—how can they do that?"

"It's an extension to the oil spill monitoring contract we have with the Coast Guard."

Laura wasn't buying it. "Yuri, what's really going on?"

"It's part of my cover. More trouble with China...the U.S. Navy needs my help."

Chapter 29

The Alaska Airlines 737 arrived at Honolulu International a few minutes before noon. TSA was a breeze for Yuri Kirov back at Seattle-Tacoma Airport. The freshly issued Washington State Enhanced Driver's License he presented to the Transportation Security Administration agent during the passenger screening process was accepted without question.

Yuri no longer feared checkpoints by the feds or even a traffic ticket. As promised, the FBI legitimized the alias that Yuri had used when he illegally entered the United States two years earlier. John Kirkwood's legend would now survive a thorough ID check. He had a Social Security number, birth certificate, work history that included FICA tax payments, and ten years of postdated federal tax returns.

Yuri rented a Ford Explorer at Hertz and drove straight to Joint Base Pearl Harbor-Hickam. He was issued a visitor's pass at the main gate and directed to park the SUV in an adjacent lot. A female enlisted sailor driving an official U.S. Navy sedan delivered Yuri to his destination.

The building was nondescript. A sign displaying a base building number was the only identifying mark on the two story structure. Yuri was met by a Marine assigned to secure the building's entrance. The Lance Corporal was all business, and he was armed—a pistol holstered on his right hip. He examined Yuri's pass as well as his driver's license. Yuri was directed to take a seat in one of the half dozen lobby chairs.

Within a minute, Yuri's contact strode into the lobby—a naval officer known to Yuri.

"Good afternoon Yur—John," said the Navy captain, suppressing a smirk as he caught himself just in time. The Marine was not in the loop regarding Yuri's true identity.

"Hello, Captain," Yuri said as he stood up.

Captain Robert Clark was in uniform—khaki button up shirt and trousers. "Any problems getting here?" Clark asked.

"No. Everything's cool."

"Good. Let's go to the conference room. The others are already here."

Yuri followed the naval officer as he led the way through a series of hallways and doors.

The first floor conference room was twenty feet square and windowless. Three males were seated at the table. One was in service khakis with a Commander insignia pin on his shirt collar. The other two occupants in the room wore civilian attire. Yuri recognized one of the pair.

"Hello," Yuri said.

"Good to see you again," said CIA officer Steve Osberg.

Yuri and Osberg shook hands. Osberg was about to introduce Yuri to the other civilian when he said, "Is Yuri okay or should I use your *nom de plume*?"

"Whatever you like."

"Great." Osberg gestured toward his companion. "Yuri Kirov, former Captain-Lieutenant in the Russian Navy, aka John Kirkwood, I'm pleased to introduce you to Jeffrey Chang. Jeff is from Langley, National Clandestine Service, Asia Desk."

Yuri gripped Chang's outstretched hand—a firm clasp. Chang was tall, almost Yuri's height but his build was slender. His black hair flowed over his ears and grazed the collar of his shirt. Like Yuri, Chang was in his early thirties.

"I've heard a lot about you, sir." Chang said. "We're all indebted to what you did here...at Pearl." There was no hint of an Asian accent."

"Thanks.

Captain Clark next introduced Yuri to Commander Scott Arnold. After the handshake, Clark said, "Scott is the reason we're all gathered here today. He's the skipper of the USS *Tucson*—a Los Angeles class attack sub. I'm sure you're familiar with the class."

"Of course."

Clark said, "Last week, the *Tucson* tangled with something that damn near sank it in the South China Sea offshore of Hainan Island."

Yuri knew instantly why he was summoned to Pearl Harbor.

Captain Clark turned to Arnold. "Commander, please provide us with a rundown of what happened."

* * * *

Commander Arnold's accounting took twenty minutes. It was currently Q & A. Yuri held an eight by ten color photograph of the damage to *Tucson's* sail. A dozen other prints were scattered around the table.

Yuri looked up, catching Arnold's eyes. "Commander, what are these marks along the aft section of the fin?" He pointed to the blemish on the photo.

"Deep cuts through the anechoic coating into the steel, almost like claw scratches."

"Hmmm," Yuri murmured.

Arnold pulled up his briefcase from the floor and set it on the conference table. He opened the case and removed a file folder filled with additional photos. He extracted a print and gave it to Yuri. "Here's a blowup of the area."

Yuri examined the damage. He glanced back at Arnold. "It must use some type of grapple to attach itself to the target."

"I agree. Very perceptive."

Yuri passed the photo to Jeff Chang and addressed Arnold. "Any idea on the length of the weapon?"

"At least twenty feet based on the damage to the fairwater, maybe a lot longer."

"So, it can wrap itself around the object it's attacking before detonating, like a boa constrictor coiled around its prey?"

"Maybe…a snake, yeah that does make sense. Its body has spikes that can grip metal to hang on with."

Yuri fought back a yawn. "I remember attending a seminar at the academy in Saint Petersburg several years ago on future ASW weapon systems. A concept design of a linear sea mine was presented. It was three or four meters long. It would attach itself to a sub's hull using magnets. When the line charge detonated, it would rip open the pressure casing like a can opener."

Yuri's story captured Captain Clark's interest. "Was the system developed by Russia?"

"No. In fact, the concept was downplayed at the seminar. Propulsion was the problem. The designers planned to tow the unit to the target area with an AUV, but noise from the AUV's propellers would likely be picked up by the target sub's sonar before the mine ever got close."

Clark turned toward Arnold. "Commander, that's a good lead in for the recording."

"Yes sir." Arnold grabbed a digital recorder from his briefcase and placed it on the table. "This is a recording from *Tucson's* passive sonar prior to the attack. It's the only warning that we had." Arnold engaged the recorder's playback mode.

Yuri listened to the faint swishing tone, puzzled. The alien sound increased slightly but as *Tucson* began to accelerate to evade the approaching sonar contact, hydraulic drag on the sub's hull and noise from the churning propeller drowned out the signal.

Yuri scratched an ear as he processed the recording.

Arnold kicked off the discussion, eyeing Yuri. "I think you'll agree that doesn't sound like a conventional AUV. It's not even close."

Yuri said, "Assuming that signal was produced from the machine that attacked your boat, it was not propeller driven."

Tucson's CO said, "I'm thinking it was some type of water jet."

"Maybe, but the jet pump would have to be super powerful to match the speed of the boat." Yuri clutched his hands. "Going back to the boa constrictor model. If the machine somehow managed to use its body to produce S shaped movements—serpentine oscillations—that might produce a similar sound print."

"Slither through the water like a snake!"

"Exactly."

* * * *

After a ten minute bathroom break, the meeting reconvened. Steve Osberg took over with a PowerPoint presentation. The first slide projected onto the wall-mounted screen was a high altitude color aerial view of China's Hainan Island. Located at the PRC's southern limit, the 12,800 square mile island bordered the South China Sea and the Gulf of Tonkin.

Here it comes, Yuri thought.

Osberg said, "As all of you know, the PLAN has been busy along the south coast of Hainan Island." The next slide displayed a bird's eye view of the shoreline. "The Yulin Naval Base is located here. This image was taken yesterday." The CIA officer used a laser pointer to highlight the naval station and turned Yuri's way. "Our colleague has firsthand knowledge of this particular facility. Yuri, would you care to comment?"

Yuri cleared his throat. "Impressive facility. Two huge quays for berthing a variety of warships."

Osberg highlighted the piers with the laser. Two aircraft carriers, dozens of frigates, destroyers, and assorted other military craft lined the docks.

Yuri said, "Besides surface vessels, the base has four piers for submarines, attack and ballistic missile boats." Osberg lased the moorage along the harbor's eastern shore. Half a dozen long and narrow black forms were visible next to the docks.

"Yulin has another highly unusual feature," Yuri said. Osberg pointed to an indentation in the shoreline about half a mile south of the moored subs. Yuri resumed, "That's the entrance to a half submerged tunnel that leads to a massive underground sub facility. It was carved out of solid rock. The Chinese use the cavern to service and hide their missile boats. Boomers as you call them."

Steve Osberg took over, addressing Commander Arnold. "I'm sure you were aware of the underground sub pens at Yulin."

"Heard about it. They also have another one in the north."

"That's right, at Jianggezhuang near Qingdao."

Arnold said, "The Chinese are tight lipped about 'em, especially the new one at Yulin. Would be interesting to know just what they're doing inside those caverns."

Osberg grinned. "Well, thanks to Yuri we now know what's going on inside Yulin."

That revelation caught Commander Arnold off guard. He frowned.

A new slide with a video link materialized. Osberg clicked on the arrow and an image of a vast underground chamber filled the screen. Three low lying black hulled behemoths moored to piers were in the foreground.

Osberg said, "Yuri managed to sneak a mini drone through the tunnel into the complex."

The next segment of the video displayed the drone's view as it hovered over one of the ballistic missile subs.

"That's one of their Jin-class boats," Arnold commented. He was trained to track and sink both Russian and Chinese boomers.

"Right," Osberg said. "Jin-class—Type 094."

Arnold along with the others watched as the drone descended through an open hatch and began to survey the interior of the top secret sub.

The tour took twenty minutes. Commander Arnold was blown away. "That's incredible. We saw virtually everything." He looked Yuri's way. "How did you manage to pull that off?"

Osberg answered. "We can't get into methods at this time but as you can imagine, this video provides our technical people with a goldmine of information on the capabilities of the PLAN's top of the line missile boats."

"No kidding."

"Yulin is important but the Chinese have been up to no good elsewhere on Hainan." Osberg clicked on the remote and a new slide flashed onto the screen. "This is a PLAN facility at Shendao, which is about six nautical miles west of Yulin." He highlighted a developed area further west. "This is the city of Sanya, about five miles northwest of the Shendao base. Resort city. Population of around 700,000—China's Honolulu."

Osberg advanced to the next slide, a high resolution aerial view of the Shendao Naval Base. A massive reinforced concrete pier jutted 2,300 feet into the breakwater protected harbor. Osberg highlighted the pier with the pointer. "This monster wharf is for mooring and servicing aircraft carriers." A 200-foot workboat moored along the south side looked like a dinghy compared to the bulk of the pier.

"So why are the carriers at Yulin?" Commander Arnold asked.

"We'll fill you in soon about the carriers. Right now, we need to focus on this facility."

Osberg called up the next slide, an oblique view of a sizeable building located upland of the aircraft carrier pier. Yuri studied the image, curious as to what Osberg was up to.

Captain Clark took over as Osberg reclaimed his seat.

"Gentlemen," Clark said. "We believe this run of the mill building represents the greatest threat to our submarine forces that the United States has ever faced."

Chapter 30

Yuri looked at the image of the Shendao installation as Captain Clark began his rundown. Yuri's immediate attention, however, was elsewhere. The revelation jolted Yuri with the impact of a mountain avalanche. *This entire briefing has been for my benefit—they want something from me! But what?*

Yuri would soon find out.

Captain Clark said, "The PLAN officially identifies this building as the Shendao Fleet Logistics and Support Center. It appears to function as advertised but it also serves another purpose, one that Beijing has gone to extremes to conceal."

Clark called up a new slide. "This is a satellite image taken during construction of the building. Note the activity in this area." He pointed with the laser, highlighting an excavated zone behind the building's foundations. A narrow but long box like reinforced concrete structure extended from the building's south end into the adjacent hillside.

"Looks like some kind of underground storage facility," commented Commander Arnold.

"That's what the Chinese want us to believe." Clark handed the remote to his colleague.

Jeff Chang highlighted the same area. "The design used here mimicked a stormwater storage vault. We use them routinely in the States to temporarily store rainfall during storms and then let it drain out over time. Helps prevent flooding. They're also sometimes used to help filter out contaminants in stormwater. From satellite monitoring of other new construction in China, we're just starting to see the use of these types of facilities. For this case, however, it's bogus."

Chang presented another slide. "This is an interior photo of the so-called stormwater vault."

Commander Arnold reacted first. "That's a tunnel."

"Correct," Chang said as he called out the obvious features. "Dedicated walkway, utility conduits, overhead lighting, ventilation system. None of these improvements would be located inside a stormwater treatment tank."

"Who took this photo?" Yuri asked.

"One of our recruits. Worked as a laborer."

Yuri started to ask a follow-up question when Steve Osberg intervened. "The tunnel connects to another facility hidden in the hillside; a cavern that we speculate was hollowed out several years before the building was constructed. We believe it houses the control center for China's new submarine monitoring system in the South China Sea, which includes deployment of ASW weapon systems."

"And that would also include whatever attacked Commander Arnold's boat?" Yuri said.

"We believe so!" Osberg signaled for Chang to continue.

Jeff Chang keyed the remote and the image of a middle aged male dressed in the uniform of a PLAN officer appeared. "This guy is Captain Zhou Jun. Naval academy graduate. Served five years as a line officer on a destroyer and was sent back to school. Received a Ph.D. in IT and transferred to the PLA's advanced weapons research group—roughly similar to our DARPA." Chang glanced toward Yuri. "DARPA stands for Defense Advanced Research Projects Agency. It's part of the U.S. Department of Defense, responsible for developing emerging technologies for use by our military."

"Thanks for thinking of me, but I'm quite aware of DARPA." Yuri grinned. "I can assure you that DARPA has and continues to generate colossal heartburn at the Kremlin."

Chang and the others laughed.

Jeff Chang resumed his presentation. "Captain Zhou is based in Sanya. His group works out of an office building in the port district. It's part of a research center operated by the Chinese Academy of Sciences." A new slide materialized, exhibiting a multistory building set on the shoreline of a modern harbor. Three oceangoing research vessels were moored to the docks fronting the marine facility. Chang continued, "Zhou has an office in the building but lately he spends most of his time at the Fleet Logistics and Support Center."

Chang again clicked the remote, returning to the aerial photo of the Shendao complex. "Our intel suggests he has operational control of all the acoustic hydrophones in the South China Sea from the underground annex. We also believe it now functions as the ASW ops center for the SCS and maybe elsewhere. Signal intercepts of PLAN comms has identified it as the South Sea Sound Surveillance System, S5 for short. Also known as China's Great Underwater Wall."

Commander Arnold reentered the discussion. "So, Zhou is the prick that ordered the sea snake thing to attack my boat—in international waters?"

"Yes, in all likelihood he gave the order."

Arnold muttered a curse.

Yuri scanned the paper pad he used to take notes before addressing Chang and Captain Clark. "Well, it appears that China has come up with an effective antisubmarine technology. I now understand your concerns so I assume you'd like my thoughts on countermeasures."

"Of course," Clark said.

"First and foremost, early detection. Your sonar picked up the two machines that attacked the *Tucson*. That's where I'd start."

"I agree and that's already in the works. But we need a way to take out those damn things at their source, not when they're about to swarm one of our boats. *Tucson* was lucky. . . if that line charge had attached itself to the pressure casing, Commander Arnold would not be here with us today. Correct, Scott?"

"Yes sir."

Yuri considered Clark's request. "Well, the best way to defeat something as radical as their sea snake machine is to get your hands on one of the units and reverse engineer it."

"We're all in agreement on that." Clark glanced Chang's way. "Jeff, go ahead and tell Yuri your plan."

"We're confident that all ASW ops for the South China Sea are controlled at Shendao. Accordingly, that's where we plan to concentrate our efforts. Our intent is to insert a recon unit onto Hainan Island with the express goal of gaining access to the Shendao ASW unit." Chang met Yuri's eyes. "Because you have intimate experience with covert ops on Hainan, your assistance is requested."

"To help plan the mission?" Yuri asked.

"That's right. We really need your hands-on experience to pull off the op."

So that's what all this is about!

Chapter 31

Nicolai Orlov was on the 21st floor of the Sun Hung Kai Centre, standing beside a window wall. The vista of Victoria Harbour in the foreground and the cluster of gleaming office and residential towers on the opposite shore awed Nick. He watched as a passenger ferry departed from a pier at its Wan Chai terminal on Hong Kong Island and began crossing the three-quarter mile wide waterway to its companion berth at Tsim Sha Tsui on the Kowloon Peninsula.

Founded in 1888, the Star Ferry Company has operated a fleet of a dozen boats on two routes that transport over 70,000 passengers a day between Hong Kong Island and Kowloon. Although a modern system of road and subway tunnels crisscross Victoria Harbour, the ferries were an inexpensive and popular way to traverse the harbor.

Noticing the vintage ferry chugging across the busy channel waters tugged at Nick's heart. He missed the daily water commute he used to make when he lived in San Francisco. He had rented a houseboat in Sausalito and took a ferry across the Bay to downtown in the morning. He would complete the commute to the Russian Consulate with a crosstown cable car ride and a brisk walk.

Nick made a mental note to take the ferry to Kowloon in the afternoon. He returned to a chair beside the oak table. He had arrived early at Russia's Hong Kong Consulate. The receptionist directed him to the conference room.

Nick retrieved his tea cup from the table and took a swallow.

His cup was almost empty when the door opened and a middle aged man with thinning brown hair and a slight build appeared.

"Nicolai! I'm so sorry to keep you waiting. I was on the phone to Moscow."

"Don't worry about it. I was early."

Nick had arrived at Hong Kong International the previous evening. His hotel was just a few blocks away from the consulate. Unable to sleep much because of jet lag, he rose early.

The two men embraced. "Good to see you, my friend," Oleg Chapev said.

"You too, sir." Earlier in Nick's career, he had worked for Chapev at the Russian Embassy in London.

Nick turned to his side and gestured toward the windows. "Incredible views from here."

"Indeed. This truly is an amazing place."

"How long have you been assigned here now?"

"Just over a year." Like Nick, Chapev worked for the SVR. He served as the SVR *resident* for the consulate. He held the rank of colonel. Seven years Nick's senior, Chapev was married and had two teenage daughters.

"How does the family like living here?"

"They love it. Really surprised me. Education system is first class. We have a gorgeous apartment with a terrific view. Evalina and the girls are fluent in English, which makes it easy to get around because it seems like just about everyone in Hong Kong speaks at least a little English. You can forget about Russian."

Nick grinned, familiar with HK's language customs from prior visits. "That's great." Nick returned to his chair and Chapev sat beside him.

Nick said, "How about you, sir—how's it going here at the consulate?"

"Busy, lots going on."

Nick crossed his legs. "I expect you're wondering what I'm doing here."

"I received notice yesterday from Center that you were en route but nothing more."

"Smirnov sent me."

"The big boss himself…I'm impressed."

"He wants an assessment of where we are with China. The Qingdao situation has everyone in the Kremlin spooked."

"That's a huge concern here too. Hong Kong likes to think it is independent of Beijing but reality's finally hitting home. Terrorists could just have easily targeted Hong Kong as Qingdao." Chapev turned toward the windows. "A nuke going off in the harbor, even a small one, would devastate this place."

"For sure."

Nick and Chapev discussed the Qingdao debacle for a couple of minutes before returning to Hong Kong issues. "Just how active is the MSS here?" Nick asked.

"Very. They have infiltrated just about every ministry, including the police. Generally, they operate in the background. Nevertheless, Beijing has clearly consolidated its grip on the entire government."

Nick said, "The specter of nuclear terrorism will accelerate the takeover."

"No doubt."

China's One Nation, Two Systems policy toward Hong Kong had provided a degree of independence for the former British colony. When the UK's lease for Hong Kong expired in 1997, China allowed Hong Kong to police itself, along with a pledge not to import mainland security forces to the enclave. That promise, along with others, evaporated. Despite vigorous protests by Hongkongers, the Ministry of State Security operated freely in the city of seven million.

"What's the gang situation like here?" Nick asked.

"Triads are active. Prostitution, illegal gambling, drug trafficking, smuggling…knockoff luxury goods."

"Contract murder?"

Colonel Chapev's eyes narrowed. "Yes, they're involved in that too. Why do you ask?"

Nick reached into a pocket of his jacket and took out a folded paper. He opened it and gave it to Chapev. "What can you tell me about this?"

Chapev scanned the photocopy of a nearly three week old Hong Kong newspaper article. It featured the murder of a prominent businessman. "This was a big deal."

"The article pointed the finger at a local Triad. Is that still the case?"

"As far as I know. Kwan Chi was a real estate developer. We heard he got crosswise with some bad people and they took him out." Chapev frowned. "What's so important about this guy?"

"We think he might have been MSS."

That took the wind out of Chapev's sails. "No—a billionaire working for the MSS?"

"Moscow believes that's the case."

Colonel Chapev hardened his posture. "Is Moscow concerned about me not knowing."

"No sir. Please relax. That's not the case at all. Center just discovered the possibility from an agent in the States. Smirnov sent me here to investigate."

Chapev took a deep breath, relieved. "Putting a hit on a highly placed MSS asset like Kwan, no triad would dare risk something like that."

"Center agrees. If a gang did it, they had no clue who their target really was."

"But who could be behind this? I'm sure Kwan had special security, being one of the wealthier men here plus working with the MSS. It's almost like he was the target of a state sponsored hit."

"Exactly, Colonel. That's what we think happened."

Chapev pursed his lips, thinking ahead. After a moment he said, "Who would risk such a thing?"

"We suspect it was a CIA op."

"But why would the Americans want him dead?"

"That's why I need your help to determine what really happened."

* * * *

Nick Orlov took in the marvels of Victoria Harbour as the *Golden Star* dashed across the waterway. Departing from a Wan Chai pier, a short walk from the consulate, the ferry was bound for the Kowloon Peninsula. The *Golden Star* was packed with tourists along with a swarm of locals this afternoon. Nick was near the stern on the lower deck. The pulse of the diesel engine vibrated the steel deck plates, transmitting mini shudders through the soles of his shoes. The churning wake surged as the ferry captain added power. The wash helped mask the high-pitched Cantonese chatter of two middle aged women who gossiped nearby.

A perpetually ravenous seagull patrolled along the starboard side of the *Golden Star,* his jet-black BB eyeballs tracking the tourists who collected near midships. The Americans munched on French fries and Big Macs from the McDonald's at Wan Chai. The gull hoped for a tasty treat to be tossed his way.

Nick embraced the salt laden fragrance of the air. And he welcomed the ship induced breeze; Hong Kong sizzled with dripping humidity. His shirt and trousers stuck to his skin like paste.

After his session with Colonel Chapev, Nick lunched with both Chapev and the Consul General at a restaurant near the Sun Hung Kai Centre. It was a courtesy meeting. On official business from SVR headquarters, Nick was not obligated to reveal the true nature of his visit to the consulate's senior diplomat. Nevertheless, it was Nick's policy to always befriend the Russian consul general or ambassador in whatever foreign country he operated. Nick traveled on a diplomatic passport and on more than one occasion foreign ministry staff had saved Nick's bacon.

During lunch, Nick explained that he was sent to Hong Kong to review the consulate's cyber security systems, which the Consul General welcomed. It was a smokescreen that Nick previewed with Chapev prior to the luncheon.

Nick would go through a perfunctory security review of the consulate for show purposes only. The CG bought in, offering whatever assistance Nick might need. Nick solidified his connection with the Consul General when he took care of the lunch bill.

Nick walked forward to the ferry's main seating area. That's when he spotted the blonde sitting in a bench seat with her back to him. Her hair was short, almost a bob.

It can't be!

With his heart pounding he stepped along the aisleway opposite the young woman. He stole a quick look—anticipating, hoping. But no joy.

What the hell are you thinking. This is the last place she would come to.

Nick took a seat a couple of rows forward of the thirty something woman. She was attractive but not even close to Elena's exquisiteness.

Elena Krestyanova, aka Nastasia Vasileva, was a former SVR operative and Nick's lover.

Nick missed Elena and thought of her often. Just a month earlier they were together and then Elena fled. She had no choice. Nick was complicit in her escape, which risked his career.

Their last mission together, sanctioned by Moscow and orchestrated remotely half a world away by Nick and Elena, resulted in a high-tech death in Hong Kong. An SVR hit team took out billionaire Kwan Chi not the CIA.

It was Nick's job to perpetuate the charade, isolating Russia from any connection to the assassination of one of China's most valued spies.

Chapter 32

Day 24—Friday

Captain Zhou Jun lay on the bed, his back propped against the bed board with a pillow. It was 12:22 A.M. The slider to the master bedroom was open to the balcony. A screened wide-open window in the kitchen on the opposite side of the apartment provided a flow path for the ocean breeze. Zhou preferred natural ventilation to the unit's mechanical air conditioning.

Overlooking the South China Sea from its hillside perch, the three-bedroom, 1,500 square foot unit was just a few years old. The PLA owned the building; it was a perk reserved for senior officers and high-level bureaucrats.

Meng Park was stretched out beside Zhou. A sheet tucked just below her neck concealed her nakedness. She slept soundly, her shallow breaths barely a whisper.

The sex was exceptional this evening. Both were ravenous. After dinner at a favorite Sanya restaurant, they rushed back to Zhou's apartment. Exhausted and sated, Park promptly fell asleep after their second round. Zhou too had dropped off but awoke after just an hour.

The naval officer slipped his legs over the edge of the bed and stood up. He removed a bathrobe from the closet and pulled it over his nude body. He grabbed a pack of Liqun cigarettes and a lighter from a dresser drawer and quietly relocated to the bedroom's lanai.

Standing near the railing, Captain Zhou took in a deep drag. The nicotine surged into his blood vessels, instantly dampening the underlying craving.

Hooked as a teenager, Zhou wanted to stop but repeatedly failed. It was one of the few life aspirations he had not yet mastered. But he had a new incentive—Meng Park.

Zhou took precautions to control his smoking habit when Meng was in town. An ardent nonsmoker, she made clear her contempt for tobacco. Zhou tempered her zeal by revealing he was working hard to cut back, which she happily encouraged. He sucked on nicotine-laced lozenges today; it helped but he continually found himself reaching for a phantom pack. And now, while Meng slept, he cheated.

The navy captain sat in one of the deck chairs. He took another lungful. The nicotine helped, as did the sex, yet trepidation persisted. Project Serpent was well underway but they were behind schedule.

Just two of the dozen planned hubs scattered throughout the South China Sea were operational. Fleet demanded daily reports on progress.

Why are they pushing so hard? Zhou wondered.

Both Captain Zhou and Dr. Meng were uneasy with the accelerated deployment program. Beijing scrapped months of the planned testing. Zhou's original schedule called for full operation in the following year.

The partial success from the Serpent attack on the American submarine had emboldened Fleet. The admiral in charge of the South Sea Fleet touted the revolutionary sub killer system to his superiors in Beijing. The Central Military Commission embraced the technology and ordered the rush deployment.

The system is not ready for full-scale operations!

Dr. Meng's analysis of the recent attack revealed a flaw in the Serpent operating code that controlled communications between multiple Viper units when they jointly pursued the same target. Exchange of targeting data between Vipers was intermittent due to the software problem. The glitch resulted in a slight delay of Viper Five's assault on the U.S. Navy sub, which Meng Park concluded led to the glancing blow and the USS *Tucson's* eventual escape. She needed at least another month to update the code to remedy the anomaly.

Fleet had overruled Meng. Captain Zhou was charged with deploying Serpent in its current state.

Something's going on but what?

Zhou heard the scuttlebutt at the officer's club. Payback was coming soon. And this time, China's enemies would pay—dearly.

Beijing was tight-lipped about the Qingdao disaster, reporting that its investigation was in progress. Nevertheless, leaks persisted despite the government's efforts to clampdown further on social media outlets.

Rumors abounded, everything from the smuggling of an Islamic A-bomb into the port aboard a Pakistani box ship to the accidental detonation of a nuclear depth charge by the PLA Navy.

Captain Zhou and several of his colleagues in Sanya knew otherwise. Analysis of radioactive isotopes from the Qingdao explosion revealed that the bomb's U-235 core originated from a uranium processing facility in the former Soviet Union. After the USSR dissolved, the cash strapped Russian Federation sold tons of the weapons grade fissile material to the United States for use as fuel in nuclear reactors. But Russia also retained a stockpile of the 90 percent enriched U-235.

One of them is responsible—but which one?

It was a delicate quandary for Beijing. Both Russia and the United States possessed the exact same fissile substance. Either one could have fashioned the low yield nuke that detonated in Qingdao.

Russia—why would they do such a thing?

China and Russia were allies, both sharing a common border and both plagued by a mutual adversary—the United States. Favorable trade relations between Moscow and Beijing were critical. More than ever, China needed Russia's crude oil and natural gas that was piped in daily from Siberia. And Russia, with over half of its national economy dependent on the sale of its vast petroleum reserves, was desperate to keep the pipelines full and the cash flowing.

Nevertheless, doubt persisted as to Russia's true intentions. Although not in that loop, Captain Zhou speculated that Beijing had contingency measures in place to punish Russia if it were involved with the Qingdao nuke.

The Americans are the real meddlers—they think they're invincible.

The United States Navy picked at the festering scab, ignoring China's territorial claims to the South China Sea. U.S. warships routinely violated the PRC's self-imposed sovereignty by patrolling within the twelve-mile limits of China's collection of artificial islands in the SCS.

What they did to Yulin is unconscionable!

The EMP attack on the Yulin Naval Base was a devastating blow to the PLAN. Zhou served as an advisor to the naval board of inquiry investigating the attack. Over thirty warships were severely impaired from the directed energy weapon that exploded in the moorage area. Both aircraft carriers would likely be out of commission for at least a year or more. And about half of the surface ships were destined for the breakers yards, the damage too extensive to warrant repairing. It was cheaper to build new ships.

Unlike the Qingdao event, Beijing succeeded in concealing the Yulin attack from the nation. China's citizenry would be furious at the affront.

Beijing would reveal the truth when it was ready, encouraging the people to vent their rage at the enemy.

All evidence pointed straight back to the United States. There was no loss of life in the attack, which matched America's tendency to employ half measures. Instead of sinking ships with missiles and bombs, the EMP device killed virtually every electronic system aboard the collection of warships assembled at Yulin.

How did they find out about Operation Sea Dragon?

Captain Zhou was privy to Beijing's grand plan. The coordinated attack on the renegade province was about to commence when Yulin was compromised. In a fraction of a second, the electronic sneak attack at the Yulin Naval Base accomplished America's goal: Derailing China's pending invasion of Taiwan.

Taiwan was now relegated to the backburner. Beijing would deal with the rebels later. The CMC charged the People's Liberation Army with evicting the American Navy from China's home waters. Project Serpent was a key element of the plan.

Serpent will shatter the American Navy's arrogance—they deserve it!

Full deployment of Serpent, even with its flaws, would severely limit U.S. submarines from operating in China's territorial waters—the Yellow Sea, East China Sea and South China Sea. Nuclear powered attack submarines represented America's first line of defense against the PRC in East Asia. Without protection from U.S. submarines, American surface warships would be too vulnerable to patrol offshore of China's coast. PRC subs, particularly ultra-quiet diesel-electric boats, were a threat. Even more concerning for the Pentagon was China's Carrier Killer. The ground launched DF-21D anti-ship ballistic missile was specifically developed to take out U.S. nuclear powered aircraft carriers. With a thousand mile range and traveling at hypersonic speeds, the missile was designed to deliver a conventional warhead to the deck of a supercarrier as it executed radical evasion measures while running at forty knots.

Denying access to China's home waters would force Washington to restrict its naval operations to the First Island Chain—Japan's Kyushu Island, the Ryukyu Islands, Okinawa, the Philippines, Brunei and Malaysia.

Future deployment of Serpent beyond the First Island Chain would force America ships and subs eastward to the Second Island Chain—Japan's Honshu Island, Iwo Jima, Guam and the Indonesian archipelago.

Beijing's ultimate goal was to curb U.S. naval operations from the Asian coastline across the Western Pacific to the Hawaiian Island chain.

Those grand plans are going to have to wait, Zhou reflected. *We're still behind with the first phase of Serpent.*

After standing, Zhou ejected the spent butt over the deck railing—disposal of the incriminating evidence. Before climbing back into bed, he would also take a swig of mouthwash. He hoped for morning sex with Park.

Chapter 33

The USS *Colorado* neared the U.S. Naval Base at Yokosuka, Japan. It was midmorning. Thick billowing clouds dotted the skies. Winds were minimal. Four-foot-high ocean swells paced the nuclear-powered submarine as it sailed northward in the Uraga Channel.

SSN 788's commanding officer, Commander Tom Bowman, and his executive officer, Commander Jenae Mauk, were in the bridge cockpit atop the Virginia class submarine's two story tall sail, each adorned in regulation parkas. Both wore communication headsets that connected with *Colorado's* control room two decks below the sail. A pair of binoculars hung from leather straps around their necks. Two additional binocular equipped watch standers were behind Bowman and Mauk on top of the fairwater.

"It'll be good for the crew to get a little shore leave," Bowman said. Although he had turned thirty-nine about a month earlier, he retained the same youthful looks he'd had when he'd graduated from the Naval Academy seventeen years earlier—close-cropped black hair without a speck of gray, square jawed, and a muscular five-foot nine frame.

"Definitely," Mauk said. "It's been a while." A petite brunette, the thirty-six-year-old mother of two was also a product of Annapolis. She'd graduated near the top of her class. When the Navy opened up subs to women, she transferred from the surface warfare program to the submarine service. After completing nuclear power school, she served on a boomer for three years before transferring to the *Colorado*. It was her dream job.

Since departing its homeport at Naval Submarine Base New London, Groton, Connecticut, the *Colorado* had been on continuous sea duty for over three months. While on its initial patrol in the Arctic, the submarine was temporarily reassigned to the Pacific Fleet. After entering the North

Pacific Ocean via the Bering Strait, its first mission was to track Russian ballistic missile submarines deployed from the Rybachiy sub base at Petropavlovsk-Kamchatskiy. Follow up missions occurred in Chinese waters and elsewhere in the Pacific. And now, with food supplies running low and just about everyone aboard suffering from "cabin fever," the forthcoming visit to Yokosuka was long overdue.

"Any new thoughts on what they have planned for us?" Mauk asked.

Several days earlier, the commander of Submarine Force, Pacific Fleet (COMSUBPAC) ordered *Colorado* to Yokosuka for replenishment. Four days of leave for the crew was promised.

"My gut tells me we're headed back to the South China Sea for more recon work."

"I think you're right, skipper. It's getting dicey down there."

Bowman and Mauk remained apprehensive from the *Colorado's* earlier encounter with a PLAN attack sub.

Captain Bowman pulled up his binocs to eye a southward bound fishing boat. Confirming the approaching vessel would pass safely to the port he lowered the glasses. "XO, you want to bring her into the harbor?"

"By all means."

Bowman keyed the mike on his headset. "Control, Captain. XO has the conn."

* * * *

"How long will you be gone?" asked Laura Newman.

"I don't know but it could be a couple of weeks."

Yuri called from his Honolulu hotel room using Facetime. It was midafternoon in his time zone. The sun was low on the western horizon in Washington State.

Yuri noted that Laura was in the living room of the Bellevue condo, sitting on a sofa; Maddy napped nearby in her playpen. Laura wore a sleeveless blouse and a pair of jeans.

"Yuri, that's what you said last time and you were gone for over six weeks!"

Yuri never tired at viewing Laura. "I know, honey."

"I suppose you can't tell me anything about where you're going and what you'll be doing."

"Sorry."

Laura massaged her temple. "What you're asking me to do is not workable. I need to be here. Too much is going on for me to leave."

Yuri had asked Laura to visit her adoptive mother in Santa Barbara while he was away. His fear that Russia or China might seek revenge against his family had not dimmed.

"I'd just feel better if you and Maddy were not in the northwest while I'm gone."

"We'll be fine in the apartment. Besides, the FBI is watching over us—right?"

"Yes."

Before committing to the mission, Yuri confirmed that FBI protection for Laura and Maddy would remain in place while he was away. Operating under a secret federal court order, FBI cyber techs hacked into the condominium tower's camera surveillance system, allowing around the clock access to every video camera in the building. FBI surveillance equipment was already in the security center of the building serving as Cognition Consultants headquarters. Digital data from both sources streamed to a fifth floor unit the FBI rented in the same building as Laura's apartment. The one bedroom flat was manned twenty-four seven by two agents.

Laura said, "I know you're not happy about this but I just can't be away right now."

"The merger?"

"Yes, we're getting close. We're hammering away on the draft agreement...countless details need to be handled."

"I get it."

"Don't worry about us. We'll be fine."

"Okay," Yuri said, deciding it was time to drop the issue. He prayed that the FBI would live up to its commitments.

They caught up for another ten minutes; it was time to end the video call.

"Please be careful," Laura pleaded.

"I will. And please give Maddy a kiss for me."

"Of course."

"I love you.

"I love you too."

Chapter 34

Day 25—Saturday

President Chen Shen and Admiral Soo Xiao lunched on the veranda of Chen's private residence. Perched on the shore of the Bohai Sea south of Qinhuangdao, the design of the sprawling estate reflected traditional Chinese architecture with post-and-lintel timber frame construction that supported majestic flowing rooflines.

Just a half hour flight from Beijing, Chen visited the compound often, especially during sweltering summers. He welcomed the ocean breezes and the stunning seascape. Located on China's most northern coast, the Bohai Sea connected with the Yellow Sea to the southeast. The Korean peninsula lay to the east.

The two men completed their meal and were now enjoying a fresh pot of green tea. Summoned by Chen for a briefing, Admiral Soo was accustomed to the president's preference to chat about family and friends before business. During lunch, Chen had doted on his three sons and their families, especially his six grandchildren.

As the offspring of a senior Party official, princeling Chen was not subject to China's former one child family policy, which had resulted in a huge nationwide surplus of males. Admiral Soo and his late wife had adhered to the edict, producing a single child—a daughter that he adored.

"You must be very proud of Genji," Chen said, wishing that one of his sons had decided to study medicine rather than business.

"I am, sir."

Dr. Soo Genji was a neurosurgeon in the last year of her residency at Peking Union Medical College Hospital in Beijing. Prior to earning her MD, Genji was awarded a Ph.D. in Integrated Molecular-Cellular Physiology from the University of California at Davis.

Chen and Admiral Soo were longtime friends. Five years previously, Chen attended the funeral of Sun Shu. Soo's wife had died without warning from cardiac arrest.

President Chen smiled. "When she finishes her residency, you watch! She will marry and soon you too will be blessed with grandchildren."

Soo said, "That will be wonderful."

A grandchild was a blessing Admiral Soo longed for yet he worried Genji might end up as a leftover. Most women in China married in their early twenties. Genji would turn thirty-four next month.

Chen took out a pack of Marlboros from his coat pocket. He pushed his chair away from the table and lit up. Facing the sea, he said, "Well, what have you got for me today?"

As the vice chairman of the Central Military Commission, Admiral Soo served as President Chen's senior military advisor. He reached into the open attaché case beside the table for a notepad. Soo scanned the outline with the ten bullet points that he needed to discuss with the president.

"Sir, I'm pleased to report that the North Sea Fleet conducted another successful test of the Dong Feng anti-ship ballistic missile system. The target was a container ship to be scrapped. Roughly the same length of an American Nimitz class aircraft carrier, the test missile was fired from . . ."

Admiral Soo's rundown on national military matters lasted almost thirty minutes. His current topic grabbed Chen's genuine interest. Soo said, "Full deployment of Serpent is underway in the South Sea. Two of the stations have been installed."

"I thought you'd be further along by now."

"They're a bit behind...some hardware issues but I still expect that the system will be operational within a month."

"So, how do you turn it on when I'm ready to do that?"

"A sonar code will be transmitted to each seafloor hub, activating the individual Viper units."

"How long will that take?" Chen asked as he lit up a fresh Marlboro—his sixth for the day.

"If ships are used, probably several days because of the distances involved. However, with a couple of patrol aircraft, all could be activated in one day by dropping buoys with sonar transmitters."

"Plan on using aircraft."

"Yes sir." The president's order triggered a question. "Will you be issuing a warning to the Americans before activating Serpent?"

"I have not decided yet. I'd like your thoughts."

Admiral Soo rubbed his temple. The stink from the cigarette smoke invaded his airspace but he ignored it. "My recommendation is to issue a warning. It does not have to be detailed, just a notice that any unauthorized submerged vessels operating in the South China Sea will be targeted. We'd have to make it very clear that surface traffic would not be impacted, just submarines."

"If I choose not to issue the warning?"

"Very risky, sir. The Americans will likely react with aggression. Remember, during the testing phase of Serpent, a Viper damaged one of their submarines. A second attack without any warning could lead to direct confrontation."

"Even if I issue a warning, Washington's going to attack us—both in the South Sea and at the UN."

"I know. But by issuing the warning, they will have at least been forewarned."

"I'll consider it and let you know my decision."

"Very good, sir." Soo glanced down at his agenda. "Mr. President, the last item I need to discuss is the contingency plan regarding the Qingdao event."

Chen nodded as he sucked in another lungful.

"The planning is complete. We're currently in the pre-operation phase. A submarine has been selected for the mission and the crew is preparing. Should you decide to proceed with the operation, the sub can . . ."

* * * *

President Chen strolled along the beach fronting his estate. His golden retriever, Blossom—*Hua*, frolicked at the water's edge. Knee-high waves washed onto the sandy beach. The meeting with Soo concluded forty minutes earlier. The admiral was currently on a military jet heading back to Beijing.

Blossom rushed to Chen's side, a hunk of driftwood clamped between her jaws and her swampy tail wagging. Blossom dropped the stick and issued a sharp bark, digging her forepaws into the sand.

"Okay Blossom, okay."

President Chen reached down and picked up the stick. Blossom woofed again. He heaved the two-foot elm tree branch waterward. Blossom charged into the surf.

Beach walking with his beloved Blossom was a cherished interlude for Chen Shen. No phones to answer, no pesky aides hovering around him, no guests to entertain, no meetings to attend. It was just him and Blossom—plus the squad of bodyguards who discreetly provided security.

The public was prohibited from accessing the beach for over two miles on either side of Chen's estate. Legions of nearby seaside residents were evicted and their homes bulldozed to enforce the security zone.

The armed sentries ensured Chen's privacy—and safety. A dozen elite special operators from the PLAN's *zhongdui* naval commando unit shadowed the president. An overwatch team occupying the top level of a six-story decorative tower near the main residence also scanned the shoreline, adjacent uplands and offshore waters for threats. A concealed radar antenna atop the tower probed the heavens for aircraft, cruise missiles and drones. If needed, a dozen man portable antiaircraft missiles were available to the overwatch unit.

Although an aerial sneak attack was possible, the principal worry for President Chen's watchers was a single individual with a high-powered rifle. Homebrewed dissidents, imported terrorists, foreign assassins, and run of the mill nutcases represented the primary sniper threats. Chen's rise to the presidency also generated legions of political enemies. Most had been dealt with, stripped of power and wealth, and in some cases imprisoned. However, outliers persisted, their hatred for Chen never abating.

Chen suspected that his greatest peril resided with the other eight members of the Standing Committee of the Central Political Bureau of the Communist Party of China, aka the Politburo Standing Committee. All had been thoroughly vetted and each had personally sworn their loyalty to Chen. Still, his gut instinct told him there was a traitor in his inner circle.

Who could it be? Chen wondered.

Blossom charged out of the surf with the reclaimed stick. Waterlogged, she ran to Chen's side and ritually shook off the wetness in a tail to nose full body convulsion. "Whoa, girl, you're getting me wet."

Blossom deposited the stick at Chen's feet, ready for another swim. Chen relaunched the branch. "Go get it," he shouted.

As Chen watched Blossom dogpaddle seaward, he sensed that it might be weeks before he could return to the beach house. China was about to go to war.

I have no choice but to proceed—the Americans have to be stopped.

China's economy had faltered. Rising interest rates, tariffs, Washington's unrelenting demands for fair trade, and the PSC's shortsighted mandate to generate jobs no matter the cost had all taken their toll. China's experimental marriage of Communism and Capitalism was in decline.

Thousands of state run enterprises had failed during the past year and the bloodbath endured. Operated inefficiently for decades and rife with corruption, the government owned companies could not compete on a global level without continual renourishment from Beijing. But with growth slashed, China's cashflow also tanked. Severe pushback from the United States on China's predatory trade practices and currency manipulation tactics further aggravated the state of affairs. The once endless gusher of renminbi was drying up.

No longer able to prop up the SREs that could not compete, Beijing had no choice but to allow the slaughter. Economic models predicted stability if half of the SREs were shut down. But the price was astronomical—tens of millions would lose their jobs.

The middle class would take the brunt of retooling China's economy. With looming massive unemployment, the Communist Party's days might be numbered. China's next revolution was already in the making, and that realization struck terror in every member of the Politburo Standing Committee.

Sea Dragon would have worked but it's too late now.

Chen and the PSC needed a diversion to gain time so China's economy could transform. Operation Sea Dragon was the designated diversion. The invasion of renegade Taiwan and its return to the homeland would galvanize the populace. Confiscating the island's assets would bolster China's wealth. Multitudes of unemployed mainlanders would take the jobs of the hapless Taiwanese. But that grand rescue plan was in shambles.

The core of the invasion fleet assembled at the Yulin Naval Base on Hainan Island was rendered impotent by an electromagnetic pulse weapon, gutting Operation Sea Dragon.

The damn Americans did it. I cannot let that stand.

Convinced that the United States was behind the e-bomb assault at Yulin, the Politburo Standing Committee would cite that event as the deciding factor for China's retaliatory actions. President Chen, of course, was on board with the PSC mandate. Yet, lingering doubts endured.

What is Russia really up to?

The MSS and the People's Armed Police Force's joint investigation of the Qingdao terror attack proceeded full throttle. Uyghur dissidents remained the prime culprits but qualms persisted. The suspected ringleader, Talgat Ramazan, had vanished. The MSS speculated that he could have been a Russian operative but had no conclusive proof.

Moscow could be screwing us right now and we don't even know it.

Fearing the experts might be wrong regarding Russia's intensions, President Chen planned accordingly. The submarine was on standby. Chen could dispatch the warship with a single phone call.

Blossom returned to Chen Shen. Spent from swimming, she dropped the stick and rested on her haunches. Her long pink tongue dangled from her mouth as she panted. Chen stooped down to massage her soft furry ears. She pushed her head back, encouraging the attention. "You getting tired, girl?"

After a two minute respite, Chen with Blossom at his side rambled southward along the shoreline.

Serpent will change everything for us!

The breakthrough technology in antisubmarine warfare couldn't have come at a better time for Chen and the PSC. Unleashing the Vipers in combination with the Carrier Killer missiles would send shockwaves through the Pentagon.

Finally, we'll get rid of the meddlers.

Denying the U.S. Navy unrestricted access to the South China Sea, followed by the same for the East and Yellow seas, would commence final atonement for China's shame.

In 1839, Great Britain's first opium war with China sparked the Century of Humiliation. London, with the world's most powerful Navy at that time, compelled China's emperor to surrender Hong Kong and Kowloon to the British Empire, as well as relinquish control of China's other key ports. Later, Russia's Czar confiscated huge segments of China's northeast territories through treaties by threatening war with China while France's navy blockaded Taiwan as a ploy to force China out of Vietnam. Imperial Japan in the First Sino-Japanese War followed up by ejecting China from the Korean Peninsula and claiming Taiwan as a trophy. Further disgrace occurred when Great Britain grabbed Nepal and Burma, replacing historic Chinese sway. And during China's Boxer Rebellion at the turn of the twentieth century, an alliance of Western powers, including the United States, invaded Beijing. Military forces from the eight nation coalition squashed the rebellion, pillaged the Forbidden City, and heartlessly ended the protests of ordinary citizens over the occupation of their country by foreigners.

The shameful century climaxed with the Second Sino-Japanese War when Japan seized the eastern half of China and ruled with brutal efficiency. The Japanese military killed, maimed and raped untold legions of innocent Chinese civilians. Only after the Allies conquered Japan in 1945 did China's Century of Humiliation end.

We will return the Cow's Tongue to the motherland!

Shortly after the end of World War II, China laid claim to nearly 90 percent of the South China Sea, citing historic use of the reefs, subtidal rocks and intertidal islets that made up the Spratly Island Group, the Parcel Islands and other quasi outcrops that barely projected above the sea surface at low tide. The claim followed China's dubious Nine-Dash line that extended southward from Taiwan following the coastlines of the Philippines and Brunei to Malaysia and looping northward along Vietnam's coast to Hainan Island. When viewed from above, the enormous swath of water took on the shape of a giant cow's tongue.

The Cow's Tongue claim ignored international agreements that recognized offshore interests of the other nations that bordered the South China Sea. Vast natural resources—subsea oil and gas fields, mineral deposits and immense diverse fisheries—were located offshore of the coasts of Vietnam, the Philippines and Malaysia-Brunei. The Cow's Tongue swallowed up the majority of those riches.

And with one third of the world's cargo, container and tank ships transiting the South China Sea every year, freedom of navigation of the sea lanes was vital to maintaining worldwide commerce. If controlled by China as proposed by the Nine-Dash line, Beijing would decide who could transit the Cow's Tongue waters and fly in the airspace above.

China disregarded the protests of its neighbors and when its Nine-Dash line claim was officially invalidated by the International Court in The Hague, Beijing ignored the ruling.

With Serpent in place, we will solidify our claim and the West can go to hell. They looted China for a hundred years. At the very least, they owe us the treasures of the Cow's Tongue.

Once the USA and its Western allies were evicted from China's home waters, Beijing would deal with its SCS neighbors. Either they would accept what pittances China offered or they would get nothing. And without the United States' naval 'Big Stick', the bordering states would be powerless to stop the bullying by China.

Besides atoning for the West's past sins, rolling the Cow's Tongue into China's official territorial borders would rocket the nation's sagging economy. Recovering the billions of barrels of crude oil and trillions of cubic feet of natural gas that underlay the seabed would greatly reduce China's dependence on imported hydrocarbons. New modern fleets of fishing vessels would now be free to harvest the fisheries within the Cow's Tongue on an industrial scale. And the taxes and fees levied on commercial vessels transiting the South China Sea would provide a new revenue stream.

Yes, this will work. China will be great again!

* * * *

President Chen was on his way back to his residence with Blossom at his side. He puffed on a fresh Marlboro. About fifty yards from the residence he spotted his wife. Chen Wu Mei stood at the seaward end of the stone pathway that connected the beach to their residence. Blossom also saw Mei and blasted ahead full speed. Chen dropped the three-quarter spent cigarette onto the saturated sand, hoping Mei did not notice. He popped a breath mint into his mouth.

Chen joined his wife.

"Did you enjoy your outing?" Wu Mei asked, now standing near the water with Blossom sitting at her side. Five-foot two with above the shoulder length jet-black hair sheared China doll style, Mei wore a flowing turquoise neck to ankle silk gown that flattered her delicate curves. Her angelic face, restored with a surgeon's skill, continued to please her husband.

"We did. It's very nice out here today." Noticing that she had traded her sandals for a pair of sneakers, Chen asked, "Would you like to walk with us for a little while?"

"I would."

"Wonderful."

Mei slipped an arm around Chen's offered forearm and they ambled northward along the shore. Blossom charged ahead, splashing through the water.

They had been a couple for thirty-four years. It was an arranged marriage but one that pleased both participants. After several minutes, they stopped and looked seaward. Chen had just tossed another piece of driftwood into the water. Blossom was in pursuit.

Mei's beauty was the natural attraction that hooked Chen but over the years, he found her counsel to be invaluable. Exceedingly bright, she functioned as Chen's sounding board. She knew everything.

"Have you decided?" Mei asked.

"Yes, I will issue a warning." Both Admiral Soo and Mei had recommended that Chen warn the Americans before formally activating Serpent.

"That is a wise decision, my darling. The Americans are weak; they will kowtow to us."

"But if they choose to ignore the warning?" Chen asked.

"Then the blood will be on their hands."

Chapter 35

Day 26—Sunday

It was midmorning at Camp David. The two men in their late fifties strolled along the forest pathway deep in the Catoctin Mountain Park. Secret Service agents roamed ahead and trailed the pair. Located in northern Maryland about sixty miles north of the District of Columbia, the military compound served as a country retreat for the President of the United States.

The sky was cloudless and the air crisp. It was early fall; the deciduous trees lining the trail had already started to turn. President Tyler Magnuson and National Security Advisor Peter Brindle chatted as they hiked.

"Just how worried is the Navy?" asked POTUS.

"Very. We've never encountered a threat like it before."

"Are all of our submarines vulnerable?"

"We don't know. The sub that was attacked is one of our remaining LA class boats." Brindle swiped a bead of perspiration from his forehead. "The *Tucson*'s old but she's still stealthy... compared to most other foreign nukes. The device that attacked it obviously detected it some distance away, which is highly alarming for the Navy."

"So how do we stop this thing?"

"Until we know more about how it works and just where it's been deployed, we can't do much to counter the threat."

"How many of our submarines are operating in the area now?"

"None. The Pacific Fleet commander judged the threat as serious and ordered all of our subs out of the South China Sea. He restricted naval ops in the sea to just freedom of navigation patrols by surface combatants."

"Do the Chinese know our subs have bugged out?"

"We don't think they do, which is good for us. We want them to think we're still operating in their backyard."

"When will the team be ready to go?"

"Soon. It's assembling as we speak."

POTUS pulled out a handkerchief from a coat pocket and blew his nose. An allergen in the air irritated his nostrils. "Pete, they can't be caught. That would be a disaster, and it'll play right into Chen's hands."

"I know, sir. The team will be so advised."

The men traveled along the path for another quarter mile. They took up a new subject.

"Lebedev has been quiet lately," commented Magnuson. "That worries me."

"He's gone through periods like this before, hanging out on the sidelines."

"He's up to no good. I just feel it." POTUS continued to reel from the nuclear detonations offshore of Hawaii and in China.

"I share your concern but so far we've not detected any new threats in the Pacific theater. Their submarines appear to be following normal operating procedures. Same for their surface fleet. They do have military exercises scheduled for next month in the Far East. They've been moving ground forces and some air assets into Eastern Siberia for those wargames."

"What about that Kanyon thing they touted—the nuclear-powered drone?" Magnuson referred to a new Russian weapon that supposedly could travel thousands of miles underwater autonomously, evading any subsea defenses before attacking a harbor or even an aircraft carrier underway.

Brindle said, "Well, sir, we still have no solid intel to judge the weapon as credible but the Navy is treating it as a possible serious threat."

"It still sounds like a PR stunt to me. You know how the Russians are with propaganda."

"Understood, sir." NSA Brindle and the Pentagon were well aware of Russia's history of inflating its technological achievements.

Magnuson and Brindle traveled along the trail for a couple more minutes before stopping beside a stream to rest. They drank from the water bottles carried in their knapsacks.

The president took a healthy swig. "Pete, I must confess that I'm having second thoughts on Project Takedown."

Takedown was the codename for a cyber attack on the Russian Federation's oil and gas infrastructure. Critical control systems across the entire nation were targeted for disruption. The scale of the pending digital hack ranged from disabling natural gas overpressure valves in transmission pipes while doubling flow pressures—resulting in burst pipelines, to sabotaging antifreeze temperature controls in Arctic and subarctic production zones, allowing crude oil to solidify and plug up the works.

Surprised, the National Security Advisor turned toward his boss. "What's the concern?"

"I know our military cyber capabilities. I'm afraid we might be too successful."

"Sir?"

"Exporting oil and gas is Russia's lifeblood. If we go ahead and crash their system, it will take months, maybe even a year or more to recover." POTUS took another swallow. "I'm afraid it might push Lebedev over the edge, similar to what happened with Japan when FDR cut off their oil supply. And we know how that turned out."

Brindle scratched the earth with the toe of his left boot. "Do you want a scaled back plan?"

"No. Once we follow that path, we need to go full speed ahead." Magnuson drained the bottle and slipped it into his knapsack. "I want Project Takedown held in reserve for possible future use after we see what happens with China."

"But what about Pearl Harbor? The terrorist attack story is starting to fall apart. There's lots of scuttlebutt on the web blaming both Russia and China for what happened."

"I'm aware of that plus Congress is antsy about it too." The President rubbed the back of his neck, responding to mounting strain. "Dammit, Pete, we're innocent in this entire matter. Chen started the whole mess and Lebedev escalated it. And now, if I make the wrong decision, we could end up in World War III."

Peter Brindle processed the President's dilemma, sympathetic to his increasingly cold feet, especially on how to respond to China's treachery. "I know you want to assess the threat from China's new ASW system before retaliating but measures could be put in place now that will expedite the response should you decide to proceed."

POTUS perked up. "What do you have in mind?"

* * * *

Seven time zones ahead, President Lebedev relaxed in Russia's equivalent to Camp David. The forested compound was located forty miles north of Moscow. A dozen modern dachas, several support buildings, and a massive guest lodge with conference center were scattered across the 300 acre site. A lake near the center of the facility made up a third of the compound's area. Reserved for the Kremlin elite, the retreat was surrounded by a ten-foot-high security fence and guarded around the clock by Army Special Forces.

Joining Lebedev in the regal library of his residence this late afternoon was a new arrival. The two men sat in plush chairs by the window wall, enjoying the twilight view of the lake and the stand of birch trees on the far shore.

"Do you enjoy trout fishing, Ivan?" asked President Lebedev.

"I do, sir. But it's been years since I've had a pole in the water." Although not in uniform today, the strapping silver haired visitor with a mottled complexion commanded all Russian military forces. Ivan Volkov had started his distinguished military career as an infantry junior lieutenant in the Red Army. Some forty years later, he ascended to its highest rank, Marshall of the Russian Federation. And then President Lebedev appointed Volkov Minister of Defense.

Lebedev said, "Well, our little lake here is chock-full of hungry trout. Perhaps you'd like to join me tomorrow morning."

"That would be fun. Thank you."

The two men discussed lake fishing techniques—bait vs. lures, which swiftly evolved to 'fish' stories. Both were 'hooked' in their teenage years. After ten minutes of trading 'whoppers' they moved onto the primary purpose of Volkov's visit.

"So, tell me how you are progressing with the contingency plan," President Lebedev asked.

"All elements of the plan are in play. Five divisions have been quietly transferred to the Far East. We've also added two hundred combat aircraft to the region."

"The Chinese will no doubt notice."

"They will, but the troop and equipment movements are consistent with the deteriorating relations with the United States—beefing up our Far Eastern defenses in response to Magnuson's aggressive behavior. Besides, it's all being orchestrated under the upcoming Home Guard wargames." Volkov referred to a colossal military exercise in Eastern Siberia scheduled for late October.

"How do you expect Beijing to respond?"

"So far, they appear not to be concerned. No significant changes with their forces along our common border."

Russia continued to play dumb. The Kremlin elite were aware that China's Navy had sabotaged a Russian subsea oil well offshore of Siberia, generating a massive oil spill in the Arctic. Later, Chinese special forces leveled a colossal $5 billion oil and gas port on Sakhalin Island. Both attacks were staged to trigger a war between the Russian Federation and the United States.

Lebedev processed Volkov's report. "What about the U.S. plan?"

"Our cyber group is close to being ready. I expect that everything will be in place within a week."

"That's excellent, sooner than I expected."

"The Americans make it easy for us." MOD Volkov smirked. "They ignore the threat. The defenses for their power grid are collectively a joke."

"How much damage can you inflict?"

"Their eastern seaboard is particularly vulnerable. When ready, we'll be able to turn out the lights from Boston to Miami. They'll be lucky to get back to normal within six months."

President Lebedev nodded his approval.

Volkov said, "I do have reservations on the extent of the attack. If we inflict too much damage, that could push Magnuson over the edge."

"Launch his own cyber attack on us?"

"Oh, you can count on that for sure."

"But I thought General Bakhtin was going to use Iran for a scapegoat." He referenced the Army general in charge of Russia's cyber warfare unit.

"He will but that will only go so far. Believe me, sir, no matter how the attack is disguised the Americans will figure it out. They will counter, taking us on as well as Iran."

"What kind of damage?"

"They have formidable skills. At least as good as ours and likely superior."

Lebedev squirmed in his chair, uncomfortable with the news. "That's not consistent with what Bakhtin has told me before."

"I understand. However, my staff report that General Bakhtin has underestimated the Americans abilities and I believe them. Bakhtin based his analysis on the assumption that the U.S. Cybercommand would limit its response to military infrastructure only. We on the other hand expect the response to be broadscale, going after both military and civilian targets."

"Power grid, communications?"

"Yes, plus financial...banks in particular, and our oil and gas infrastructure."

The last item resonated with President Lebedev. "I thought our petroleum industry was protected."

"For our newer installations, substantial safeguards are built into both software and firmware systems. But our older equipment has not been upgraded and it will be easy for the Americans to inflict major damage."

"Just how much is vulnerable?"

Minister Volkov moped. "About sixty percent of our entire oil and gas infrastructure."

President Lebedev looked away, stunned—and furious with the oversight by the commanding officer of the Cyberwarfare unit. After ten seconds, he faced Volkov, his anger checked. "General Bakhtin should have told me about that threat. We can't afford to have that much of our operations shut down. I need to rethink our response to the Americans. Cyber may not be the way to respond."

"I understand, sir." Volkov shifted in his chair. "I've discussed this issue with General Bakhtin. He's adamant that the American's response would be timid."

"I can't rely on that assurance—not with the potential exposure."

"I intend to replace Bakhtin but it will take time to find the right man. Should you decide to use cyber, he needs to stay in command."

"Yes, fine. Whatever you think."

"Very good, sir,"

President Lebedev decided to revisit his principal worry. "Please update me on the Chinese response."

"Good news on that front. The Navy is ready to proceed with Vortex."

"Excellent. How long will it take to have our asset in place?"

"Once authorized, it will take about eight days for the submarine to reach the target zone."

"Consider this your authorization."

Chapter 36

Yuri was beat. Meaningful sleep eluded him during the eight hour flight from Joint Base Pearl Harbor-Hickam to Yokota Air Base. The C-17 Globemaster III touched down at the U.S. Air Force and Japan Air Self-Defense Force base near Tokyo at eight o'clock the previous evening.

After deplaning at Yokota, Yuri climbed aboard a bus with two dozen other passengers from the C-17—a mix of sailors, Marines and civilians. After a two hour bus ride, he arrived at the Yokosuka Naval Base. Yuri was assigned a room at the base guest quarters. He managed to sleep six hours but it wasn't enough.

Yuri was seated in a well-worn chair in the lobby of an unremarkable two story building that could have been located on just about any U.S. military base worldwide. The receptionist—a brawny Marine with a sidearm—offered Yuri coffee, which he happily accepted. He needed the caffeine.

Yuri was on his last sip when a familiar face appeared. "Good morning," Jeff Chang said.

"Hi Jeff," Yuri said, addressing the CIA officer.

Jeff was on the same flight as Yuri. Jeff's boss, Steve Osberg, along with Captain Clark returned to the East Coast. Commander Arnold spent a couple of days with his family in Honolulu before flying back to Guam to oversee the repairs to the *Tucson*.

"Sleep okay?" Chang asked.

"So so."

"Jet lag sucks."

"For sure."

Chang gestured to a nearby door. "Well, the team's here and they're all eager to meet you."

Here it comes! Yuri thought.

* * * *

The conference room turned out to be a windowless twenty-foot by thirty-foot room with a couple of folding tables pushed together in the center surrounded by a dozen empty chairs. The room's occupants were clustered in a far corner standing beside another waist high table. They were all dressed in civilian attire, blue jeans and T-shirts and short sleeved Hawaiian shirts.

Yuri and Chang approached the U.S. Navy SEALs.

"Gentlemen," Jeff Chang said, "I'd like to introduce you to our consultant, John Kirkwood."

The five man unit with the codename Ghost Riders turned away from the table. Yuri caught a glimpse of the scale model on top of the table.

The closest man approached Yuri. "Brent Andrews," he said. The officer was about Yuri's age. Beefy, he was clean shaven and his black hair cut to regulation length.

As Yuri shook Andrews's offered hand, Jeff Chang chimed in. "Lieutenant Commander Andrews is the team leader." Andrews graduated in the top ten percent of his class at Annapolis, which allowed him to select his career path—U.S. Navy Special Operations.

"Nice to meet you Commander," Yuri offered.

"Likewise."

Yuri exchanged greetings with the other team members, each man only offering his first name or handle. They were a motley crew ranging from a Texan who followed the rodeo circuit before enlisting to a rich kid Malibu surfer who managed to "hang ten" whenever he could. All were at minimum chief petty officers (E-7). As special operators, the Ghost Riders were not subject to normal U.S. Navy grooming standards. Facial hair and extended manes were tolerated. Their age ranged from late twenties to early forties. Each man appeared exceedingly fit; their well muscled shoulders, biceps, thighs and calves reflected a rigorous regime of weight lifting and running.

The group reassembled at the tables. Jeff Chang dimmed the room lights and commenced the briefing, standing beside a slide projector. "Well, gentlemen," Chang said, "I know you're all curious about the mission."

Other than Lieutenant Commander Andrews, all the team knew was the mission would take place in Southeast Asia. Chang glanced at those assembled and dropped the nuke. "We'll be operating in China."

A rush of suppressed mutterings issued from the SEALs; the men clearly taken aback at the news. None had operated inside Chinese territory.

The first PowerPoint slide appeared on the wall-mounted screen. Yuri instantly recognized the image: a bird's eye view of the southern shoreline of Hainan Island.

"This is an overview of the area where our objective is located." Chang used a handheld laser pointer to highlight the slide. "This is the city of Sanya on China's Hainan Island. It borders the South China Sea."

Chang clicked a new slide: a blowup view of the southern section of the previous photo, highlighting the shoreline. "This is the objective area. It's called Shendao."

"That's a huge pier! What's it for?" asked CPO Don Dillon aka Driller. He had the longest hair of the group; mahogany locks secreting his ears. Due to his good looks, toned physique and his youth—just twenty-eight, he could have been a cover model for a bestselling romance novel.

Chang said, "Shendao serves as the designated aircraft carrier homeport for the PLAN's South Sea Fleet."

Senior Chief Aaron Baker spoke next. "Isn't there another naval base nearby?" The thirty-seven-year-old burly African-American with a grizzled beard and a jet-black thatch hailed from Atlanta. Baker secured the moniker of "Runner" from the marathons he ran for fun when off duty.

"Correct," Chang said. He returned to the first slide. Using the remote he lased the right side of the photo. "This area is where the Yulin Naval Base is located. A huge facility that moors both surface combatants and subs."

Chang returned to the Shendao photo. He highlighted an area of the uplands near where the aircraft carrier pier connected with the shore, circling the pointer's laser dot around the south end of a large building. "The entrance to the objective is located in this section of the building. It runs underground in a tunnel that leads to a cavern carved out of rock inside the hillside. The cavern functions as the operations center for a new ASW system the Chinese are in the process of deploying in the South China Sea. Your job, gentlemen, is to get me inside that center so I can get access to the computer system."

"How big is this op center?" asked Master Chief William "Wild Bill" Halgren. The most senior member of the team, the Texan was also the largest at six-foot four and 240 pounds. Cleanshaven with an old school crew cut, Halgren could have easily fit in during the nineteen fifties and early sixties. He earned his handle from his pre-Navy cowboy stint, competing as a saddle bronc rider and a bull rider. Hardened from wrestling half-ton beasts determined to maim him, Halgren aced BUDS—Basic Underwater Demolition/SEAL training at Coronado, California, launching his esteemed military career.

"Sorry Master Chief," Chang said, "we don't have intelligence on what's inside. We'll have to play it by ear."

That comment generated another collective groan from the assembled.

"Well excuse me, sir," Halgren said, "that means we won't have a clue as to what we're up against. That's not acceptable."

Lieutenant Commander Andrews joined in. "Master Chief, both Command and I understand your concern. We don't like it either but given the circumstances, we have no choice but to go in blind."

Halgren folded his arms across his chest. "What circumstances, sir?"

Andrews took a couple of seconds to compose his response. "This will be a tough mission. And you all deserve to know what's at stake." He scanned the others sitting around the table. "The Chinese have developed a radical new weapon that is designed to takeout our subs. One of our Los Angeles class boats was attacked a couple of weeks ago in the South China Sea. It came within a whisker of sinking."

Several expletives were muttered. Andrews resumed, "Gentlemen, our goal is to obtain as much intel as we can on how the system works so that our people can come up with countermeasures. Right now, we have nothing, which means our entire game plan for dealing with the PLA Navy in Southeast Asia is in jeopardy."

Jeff Chang continued the briefing. A blowup of a spy satellite photograph of Shendao filled the screen. It depicted the offshore waters of the Chinese naval facility. "As you can see, the offshore breakwater system protecting the carrier pier has two openings. The gaps allow vessel ingress and egress to the harbor area."

"What's the water depth at those entrance channels?" asked Halgren.

Chang said, "Around fifteen meters, which should allow covert access for an SDV, especially when running at night."

The muscular blond with a bushy beard piped up next. "What kind of bottom sensors can we expect?" CPO Ryan Murphy, aka Malibu Murph, was the team's tech-head. One of his specialties was defeating underwater intruder detection systems. Having spent much of his early privileged life surfing, skin diving and lifeguarding, Murphy was also right at home with in-water SEAL operations. He was adept at operating the U.S. Navy underwater craft used to transport the Ghost Riders—the SDV aka SEAL

Delivery Vehicle. Also comfortable underwater, Runner and Driller shared Murphy's skillsets. Wild Bill, on the other hand, a true landlubber, stomached wet ops, leaving driving of the SDV to the other team members.

Chang responded to Murphy's inquiry. "We don't have any specifics on bottom sensors but suspect sonar based anti-diver systems are in place." The CIA officer looked Yuri's way. "John, perhaps you'd like to jump in here." Chang addressed the team. "Our guest has actual knowledge of the Sanya area."

Yuri cleared his throat. He gazed at the team members sitting around the table. "Gentlemen, you can expect that this facility will have the best underwater detection system that money can buy. Your submersible vehicles are well designed and stealthy but I do not recommend trying to penetrate this harbor through the channel openings in the seawall system. Your vehicle will likely be detected and attacked by a swarm of unmanned patrol boats—drones. It's highly doubtful that your minisub would survive such an attack. And your mission, of course, would fail before it started."

"With all due respect, sir," Halgren said, "what do you know about our equipment and capabilities? And just how do you know what the Chicoms have at this place?"

Yuri turned toward Chang for direction. Jeff nodded. Yuri looked back at Halgren. "About a month ago, I ran an op at the Yulin Naval Base, just down the coast from Shendao. We came in underwater in a mini, deployed from an attack sub…a Russian boat named the *Novosibirsk* out of Vladivostok."

"Holy shit," muttered Master Chief Halgren. "Who the hell are you?"

Chapter 37

Yuri made eye contact with Master Chief Halgren. "Until just recently I was an intelligence officer with the Russian Navy. My specialty was underwater reconnaissance."

"You're shitting me, right?" Halgren said, thunderstruck.

Jeff Chang took over, addressing the entire team. "John here is the real thing. He was a Captain Lieutenant in the Russian Navy—a two and a half striper. He has extensive experience aboard subs and he's run a number of covert underwater ops."

Runner said, "You were a Russian spook but you now work for us?"

"I was offered political asylum. Assisting your navy is part of that process."

Murph rejoined the interrogation, "Did you spy on us—in the States?"

Yuri started to respond when Lieutenant Commander Andrews intervened. "Our friend is not at liberty to divulge that type of intel at this time. What he can talk about is his experience in penetrating the Yulin Naval Base, which is just a hop, skip and jump away from our objective. His knowledge is golden, gentlemen, and he's here for our benefit so let's make use of the opportunity."

Jeff Chang, still standing beside the table, clicked to a new slide—a high resolution photograph of the Yulin base. "John's going to take over now. He'll brief you on his Yulin op, which I believe all of you will find invaluable for the mission at Shendao."

* * * *

It took Yuri forty minutes to retrace the Yulin mission. It was a true eye-opener for the SEALs. Jeff Chang already knew everything. Andrews had been provided a brief summary of the mission back at Pearl but was not provided any details—the real red meat. It was the meat that the SEALs pounced on.

"I didn't realize the Chicoms have ASV's that worked that well," CPO Murphy said, addressing Yuri. He referenced the autonomous surface vessels—robotic sentries—that guarded the Yulin base. The drones hunted together, using their AI brains to swarm intruders.

"They're formidable and you can expect that they will be in use, especially if they move the aircraft carriers from Yulin to Shendao."

That prompted a question from Chief Dillon. "Are both carriers still dead in the water?"

Chang answered. "Yes. We believe they're trying to repair each carrier's power plant so they can maneuver on their own. However, based on intercepts of PLAN comms, it appears they may be planning to tow at least one of the carriers to Shendao to expedite repairs. The pier and support facilities at Shendao are serviceable unlike Yulin."

Senior Chief Baker joined the Q&A. "Just how big was that e-bomb you guys set off?"

"Man portable," Yuri said. "The two man team carried the device and balloon in one trip."

"That's impressive," Baker noted. "A modest package like that inflicting such enormous damage…and without loss of life. Just incredible."

Yuri fielded additional questions on the e-bomb element of the Yulin mission, careful not to claim credit for that portion of the op. The FSB OSNAZ *Delfin* operators, impersonating naval *Spetsnaz*, had lied to Yuri about the true nature of their work.

Dillon spoke up next. "Could you show us that video of the underground sub base again?"

"Sure." Yuri clicked on the remote, reversing the slides. The requested slide materialized. It contained an embedded video, which started automatically. The clip was a minute long; it consisted of a 360-degree view of the interior of a huge grotto carved out of solid rock. The mini drone that captured the video hovered over one of the three PLAN ballistic missile submarines that were moored inside the mountain.

"That's just fricking amazing," Dillon said. "Sneaking that drone into the base with a fake crab…what did you call it?"

"Crawlerbot."

"Yeah, crawlerbot." Chief Dillon grinned. "I'm wondering if we can do something like that at Shendao. My dad was a mining engineer and when I was a kid, he took me to some of the mines he was working on in Georgia and other places in the South. Coal and copper. Anyway, one of the things I remember him telling me was that whenever they carved out a large underground cavern, they usually drilled extra ventilation shafts from above for air circulation, venting smoke if there's a fire, and in some cases, using the shafts as emergency exits." Driller smiled again. "So, I'm wondering if the Chinese did the same for their ASW control center."

Yuri caught on. "Clever, Chief. Send a mini aerial drone down a shaft for a remote recon."

"That's it!"

Jeff Chang rejoined the conversation. "How big would these shafts be?"

"It all depends," Dillon said. "Probably at least a couple of feet in diameter."

"Maybe you guys can slither down something like that," offered the CIA officer.

That comment generated an instant group response—all negative.

As the SEALs bantered, insulting each other as to who's butt was too big to fit down a pipe, Yuri clicked through the slides until he found the close-up aerial of the objective. He turned to Dillon. "Do you see anything in this photo that might be a vent?" Yuri pointed to the hillside behind the Shendao Fleet Logistics and Support Center building. Thick green vegetation covered the slope.

Chief Dillon scrutinized the screen image. "I don't see anything obvious. But since this is a highly secure facility, the vents, if they exist, would be camouflaged—like what we'd do."

"What about temperature differences?" Murphy asked. "If the underground base has some type of ventilation system, there's probably a difference in temperature at the discharge vent compared to the surrounding air."

Jeff Chang responded. "Great idea. I'll check with Langley to see if we can get one of our recon birds to run a thermal scan of the base."

* * * *

After a fifteen minute break, Yuri, Jeff Chang and the SEALs gathered by the scale model set up in a corner of the meeting room. The model was the size of two ping pong tables connected lengthwise. Chang arranged for construction of the segmented model back at Langley. It arrived at Yokosuka the day before via military air transport.

The model depicted in three dimensions the rugged coastline of Hainan Island and the adjacent uplands from Sanya Bay to Yalong Bay. The Shendao Naval Base was positioned at the model's center, which included replicas of the aircraft carrier pier and the harbor breakwaters. In addition to displaying a duplication of the Fleet Logistics and Support Center building and adjacent hillside, the model provided offshore bathymetry. The underwater topography was especially important to the SEALs.

The current discussion focused on Yuri's mission at the Yulin Naval Base in Yalong Bay, which the model reproduced on the right side of the table.

"Where did those drones swarm the mini?" asked Master Chief Halgren.

Yuri pointed with a finger. "Right here."

"That's a shallow area. You were lucky to have escaped."

"We were; it was close—too close."

Baker commented next. "I can see why you avoided bringing the mini into the harbor. All they would have to do is station one drone at each of the two entrance channels and they'd have you trapped. The rest of those damn things would be able to hunt you down at will."

"That's right, Senior Chief," Yuri said. The African-American's observation provided Yuri the opportunity to refocus on his prior recommendation. He gestured at the center of the model. "A similar issue applies to Shendao Harbor. If you sneak in through one of the entrances with your SEAL delivery vehicle, you could be trapped the same way."

"What about exiting the SDV here and swimming underwater to the shore in this area?" asked Andrews. The officer pointed to the shoreline adjacent to the landward connection of the southern breakwater.

"That's certainly possible, Commander. However, in light of what occurred at Yulin and Qingdao, I expect the PLAN is ultra-paranoid about diver intrusions at any of their facilities. That means you can expect extra underwater sensors and increased drone patrol boat activity coupled with equivalent upland security measures including troops patrolling the shoreline."

Jeff Chang rejoined the discussion. "He's right. Our onsite sources have verified a significant uptick in security measures at both Yulin and Shendao."

Several of the SEALs uttered groans at Chang's comment.

Andrews said, "We're open to any recommendations about accessing the objective."

Yuri flashed a friendly smile. "I do have a suggestion." He took a step to the right. "I'd avoid Shendao Harbor and its offshore waters entirely."

He pointed to a pocket beach in a bay east of Shendao. "I strongly suggest that you come ashore in this area here and hike overland to the objective." During the break period, Yuri had studied the model.

"What's around the beach?" asked Murphy.

"It's quite isolated. Apparently, the resort developers have not yet been granted government access to the property." Yuri pointed to a cluster of buildings east of the subject beach located on the opposite side of a rocky peninsula. "A couple of resorts border Yalong Bay here. As I recall one of 'em is a Hyatt. It's about two miles from the beach over this hill."

"I like this beach," Lieutenant Commander Andrews said. "Looks like it's not used much."

"Right," Yuri replied. "There's only one obvious structure." He pointed to the uplands located near the center of the beach. "Appears to be a house, possibly abandoned. You'd want to keep your distance from it regardless."

Andrews nodded his agreement. "How far is the beach from Shendao?"

Yuri had previously calculated the distance. "It's a little over a mile. Elevation change is around 450 feet. From my experience at Yulin, I expect the biggest obstacle would be dealing with brush. It's likely to be dense, hard to penetrate."

Andrews chortled. "No problemo…right boys?"

The SEALs echoed their leader's comment with gusto.

Chapter 38

It was early evening at the Admiral Arleigh A. Burke Officer's Club in Yokosuka. Yuri sat at a table in a quiet corner of the dining room with Lieutenant Commander Brent Andrews and Jeff Chang. They had just ordered their meals; all three sipped chilled beers.

Yuri would have preferred to return to his quarters and sleep. But he couldn't turn down Andrews's invite.

"I think the team took a liking to you today," Andrews said, addressing Yuri.

"They're probably more curious about me than anything else."

"I think they were a little awestruck. It's not very often they get to team up with a former adversary, especially one that has been involved in a major op in their own backyard."

Back at the meeting room during the afternoon, Jeff Chang authorized Yuri to fill in the four CPOs regarding Yuri's Pearl Harbor mission; Andrews had been briefed earlier. Astonished was an understatement of the SEALs' reaction. Chang's purpose in revealing details of the operation was twofold. First, demonstrate Yuri's technical skills. Second, provide a convincing reason why Yuri defected to the U.S.

Yuri took a swig from his beer, sensing it was the right time to ask a few questions about Andrews and his men. "Would you mind filling me in on how the team functions. Its overall organization, chain of command... those kinds of things."

Andrews took a quick look around the room. The nearest occupied table was about ten feet away. The two uniformed officers, both O-5s, were busy chatting and appeared to have no interest in their neighbors.

Turning back to Yuri, he said, "We're part of the Naval Special Warfare Development Group. DEVGRU for short."

"SEAL Team Six?" Yuri asked.

"Used to be called that but we go by DEVGRU now."

"Got it."

"DEVGRU consists of Tier One special operators. Top performing individuals from other SEAL units compete for a space in DEVGRU. As you can imagine, it's extremely competitive."

"Best of the best," Yuri said.

"Correct. It's a screening process. DEVGRU is broken down into squadrons, varying from assault to recon and training. The individual squadrons are color coded. Our group is part of Black Squadron."

"Let me guess, you're in a recon squadron."

"That's right. Our specialty is reconnaissance, surveillance and general intelligence gathering." Andrews grinned. "Kind of like what your unit must have been like."

Yuri chuckled. "Sounds familiar all right."

"Black Squadron consists of three troops. I have command of one of the troops, which is further divided into three recon teams. The team with me here is the best in the entire Black Squadron. Their handle is Ghost Riders." Andrews took a swallow of beer. "This particular team is unique… cross-trained to operate underwater craft without the need for a dedicated SDV unit to transport them ashore. They're also well experienced in high-risk surveillance operations."

"Thanks. That helps." Yuri intertwined his fingers. "Will both of you be going on the mission?"

Andrews turned toward Jeff Chang and winked.

Yuri caught the signal and immediately stiffened his posture.

Jeff Chang said, "Yes, Brent and I will be accompanying the Ghost Riders. And we'd like you to come along with us, too."

Govnó!

* * * *

Yuri returned to his room at the base guest quarters. It was 10:05 P.M. After showering, he lay on the bed with his spine propped against the bed board. He wore a pair of boxers and a T-shirt. The television on the opposite wall was tuned to an English-speaking channel. An attractive young Japanese female recited the day's news.

Yuri soon lost interest in the broadcast and switched off the TV. He yawned, fatigue finally settling in. He reached for his cell phone on the nightstand, about to call Laura when he reconsidered. Yuri was sixteen time zones ahead; it was still early in Washington State. He returned the phone to the table, deciding to make the call in the morning when he woke up.

After turning out the light, he settled into the bed, expecting instant sleep. Not so. Yuri reeled from the dinner conversation with Chang and Andrews.

They want me to go on the Shendao mission—that's not what I agreed to do in Hawaii!

During Yuri's previous meeting at Pearl Harbor with Chang and the U.S. Navy, reviewing the USS *Tucson* incident, Yuri's role was described as a 'technical advisor.' There was no discussion regarding actual mission participation. But over dinner this evening, CIA officer Chang made his case, backed up by the SEAL team commander.

Yuri was the ideal candidate for the mission. He had in-water and on-land knowledge of the target area, something no other U.S. military officer or NCO could claim. He was also an expert diver with training that far exceeded SEAL qualifications. And most important of all, Yuri was an expert in underwater robotic systems. Whatever innovations the Chinese had created with their new and deadly autonomous antisubmarine weapon, Yuri was the most qualified of anyone on the team to identify what was important and what was not.

This must have been their goal from the very beginning.

While the trio had munched on their seafood platters, Yuri launched a vigorous rebuttal to Chang and Andrew's proposal. He tried in vain to talk himself off the mission but got nowhere.

They should bring in someone else from their own weapons research program—they don't need me!

Yuri had argued that plenty of other U.S. Navy and/or DoD personnel could identify the key components of the PLAN weapon system. Chang countered that none of the other potential candidates were trained to take on such a mission. It might take weeks of physical training and dive certification before a candidate was capable of carrying out the mission. Time was of the essence and Yuri was the only one primed to go.

I can't believe they're going to let me go aboard one of their new subs.

Yuri was flabbergasted when Andrews reported that he had been cleared by the Secretary of Defense to accompany the Ghost Riders aboard a U.S. Navy nuclear powered submarine. The Virginia class boat would transport the SEALs and their SEAL Delivery Vehicle to within a few miles of Hainan Island. Yuri could not imagine such an event occurring in the Russian Navy—allowing a former spy access to one of the nation's most valued and secret weapons.

This whole mission is crazy. The risk is way beyond what we did at Yulin.

Yuri knew his fate had been predetermined. To preserve his dream of living a normal life with Laura and Maddy, he had no choice but to join the mission.

Just before yielding to fatigue, Yuri's last thought centered on what was coming. *I might not make it out of this one.*

Chapter 39

Day 27—Monday

Dr. Meng Park's stomach roiled. She was on the verge of vomiting as the *Lian* wallowed in the swells. Forty knot gusts buffeted the ship. Drenching rain soaked everything. The South China Sea was in turmoil this morning as a tropical front flowed through the region.

The 308-foot research ship was 430 nautical miles southeast of Hainan Island. Meng and her team were in the process of deploying their third installment of the Serpent ASW system.

Clad in canary yellow rain gear with a hard hat and life jacket, Dr. Meng stood on a portable ladder and leaned over one of the containers housing a coiled Viperina. She checked the LED control panel at the exposed end of the eighty-two-foot-long device, verifying the serpentine robotic sub killer was primed and ready for deployment."

Meng climbed down to the ship's deck. Standing beside the steel cradle that held the six Viper units, she faced the installation supervisor, a mid-twenties PLAN officer. "They're all okay. Let's go ahead and deploy."

"Ma'am, the ship's movements exceed safe protocols for operating the winch system."

Meng glowered. "How long?"

"The latest weather report indicated that this system will pass out of our operating area within the next hour." The lieutenant junior grade checked his wristwatch. "I expect that the seas will be within acceptable operating limits around twelve hundred."

Disappointed, Meng said, "I guess we have no choice but to wait."

"Very good, ma'am. We'll secure the system and reschedule deployment. I'll let the captain know."

"Okay, thanks."

Meng Park turned and began walking forward. If she was going to puke, better to do it in the privacy of her own cabin than on an open deck with half a dozen sailors nearby.

As the only female aboard the ship, and a particularly attractive one, Park couldn't help but notice the stares, especially from some of the older men. The *Lian's* entire crew was military, under the direct authority of Captain Zhou Jun.

Park took precautions. She wore her glasses instead of contacts. The baggy coveralls she wore were a couple of sizes too large. She kept her hair in a plain bun. When accessing the interior of the *Lian*, she avoided dead-end passageways and confined spaces. And when inside her cabin, she always double locked the door.

Park wished that Zhou Jun had accompanied her on the voyage. Tasked with completing the integration of the Serpent operating system with the S5 surveillance network, he and his staff had their hands full. Fleet harassed Zhou with requests on the timeframe for full implementation of Serpent.

Park was behind schedule too. She needed to oversee the deployment and installation of all six Viper stations before she could return to Sanya. Another PLAN crewed ship worked the southern basin of the South China Sea. It had installed one station so far.

Why is Beijing pushing so hard?

Both Meng and Zhou had asked the same question on numerous occasions before.

The Americans must be up to something!

Park worried that Beijing's rush to full-scale deployment of Serpent was in response to a threat from the United States. From pillow talk with Captain Zhou, Park knew that despite tough talk from Beijing, China's Navy elite still feared the U.S. Navy, particularly its submarine force.

Dr. Meng Park was not a pious person. But as she made her way forward, she prayed to Buddha.

Please, let Serpent work!

* * * *

"Hi sweetie!"

"Yuri!" Laura Newman called out.

Yuri telephoned from his room. It was 8:05 A.M. in Yokosuka; 4:05 P.M. the previous day on the U.S. West Coast.

"Where are you?" Laura asked. She and Maddy resided in the condo apartment in downtown Bellevue; Laura decided to avoid the Sammamish home until Yuri returned.

"I can't talk about that."

Laura uttered an audible sigh. "Can you at least tell me if you are in the States or out of the country?"

"Out."

Recognizing that it was useless to pursue Yuri's whereabouts, Laura shifted tactics. "So, how's it going, whatever you can tell me?"

"Okay. Lots of meetings, kind of boring at times." Yuri attempted to downplay his absence but Laura was suspicious.

"Just meetings, nothing else?"

"I'm a consultant. That's all." Yuri changed gears. "So, how have you and Maddy been?"

"We're both good. She's starting to . . ."

Yuri and Laura caught up for the next few minutes on family matters before returning to his current situation.

"When will you be coming home?" Laura asked.

"Probably a couple of weeks."

"Are you in danger, or will be?"

Aware that the FBI and/or National Security Agency might still be eavesdropping on their cellphones, Yuri followed protocols established by Special Agent Michaela Taylor—absolutely no discussion of operational matters over unsecured communications.

"No way. I'm just pushing paper." Before Laura could react, Yuri asked, "How's the merger going?"

The diversion worked. Laura spent the next couple of minutes briefing Yuri on the continuing discussions between Cognition and its Fortune 100 suitor. Their call ended with a promise from Yuri that he would return home as soon as he could.

After Yuri pocketed his cell, trepidation resurfaced as the memory kicked in. He'd slept soundly for several hours until the nightmare woke him. A couple of weeks had passed since the last eruption.

About six months earlier while aboard a yacht in Vancouver, B.C., Yuri had fired twice, both rounds striking the target. It was a split-second decision. Yuri's foe fired simultaneously but missed him; instead, the errant round plowed into another person.

The awful truth that Yuri took another human being's life haunted him. And now with the pending return mission to China, Yuri's angst mounted.

The SEALs are going to walk into a snake pit, dragging me along. No way we're not going to get bitten.

Yuri brushed away the troubling premonition. He checked his watch. *Time to go.*

He and Jeff Chang had arranged to meet for breakfast. The café was a five minute walk away. Yuri intended to press Chang hard before meeting with the Ghost Riders for another round of pre-mission planning.

Somehow, I've got to convince him they don't need me.

* * * *

Captain Petrovich was atop the *Novosibirsk's* sail as the submarine cruised under the bridge spanning the Bosfor Vostochnyy and entered Ussuri Bay. The magnificent cable stayed Russky Bridge with its twin sculptured towers linked the Russian mainland with Russky Island. The seas were mild this afternoon, just one meter high swells rolling in from the southeast. The chilled sea breeze reminded Petrovich that autumn had just commenced. He was thankful he wore his wool sea coat instead of a windbreaker.

The three watch standers on the bridge behind Petrovich were each assigned a section of the surrounding waters to monitor. Petrovich scanned the approaching sea. Two kilometers ahead—about a mile, a tankship laden with twenty million gallons of diesel fuel, gasoline and jet fuel preceded the warship's departure from Vladivostok. The tanker was bound for Petropavlovsk-Kaminsky, some 1,500 nautical miles to the northeast. The tankship would soon transit Peter the Great Gulf and enter the Sea of Japan where it would commence its northbound journey. It would follow the Kuril Island chain to the Kamchatka Peninsula.

Standard protocol called for the *Novosibirsk* to also cruise northward where it would pass between Japan's Hokkaido Island and Russia's Sakhalin Island to reach its normal patrol area—the North Pacific Ocean. However, Captain Petrovich's orders called for a different route.

Petrovich estimated it would take eight days to reach the target area. For this mission, all but four of the normal charge of torpedoes were offloaded. Thirty 'specials' were stored in the weapons bay instead.

Novosibirsk's orders were personally delivered by Admiral Belofsky. The commander of the Pacific Fleet was unable to offer Petrovich an explanation as to the purpose of the radical mission parameters, only that the edict had originated from the Kremlin. Knowing he had no choice in the matter, Captain Petrovich accepted the mission.

As Petrovich eyeballed the tanker ahead, he couldn't shake the dread that nibbled away at his well-being. It started with his prior mission, which took the *Novosibirsk* deep into hostile Chinese waters and later to Hawaii. From that excursion, Petrovich learned firsthand what his masters in the Kremlin were capable of.

And now he was tasked with raising the stakes even higher.

* * * *

Yuri returned to the same meeting room from the day before, accompanied by Jeff Chang. Lieutenant Commander Andrews and the Ghost Riders were already waiting. The group gathered beside the scale model of the Shendao harbor. Jeff Chang reported the latest update from the Pentagon.

"Good news, gents," Chang said. He held an eight by ten infrared color photograph in his hands. "NRO re-tasked one of its birds last night." He referred to the National Reconnaissance Office. "It scanned the Shendao area as we requested." Chang turned the photograph toward the group. "See these two white streaks here?" He pointed to the aberrations on the otherwise bluish background. "That's hot air. Langley said the signature is consistent with air vents for an underground chamber."

"All right!" CPO Dillon said, pleased that his suggestion bore fruit.

Lieutenant Commander Andrews commented next. "Is that in the area where you think the command center is located?"

"It is." Chang handed the photo to Andrews and removed another print from an envelope he held. "NRO also scanned the subterranean sub facility at the Yulin Naval Base for a comparison check." He displayed the photo. "Several ventilation stacks are visible on the east side of the hill. They had similar thermal signatures to Shendao."

"Any idea on the diameter of the vent?" Andrews asked.

"The actual vent is surrounded by vegetation. That's why it doesn't show up in the photos. But by analyzing the discharge plume, NRO was able to come up with a rough estimate of the vent diameter, which is around three-quarters of a meter, maybe thirty inches."

"That'll work," Dillon aka Driller said. "Even Murph's big ass could make it down the tube."

That drew a few laughs but not from Yuri. "Based on my experience," he said, "there's no way that the PLAN would allow direct access from the hillside into that vent. At a minimum, it will be screened to keep wildlife out. You should plan that it will also have sensors around the opening and possibly inside."

"Good points," Andrews chimed in. "We'll need to thoroughly check it out before attempting to use it as an entry point."

Yuri said, "I recommend a backup in case the vent doesn't work."

Andrews turned toward Chang. "Jeff, you got any ideas on that?"

The CIA officer half smiled. "If we can't use a ventilation shaft to gain entry to the underground control center, our only option will be to use the front door."

"How will that be done?" Andrews asked.

"With this little black box of magic." After reaching into his pocket, Jeff presented an electronic device about the size of a pack of cigarettes.

"What is it?" Master Chief Halgren questioned.

"ID card reader. We know all personnel accessing the Shendao logistics building use individually issued proximity cards. No need to swipe the prox cards through a reader, just stand near the door. All we need to do is place this gadget near one of the door readers. It'll pick up the current codes. I can then duplicate them at will."

"Cool," Halgren said, "but what if they use different prox cards to access the underground command center?"

"I expect that will be the case. But once we get inside the building, I'll have access to the computers. That'll be our way into S5."

Murphy jumped in. "How do you crack the passwords to the PCs?"

"I don't need the passwords. I know how to bypass the memory and get direct access to the files."

"Sounds good," Murphy said.

"What're the ROEs?" asked Senior Chief Baker, referring to the rules of engagement.

Andrews responded. "First and foremost, no engagement. In order to accomplish the mission, the team can't leave any traces behind."

That prompted Yuri to comment. "I'm sorry, Commander, but that's not a realistic expectation. You may be able to get around electronic locks and security measures but my experience and training regarding the Chinese military is that they will have multiple systems in play to guard that command center—similar to what the Russian military does. That means a labyrinth of electronic sensors supplemented by numerous human guards."

Jeff Chang joined in. "Your points are well taken. But we do have solid intel on the personnel using the facility." He turned toward the model and pointed to the replica of the Shendao Fleet Logistics and Support Center building. "One of our agents installed miniature cameras to surveil the three ingress and egress points. Without going into details, we've been observing everyone coming and going into the building twenty-four seven for over a month. We estimate that at this time the Shendao antisubmarine facility—S5—has a staff of thirty-eight. During a typical daytime shift, it has around two dozen personnel including guards. But that drops to just a handful between midnight and six in the morning. That's when we'll be going in."

"That's surprising," Yuri commented. "From what happened at Yulin I would have expected a large around the clock security team guarding S5."

Chang nodded. "We think the PLAN believes they managed to hide their ASW control facility, using the mundane service building as a cover... hiding in plain sight."

"And that's very good news for us," added Commander Andrews.

The Ghost Riders all echoed their concurrence.

"Sounds good," Yuri said. But reservations remained.

Sounds too good.

Chapter 40

Commander Yang Yu observed from the deck of the pressure casing. The squad of technicians scurried around the aberration bolted to the exterior skin of the *Heilong*. It was positioned on the submarine's hull about sixty feet astern of the sail. Around thirty feet long and six feet in diameter, the steel cylinder had the appearance of an oil tank on its side. The aft hemispherical door to the tube was swung open to the port, revealing the interior of the pressure resistant chamber. A retractable steel frame cradle protruded twenty-five feet from the opening; its solid rubber support wheels rested on the steel deck. The "package" hovered above the cradle, suspended by steel cables from an overhead monorail crane.

The monorail system was bolted to the rock ceiling of the grotto. The *Heilong* floated inside the secret subterranean sub base at Jianggezhuang near Qingdao.

"Captain, permission to lower the unit into its cradle?" The officer in charge of the installation stood beside Yang.

"Proceed, Lieutenant."

"Yes sir." The officer turned about and began issuing commands to his work crew.

Yang watched as the package gradually descended. It had the shape of a drainage pipe, roughly twenty-five feet long and just over three feet in diameter.

The package made a soft landing in the cradle with its bow positioned aft toward the *Heilong's* stern. Designated *Shing Long*—Victory Dragon, the machine represented the People's Liberation Army-Navy's latest autonomous underwater vehicle. Coated with a jet-black sound absorbing rubberized veneer, the AUV had a bullet shaped nose cone, stubby tailfins, and a ducted propeller.

After verifying that the *Shing Long* was positioned correctly, the officer in charge directed his team to engage the two metal straps that secured the AUV to the cradle. Next, the cradle was rolled back into the pressure chamber.

The excessive diameter of the *Shing Long* prevented launching it from any of the *Heilong's* eight torpedo tubes or dozen vertical missile cylinders, necessitating the external cargo container.

Commander Yang walked to the open end of the pressure chamber, seeking a close-up view of the *Shing Long*. Standing beside the nose cone, he ran a hand across the curved surface. It was chilly to the touch. Like most weapons, the explosive was positioned in the forward end of the AUV.

Yang moved aside as the installation team leader connected a pencil sized cable to a remote release external port on the AUV's side near the nose cone. The opposite end of the cable connected to a through hull fitting in the top of the *Heilong's* pressure casing. The cable supplied electrical power. It also contained multiple fiber-optic communication lines, which allowed remote monitoring and activation from the submarine's attack center.

The lieutenant wore a headset that was linked to the weapons console in the attack center via a hardwire connection port inside the chamber. He looked up, making eye contact with Yang. "Sir, the weapon's officer verified that all systems for the *Shing Long* are within normal parameters."

"Very well, go ahead and complete the installation."

"Aye, Captain."

It took ten minutes before the hefty hemisphere door to the containment chamber rotated to the closed position and sealed. Rated for a depth of three thousand feet of seawater, the cocoon housing the *Shing Long* exceeded the crush depth of the *Heilong*.

Satisfied with the operation, Commander Yang dismissed the install crew. The men descended into the hull through the aft escape trunk hatch. Yang waited behind.

It was eerily quiet inside the partially submerged cave this afternoon. The other three submarines moored inside the underground base were devoid of human activity on their exterior decks.

The device now attached to the submarine was unlike any weapon Commander Yang had worked with in the past. The North Sea Fleet command provided Yang with minimal background on the *Shing Long's* mission. Nonetheless, he had pieced together the mission profile.

It has to be in response to Qingdao!

The seaport city endured aftereffects from the nuclear detonation. The Badaxia and Taixi residential districts near the mouth of Jiaozhou Bay suffered the most from radioactive fallout. The peninsula northward from Tuandao to the borderline with the Yunnan neighborhood was evacuated. Decontamination crews worked three shifts a day to washdown every structure in the hot zone.

Traffic in the already congested port city had evolved into nightmarish gridlock. The Jiaozhou Bay Bridge opened a week after the bomb blast but commuters shunned the crossing, knowing the structure was just a couple of miles from ground zero. The Qingdao Jiaozhou Bay tunnel system at the juncture of the bay and the Yellow Sea was not directly impacted by the detonation. However, a tanker truck filled with fifteen thousand gallons of concentrated decontamination fluid laced with nuclear isotopes overturned in the outbound tunnel. The tunnel was still closed.

Tao is going to be okay!

Knowing the *Heilong* would be departing soon, Yang Yu and Sun Tao rendezvoused the previous evening in a hotel room near Sun's restaurant in Qingdao's financial district.

Yang's lover had relocated his family from their Badaxia home to an apartment building in the Hushan Road Residential District in north Qingdao. Sun owned four units in the fifteen story building. He evicted the tenant in the best unit. The $20,000 bribe he paid to a local party official expedited the process. The hapless renter received $500 for relocation expenses.

Sun Tao paid an additional $20,000 to another Communist party hack to have the Badaxia building his family resided in booted up to the top of the decontamination list. Even with that bribe it would be weeks before they could return. Other rich Qingdaoians had beat out Sun in the kickback race.

At least I don't have to worry about Mom and Dad for a while!

Commander Yang's parents resided in his hometown of Langfang, located thirty miles south of Beijing. His father, Yang Jin, recently lost his job after the company he had worked at for decades folded. A victim of Beijing's decision to allow underperforming state-owned enterprises to fail, the company that manufactured knockoff replacement parts for American manufactured automobiles and trucks fired the entire staff of eight hundred and fifty.

With their life in shambles and Jin out of a job, Commander Yang's mother, Ling, had hinted strongly that they wanted to sell their home and move in with their son. Yang had a spacious two bedroom apartment with a water view, and he was often away at sea for months at a time.

All along, Yang had planned to care for his parents and was prepared to make the transition. But Ling's persistent talk about moving stopped abruptly after the bomb exploded. To help ease their transition into retirement, Commander Yang arranged for ten percent of his monthly pay to be sent to his parents.

Yang took a last look at the sealed pressure chamber housing the *Shing Long*. It was time to return to the *Heilong's* attack center. The submarine was scheduled to depart at 2200—10 P.M. In the interim, Yang and his crew had a host of pre-mission tasks to complete.

Beijing wants blood and I've been ordered to hurl the spear.

As Commander Yang approached the nearby open hatch, he couldn't help but think about the unimaginable power of the weapon inside the *Shing Long*'s warhead compartment. Four times the yield of the weapon detonated at Qingdao, the atomic bomb would wipe the Russian submarine base at Petropavlovsk-Kamchatskiy off the chart.

Chapter 41

Day 28—Tuesday

"I don't like the idea of that guy coming aboard," Commander Tom Bowman said. He stood beside a counter inside the USS *Colorado*'s wardroom, coffee pot in hand.

"What do you know about him, skipper?" asked Jenae Mauk. *Colorado's* executive officer clutched a coffee mug while sitting at the mess table. The pair were alone.

"He's some kind of a defector, a former Russian naval officer." Bowman poured the brew into his mug.

"Submariner?"

"Fleet intelligence—GRU. Apparently, he was assigned to subs."

"Wow, a Russian naval spook. This should be interesting."

Colorado's commanding officer returned to his seat at the table. Bowman took a swallow from the mug. "I don't like it. Letting a spy aboard, even if he supposed to be working for us. Just doesn't sit right with me."

"Why is he part of the SEAL op?"

Commander Bowman picked up a manila file stamped TOP SECRET. It contained *Colorado's* orders from COMSUBPAC. Bowman paged through the document. "Says here he has local knowledge of the target area. Plus, he's an expert with AUVs."

"Maybe he can enlighten us on what the Russians are up to with their underwater robotic gear?"

"Maybe. But what I'd really like is some hard intel on what the PLAN has in the water around Hainan Island." He returned the file to the table.

Mauk said, "I expect it's similar to what we encountered at Qingdao."

"That's a minimum. But after what happened at Yulin, plus the nuke going off, the Chinese Navy has to be going nuts with boosting underwater defenses at all of their bases."

Bowman's comment sparked a new thought for XO Mauk. She reached for the file. She remembered an item during her first reading of the ship's orders. It took half a minute to find the citation. "This says that our guest is an expert diver who has conducted numerous underwater clandestine missions." She found a separate comment in another section of the report. "Like you mentioned, he apparently also has local knowledge of the target area." She looked up, meeting Bowman's gaze. "How do you suppose that happened?"

"Hmmm," Bowman muttered as he processed Mauk's question.

"I wonder if this guy was somehow involved in what happened at Yulin."

Commander Bowman rubbed his temple. "That's an interesting thought." As the revelation gelled he offered, "Maybe the Russians are the ones that took out Yulin."

What occurred at the Yulin Naval Base was an enigma to most in the U.S. military. The rumors circulating around the Pentagon centered on the accidental detonation of a Chinese EMP weapon stored aboard one of the ships moored at the base. It was a rumor the White House encouraged. Alternative gossip blamed the Kremlin.

Commander Mauk said, "If there was no accident, an attack from the sea makes sense to me. A sub delivers the assault team offshore. The divers sneak into Yulin. They deploy the EMP device and return to the sub."

Bowman nodded, his lips pressed together as he gauged his executive officer's bombshell scenario.

Commander Mauk located the eight by ten color photograph in the file. She turned the image of Yuri toward her boss. "If the Russians were behind the Yulin attack, then just maybe Captain Lieutenant Yuri Kirov was responsible. If so, he could have a treasure trove of info for us."

"Definitely."

* * * *

Yuri Kirov and Jeff Chang were alone in the team meeting room at the U.S. Navy's Yokosuka Naval Base. Lieutenant Commander Andrews and his SEAL operators were training elsewhere on the base.

"I just received confirmation from Langley. We leave tonight. The weather forecast will help provide cover for us. A storm front will be moving through at that time," Chang said.

"Satellites?"

"Yep. The Chinese and Russians both keep a close eye on Yokosuka. Our Navy likes to keep 'em guessing on our submarine movements, especially boats carrying external pods."

"What about SAR?" Yuri referred to satellites equipped with synthetic aperture radar. SAR penetrates clouds to create images of objects located on the earth's surface, both land and sea.

"We have a two hour interval at the departure time where no SAR equipped birds will be overhead. Once the sub is in Uraga channel, it will dive."

"Sounds like a good plan," Yuri said. "What can you tell me about the boat we'll be on?"

"Her name is *Colorado*. One of our newer subs. Virginia class."

"What does the captain know about me?"

"The basics, former Russian Navy intel officer. That you're working with me as a technical advisor."

Yuri looked away from the table, studying the navigation chart taped to a nearby wall. It depicted the western Pacific Ocean from Japan to Vietnam.

"How long will it take?"

"The captain estimates the trip will be around five days."

While still eyeing the chart, Yuri unconsciously shook his head. Chang noticed. "What's wrong?"

Yuri said, "I'm just tired. Still not sleeping all that well." That was true but Yuri neglected to mention his underlying trepidation. Nearly seven weeks earlier, he'd barely survived an incursion into Chinese territory. And now he was about to return to the same hostile waters.

"Well, you'll have plenty of time to rest up on the trip."

"Right." But Yuri doubted he'd relax much. Submarines were unvaryingly crowded with equipment and people. Privacy was nearly nonexistent. And despite reassurances from Chang, Yuri expected his presence aboard the U.S. warship might not be welcomed by all aboard.

The CIA officer grinned. "I've been told that the food is fantastic on the *Colorado*. Submarines have the best chefs in the Navy. I think you'll like that."

"I look forward to it." The fare aboard Russian submarines was adequate but nothing to write home about.

Chang checked his watch. "We'll get a chance to check it out in about an hour."

"What?"

"The captain invited us for lunch. He wants to meet you."

* * * *

The Rueben sandwiches were superlative. Served with delicious tossed green salads and chilled glasses of iced tea, the lunch was exceptional—just as Jeff Chang promised.

Yuri was seated at the mess table in the *Colorado's* officers' wardroom with Chang and the submarine's two senior officers.

Yuri was aware that the U.S. Navy allowed females to serve aboard submarines. Still, it came as a surprise when he climbed down the hatchway and entered the sub's accommodations compartment. XO Jenae Mauk welcomed Yuri and Chang aboard and directed them to the wardroom.

During the meal, the conversation was casual. At first, Yuri detected a hint of hostility from Commander Tom Bowman. He was polite but reserved. Mauk in contrast was friendly and inquisitive. The tension in the wardroom unwound when Yuri, prompted by Mauk, described his experiences at the Russian Navy's Higher Naval Submarine School at St. Petersburg. The school was similar to the U.S. Naval Academy at Annapolis but with a five-year curriculum directed toward training future submarine officers.

Both Bowman and Mauk were graduates of Annapolis. Yuri and the two officers traded tales about their academy life. CIA operative Jeff Chang took it all in, pleased that the three sailors had something in common to share.

Lunch was over. The two U.S. Navy officers drank coffee from mugs. Yuri and Chang worked on iced tea refills. Chang briefed Bowman and Mauk on the latest mission details.

"John," Bowman said, using Yuri's alias, "I understand you have experience with Chinese underwater sensors in shallow waters, anti-sub and anti-diver modes. What can you tell us about them?"

"High quality. They have access to the best hardware available. Cost isn't a concern."

"European?"

"Yes, that was our conclusion."

Mauk followed up with technical questions regarding sensor types, likely deployment strategies, and possible ways to defeat submerged detectors. Yuri provided his opinions.

Bowman asked a couple of follow-up questions to Yuri's response. Satisfied, Bowman said, "Our mission orders noted that you apparently have some local knowledge regarding the target area. Could you elaborate on that for us?"

Yuri expected the question; Chang had already cleared Yuri to answer if the subject came up.

Yuri said, "I was part of a naval *Spetsnaz* operation directed against the Yulin Naval Base on Hainan Island."

"Hmmm," muttered Bowman as he made eye contact with Mauk.

Yuri spent the next half hour reciting the details of the operation. Bowman and Mauk were skeptical at first but converts when Chang verified Yuri's storyline. The kicker was how effective the directed energy weapon was, and that it had been deployed by divers.

"So," Bowman said, "the minisub was detected after your team locked out?"

"Yes. We had no indication the *P-815* was detected when we approached the island."

Commander Mauk asked, "Were drone boats patrolling in the area when you came in?"

"We didn't detect any surface vessels at that time."

"How stealthy are the drones?"

"They're not. High performance diesel engines. Noisy on the surface and below. You can hear them from quite a distance."

Bowman rejoined the discussion. "Any idea where the sensor was located that detected your mini?"

"The *P-815* is ultra-quiet," Yuri said. "It must have been right over the sensor, probably in shallow water. Might have picked up the propeller." The Russian minisub was powered by a bank of lithium-ion batteries. Its acoustic signature was virtually nil when operating in stealth mode.

Commander Mauk said, "I assume you didn't encounter any mines during your approach to Yulin."

"Correct. The mini didn't detect any moored mines. Same for the *Novosibirsk*." Yuri reflected further on the XO's inquiry. "There's a lot of recreational boat traffic in the area from the Yalong Bay resorts. Adding minefields around the bases would be a nightmare to manage."

"I agree."

Yuri turned toward Bowman. "If I might ask, Captain, just how close in are you planning to bring the *Colorado*?"

"It hasn't been decided yet but likely within five to six miles. The closer in the better it will be for the SEAL detachment."

"Hmmm, that's close. During our excursion, the *Novosibirsk* remained in international waters—twelve nautical miles offshore in deeper water."

"We don't have that limitation for this mission. Besides, the *Colorado* and her sister ships are designed to operate in shallow, nearshore waters."

"Impressive. Russian nuclear subs do not have that capability—yet."

The wardroom briefing ended ten minutes later when Commander Bowman announced that he had to leave for a shore meeting. After Bowman departed, Commander Mauk took Yuri and Chang for a tour of the ship.

Yuri was able to see virtually every key system aboard the supersub, except the nuclear reactor. Awed by the marriage of technology and function, he concluded that the *Colorado* was at least one generation ahead—and perhaps two—of Russia's latest nuclear submarine.

After Yuri climbed an internal ladder and exited the hatch just behind the sail, he waited for Chang to emerge. The CIA operative lingered below chatting with Commander Mauk.

Yuri peered aft, looking over the long smooth lines of the *Colorado's* hull. The dry deck shelter was mounted over the logistic plug trunk about thirty feet away. Installed the previous day, the DDS looked like a giant wart on the otherwise sleek deck. It was nine feet wide, nine feet high and thirty-eight feet long. A portable awning covering the DDS shielded it from overhead spies.

The U.S. Navy Shallow Water Combat Submersible was housed inside the DDS. The vehicle would transport Yuri, Chang and the Ghost Riders from the *Colorado* to Hainan Island.

The SWCS was tiny compared to the minisub that transported Yuri and the *Spetsnaz* team to the Yulin Naval Base earlier in the year. The Russian mini, the *P-815*, also had vastly superior capabilities compared to the U.S. Navy's submersible. Yuri's chief concerns were the snail's pace of the SWCS's electric drive propulsion system, its limited battery life and the need for the passengers and crew to wear full diving gear during the mini's excursions.

The perpetual knot in Yuri's belly tightened a notch. He sensed disaster ahead.

They're pushing too hard and too fast. This mission is all wrong.

Chapter 42

Nick Orlov had the code room to himself. It was midafternoon at the Russian Consulate in Hong Kong. Nick's boss, SVR Director Borya Smirnov, was on the other end of the encrypted satellite telephone circuit. It was late morning in Moscow.

After requesting a briefing on Nick's activities at the consulate, spymaster Smirnov broached the real purpose of his call—Yuri Kirov. "Our people in Seattle have not been able to locate him for the past week," Smirnov said.

"I'm not surprised. The company he works for has a lot of work in Alaska…that's probably where he is."

"We think the CIA has him someplace, conducting a debriefing."

"I suppose that's possible but my bet is that he's busy working out of the state."

"He knows too much, Orlov."

I knew it, Nick thought. "Well, sir, all he wants is to stay in America with his lover. Apparently, requesting political asylum was the only way he could make that work."

"He's a potential traitor."

Before responding Nick sucked in a deep calming breath. He slowly exhaled. "Director, as I said, all Kirov wants is to be left alone—by us and by the Americans. In my mind, he's earned it. By his efforts, we avoided war with the Americans earlier in the year and he saved the *Neva's* crew before that. That's got to count for a lot of goodwill toward Russia on his part."

Smirnov ignored Nick's plea. "I want you to contact his woman—the software executive—to find out where Kirov is."

"I'll try, sir, but I don't think Laura Newman is going to be cooperative."

"Push her hard. Threaten her if you have too."

"Threaten her with what?"

"They'll never have peace until we get what we need from Kirov."

What the hell is going on? "Can you provide some detail? It might help when I talk with her."

Smirnov said, "On his last mission for the Navy he arranged for highly classified data to be transmitted to fleet headquarters in Vladivostok. The Navy received the data but it's encrypted. Kirov changed the passcode. They have not been successful in their attempts to decrypt the data files."

Everything clicked for Nick. He knew that Yuri was in China, spying on naval facilities. *Yuri held back the decrypt key for insurance. That must be Yuri's secret!*

"Thanks, that helps. I'll get right on this."

After signing off, Nick tipped his chair back. Teetering, he thought of his friend.

Yuri, what are you really up to?

* * * *

"How'd it go?" asked Commander Jenae Mauk. She stood in the threshold to Commander Tom Bowman's stateroom. The captain and XO's cabins were located side by side at the aft end of the control room.

"Come on in," Bowman said from his desk chair.

After closing the door, executive officer Mauk leaned against a cabinet. The cabin was barely large enough for one occupant. *Colorado's* commanding officer had just returned after his shoreside meeting at the Yokosuka Naval Base's submarine operations center. The video conference with COMSUBPAC staff in Pearl Harbor took nearly an hour.

"We're good to go for tonight. Depart at twenty-three thirty. That'll give us plenty of time to exit the harbor and submerge before the next spy bird shows up."

"Very good, I'll begin implementing the departure plan."

"Were the charges delivered?" asked Bowman.

"They were. A dozen units are stowed in the torpedo room."

"Good."

The special cargo arrived while Bowman was ashore. The compact explosives were taken aboard through the weapons loading hatch.

Mauk crossed her ankles. "Did COMSUBPAC specify a deployment schedule for the charges?"

"It's still fluid but probably after the SEALs complete their mission."

"I'll start working on the mechanics of deployment with Weps."
Bowman nodded.

"Any new developments in the mission area?" Mauk asked.

"No. NSA and CIA both report minimal vessel activity. I did,
however, get feedback about one of our contacts from the last patrol...the
Heilong's at sea again."

"What's it up to this time?"

Colorado had tracked the People's Liberation Army-Navy nuclear
attack sub from the South China Sea to within several hundred miles of
Hawaii before forcing it to return to China.

"IUSS picked it up earlier today. Probably departed Jianggezhuang
late last night." The U.S. Navy's Integrated Undersea Surveillance System
was responsible for detecting and tracking submarines. A vast network of
underwater hydrophones scattered across the Pacific (and other oceans)
monitored subsea sounds around the clock.

"Returning to the South China Sea?" Mauk asked.

"Not sure yet. It's heading southeast in the shipping lanes across the East
China Sea, possibly toward the Ryukyus." The Ryukyu chain of islands
extend from Japan's southern island of Kyushu to Taiwan. Commercial
vessels laden with Chinese exports for North American markets cross
through the Ryukyu Islands to enter the Pacific Ocean.

"You don't suppose it's going to try Pearl again?"

"COMSUBPAC isn't taking any chances. If *Heilong* pokes her nose
into the Pacific, she'll have company."

"Which boat?"

"*Mississippi.*" Bowman referred to the USS *Mississippi,* a sister
sub to *Colorado.*

"I like it." Mauk fingered her hair. "You know, skipper, I wonder if it's
headed back to Petro." *Colorado* first detected the *Heilong* when it spied
on the Russian submarine base located on the Kamchatka peninsula.

"Could be." Bowman stretched out his arms. "IUSS did detect an
anomaly with the *Heilong's* signature, an increase in hull turbulence
since we tracked her. IUSS thinks that it might have an external package."
Colorado's sonar unit had provided IUSS selected recordings of the Chinese
submarine's acoustic signature under a variety of operating conditions.

Mauk said, "You mean like what we've got—a dry dock shelter?"

"They don't know. I suppose the PLAN has something like that in
their inventory. Anyway, I thought you might find that tidbit interesting."

"Thanks."

After exiting Bowman's stateroom, Commander Mauk made her way aft to check on a maintenance operation underway in the engine room. Her discussion with the captain about the *Heilong* lingered.

That Chinese boat is up to no good. I just know it!

* * * *

"Status report," Captain Petrovich said, addressing the *Novosibirsk's* sonar technician. Petrovich just entered the submarine's sonar compartment.

The chief petty officer turned away from his console and slipped off his headphones. "Captain, the container ship is now twenty four hundred meters to the east, proceeding north at fourteen knots. The cluster of southbound fishing vessels to the southeast are moving between five and seven knots. The nearest is twelve kilometers away."

"Nets?"

"No. They're all longline operations." He referred to a commercial fishing system that used a long line with baited hooks on branch lines uniformly spaced along the main line's length.

"I want to know immediately if we have the potential for any type of fishing vessels overhead." A submarine that Petrovich was assigned to as a junior officer had an encounter with a bottom trawl net. It was an experience he never wanted to repeat.

"Aye, Captain."

"Very well."

Petrovich exited sonar to continue his roving patrol. It was part of his routine, circulating between key compartments aboard the nuclear-powered attack submarine. While his XO took charge of the central command post, aka attack center, he toured the boat twice a day. It allowed him to assess the overall condition of his command as well as make personal contact with the crew. Next stop was the ship's mess. He planned to have a cup of tea with off duty sailors that were having a meal.

So far, so good, he thought.

The *Novosibirsk* ran southward at a depth of 450 meters—1,476 feet. Underway for a full day, it paralleled the eastern shoreline of the Korean Peninsula. Aware of IUSS hydrophones in the Sea of Japan, Captain Petrovich took extreme care to avoid detection by the Americans. The *Novosibirsk's* acoustic signature was minimal, thanks to advances in hull and machinery sound proofing. It was quieter than the newest Chinese nuclear subs and comparable to U.S. Navy *Los Angeles* class boats.

To ensure maximum stealth, Petrovich had throttled back *Novosibirsk* to just ten knots and dove deep into the Sea of Japan. Although well hidden, Petrovich had concerns for what lay ahead for his ship

Compared to the Sea of Japan, the East China Sea was a bathtub. The shallow waters multiplied the chances of detection.

* * * *

While the *Novosibirsk* cruised southward toward the East China Sea, the *Heilong* was nearly halfway across the East Sea, hugging the shallow bottom. After departing from the subterranean sub base at Jianggezhuang, the People's Liberation Army-Navy attack submarine crossed the Yellow Sea into the East China Sea. It traversed the progressively deepening sea on a southeasterly heading running at fifteen knots. It followed in the wake of a massive box ship that had departed from Qingdao. The China COSCO Shipping vessel was bound for Los Angeles. The sound energy radiating into the water column from the 1,200-foot-long ship's hull and its twenty-seven foot diameter propeller helped mask the *Heilong's* acoustic signature.

Once the container ship navigated through the Ryukyu Island chain, the *Heilong* would commence its northward track in the North Pacific Ocean. It would follow the Japanese coastline and the Kuril Island chain to Petropavlovsk-Kamchatskiy.

To evade Japanese, U.S. and Russian subsea listening posts in the Pacific, the Chinese warship would dive to a depth of 300 meters and run at no more than sixteen knots. Such procedures were prudent but ineffective. Thanks to tracking data supplied by the USS *Colorado* from its previous mission, the American Navy would monitor the *Heilong* during its entire 2,700 nautical mile, seven plus day voyage.

Hydrophones installed on the seabed offshore of South Korea recorded the underwater racket produced by the COSCO behemoth as the ship charged through the Yellow and East Seas. Cutting edge software developed by the U.S. Navy filtered out the extraneous noise, unmasking the *Heilong's* unique sound print. Bottom sensors in the Pacific would continue to track the submarine once it turned left and sailed up coast to the Kamchatka peninsula. Because COMSUBPAC was ever more suspicious of China's intent, tracking data from IUSS sensors was supplemented.

The USS *Mississippi* was already on station. Once the *Heilong* sailed into the Pacific, the *Mississippi* would stalk the PLAN warship with diligent and dogged care, ready to send it to the bottom if ordered.

Chapter 43

Day 29—Wednesday

The *Colorado* departed from Yokosuka on time. Underway for an hour, the submarine was three hundred feet below the surface running at ten knots. It was 12:33 A.M.

Yuri and Jeff Chang observed from the aft end of the control room as the crew executed their duties with practiced efficiency.

"Amazing place," Jeff whispered.

"Absolutely," Yuri replied.

All consoles and work stations were crewed. Lighting inside the compartment was subdued for nighttime running conditions. Control panels, computer stations and flat panel displays populated the space. The officer of the deck issued crisp commands; the recipients acknowledged with businesslike responses.

It was a familiar routine for Yuri. Russian submarines, as well as most other navies, had similar operating protocols to the U.S. Navy. What was not comparable, however, was the sophistication of the *Colorado's* nerve center. Yuri was truly dazzled by the electronics. The sonar unit was integrated into the control room along the portside of the hull, allowing the captain instant access. Yuri was aware that older U.S. subs housed the sonar team in a separate room.

Equally impressive as the sonar were the photonics and navigation systems, located adjacent to sonar. The ship's control station, manned by the pilot and copilot, was located at the forward end of the control room. A simple joystick controlled the direction and depth of the submarine.

The ship's command center console was located just aft of the pilots. Behind the command center was the horizontal large screen display (HLSD). The flat-panel screen built into the waist high table provided easy access to electronic navigation charts and other digital media.

The combat control center was located on the starboard side of the control room next to the command console. Torpedoes and cruise missiles were controlled from this unit.

The radio room and the electronic surveillance measures room were situated along the starboard section of the hull opposite the combat center.

Commander Bowman hovered over the HLSD. He looked up and made eye contact with his guests. He gestured for them to come forward.

As Yuri and Chang joined *Colorado's* CO, Bowman said, "I thought you gentlemen would like to see our planned route."

"Great," Jeff Chang said.

Yuri studied the screen, which displayed a digital chart of the Uraga Channel. Superimposed on the chart was a blue submarine icon, which represented the *Colorado's* current position. The warship was about to exit the channel and enter the ocean.

Bowman manipulated the display's touch screen. The chart disappeared, replaced with a color worldwide image of the western Pacific Ocean. Overlaid on the image was a solid red line that extended from Yokosuka to Hainan Island.

Bowman pointed to the screen. "We'll parallel Japan's southern coastline and head southward along the Ryukyu Islands. Once we're opposite Taiwan's southern tip, we'll cross the Luzon Strait, enter the South China Sea and proceed westward to Hainan."

"How far is it?" asked Chang.

"About two thousand nautical miles."

"Still planning on five days?"

"Correct."

Yuri made eye contact. "Captain, what do you know about China's bottom sensors in the South China Sea?"

Commander Bowman grinned. "Quite a lot." He again manipulated the HLSD and a new overlay snapped into focus. "Gentlemen, behold China's Great Underwater Wall." A spider web of icons and lines crisscrossed an enlarged view of the South China Sea. Bowman pointed at the screen. "The red triangles represent hydrophones on the bottom. Red lines are submarine comm cables from the hydrophones that connect to a deepwater buoy system. The yellow circles are so called Chinese tsunami warning and weather station buoys but they also serve as relay stations for transmitting hydrophone data to PLA satellites." Bowman fingered the southern end of Hainan Island near Sanya. "This entire network is controlled from here—the PLAN's South Sea Sound Surveillance System. Also known as S5."

"What are these for?" Yuri asked. The crimson skull and crossbones icons were scattered across the South China Sea.

"Those are the problem, gentlemen. They represent the seabed locations of China's new ASW system."

"The snake thing?" Chang asked.

"That's right."

Yuri said, "Can we avoid them?"

"Yes, we'll tread lightly around them but it's likely more will be in place by the time we reach Hainan. The PLAN is busy installing the damn things."

"They're getting ready for a confrontation," Yuri suggested.

"COMSUBPAC thinks they're preparing to evict us from their home waters. I'm afraid it's going to be dicey for all of us soon."

* * * *

As the USS *Colorado* commenced its voyage, the *Novosibirsk* crept toward the Korea Strait. The one hundred nautical mile wide passage separated the Korean peninsula from Japan. Captain Petrovich elected to use the western channel of the strait, which extended from South Korea's southern shore to Japan's Tsushima Island. The island was located near the center of the Korea Strait.

To avoid detection, the submarine's power plant was throttled back to maintain an average over the bottom speed of seven knots. Accounting for the ebb and flow of the tide, Petrovich estimated it would take three days to navigate through the Korea Strait, the East China Sea and the Ryukyu Island chain before it finally reached the Pacific. The *Colorado* and its sister sub, the *Mississippi*, along with the *Heilong* would all be long gone before the *Novosibirsk* sailed into the ocean.

It was a prudent plan. Unlike the *Heilong*, the *Novosibirsk* would not be detected by American, South Korean and Japanese underwater listening posts during its voyage through the shallow and confined waters of the Korea Strait and the East China Sea. Ditto for Chinese hydrophones.

Once the *Novosibirsk* reached the deep blue ocean waters, it would commence a southbound speed run, following a similar course taken by the *Colorado*.

* * * *

Yuri and Jeff Chang were in the officer's wardroom. Although it was 2:05 A.M. neither was ready for sleep. It was time for a break. Both had been on the go all day preparing for the mission. The SEALs were already bedded down in the special operations compartment located aft of the maneuvering room near the *Colorado's* stern.

Instead of helping themselves to the always available pot of coffee, Yuri and Chang elected to have green tea which Jeff brewed in a teapot. They were alone.

Thanks," Yuri said after Jeff filled Yuri's mug. The high quality porcelain cup was decorated with the *Colorado's* crest—the head of a charging mustang with the profile of the submarine's hull superimposed on the image. Also embedded in the emblem was the ship's motto: *Terra Marique Indominta*—By land and sea, untamed.

Chang took a seat at the mess table next to Yuri, carrying a duplicate ship's mug. "This is quite a machine, isn't it," Jeff offered after a cautious taste of the steaming brew.

"I'm impressed. This boat is superior to anything Russia has—and China too."

"That's good to hear."

After taking a sip, Yuri said, "I assume you've been aboard subs before."

"I have…a Los Angeles class."

"They're still excellent boats, very difficult to detect."

Jeff stretched his arms out. "The *Colorado* is larger than the one I was aboard. The extra space is nice."

"If I may ask, what kind of mission were you on that required you to travel by submarine?"

Chang smiled. "Let's just say that I was part of a team that helped extract a high value asset out of harm's way."

Yuri chuckled. "Okay, I get it." He took another swallow from his mug. "I know you're a diver but can you elaborate on your experience."

"Started off with basic scuba, which was part of original training at the CIA. I took additional training with rebreathers."

"What's your deepest dive with a rebreather?"

"Shallow. One hundred and twenty feet max."

"Helium and oxygen mix?"

"Yes." Chang rested an elbow on the table. "How about you?"

"Numerous hundred meter plus operational dives."

The CIA officer did the math. "Wow, almost three hundred and thirty feet. That's crazy deep. What were you doing?"

"Installation and retrieval of surveillance equipment."

Chang suppressed a laugh. "That wouldn't happened to have taken place in U.S. waters, would it?"

Yuri just smiled.

Yuri suspected Chang had a detailed digital file on his background, compiled by the FBI, CIA and various DoD agencies. Yuri had zilch on Chang. He was more than curious about the CIA operative's background. He decided to probe.

"Did you grow up in America?"

"I did. In Seattle, which I guess is also your adopted hometown."

"We live east of Seattle in the suburbs."

"I know. Your partner has a home that overlooks Lake Sammamish. Very nice area to live in. I have a brother who has a home nearby in Issaquah."

"What does he do?"

"Software engineer for Microsoft."

Yuri and Chang chatted several minutes about suburban life on the eastside of Lake Washington before Yuri relaunched his probe. "I take it you live in the Washington, D.C. area."

"Virginia. I have a condo in Arlington."

"Married?"

"No. My present situation doesn't allow for any long-term relationships."

"I know how that is."

Yuri and Chang spent a couple more minutes comparing their nomadic lifestyles, Yuri as a young officer in the Russian Navy and Jeff as a fledgling CIA case officer. Yuri learned that Chang had spent time in the U.S. embassy in Beijing and the consulate in Hong Kong. Fluent in both Mandarin and Cantonese, his language skills helped advance his career.

Yuri switched to a new tack. "Tell me about your parents."

Caught off guard, Chang said, "What do you mean?"

"I'm just curious. What does your dad do for a living?"

"He's retired now but he used to work as an engineer. His specialty was structural engineering. Worked mainly on the design of high-rise buildings throughout the West Coast."

"That's impressive, you must be very proud of his accomplishments."

"I am. He was also a partner of the company, which is based in Seattle. It has several hundred employees and a couple of branch offices."

"Was he an immigrant?"

"No. He was born in Seattle, like me. But his father, my grandfather, immigrated from China before World War II."

"Hmmm…so he managed to get out before Japan invaded China?"

"Yes. Granddad had earned a degree in civil engineering in China and was able to find work in Seattle."

Yuri considered Chang's lineage. "Why didn't you pursue engineering? Your grandfather, father and brother are all engineers."

"I'm not wired like them. I'm competent in math but I'm not wild about it. Plus, what engineers do just doesn't interest me."

That provided a transition to the real purpose of Yuri's soft interrogation. "So, how did you end up working for the Central Intelligence Agency?"

"Well, my mother indirectly pointed me in that direction."

That statement captured Yuri's attention. "Really."

"Mom's an attorney, a partner in a Seattle firm. She's ten years younger than Dad and still practices law." Jeff fought off a yawn. "I was in my sophomore year at the University of Washington in a liberal arts program, majoring in English. I already had basic Mandarin skills because of my mom. She emigrated from Shanghai with her family when she was ten. She suggested that I take a minor in Asian languages, which I did. It came easy to me so I became fluent in Mandarin as well as Cantonese. I also speak passable Japanese and Korean."

Yuri connected the dots. "I take it the CIA recruited you out of school?"

"Eventually, yes. I had just completed a master's degree program at Yale. History of Asian languages. I was thinking about continuing on with a doctorate program to pursue an academic career when I was pitched."

Yuri grinned. "Let me guess, see the world, protect your nation, work with highly motivated patriots."

"Close. But when I really thought about it, I just couldn't see myself spending the next thirty years teaching Asian language history to undergrads who more than likely could care less."

"Itchy feet, right?"

"You got it. I signed up with the Company, spent time at the Farm, and then started work at Langley. I've never looked back."

Yuri's thoughts coalesced. *This guy's a hardcore spook—just like me.*

Chapter 44

Day 30—Thursday

Dr. Meng Park was alone inside the *Lian's* radio room. Located just aft of the bridge, the compartment contained an array of cutting edge communication equipment. This morning she used the satellite phone system. The unit was military grade, employing the PLA's latest encryption technology.

Captain Zhou Jun was on the other end of the satellite link in his S5 office at the Shendao Naval Base. He initiated the call, summoning Park from the aft deck where she supervised the installation of the Serpent antisubmarine system.

"Fleet continues to pester me about your progress," Zhou said.

"Well, we're finally at Station Five. The weather is rough again so we're currently waiting for the wind and seas to die down. We might have a six hour window coming up in midafternoon."

The *Lian* was approximately five hundred miles east of Sanya, located about half way between Hong Kong and the north shore of Luzon Island in the Philippines. The ship hovered near the peak of a seamount along the northern rim of the South China Sea. Water depth over the rise was about 1,000 feet. Two miles to the northeast in 2,900 feet of water lay the hulk of the *Toyohi Maru*. Two miles southeast of the seamount was the *Shoryu Maru;* the wreck rested on the bottom 3,500 feet down. Both Japanese cargo ships were sunk by U.S. submarine action on May 4, 1944.

"Okay," Captain Zhou said, "Assuming you're able to deploy the Viper Five station today, what's your estimate regarding Six?" The planned location for the Viper Six subsea station was approximately two hundred miles to the south.

"Late tomorrow—if we're lucky."

Installation of Serpent was critically behind schedule. The other ship operating in the southern half of the South China Sea basin had deployed only two of its six VIPER subsea stations. Plagued with equipment failures and delayed by the same crappy weather as the *Lian*, the ship was currently moored at a PLAN naval facility in the Spratly Islands undergoing repairs. The illegal Chinese base covered almost seven hundred acres, nearly all of it manmade.

For several years, a fleet of dredges had dug up the bottom surrounding the original rock outcrop marked on charts as Fiery Cross Reef. The reef was named for the British tea clipper *Fiery Cross* after it impaled itself on the shoal in 1860.

"I know you're working hard," Zhou said. "If you can deploy Viper Six, at least we'll have the north half of the basin covered. That should help appease Beijing."

"Thanks. Everyone aboard is aware that the clock is ticking." Dr. Meng massaged the back of her neck. She was worn out and had slept poorly the previous night. "So, how's it going on your end?"

"Very well for a change. We've managed to integrate the four units you've deployed and the two from the other ship into the S5 command structure. The system appears to be working as planned."

"You haven't gone live yet, have you?"

"No. It's still in test mode only."

"Good. Just remember that when I get back to Sanya, I need to run final diagnostics on the integrated system before activation."

"I know. Don't worry, it's all going to work out."

"Okay," Meng Park said.

Before signing off, Zhou promised to pick up Park when the *Lian* returned to Sanya. Despite Zhou's optimism, she worried, her downbeat thoughts racing.

The system is not ready for combat!

The flaw in the Serpent's operating code that controlled communications between multiple Viper units was her chief concern. Her team managed to code a workaround to the problem but it had not been tested.

This is crazy—we could easily lose control of the system and not even know it.

Meng feared that one or more of the deployed Vipers might end up going rogue, attacking a civilian merchant vessel. Dozens of container ships, tankers and cruise liners sailed through the South China Sea every day. Even worse, China's own submarines and surface warships might be targeted.

Meng based the code for Serpent on proprietary software that she stole while conducting research in the United States. It was a coworker's project funded by the United States Air Force that developed complex algorithms to control swarms of aerial drones. The classified code was accessible with her credentials. The Chinese software engineers assigned to Serpent were confident with their adaptation of the purloined code. Still, Meng had her doubts.

If we have problems, I'll have to shut it down.

Meng had inserted a backdoor in the Serpent operating system, which was known only to her. For security purposes, the PLAN admiral in charge of Serpent mandated that control of the system rest with S5 headquarters at Shendao and nowhere else. Meng violated the protocol as a safety measure during deployment operations. If a Viper unit malfunctioned while at sea, she wanted a way to swiftly shut down the weapon. Relying on S5 to implement the abort procedure was judged as too risky by Meng. She also did not trust the acoustic shutdown code developed by the S5 programmers; field tests of the abort algorithms, including acoustic countermeasures by a target vessel, revealed serious flaws that had not yet been remedied.

Meng's secret abort signal was also acoustic but it was designed to "kill" a rogue Viper on the spot rather than sending it home. The signal could be directed to an individual Viper unit or an entire subsea base station. She kept a copy of the abort key recording on the cell phone she carried while aboard the *Lian*—just in case one of the Vipers decided to target its host. Using the ship's internal communications network to access the main hydrophone mounted to the keel, Meng could playback the abort recording. Boosting the signal strength a hundredfold, the hydrophone would broadcast the kill code into the deep where the Vipers ranged at will.

Once we're done, I'll seal the backdoor. No one will ever know.

After the twelve Serpent subsea stations were installed and tested in the South China Sea, Meng Park would delete the abort code from the network.

* * * *

Fifteen times zones behind the *Lian*, it was 8:05 P.M. in downtown Bellevue, Washington. Laura Newman was in the living room of the high-rise condominium apartment she rented. Madelyn slept in her bedroom. Maddy's nanny spent two to three evenings a week at her boyfriend's residence in Redmond, returning to the condo early in the following morning to start work.

Laura sat cross-legged on a sofa composing a Cognition memorandum with a laptop when her iPhone chimed, signaling an incoming text message. She picked up the cell from a side table. The text was one word long: HERCULES.

What's this about? she wondered, staring at the display.

Laura checked for the source of the message but there was no sender name or mobile telephone number, not even a four or five digit sender code.

Hercules—what's that supposed to mean?

Chalking up the mystery text as a fluke, Laura returned the phone to the table and continued working on the memo. About five minutes later, the revelation hit with the impact of a sledgehammer.

Hercules—that was the name of the workboat we used at Point Roberts!

Laura set the laptop aside and turned toward the nearby window wall. She ignored the dazzling night vista. Instead, her mind raced at supersonic speed.

Who sent it? What do they want? Is it about what happened to Dan Miller?

Miller was the captain and owner of the MV *Hercules*, a ninety-six foot workboat that Laura chartered to help Yuri rescue the survivors from a Russian submarine accident. The *Neva* sank offshore of Point Roberts, Washington near Vancouver, B.C. The marooned *Neva* had rested on the mud bottom over seven hundred feet deep.

Laura had just about convinced herself that the text was about Miller— and his demise when another possibility registered.

Could this be about Ken?

Ken Newman was Laura's ex; almost two years earlier he had stalked Laura while she hid out at a beach house in Point Roberts. Yuri and Ken had collided—violently.

Ken's mother hired a private investigator to look into Ken's disappearance. The P.I. made a couple of trips to Point Roberts.

Oh, dear Lord, maybe the P.I. traced Ken to the Hercules!

Laura thought through that scenario and dismissed it. *No way. No one else would have ever seen Ken on the* Hercules. *It was just Yuri and me...and Nick!*

Finally, it all clicked. *It's Nick!*

Nicolai Orlov assisted Yuri and Laura at Point Roberts. He also saved them from Ken's treachery. Earlier this year, Nick had sent Laura another one word text: NEVA. It was a code.

Laura worked her laptop. She logged onto the anonymous Gmail account that she and Yuri shared with Nick, ignoring Yuri's warning to avoid using it.

She opened the draft folder and discovered the unsent message.
It is from Nick!

Chapter 45

Day 31—Friday

Underway for over two days, the USS *Colorado* was southbound in the Pacific. It followed the Ryukyu Island chain, presently running at twenty knots six hundred and fifty feet below the surface. The Japanese island of Okinawa was about fifty miles away to the northwest.

Yuri Kirov and Jeff Chang were in training. They stood inside the submarine's lockout trunk with two SEALs from the Ghost Riders recon team. The combination emergency escape trunk and special ops lockout-lockin compartment was located on the *Colorado's* top deck level just aft of the sail. The airlock was designed to allow a nine man SEAL assault team to egress and ingress the submarine during one cycle of flooding and draining of seawater.

Yuri and Jeff had spent time in a pool back at Yokosuka with the SEALs training with the diving gear. This morning was their last exercise. Neoprene dry suits covered Yuri and Jeff from head to foot. Rebreather packs were strapped to their chests. Gloves, facemasks, weight belts and buoyancy compensators completed the ensembles. The two SEALs were similarly adorned.

Master Chief "Wild Bill" Halgren was in charge, assisted by CPO Ryan Murphy, aka Malibu Murph.

"Okay gents," Halgren said, "you know the drill. I'm going to flood the chamber to the equivalent pressure of forty feet of seawater. I want you to hang onto the handholds, no swimming around until I give the okay signal. Got it?"

"Understood," Yuri said. Jeff Chang echoed Yuri.

"If either of you have any problems, signal us immediately." Halgren looked Yuri's way. "I'm going to watch you." He gestured to Jeff. "Murph's got your six.

Yuri and Jeff acknowledged their understanding.

"Okay, let's do it."

All four prepared for flooding. They slipped on their facemasks, covering eyes and noses. Next, each man retrieved his closed-circuit rebreather gas hose and clamped down on its rubber mouthpiece. The divers inhaled and exhaled, verifying gas flow.

When prompted by Halgren, Yuri and Jeff hand signaled they were okay.

Seawater began to flow into the compartment. Yuri expected to hear the usual racket of rushing water but he heard just a whisper. *Amazing,* he thought. *They employ sound suppression techniques on virtually everything on this boat. No wonder no one can hear them.*

As the water level in the compartment surged over Yuri's head, he gripped the handhold. He was buoyant and needed to release air from the horse collar buoyancy compensator draped around his neck. He made eye contact with Halgren and pointed to the purge valve on the BC.

The master chief formed a circle with the thumb and forefinger of his right hand and extended the remaining fingers.

Yuri pressed the valve. Compressed air squirted into the water, releasing a cascade of bubbles.

Now neutrally buoyant, Yuri checked the rebreather's electronic readout unit strapped to his left forearm. Oxygen and carbon dioxide levels were in the green. Yuri again made eye contact with Halgren and signaled he was okay.

Granted permission to move onto the next element of the exercise, Yuri began to move about the narrow compartment. He swam up the ladder that was partially enclosed by a round pipe-like combing and entered the lockout trunk hatch chamber. After a quick look at the sealed hatch mechanism, he descended. Jeff Chang repeated the same procedure.

Just as Jeff emerged from the upper hatch chamber, dropping feet first with his hands on the ladder, Murphy came up from behind and yanked off Jeff's facemask. It sank to the bottom of the compartment.

Govnó, Yuri muttered to himself. That part of the drill was not expected. But then he remembered. While undergoing military dive training at Sevastopol on the Black Sea, he experienced similar terror tribulations. They were designed to test how well a student diver reacts to the unexpected.

Jeff Chang gripped the ladder with both hands, momentarily stunned from the sting of seawater in his eyes.

Yuri watched, worried how the CIA officer would react. *Come on, Jeff. You know what to do!*

Chang regained his composure and followed the ladder down to the bottom of the compartment. He retrieved his facemask, pulled it back into position and purged the water.

Attaboy! Yuri said to himself.

* * * *

Laura Newman was in downtown Seattle sitting at a small conference table inside an elegant office. Facing Elliott Bay, the unobstructed water view from the fifty story tower was overwhelming. Ferries darted across the bay while tugboats, yachts and a massive box ship cruised the waters.

Across the table from Laura sat her attorney. Tim Reveley was in his early fifties. Tall with a brawny torso, he was within just ten pounds of his college weight when he had played first-string quarterback for USC. Tanned from golf and tennis, his bronzed complexion and sun bleached brunet hair flattered his ruggedly handsome face.

It was the noon hour. To ensure privacy, they avoided restaurants. The catered lunch had just been delivered to Reveley's office. Laura enjoyed a Caesar salad; Tim munched on a ham and cheese sandwich. Fresh coffee was also provided.

"Are you sure this is the same person?" Reveley asked.

"It has to be. Just Yuri, me and Nick know about the Gmail account."

"Did either you or Yuri mention this Gmail account to the FBI?"

"Maybe. I just don't remember—they asked so many questions." Laura dabbed her mouth with a napkin. "Anyway, Yuri told me not to use it because he didn't want Nick implicated for what he'd done—seeking asylum in the U.S."

"Yet, apparently this Nick fellow reached out to you."

"Yes."

"What does he want?"

"He wants to speak with Yuri."

"About what?"

"The draft email didn't say, only that it's urgent that Yuri call him on the burner phone Nick provided for him."

"Do you have access to the phone?"

"No. Yuri destroyed it."

Tim took a swallow from his coffee cup. "When will Yuri be back?" Earlier, Laura told Reveley that Yuri was out of town on business.

"At least a week, maybe longer."

"Is this NSD work?"

"No."

"Oh," Reveley said, surprised. "He's already been put to work by the government?"

"Yes. They didn't waste any time."

"Laura, this is serious stuff. I know you care about the welfare of Orlov but you and Yuri cannot have any kind of contact with a foreign intelligence officer. It will jeopardize the agreement we worked out with Justice."

Laura slumped in her chair.

Tim noticed. "What's wrong?"

"A couple of weeks ago Nick showed up without any warning at Yuri's office in Redmond. They had lunch together."

"Oh jeez! I hope he reported that to the FBI."

"No, he didn't. Yuri said he didn't want to get Nick into trouble. Apparently, he entered the country with a false ID."

"That was a mistake. If the FBI finds out he talked with that guy and didn't report it they're going to be really suspicious. And now with this second attempt to contact Yuri, the intelligence agencies may start to believe he's really a Russian mole instead of a defector."

Laura stared at the desk while massaging the back of her neck. "Tim, what should I do?"

"Ignore the text. Don't ever access that Gmail account again."

"Should I tell the FBI?"

"Normally, I'd say yes. But if you did that, you'd have to also reveal the prior contact Yuri had with Orlov." Reveley tilted his chair back a few degrees. "The FBI said they would stop surveilling your phones and computers when Yuri agreed to work for the government but they could be lying." Tim returned his chair to the upright position. "If they're still monitoring your phones, how do you suppose they'd react to the codeword—what was it again?

"Hercules. I told them about the workboat we used at Point Roberts, so they might piece it together."

"Let's do this: If the FBI contacts you about the text, just tell them what happened. But make sure to emphasize that you did not act on it and we'll see what develops from that."

"Okay."

Chapter 46

Day 32—Saturday

The tension inside the *Colorado's* control room was intense. The crew's stress level ratcheted up several notches eight hours earlier when the submarine cruised through the Luzon Strait and formally entered hostile waters—the South China Sea. All consoles and workstations inside the compartment were staffed. Conversation between individuals was all business.

Yuri studied the control room's horizontal large screen display. A digital chart of the northern half of the South China Sea filled the waist high touchscreen. *Colorado's* current position and its projected course were superimposed on the display. It was six hundred feet below the surface running at a stealthy sixteen knots.

Commander Tom Bowman was next to Yuri. *Colorado's* CO gestured toward the high definition screen. "One of those new bottom stations is right here."

"How far away are we from it?" Yuri asked, noting the skull and crossbones icon that marked the location of the Chinese seabed-based antisubmarine weapon system.

Bowman touched the screen. "Right now, it's sixty-four nautical miles away."

"How close can we come to it?"

"COMSUBPAC's latest report ordered us to maintain a minimum separation of forty nautical miles but we'll be around forty-five."

Bowman referred to a scheduled radio check-in with the commander of Submarine Force, Pacific Fleet. While underway, *Colorado* deployed its floating wire to intercept encrypted VHF radio transmissions originating from Pearl Harbor. The very high frequency waves penetrate the ocean surface to a depth of five to six feet, allowing reception by the sub without the need to raise a radio antenna.

Yuri noted that the proposed route on the display bisected two additional death's-head icons located eastward of Hainan Island. "So, two more of those things to go along our route after this one?"

"That's right."

"Which one did *Tucson* tangle with?"

"The one southeast of Sanya, just north of the Parcel Islands." Bowman pointed with a finger.

Yuri looked up. "How close to that station did *Tucson* come?"

"About thirty-five nautical miles but as you'll recall, *Tucson* only detected those things ascending from just a couple miles away. My gut tells me those two units were in active patrol mode when *Tucson* showed up."

"That makes sense," Yuri said, nodding. "How many more bottom stations?"

"At last count, eight confirmed installations in the South China Sea, six in the north basin and two in the south. But it's likely going to increase." Bowman kneaded his nose. "The PLAN has had two ships installing the damn things."

"You must be tracking them by satellite."

"We are, plus we have our own SOSUS network that allows us to monitor what the ships are up to twenty-four seven." Bowman referred to the U.S. Navy's Sound Surveillance System, a network of underwater listening posts.

"In the South China Sea?"

"That's right."

Bowman's revelation was new to Yuri. "Do the Chinese know?"

"We don't think so. We were careful during deployment. The PLA Navy needs to remain in the dark about our network."

Yuri put it together. "You used subs to install the hydrophones."

"No comment," Bowman said with a smirk.

* * * *

The *Novosibirsk* breached the northern Ryukyu Islands on schedule, passing between the Japanese volcanic islands of Kuchinoerabu-jima and Kuchino-shima. The Russian attack submarine crossed the Yaku-Shin Bank and entered the Pacific Ocean. The *Novosibirsk* was currently southbound.

With the troubled waters of the Korea Strait and the East China Sea now in *Novosibirsk's* wake, Captain Petrovich took the opportunity to leave the attack center, where he had "camped out" for the past three days. He just arrived at the torpedo room.

The watch officer snapped to attention as *Novosibirsk's* commanding officer approached. "What's the status of our 'specials,'" Petrovich asked.

"They all check out, Captain. No problems." The twenty-seven year old lieutenant was a recent transfer to the *Novosibirsk*.

"Excellent."

The *Novosibirsk* typically carried thirty heavyweight torpedoes but for this mission only four were aboard. The "war fish" were loaded in four of the sub's ten torpedo tubes. Occupying the weapon's bay racks were thirty self-propelled anti-ship mines. Nearly the same length as the torpedoes, the mines consisted of a propulsion unit and a mine package. Once ejected from a torpedo tube, the mine was designed to swim to pre-designated bottom coordinates where it would settle onto the bottom and wait.

"Ah, Captain, will the deployment water depths still range from twenty to forty meters?"

"That's the current plan—why do you ask?"

"Just concerned about possible discovery because of the shallow water."

"Your job is to ensure that the units are deployed as planned and that they will detonate."

"Understood, sir," the assistant weapons officer said. But he was not finished. "It's just that these units are foreign made. I don't know how reliable they are."

"Fleet vetted the mines prior to our mission. They're based on our own SMDM mine system but with improvements." The GRU purchased the Chinese exports through a host of middlemen and cutouts, ensuring that the trail would not lead back to the Kremlin.

"The SMDM—but how?"

"Not your concern. Any additional questions?" Petrovich asked with an edgy tone.

"No sir."

"Very well, carry on."

"Aye, Captain."

Petrovich exited the torpedo compartment, deciding to pay a surprise visit to the engine room. As he headed aft, he considered his conversation with the weapons officer. The lieutenant's concerns about the mines were justified. Fleet engineers at Vladivostok assured Captain Petrovich that the Chinese mines were functional, which was not a surprise to Petrovich. The buzz circulating within the senior naval officers at Pacific Fleet Headquarters shed light on the origins of the "specials."

A civilian engineer in Saint Petersburg working for the Russian Navy sold the complete SMDM design package to an MSS agent. Chinese engineers in Shanghai took the plans and specs and improved on the design. The knockoff units actually worked better than the original Russian manufactured torpedo mines.

After confessing to an FSB interrogator, the engineer was sentenced to thirty years of hard labor at a Siberian prison camp.

Petrovich and his colleagues all agreed that the traitor should have faced a firing squad instead.

* * * *

The *Heilong* progressed northward, following the east coast of Japan's most northerly island of Hokkaido. The fisheries city of Nemuro was one hundred and seventy nautical miles to the west. The submarine cruised at twenty knots just over a thousand feet below the surface. Water depth in this region of the ocean was around three miles deep.

Operations aboard the Chinese submarine had evolved into a routine of around the clock watch standing, endless drills, continuous maintenance, and constant surveillance. Of particular concern to *Heilong's* commanding officer this day was the sonar report of a surface contact. Commander Yang Yu discussed the contact with *Heilong's* executive officer, Lieutenant Commander Zheng Qin.

"What do you make of this?" asked Yang.

"It does appear to be following our track, matching our speed and heading." Zheng was thirty-one, scrawny with jet-black hair cut to regulation length. Pockmarked from severe acne as a teen, his face mimicked the surface of the moon.

The two officers peered at the plotting table in the *Heilong's* attack center. The electronic chart displayed the submarine's current position and the sonar contact. Sonar identified the ship's acoustic signature as a Japan Coast Guard cutter.

Commander Yang checked his wristwatch. "It's been on the same course for an hour now."

"But how could it detect us at this depth, Captain?"

"It shouldn't."

"It may just be a coincidence," Zheng offered. "The ship's likely on a routine fisheries patrol. Sonar reported over a dozen fishing vessels in the general area."

"You're probably right." Yang stared at the digital chart. "We'll continue as we are for the next hour. If it still follows, we'll reevaluate our options at that time."

"Very good, sir."

The Japanese patrol ship changed course to a westerly heading twenty minutes before Yang's time limit. Relieved that the sonar contact was a false alarm, Commander Yang decided to return to his stateroom for a nap. XO Zheng commanded as Yang rested.

In the *Heilong's* wake some twenty miles away, a predator stalked its prey. The USS *Mississippi,* ever vigilant, was ready to strike if ordered.

Chapter 47

The *Lian* returned to Sanya a few minutes before three in the afternoon. Dr. Meng Park was one of the first to disembark. After eight days at sea, she was more than ready for shore leave.

Captain Zhou Jun waited on the pier adjacent to the gangway that connected *Lian* to the dock. He watched Park as she walked down the ramp, towing a wheeled suitcase and carrying her briefcase. She had traded her bulky coveralls for a pair of skintight blue jeans and a short sleeved silk blouse that flattered her breasts.

"Welcome back, Dr. Meng," Zhou said.

"Thank you, Captain."

"I need an immediate debriefing before you return to your hotel. Do you mind?"

"Not at all."

"Good, my vehicle's close by."

"Okay."

Captain Zhou reached forward and grabbed the handle of her suitcase. "Let me get that."

"Thank you."

The businesslike greetings were a charade for the benefit of the dockworkers and *Lian's* crew that milled about the pier and along the decks of the ship. During the ten minute drive to Zhou's apartment, Meng would indeed provide a summary rundown on the installation of the Viper network. But that was a pretext for the real purpose of their encounter.

Both were ravenous. They would spend the rest of the afternoon in bed before finally taking a break. Zhou had reservations at a nightclub in downtown Sanya.

* * * *

Commander Bowman summoned Yuri Kirov and Jeff Chang to the *Colorado's* wardroom. Yuri and Jeff were seated at the mess table when Bowman and Lieutenant Commander Andrews entered the compartment. It was 3:07 P.M., local time.

SEAL team leader Andrews took a chair next to Chang. After Bowman filled his mug with fresh coffee, he claimed his chair at the head of the table. Glancing toward Yuri and Jeff, Bowman said, "Thanks for joining us." He took a taste. "We're currently about sixty nautical miles out, still in deep water. But it's going to get shallow soon so we'll be reducing our speed accordingly." *Colorado's* CO glanced at his wristwatch. "The current plan is to launch the SDV at zero one hundred hours this coming morning."

"How close to shore will we be?" Yuri asked.

"Six miles."

"Water depth?"

"Around two hundred thirty feet."

Yuri did the math—seventy meters. "I assume we'll be near the surface when the submersible is launched, otherwise we might need a decompression stop."

"Correct. The launch sequence has been set up to avoid the need for decompression."

"Good," Yuri said. "One less issue to worry about."

Andrews commented next. "It'll be slack tide so the trip in should take no more than an hour."

"Any change regarding surf conditions at the beach?"

"No. One half meter high waves."

"Okay."

After another taste of coffee, Commander Bowman rejoined the conversation, addressing Yuri. "When you launched the mini from the boat you were on, how far offshore of Yulin were you?"

"About twenty kilometers."

"So, just outside of China's territorial waters."

"That's right. Moscow ordered the *Novosibirsk's* captain to keep the boat out of Chinese waters."

"How close to the base were you when you and your team locked out of the mini?"

"It was close-in, about half a kilometer from the island." Yuri wondered where this line of questioning was going. He decided to ask. "What's the concern, Commander?"

"We just received an update from COMSUBPAC. Four autonomous surface drones were observed exercising in the Shendao harbor area yesterday afternoon."

"New ones, in addition to those at Yulin?"

"Yes."

Yuri muttered a Russian expletive.

"I'm worried about the sea drones," Bowman said. "If the PLAN gets just the slightest whiff that we're in their backyard, the mini won't stand a chance against those things."

Open to the sea with just a thin sheet of aluminum to protect the occupants, a single depth charge detonated a hundred yards from the Shallow Water Combat Submersible would scramble brains and macerate guts.

"Are they patrolling near our route to the beach?" Jeff Chang asked.

"No. As of yesterday, all drone activity was confined to waters within the harbor's breakwaters. But that could change."

Chang scowled while taking in the news. "Any idea what caused them to supplement harbor coverage at Shendao?"

"COMSUBPAC did not elaborate."

"I think I have an idea what might be going on." All eyes turned Yuri's way. "It's the carriers. They might be planning to move them from the Yulin Naval Base to Shendao. The drones will be in place for supplemental security."

"Move them how?" Chang asked. "Aren't they dead in the water?"

"Towing. It's a short trip, just a dozen kilometers or so. Piece of cake with good weather." Yuri picked up the cake idiom from Laura. He glanced at Bowman. "Any reports regarding the propulsion systems on the *Shandong* and the *Liaoning.*"

"We've received no recent reports about the carriers."

"My guess," Yuri said, "and that's all it is at this time…is that the PLAN has given up trying to restore ship power for both carriers at the Yulin base. The EMP damage to the utilities systems on the piers and shoreside facilities was catastrophic. However, the pier and upland system at Shendao were not damaged. In fact, the pier was specifically designed to service aircraft carriers."

"Hmmm," Bowman mumbled. "That does make sense."

"If they move the carriers," Chang said facing Bowman, "they might pass right over the *Colorado*."

"We'll be listening. If that happens, we'll head back into deep water until they're out of the way."

"That makes sense." The CIA officer turned toward Andrews, "What's the latest intel about our target area?"

"Nothing new has been directed our way about S5. When we arrive at the launch site, we'll get another update."

"Okay, thanks."

After the briefing broke up, Yuri returned to the compact quarters he shared with Chang. As Jeff showered, Yuri stretched out on his bunk. Lieutenant Commander Andrews suggested that they both try to rest before the mission started.

Yuri stared upward at the bottom of Jeff's bunk. Yuri's comfort level with Chang and the Ghost Riders increased each day he spent aboard the *Colorado*. He was also impressed with Commander Bowman and his crew. *So far, so good.*

Yuri hoped for a smooth mission—a quick in and out without detection. *Maybe we can really pull this thing off.* That was Yuri's last conscious thought before drifting off.

After ninety minutes, the familiar nightmare abruptly returned Yuri to reality.

This mission is all wrong!

* * * *

While the USS *Colorado* crept toward Hainan Island, the Russian attack submarine *Novosibirsk* approached the Luzon Strait at twenty knots. The waterway extended from Taiwan's southern coast to the north shore of Luzon Island. *Novosibirsk's* planned route across the passage was about eighty nautical miles south of the path *Colorado* had navigated the day before.

Captain Petrovich caucused with his key officers in the wardroom. A bulkhead mounted HD wide-screen monitor at the aft end of the room displayed the digital image of a navigation chart of another sea passage—the *Novosibirsk's* final destination.

"Gentlemen," Petrovich said, "this is the area where I intend to begin our seeding operations." He clicked on a handheld laser pointer, highlighting the waters near the island city-state of Singapore and the the eastern end of the Strait of Malacca. Sandwiched between the Malay Peninsula and the Indonesian island of Sumatra, the Strait of Malacca was the world's most frequently traveled shipping channel. Nearly a hundred thousand commercial vessels navigated the passageway each year.

"It's very shallow in that area, Captain," the navigation officer noted. "How close in do you plan to bring the boat?"

"We'll stay within our normal operating parameters plus all seeding ops will occur at night."

The Strait of Malacca and the connecting Singapore Strait were both shallow. With a hull diameter of almost fifty feet, the *Novosibirsk* needed to take care not to run aground while submerged. And to avoid visual detection of the hull by aircraft and watercraft, night operations were mandatory.

"Magnetic fuses still the plan?" asked weapons.

"Correct. All of the targets are merchantmen with steel hulls. No concerns over degaussing with them." Degaussing was a procedure to reduce the magnetic field of a ship, typically used for submarines and surface warships.

Petrovich keyed the pointer again. "I want to place the first units in the main channel in this area. After seeding that channel we'll proceed . . ."

The installation procedure for each grouping of the mines was finalized and the briefing ended.

The goal of Operation Vortex was to create mass confusion and terror within the world's shipping community. The indiscriminate mining of one of the globe's most vital marine transportation corridors was designed to paralyze China's already delicate economy. Until the mine threat was eliminated, oil laden tankers from the Middle East and gigantic container ships loaded with Chinese goods bound for European markets would avoid the route that linked the Indian and Pacific oceans.

Conceived by the Kremlin, Vortex was designed to deter China from seeking revenge for the nuclear detonation in Qingdao and the e-bomb attack on the Yulin Naval Base. Simply put, Moscow's message to Beijing was: Don't think of attacking Russia. We can repeat the mining operation anytime we choose.

Vortex was a bold plan, one that appeared bulletproof to the Kremlin and Russia's military elite. To achieve success, however, it required Russia's most modern and stealth attack submarine to cross the South China Sea unnoticed.

A PLAN bottom mounted hydrophone in the Luzon Strait detected the faint acoustic signature of the *Novosibirsk's* propeller as it cruised into the South China Sea. It took just a minute to relay the alert via encrypted subsea and satellite comms to S5 headquarters on Hainan Island.

Chapter 48

The submersible skulked through the gloom. Yuri was jammed inside the passenger compartment with Jeff Chang and SEALs Halgren and Murphy. In the forward end of the Mark 11, Senior Chief Aaron "Runner" Baker piloted the midget sub while Chief Don "Driller" Dillon operated sonar and comms.

The U.S. Navy Shallow Water Combat Submersible, designated as the Mark 11 SDV, was twenty-two feet long and about five feet in diameter. The battery compartment took up the center of the craft, separating the cockpit from the four person passenger compartment. The lithium-ion batteries supplied the juice that powered the electric motor in the stern. The motor turned the propeller.

Operating as a wet vehicle, the interior of the Seal Delivery Vehicle was flooded with seawater. All occupants wore diving equipment and breathed compressed air from onboard storage tanks.

The Mark 11 departed from the *Colorado* half an hour earlier. It was 1:32 A.M. local time. Running at six knots and thirty feet below the surface, it would take the submersible another half hour to reach shore.

Yuri was uneasy with the ride sandwiched inside the aluminum shell with no viewports. The dim interior illumination from a bulkhead light didn't help either. A tinge of claustrophobia eroded his well-being.

The four Ghost Riders wore full face masks with communication gear, allowing them to talk with each other. Yuri and Jeff, however, were each equipped with an earphone inside the hood of their dry suits. Watertight leads from the earphones plugged into the onboard intercom system. They could listen but not speak to the SEALs. Switching from full face masks to rebreather gear prior to exiting the SDV required considerable expertise, which Chang lacked. Yuri had the skillsets but didn't mind joining Jeff.

Other than occasional SEAL chatter, all Yuri could hear was the chorus of expanding bubbles from the exhalations of his fellow passengers. When the minisub was half a nautical mile from the shore, the passengers would switch from onboard air to their rebreathers, reducing the telltale trail of bursting bubbles on the surface.

Yuri tried to relax but failed. Pre-mission jitters prevented any meaningful rest. Although tired, what really taxed Yuri was his sense of impending doom.

This mission is insane, Yuri reflected.

What lay ahead was a true mission impossible. Sneaking into one of the People's Republic of China's most secure military installations to steal state of the art antisubmarine warfare technology was beyond the pale for Yuri.

A million things can go wrong—will go wrong!

Other than satellite photography, the route ahead to the secret facility was unknown. Yuri worried that the hillside housing the underground headquarters for S5 was littered with intruder warning devices and surveilled by roaming armed security forces.

They rely too much on remote comms.

Communications was another worry for Yuri. Once the shore team deployed, the submarine would retreat beyond the twelve mile limit and commence hovering several hundred feet below the surface. A tethered buoy would be released from the sub. The low profile antenna buoy, constructed to mimic an indigenous fishing float, was designed to connect with the constellation of U.S. military satellites orbiting the Western Pacific. The satellites would in turn connect to the tactical multiband networking SATCOM radio Murphy carried.

Andrews should be with us—not sitting on the sub.

The officer in charge of the mission, Lieutenant Commander Andrews, remained aboard the *Colorado*. Andrews would use the radio relay system to monitor and manage the shore team from a console inside the *Colorado's* control room. He would also coordinate with the U.S. Indo-Pacific Command in Hawaii and the Joint Special Operations Command at Fort Bragg, North Carolina on mission progress. It was an impressive arrangement, allowing the team to obtain near instant intel on mission critical issues. But just one glitch in the elaborate tag team scheme would render the shore team deaf, dumb and blind.

Yuri also worried about the PLA-Navy SIGINT unit at Lingshui Airbase. Located on Hainan Island's southern coast forty statute miles east of Sanya, the facility was staffed with over a thousand signals intelligence analysts. Their principal task was to monitor downlinks from commercial communication satellites.

They might pick up our own comms.

Lingshui staffers were also responsible for monitoring communications from U.S. naval forces operating in the South China Sea, which Yuri construed to mean their mission. Andrews wasn't concerned that mission comms would be detected by Lingshui, alluding to non-specified secret procedures that would be used. Yuri still had his doubts.

We're light on weapons. If we get into a firefight with security forces, we're screwed.

Yuri would have preferred that Runner and Driller accompany the shore team instead of returning the Mark 11 to its bat cave on the *Colorado*. But Andrews vetoed Yuri's suggestion of parking the submersible on the bottom offshore of the landing site, which would have allowed the two additional SEALs to join the ground team.

Andrews noted that the shallow tropical waters at the debark point were crystal clear, which meant that a bottomed-out Mark 11 might be visible from above during daylight hours. But more to the point, Andrews reminded Yuri he was on a reconnaissance mission. Additional men ashore beyond the four man team increased the probability of detection. Washington mandated that contact with the enemy be avoided at all costs. There would be no overhead drones armed with Hellfire missiles to terrorize the enemy or QRF—quick reaction force—helicopters to extract the team should they run into trouble.

The only way out for the shore team was to follow protocols—avoid detection, secure the intelligence, retreat to the underwater extraction point, and return to the *Colorado* aboard the Mark 11.

Yuri couldn't fault Andrews's reasoning but his gut told him the SEAL officer should be with the shore team. *One more man ashore would—*

Yuri's thoughts were interrupted as Chief Dillon's voice broadcast from the earphone inside Yuri's neoprene hood. "Heads up, gents. We're five minutes out. Switch to rebreathers and prepare to disembark."

God, please watch over us!

* * * *

"Jun...Jun, wake up! Someone's at the door."

Captain Zhou Jun rolled onto his back and looked up. Meng Park was at his side leaning over his chest; her breasts brushed his skin.

"What's wrong?"

"Someone is banging on your door."

Zhou heard the racket. He checked the clock on the bedside table: 2:02 A.M. He swore as he swung his legs onto the bamboo flooring. "Stay in here," he ordered as he grabbed a bathrobe.

Furious, Zhou yanked open the front door to his apartment.

A junior officer from S5 stood in the hallway.

Zhou was about to reprimand the ensign when the twenty-three year old blurted out, "Sir, we've been trying to reach you for over an hour but your phone just goes to voicemail. I was sent here to summon you...the duty officer needs you back at once."

"What's going on?"

The ensign peered down the hallway. It was deserted and none of the other residents had opened their doors. "We have a positive track on a foreign submarine. It was detected in the Luzon Strait."

Zhou gestured for the ensign to enter. After Zhou shut the door he said, "Is it American?"

"No, sir, Russian. Nuclear attack boat, Yasen class."

"You're certain?"

"Lieutenant Wu is, sir."

"Where's it headed?"

"It was on a southwest heading when I left."

Captain Zhou massaged his temple as he processed the news. "All right, you may return to base. Tell Wu I'll be there in forty-five minutes."

"Yes sir. But Lieutenant Wu instructed me to tell you that Fleet was automatically notified of the sub intrusion. We've been ordered to activate Serpent."

"What? Who gave that command?"

"I don't know, sir."

After the ensign left, Captain Zhou returned to the bedroom.

Meng Park stepped out of the bathroom, a towel covering the essentials. "What's going on?" she asked.

Zhou briefed her on the news and she reacted. "Serpent is not ready yet for combat."

"I know but we don't have any choice."

Park sat on the edge of the bed as Zhou retrieved his cell phone from the dresser top. He had switched it off several hours earlier, not wanting any interruptions during sex with Park. He powered up the phone and turned toward Park. "I'll drop you off at your hotel on my way to the base."

"Maybe I should come with you now to S5."

"No. It'll be better if we arrive separately. When I drop you off at your hotel, wait ten minutes or so and then take a cab. I'll let staff know that you've been asked to come in."

"Okay."

Captain Zhou and Dr. Meng exited the apartment building parking lot in the BMW. As Zhou drove through the deserted streets of Sanya, he also held his cell phone to an ear. He called the S5 duty officer, requesting an update.

At first, Park half listened to the one-sided conversation but her thoughts soon wandered. Trepidation seeped into her well-being, corroding her confidence.

They're going to test the system with another real target!

But Serpent is still not ready.

What if it doesn't work?

What if it does?

* * * *

The four phantoms emerged from the murk in unison. It was ten minutes past two o'clock in the morning. Standing in chest deep water, Yuri Kirov and his companions scanned their surroundings. Each man had pulled down his facemask, letting it hang around the neck. The setting moon hung low on the horizon, providing a modicum of illumination. Forty feet ahead, knee-high waves rolled onto the sandy beach with a muted rush. The night air was motionless and sticky hot at ninety degrees Fahrenheit—ten degrees warmer than the ocean water.

Master Chief Halgren used a gloved hand to signal the others to stay put. He then thrust his bulk landward through the water.

Before surfacing, the entire team had clipped their dive fins to D-rings on the chest harnesses they wore under the rebreathers and BCs. Reinforced rubber booties, part of the jet-black lightweight dry suits that covered the men, protected feet from fragments of coral and rock that littered the otherwise sandy bottom. Bulky rucksacks stuffed with gear and supplies were strapped to each man's back.

Halgren waded forward twenty feet when he stopped abruptly. He turned to his companions, signaling danger.

Ryan "Malibu Murph" Murphy planted the butt of his Colt M4A1 in the socket of his right shoulder, aiming the sound suppressed assault rifle downrange—cover for Halgren. That's when Yuri heard it. Music—rock and roll, Chinese style. *What the hell?*

Jeff Chang pulled out a monocular night vision device from a waterproof pouch. He peered at the beach. Yuri noted that Halgren had deployed his own NVD goggles.

Chang gave Yuri his scope and pointed to the right of Halgren's position.

Yuri homed in on the target. A twenty-four-foot fiberglass speedboat with huge twin outboards bobbed just beyond the surf zone, held by an anchor line that extended offshore. Beyond the watercraft, the glow from a roaring campfire on the beach illuminated the silhouettes of targets. Yuri counted at least nine—bikini clad females and bare chested males in swim trunks. Some danced, others staggered about holding beer bottles, a few lay prone on the sand, embracing.

Yuri assessed the situation in a heartbeat: Drunken teenagers from one of the resorts throwing a late night beach party. *Now what do we do?*

Halgren backtracked to the team. "Kids partying," he whispered. "We need to relocate two hundred meters to the southwest. Gear up and follow me."

After swimming to the alternate landing site and verifying the beach was clear of partygoers and other interlopers, the four men emerged from the ocean. They crossed the beach and assembled in the uplands. Murph used one of his dive fins to brush away the footprints they left on dry sand.

Hidden by thick clumps of brush, Halgren briefed the team, his voice a whisper. "The ravine is about eighty meters to the north." He held a GPS receiver. "We need to bury our dive gear here first." He pressed a key on the machine, registering the earth coordinates. He next made eye contact with Yuri and Chang. "Look around and become familiar with this location. Your lives might depend on it. You can't rely on GPS alone."

Murph removed a digital tablet from a watertight pack he carried. He called up an aerial photo of the site. After entering the GPS coordinates, he pointed to the screen. "We're right here. The partygoers over here. The ravine is up here."

"What about that building?" Yuri said, noting a structure several hundred feet west of their location.

Halgren answered. "Supposed to be abandoned but don't count on it. We're going to give it a wide berth."

"Got it," Yuri said.

"All right. Let's get out of our dive gear."

The men unstrapped their rebreathers and the other apparatus they had carried ashore. They next shed their dry suits, each thankful to be rid of the covering due to the warm conditions. Underneath the dive garments, the men wore long sleeved shirts, tactical camo pants and socks. Lightweight camo jackets and jungle boots carried ashore in watertight backpacks completed their attire.

The team spent the next ten minutes digging a three-foot deep pit in the sandy soil, using collapsible spades they carried. Each man's diving gear including dry suit was encased in plastic bags and backfilled with excavated soil. Clumps of brush were cut and placed over the work zone.

Satisfied with the concealment, Halgren said. "Okay guys, let's proceed to the objective."

Chapter 49

"Captain, this is Security. Dr. Meng has arrived."

"Grant her entry and have an escort bring her to my office."

"Yes sir."

Meng arrived five minutes later. "Any problems?" Zhou asked.

"No. It all went as you planned." Before taking the cab ride she had changed to casual garb, fitting for the early hour of the morning. Meng took a chair fronting Zhou's desk. "What's the latest?" she asked.

"I've reviewed the hydrophone data. It's definitely a Russian boat, Yasen class. We suspect it's the *Novosibirsk*. Satellite imagery confirmed that the *Severodvinsk* is in Petropavlovsk but the *Novosibirsk* is no longer in Vladivostok."

"When did it leave port?"

"Our last satellite data suggests it departed a week ago."

"Plenty of time to get here."

"I agree."

"So, what's it up to?"

"It's current heading suggests that it's bound for Singapore."

"Speed?"

"Still running at twenty knots."

Dr. Meng digested the info. "So, he's either foolish or the Russians don't know our tracking capabilities."

"I expect the latter."

The S5 surveillance network was a work in progress. The hydrophone array in the Luzon Strait that detected the Russian submarine had been operational for just a couple of weeks.

Captain Zhou continued the rundown. "We're lucky to have picked the boat up. We're right on the edge with our sensors. If he'd dropped his speed to fifteen, sixteen knots, it's unlikely we would have heard him."

"They're that quiet?"

"Yes, the Yasen are at least as quiet as the American Los Angeles class."

"What are your orders?"

"Continue tracking, prepare for possible interdiction."

"With Serpent?"

"The CMC has not made a decision. We're on alert for possible air attack as well as Serpent. I have a Y-8 on alert at Lingshui if an aerial attack is ordered.

"Where is the sub now?" Meng asked.

Zhou rotated the monitor on his desk. She eyed the screen and said, "It's headed toward Station Six."

"That's right. It's a perfect set up."

Meng frowned. "But why would Beijing want to take out a Russian boat? They're supposed to be our ally."

Captain Zhou had the same thoughts. "I don't know. There's a lot more to this than either of us will probably ever know."

* * * *

The trek to S5 was only a mile long but it turned into a slog. The brush under the tropical forest canopy was exceptionally thick, requiring frequent diversions to the pre-planned GPS route. Halgren and Murphy took turns on point, both on constant lookout for possible ground sensors that might alert security forces to the team's presence. Wildlife was another issue. Hainan Island was home to several species of venomous snakes, including cobras and pit vipers. Wasp nests were also a hazard. But the biggest hassle was the swarms of mosquitos. They plagued everyone.

At half past three in the morning, Halgren confirmed with his GPS unit that the team had arrived at their destination. Perched on the slope of a hillside overlooking the breakwater protected harbor, the observation post was about eight hundred feet upslope from the Shendao Fleet Logistics and Support Center building. Sparse interior lighting from the PLAN facility suggested it was currently not in use.

Seaward of the logistics building, the huge aircraft carrier quay jutted into the harbor. The pier's platoon of pole mounted floodlights lit up the reinforced concrete deck with more than enough light to play pro soccer.

Near the center of the quay was a long and narrow office building. Stationed on the north side of the pier opposite the building was a track mounted traveling crane with a towering derrick. Several pickup trucks scurried about the 2,300-foot-long pier. Parked near the center of the 400-foot-wide deck was a fleet of semi-trailer trucks. Other than a small workboat tied up on the south side of the monster pier near the shoreline, no other vessels were moored to the structure.

"What do you think they're up to?" Murphy whispered to Halgren. The SEALs peered downslope, using the lush vegetation as cover.

"Looks like they're getting ready for something."

Yuri peered over Murphy's shoulder. "I suspect they're planning to bring one or both of the carriers over from the Yulin base."

"I think you might be right," Halgren said.

"So, what does that mean for us?" asked Jeff Chang.

Master Chief Halgren faced the CIA officer. "Probably a lot more activity on the pier, maybe also with the logistics building. Around the clock work on the ship is likely, too." He pointed toward the pier. "See all of the truck trailers lined up near the building. They're there for a reason."

Jeff nodded without commenting but Murphy added his two cents. "If they're anything like what we do when a carrier's in port, security will be up the wazoo. That means we've got be really careful not to call attention to ourselves."

CPO Murphy's observation resurrected a memory for Yuri. "Something else to be aware of guys," Yuri said. "If the carriers do show up here, the drone patrol boats will likely be swarming around the harbor. If we have to abort from our planned out, just remember that getting out through the harbor will be a bitch with those things around."

"Can they detect the Mark Eleven?" Murphy asked.

"Count on it. They're equipped with cutting edge sonar designed for anti-sub and anti-diver ops. They use both active and passive sensors. They also carry depth charges and torpedoes plus a deck mounted gun."

Malibu Murph cursed. "How are they controlled?"

"They're autonomous, that's what makes them so dangerous. Three of those bastards executed a coordinated attack on their own against the mini we used at Yulin. It was just luck they didn't sink it."

Halgren said, "Thanks for the heads up." He turned to Murphy. "Let's get comms set up. I need to let Andrews know we're operational."

"Okay boss."

Halgren directed his attention to Yuri and Chang. "The sun will be coming up in a couple of hours. I suggest you guys catch a little sleep."

They took advantage of Wild Bill's offer. Jeff lay on his left side atop a plastic ground cloth. Mosquito netting shielded his head. Two applications of bug repellent covered his hands, face and neck. Somehow, he managed to fall asleep.

Yuri was beside Chang with his spine propped against a tree trunk. Also lathered with anti-insect goop, he was wide awake. Despite the successful infiltration, trepidation contaminated his well-being.

What the hell am I doing here?

* * * *

The *Novosibirsk* proceeded southwest across the South China Sea. Luzon Island was eighty nautical miles to the east. The submarine navigated through the abyss nearly a thousand feet below the surface. The bottom under the keel was over two miles deep.

Captain Petrovich was seated in his command chair inside the submarine's central command post. He sipped from a mug of tepid tea while reviewing daily department reports on his digital tablet. It was boring work but part of his duties as commanding officer. He finished the Engineering Department report and was about to start on Weapons when he was interrupted.

"Captain, I have a recommendation regarding our speed." First officer Captain Third Rank Fredek Yermakov viewed the plot table a couple of meters away from Petrovich. Thickset with a wrestler's bearing, the thirty-seven-year-old father of twin daughters had red hair and a sprinkling of freckles across his forehead and cheeks, which during his tenure as a cadet at the naval academy had earned him the moniker of "Red."

Petrovich set the tablet aside and joined the XO. A digital chart of the South China Sea filled the wide-screen display. A flashing red submarine icon marked *Novosibirsk's* current position. "What've you got, Fredek?"

"As you'll recall, yesterday Fleet sent us an updated intel report on PLAN ops in the South China Sea."

"Yes, and our projected route was clear."

"Correct, but I read the report again. There haven't been any Chinese naval operations but an oceanographic research vessel was in the area that we're now approaching."

"When?"

"Three days ago." Yermakov keyed in a command on the keyboard that operated the horizontal digital chart table. A color satellite image of the northern half of the South China Sea appeared on the display. It matched the scale of the underlying chart. A white circle was superimposed on the image. He pointed to the ring. "Fleet marked the ship's location here." Yermakov worked the keyboard again. The resolution of the digital image expanded until the hull of the ship materialized. Several personnel standing on the stern deck of the ninety-four-meter-long research ship were visible.

"What is that ship?" asked Petrovich.

"Fleet identified it as the *Lian*. Operated by the Chinese Academy of Sciences."

"So, what was it doing?"

"Unknown, sir. But there's a seamount nearby. The summit is only a couple hundred meters below the surface."

Petrovich connected the dots. "Perfect place to install a hydrophone array."

"Yes. The PLAN might be using that ship as cover to install bottom sensors. That's why I think it would be a good idea to reduce speed."

"By how much?"

"Cut it in half…to ten knots. At that speed we're a hole in the water."

Petrovich considered Yermakov's recommendation. The *Novosibirsk* was already behind schedule, due in part to the precautions Petrovich had taken to navigate through the Korea Strait and the East China Sea.

"I'll go with reducing our speed to twelve knots. Once we're past that seamount we'll pick it back up."

"Very good, sir. Permission to execute the speed reduction."

"Granted."

* * * *

"Hey, it just rounded the point."

"Wow, it's a big sucker."

"Yeah, but it's not even close to one of ours."

Yuri woke to the banter between Murphy and Halgren. He checked his wristwatch: 7:23 A.M. Amazed that he managed to sleep for several hours, he joined the SEALs. Both men peered toward the southwest with field glasses. Jeff Chang hovered beside the sailors. He also had a pair of binoculars.

"What's up?" Yuri asked.

Jeff turned toward Yuri, lowering the binocs. "You were right. Take a look." He handed the glasses to Yuri and then pointed with an outstretched arm.

Yuri spotted the ship as it rounded the distant headland that defined the southern boundary of the Shendao harbor. He pulled up the binoculars for a close-in view of the People's Republic of China aircraft carrier. "I think that's the *Shandong*," Yuri announced.

"I count five tugs," Halgren said. "Three on the bow and two astern."

"It must be dead in the water all right," Murphy added.

"Right, I don't see any smoke coming out of its stack." Halgren faced Yuri. "Your people sure did a number on that thing"

"Yes."

Yuri was tempted to remind the SEALs that he was not responsible for detonating the Yulin e-bomb but refrained. Regardless of what Yuri said, the U.S. Navy's special operators would forever link him to the mission that took out half of the PRC's South Sea Fleet with a gaggle of supercharged microwaves.

While the rest of the team watched as the 1,000-foot-long ship approached the entrance to the harbor between two breakwaters, Yuri turned his attention to the nearby pier. He noted that additional semi-trailer trucks had parked on the massive concrete deck while he slept. Two mobile cranes had also arrived, one positioned on each side of the pier near the midpoint.

No longer sparsely populated, the pier was a beehive of activity. Dozens of workers in civilian attire scurried across the twenty-one acres of concrete deck. The pier was so vast that some of the men rode bicycles to get around. Uniformed sailors and the occasional officer were also observed moving about. But it was the armed sentries that captured Yuri's attention. He counted twenty-four guards, spaced evenly along the north, west and south sides of the pier. Each man wore camouflaged fatigues and carried an assault rifle.

After scanning the nearby downslope Shendao Fleet Logistics and Support Center building and its adjacent parking lot, Yuri returned the field glasses to Chang. "Anything happening with our target area?"

"It's been quiet. Staff coming and going, appears routine."

Yuri turned his attention to Halgren. "Thanks for letting me sleep."

"No problem."

"What's the plan for today?"

"Me and Murph are going exploring." He grinned. "We're going to check out the ventilation shafts."

"During daylight?"

"Yeah, it'll be easier for us to spot sensors and other surprises the PLAN might have placed around the vents. I don't want to try the initial recon in the dark."

"Makes sense to me."

"You and Chang will hold the fort here. We'll maintain contact with our field comms." He referred to the encrypted shortrange radio headsets that each team member carried with their gear.

"Okay." The reference to comms sparked a new question. "What's the latest from Andrews?"

Halgren eyed his wristwatch. "Checked in with *Colorado* about an hour ago. They gave us the heads up on the carrier. It was already on the move. The skipper decided to bugout to deeper water. Too much activity in the area."

"Thanks for the update."

Yuri returned to where he had bedded down. After sitting on the tarp he'd placed on the ground before sleeping, he opened his backpack and searched for the food packet. As he breakfasted on the energy bar, another wave of apprehension hit. With the crippled pride of the South Sea Fleet about to arrive at its homeport, the Shendao fleet logistics complex would be under increased monitoring by PLAN security forces. *How are we ever going to pull this off?*

Colorado's retreat amplified Yuri's concern. If the team were forced to abort—or worse was discovered, the submarine was their only way out.

Nothing ever goes as planned.

What's going to go wrong next?

* * * *

Four hundred and fifty feet down the hillside and over two hundred feet underground from Yuri's position, Captain Zhou Jun and Dr. Meng Park monitored a wide-screen display in the Serpent Operations Center of S5's lower level. The home theater sized screen presented an overview of the Serpent antisubmarine network for the northern half of the South China Sea.

"Jun, I don't think this is a good idea," Ming Park said. "We don't know where that sub is now."

"I share your concern but I've been ordered to proceed."

Several hours earlier, the S5 hydrophone network lost track of the *Novosibirsk* when it reduced speed. After numerous attempts to find the submarine with acoustic sensors, Captain Zhou reported the loss of signal to the Central Military Commission headquarters in Beijing. He recommended delaying any action until the *Novosibirsk's* sound print was reacquired. The CMC ignored Zhou's suggestion. He was ordered to prosecute the attack based on the sub's projected course. Serpent Station Six was activated.

Dr. Meng checked the screen. A solid red line marked the Russian submarine's route from the Luzon Strait into the South China Sea, covering a distance of almost sixty nautical miles. Beyond that point, the line changed to a dashed red line—the projected course of the *Novosibirsk*. Scattered across the sub's estimated course were dozens of sonar contacts—commercial ships, fishing vessels and yachts.

Meng pointed to the dashed line. "Look at all these surface contacts. One or more of the Viperinas might attack them instead of the target. The system has not been tested enough to exclude that possibility."

Captain Zhou heaved a sigh. "My hands are tied, Park. Besides, the scenario you're worried about has been tested. None of the units ever malfunctioned like that."

"That's because the tests were run with single units. We've never run a test with multiple Viperinas prosecuting a coordinated attack while several surface craft operated above them."

"You're still worried about the unit to unit comms?"

"Yes. I've never been happy with the workaround. The American code was just patched. It should have been reprogrammed specifically for our use and then thoroughly tested."

After reflecting on Meng's apprehension, Zhou said, "Help me get through this current situation and then I'll request that Fleet address this specific issue, citing your concerns. If the testing reveals a problem, I'm sure Fleet will approve complete vetting of the code."

"All right."

While Captain Zhou conferred with one of his subordinates at a nearby console, Dr. Meng stared at the giant screen, focusing on an icon marking the location of Serpent Station 6. Her career was on the line, controlled by half a dozen autonomous killers patrolling the ocean depths in search of prey.

Chapter 50

From the S5 command center on Hainan Island, Captain Zhou authorized the attack command. A parabolic antenna mounted on the roof of the Shendao Fleet Logistics and Support Center building transmitted the encrypted signal to an overhead PLAN satellite. The satellite relayed the command to Tsunami Warning Buoy Station Four located in the northeast quadrant of the South China Sea. The moored buoy's microprocessor converted the radio signal to light impulses and forwarded the message via fiberoptic cable to Hydrophone Array 42. Located on the bottom two miles deep and 20 miles northeast of Stewart Seamount, the undersea station's principal function was to listen for submarines and report its findings to S5. It also served as S5's link to Serpent Station Six, which rested on the north slope of the seamount in 1,600 feet of water.

Although the majority of HA-42's equipment consisted of passive acoustic receptors, it also contained two active sonar transmitters. Responding to the S5 directive, the primary sonar unit communicated the attack code to Serpent 6 using an encrypted signal.

Station Six's hydrophone unit detected the acoustic broadcast and activated all six Viperinas. The weapons were released. They hunted in pairs.

Vipers 1 and 2 swam toward the projected course of the *Novosibirsk*. Vipers 3 and 4 took up position five miles to the northwest. V-5 and V-6 repositioned five miles to the southeast.

Upon reaching their assigned attack coordinates, each set of vipers deployed into tracking mode. One unit extended its full length horizontally— eighty-two feet—while its companion deployed vertically. The vipers eavesdropped, each set of eighty omnidirectional mini hydrophones searching for game.

Ninety-three minutes after deployment, Vipers 1 and 2 detected the *Novosibirsk's* propeller. The Russian submarine was seven nautical miles to the northeast, closing at twelve knots.

V-1 and V-2 converted to attack mode and sprinted ahead.

* * * *

Aboard the *Novosibirsk*, a bulkhead speaker in the central command post blared. "Captain, sonar. Contact dead ahead, range four kilometers."

"Sonar, Captain. What is it?" Petrovich replied using a handheld microphone.

"Unknown. No propeller cavitation or mechanical signals. More of a hydraulic flow tone. Possible biologic."

"A whale?"

"It's not like anything I've—check that. I now have sonar contacts from both the east and west of the primary. All three appear to be converging on our heading…Captain they're accelerating. Speed thirty plus knots."

"Standby sonar." Captain Petrovich turned to the officer of the watch. "Battle stations, torpedo. No drill."

The watch officer relayed the captain's order ship wide.

Novosibirsk's commanding officer turned his attention to the weapons officer at a nearby console. Petrovich fired off a series of orders.

A minute and a half later, first officer Yermakov raced into the central command post. He had been in his stateroom showering when the battle order was issued. "Captain, what's happening?" His crimson scalp was damp.

"We're about to be attacked." Petrovich pointed to the horizontal plot table. The track lines of the approaching sonar contacts inched toward the submarine icon that marked the *Novosibirsk's* location.

"Torpedoes?"

"Not like anything we've seen before. It's something new—the bastards!"

"Chinese?"

"Who else?" Petrovich turned away from Yermakov to engage the weapons officer. "Weapons, status report."

"Captain, tubes one through four ready in all respects."

"Match sonar bearings and shoot tube one, Target One."

"Match sonar bearings and shoot tube one, Target One, aye, sir."

Petrovich repeated the order for tubes two and three, directing the torpedoes toward Targets Two and Three respectively. Tube four was held in reserve.

Petrovich fired off another series of commands to the officer of the watch.

* * * *

Viperinas 1 and 2 swam parallel through the abyss six meters apart, their slender bodies undulating with synchronized serpentine locomotion. Starting at the head, each viper's linear network of mechanical-electrical muscles contracted and expanded, thrusting the body from side to side in a series of S-shaped curves. By pushing against the water at maximum output, V-1 and V-2 sprinted forward at thirty-eight knots. They communicated optically, lasers in each Viper's head trained on a band of light receptors located half a meter behind the head of its companion.

Although the sonar sensors in each Viper had locked onto their prey, a new contact was detected. V-2 signaled to its partner that it would engage the new target. V-1 diverted to the east.

V-2 prepared to attack the approaching target when the torpedo detonated.

* * * *

"Target One destroyed, Captain," shouted *Novosibirsk's* weapons officer.

"Status on Fish Two and Three." Captain Petrovich stood beside the weapons officer's console.

"Both tracking targets. Fish Two should—shit!"

"What?"

"Target One, it somehow escaped the blast. It continues to close. I don't understand . . ."

Petrovich read the tactical situation in a flash. "Two of those things might be running in tandem, possibly the same for the other directions."

"Oh God, Captain! We don't have enough torpedoes."

"Snapshot on Target One with tube four. Now!" ordered Petrovich.

"On the way!"

The *Novosibirsk's* last torpedo raced out of the tube.

* * * *

Viperina 1 was just 550 feet away when its mate, V-2, blew up. The ensuing underwater shockwave knocked out V-1's primary sonar system, leaving only the search sonar. After V-1's computer brain rebooted its sonar system, it reacquired the primary target, which had altered course and increase speed. The *Novosibirsk* sprinted eastward toward Luzon Island.

V-1 recalculated a new intercept course. The active sonar transmitter pinged the target. V-1's single remaining sonar receiver homed in on the sound reflections from the fleeing submarine. It ignored the litany of other underwater sounds that propagated through the deep, including the torpedo that closed from the northeast.

Twenty-six seconds later, 300 kilograms of high-explosive inside the warhead of the wire-guided Fish 4 from the *Novosibirsk* detonated.

* * * *

"We got it, Captain!" shouted the *Novosibirsk's* weapons officer. Everyone aboard heard the explosion, which occurred less than a mile away.

"Status on Fish Two and Three," Captain Petrovich said.

Weps started to respond when a bulkhead speaker erupted. "Captain, sonar. Fish Two and Three just detonated."

Petrovich grabbed a microphone. "Are the targets destroyed?"

"Unknown, Captain, we're moving too fast for our sensors."

"Very well. Standby."

Captain Petrovich joined his first officer at the plot table. "Recommendations, Fredek?" Petrovich asked.

"I think we should continue at flank for another ten minutes to make sure we outrun any survivors. We can then slow up and run a detailed sonar scan to check."

"I concur."

* * * *

Viperina 6 continued its pursuit after V-5 intercepted the torpedo—Fish Three. Anticipating its prey's retreat, V-6 continually calculated attack parameters. The underwater racket generated by the submarine running at thirty-five knots—forty miles per hour—provided a beacon for V-6's sonar sensors to track the target.

V-6 was in sonar contact with the other survivor—Viperina 3. V-3 was three miles west of V-6. V-3's hunting partner, V-4, had tangled with Fish Two.

The two surviving autonomous killers coordinated the hunt with sonar, utilizing algorithm's based on observations of how a wolf pack takes down elk and caribou. V-3 tracked from the west while V-6 approached from the south.

* * * *

"Officer of the watch, reduce speed to twenty knots."

The watch officer repeated Captain Petrovich's order and relayed the command to maneuvering.

"Sonar, Captain. Make a complete scan."

"Sonar, aye."

* * * *

Viperina 6's sonar detected the reduction in the turn rate of the *Novosibirsk's* propeller. V-6 slowed to reduce its sound print. Viperina 3, however, continued the pursuit.

* * * *

"Captain, sonar. Target bearing two four five degrees relative, range two point nine kilometers. Speed thirty-five knots."

Captain Petrovich fired off a series of commands to the watch officer. Within half a minute, the *Novosibirsk* turned southward, away from V-3, and accelerated to flank speed.

* * * *

Viperina 6 hovered, the trap now set. V-3 provided the diversion, driving the prey towards its hunting partner.

* * * *

"Captain, there might be more than just one of those things still left."

"I know. We'll stay on this course for five more minutes and then proceed west."

Captain Petrovich and first officer Yermakov stood caucused at the plot table. Without additional torpedoes to fend off the attack, the *Novosibirsk's* only hope for survival was to outrun the alien weapon. Or maybe not.

"Perhaps we can create a diversion," Yermakov offered.

"What do you mean?"

"Eject a couple of mines. Maybe it will home in on one of them. We'd have to slow down to eject 'em."

Petrovich pounced on the plan. "Excellent idea Fredek."

* * * *

Viperina 6 intercepted the *Novosibirsk* before the first mine could be ejected. V-6 wrapped its eighty-two-foot-long form across the top of the hull aft of the sail, straddling the missile compartment. Two dozen cruise missiles were housed inside the vertical launch tubes. Despite the submarine's velocity, V-6's half inch long titanium spikes gripped the steel hull with the vigor of a thousand pit bull terriers. Ten seconds after securing itself to the target, V-6's computer issued the detonate command to the shaped charges embedded within the length of the weapon.

All fifty-two of the individual two kilogram semtex charges ignited simultaneously, propelling hundreds of half inch diameter copper projectiles embedded within the plastic explosive into the pressure casing. Superheated slugs of molten copper sliced through the hull's high strength steel alloy. Dozens of slugs penetrated the missile compartment, one impacting the warhead of a *Kalibr* anti-ship cruise missile. The 200 kilos of high explosives detonated.

The blast triggered half a dozen other missile warheads inside the compartment. The resultant sympathetic explosions obliterated the submarine's midsection, destroying the adjacent nuclear power plant and most of the accommodations section—the crew's living quarters.

The *Novosibirsk* descended in a death spiral.

Chapter 51

"Skipper, is that what I think I'm hearing?"

Commander Tom Bowman grimaced as he responded to *Colorado's* executive officer. "It's breaking up, heading to the bottom."

"Dear Lord," muttered Jenae Mauk, horrified as the din of torn metal and collapsing bulkheads broadcast over the control room's public address system.

The *Colorado* monitored the undersea combat that took place offshore of Luzon Island in the Philippines. The submarine's network of hydrophones and sonar sensors picked up the clash, transmitted across the expanse by multiple convergence zones within a deep sound channel. Commander Bowman had directed the chief sonar tech to amplify the battle clamor so everyone in the control room could hear.

When the *Novosibirsk* bolted and launched its torpedoes, the sounds of cavitating propellers lit up *Colorado's* sonar consoles. It took just seconds for the sonar team to identify the boat as Russian—Yasen class.

"What do you think happened?" asked XO Mauk. *Colorado* heard part of the conflict. The weak acoustic sound prints from the Viperinas were lost in the background clamor from the churning submarine and its weapons. The actual battle location, however, was unknown to Colorado. Its sensors could only estimate the general direction of the underwater skirmish—from the east.

"I don't know. There was no sign of another boat."

"It was like it was fighting a ghost."

Mauk's revelation registered with Bowman. "Damn! That Russian boat might have been attacked by what *Tucson* tangled with."

Commander Mauk was about to respond when the sonar supervisor interrupted. "Captain, I'm picking up something new."

Petty Officer Second Class Richard "Richey" Anderson manned his console just a few steps from where Bowman and Mauk caucused.

"What have you got?" Bowman asked, now standing beside Anderson.

Built like a fireplug, the late twenties tech pointed at his sonar display. "Something appears to have been ejected from the hull."

"Escape capsule, skipper?" Mauk offered.

"That could be it. Yasens are rumored to be equipped with escape pods that can accommodate the entire crew." Bowman made eye contact with the sonar tech. "Richey, where's that contact now?"

"I don't know, Captain. We picked up what I assume was the initial separation but that was it. If it's heading to the surface, it's not making enough noise for us to hear."

Bowman swiped a bead of perspiration from his forehead. "Let's hope the crew made it out."

"Amen to that," Mauk said.

* * * *

Captain Petrovich and seventeen other survivors were crammed inside the top level of the escape capsule as it ascended through the deep. The four meter diameter by six meter high cylinder was formerly housed in the *Novosibirsk's* sail, aft of the bridge.

After the missile compartment exploded, it took just seconds for Captain Petrovich to assess the condition of his command. Powerless and with catastrophic flooding in the aft compartments, emergency blowing of the surviving ballast tanks could not overcome the inundation.

Petrovich issued the abandon ship command over the sub's intercom, directing all crew to the escape chamber. Most of the central post crew made it along with a handful of men who were near the sail. Shock damage to passageways and hatch doors aft of the sail doomed the few that had not already been shredded by the blast or drowned by surging seawater.

Half a minute before *Novosibirsk* reached crush depth, Petrovich sealed the capsule hatch door and triggered the explosive bolts that secured the steel chamber to the hull. Ejected from the sail, the pod began its ascent.

First officer Yermakov monitored the chamber's control panel, calling off depth levels. "Five hundred meters...four hundred... three hundred . . ."

Captain Petrovich smiled at the men clustered at his side. "It won't be long now, boys, and we'll be topside."

"One hundred meters," Yermakov called out.

Petrovich watched as the terror creased faces of his crew began to subside.

"Fifty meters."

Petrovich spotted a couple of grins. "Almost there now," he called out, his voice reassuring.

"Twenty meters."

"Hang on, boys," Captain Petrovich shouted. "When we break the surface, it might be a little rough."

The top section of the capsule emerged from the sea, abruptly ending its seventeen hundred foot ascent. All eighteen men cried out their joyous salvation in a chorus of laughter, thanks and prayers that lasted a minute.

Yermakov grinned. "We made it, Captain! A true miracle."

"Indeed."

* * * *

After registering V-6's kill, Viperina 3 rose from the depths. Its sonar detected the escape capsule when it separated from the sinking hulk of the target. V-3's AI brain construed the ascending remnant as a pending threat and returned to attack mode.

Chapter 52

"What have you got?" asked Commander Bowman. He had been summoned to *Colorado's* radio room, located adjacent to the control room. XO Mauk accompanied him.

The twenty-six-year-old radio room tech looked up from his seated position at the comms console. *Colorado's* disguised floating surface radio antenna maintained a secure link to Pearl Harbor. "Sir, COMSUBPAC just reported picking up an emergency DISSUB beacon. GPS coordinates are consistent with the Russian boat's operating area."

"Advise COMSUBPAC that the beacon might be from a Russian submarine escape pod."

"Aye, aye, Captain."

Bowman and Mauk returned to the horizontal large screen display in the control room.

"Maybe the crew survived," Mauk said.

"The beacon is a good sign."

"Who do you think is going to rescue them? I don't know of any nearby Russian assets."

"Probably the Philippines. I expect COMSUBPAC will be talking with Manila soon, issuing an international disabled sub alert."

"Skipper, what if the PLAN shows up instead? I don't think that will go over well with the survivors."

"That would be ironic alright."

* * * *

Captain Zhou Jun, Dr. Meng Park and a dozen staff were inside the S5 subterranean operations center at Shendao, Hainan Island. They all focused on the flat-panel wide-screen display secured to a nearby wall. Live video images transmitted from a Y-8FQ PLA-Navy maritime patrol aircraft filled the monitor.

"There it is," shouted the S5 duty officer, pointing to the upper left corner of the screen. The escape pod surged through the water-air interface in the morning sun, rising beyond the midpoint of the vertical steel cylinder before re-submerging. The pod repeated the oscillation several times before reaching buoyant equilibrium. The crown of the twenty foot high capsule was about four feet above the sea surface.

"The Vipers took out the sub!" announced Captain Zhou, officially confirming the kill.

Jubilation erupted from the assembled. Handshakes and high fives broke out.

Zhou saluted Meng Park as the S5 watch officer approached. "Congratulations, Captain. Serpent worked perfectly."

"The thanks belong to Dr. Meng. This whole project is her brainchild."

Zhou's deputy turned toward Meng and bowed. "Brilliant concept, Dr. Meng."

Meng Park smiled. "Thank you." She turned back to view the screen; it displayed a close-up view of the bobbing escape pod.

Dazzled by what had transpired, euphoria flooded Meng's senses. *It really worked!*

Meng and Zhou had observed Serpent's attack remotely. The network of seafloor hydrophones scattered throughout the South China Sea allowed real time monitoring of the hunt. Zhou had supplemented the bottom listening stations with sonobuoys dropped from the Y-8FQ that orbited above the underwater battlefield. Terabytes of acoustic energy data poured into S5 every minute via satellite, allowing the S5 supercomputers to generate three-dimensional positions of all six attacking Viperinas and the Russian sub. Unlike the *Novosibirsk* or the *Colorado,* S5 had the decrypt key that allowed eavesdropping of the Vipers' machine to machine acoustic comms.

Meng focused on the rescue capsule, wondering when the survivors would open the top hatch. She was about to ask Zhou a question when she noticed the disturbance in the water near the pod. Something was just below the surface, orbiting the pod in steadily decreasing radii.

"Oh my god!" Meng screamed.

* * * *

"What's that noise?" called out one of the submariners inside the escape capsule.

Captain Petrovich heard the scraping racket, too. "Quiet everyone," he ordered. He touched the steel wall of the chamber. He could feel the vibration in the tips of his fingers. *What's that?* he wondered.

With a suppressed tone, Yermakov said, "Captain, maybe someone from a passing boat is securing a line to the pod."

"Let's hope so."

The metallic rasp stopped, rendering the interior of the capsule silent. To a man, the bliss of impending rescue was the universal—and last—thought of the *Novosibirsk's* survivors.

* * * *

"WOW!" shouted the *Colorado's* sonar supervisor.

"What?" demanded Commander Bowman. He stood next to the horizontal large screen display. Executive officer Mauk was at his side.

"Captain, I just picked up another explosion." Petty Officer Anderson pulled down his headphones.

"Where?" Bowman asked as he and Mauk joined the sonar supervisor

"Same general area as the Yasen," Anderson said.

"Ordnance detonating in the bottom wreckage?"

"No sir. It was a surface blast."

"The rescue capsule?"

Anderson looked up, facing the captain. "Maybe. I'm going to replay the event." He worked his keyboard and the sharp crack of an explosion broadcast from an overhead loudspeaker.

"My god, Tom," muttered Mauk. "They wouldn't self-destruct, would they?"

Commander Bowman did not respond, lost in his thoughts. *What the hell's going on?*

Chapter 53

"Park, are you okay?"

Meng Park knelt at the toilet bowl and retched again.

Captain Zhou Jun stood on the other side of the lavatory door. "Let me know if I can help."

After five minutes, Meng joined Zhou in the corridor. They were alone. "I'm sorry," she said. "I couldn't help myself."

Zhou slipped an arm around Park's waist and pulled her close. "I regret you had to witness that."

Seared in Dr. Meng's memory, the horror endured. Viperina 3 had swirled around the escape pod just below the water surface. Like a gargantuan boa constrictor, V-3 gripped the cylinder's steel hull with its metallic claws. The PLAN patrol aircraft had swooped in for a closer view of the pod when the weapon detonated. The shockwave from the blast rocked the four engine plane with the vengeance of a Cat 5 hurricane. The live video feed from the Y-8FQ had flashed to a sheet of static on the wide screen monitor in the S5 ops center.

It took the airborne camera operator about a minute to reboot the system before new images materialized on the S5 video display. The rescue pod had vanished. In its wake, several corpses and a collection of body parts littered the frothy waters.

"It should never have come to the surface," Park said.

"I understand. We'll figure it out and fix it."

"All of those men—torn to pieces."

Zhou again hugged Meng. "Just give it time," he whispered. "The bad memories will fade."

Park buried her brow in Jun's shoulder. He comforted her as best he could. But he too suffered.

During Zhou's twenty plus years as an officer in the People's Liberation Army-Navy, he had never experienced combat. The visceral images he witnessed today would remain with him for the rest of his life.

* * * *

While Meng and Zhou embraced, Yuri Kirov stepped gingerly on their native ground about one hundred feet above the couple. He followed Master Chief Halgren. It was late morning.

Jeff Chang and Murphy were one hundred and thirty yards upslope, serving as lookouts. They kept an eye on the nearby Fleet Logistics building but a new arrival captured most of their attention. The *Shandong* loomed beyond the three story structure. The wounded aircraft carrier had docked several hours earlier. The Shendao pier buzzed with activity as work crews boarded the ship and sailors milled on the pier deck.

Yuri and Wild Bill approached one of the shafts that ventilated S5. The holes were concealed within the dense undergrowth of the tropical canopy. Four 0.75-meter (30-inch) diameter vertical steel tubes extended downward from ground level to the ceiling of the underground complex. Two downhill shafts served as air intakes. The uphill tubes discharged excess heat and stale air.

Halgren stopped beside the vent. Yuri joined the SEAL. The rush of warm air flowing from the pipe brushed Yuri's cheek.

"This is the one we want to use," Halgren whispered. He and Murphy had located the shafts earlier in the morning during a recon patrol.

Yuri examined the open end of the exhaust port. The pipe jutted two feet above the ground. A galvanized steel mesh matching the diameter of the pipe lay on the dirt. During the SEALs earlier look-see, they had disconnected the anti-critter mesh. They also checked the vent and the surrounding grounds and vegetation for electronic sensors, motion and ground pressure detectors in particular. Finding nothing, both operators hoped they had not missed something.

Yuri peered into the tube—a black hole. He grabbed his flashlight and illuminated the pipe's interior. That's when he spotted the steel grill twenty feet down. One inch diameter steel dowels welded to the pipe and spaced every five inches provided a low-tech access barrier while allowing for the flow of exhaust.

"Govnó," Yuri muttered. He turned to Halgren. "You're right. That's going to be a bitch to get through."

"We've got thermite, which will blow through those bars. But that damn stuff will keep going. If it gets into the ventilation fans below, who knows what kind of alarms that will set off."

"Maybe we can work out a way to capture the excess."

"I don't know...that shit is wicked, burns through everything."

Maybe not everything, Yuri thought. "Let me think on it some more. Anyway, let's run the camera down and take a look."

"Okay."

****

Dr. Meng and Captain Zhou were next to Zhou's BMW in the Fleet Logistics parking lot.

"I just need to rest for a while," Meng said.

"If you're too tired for dinner tonight, that's okay with me."

"No. I'm looking forward to that."

"Okay, great." He gave Park the key to his sedan.

"I'll come back and pick you up," she offered.

"Don't bother. I'll get a ride to Sanya from one of my staff. Seven o'clock okay with you?"

"Fine." Meng kissed Zhou on the cheek. "See you tonight." She opened the door and climbed into the automobile.

****

"I don't frigging believe it," Jeff Chang said as he watched the BMW exit the parking lot.

"What?" asked Murphy. He squatted nearby, working on an MRE— Meal Ready to Eat.

The CIA officer and the SEAL staffed the team's observation post. Yuri and Halgren were still downslope, investigating the S5 vents.

Chang lowered the Nikon 35 millimeter camera with a telephoto lens. "I just noticed something very interesting in the parking lot."

"Oh yeah," Malibu Murph said now peering through an opening in the vegetation. The asphalt lot was only a quarter full. Maybe twenty vehicles. He observed a uniformed male walking toward the Fleet Logistics building.

Chang pointed west. "That officer walking back to the building runs S5. Captain Zhou Jun."

"Son of a bitch!"

Zhou was in charge of the South Sea Sound Surveillance System. But it was the female who had accompanied the navy captain that supercharged Chang's interest.

Jeff worked the Nikon, retrieving one of the dozen images he had just recorded. "Hello there, little sea turtle!" Jeff muttered as he studied a digital blowup of Meng Park's lovely face.

* * * *

Yuri and Halgren returned to the observation post. The two SEALs and Yuri currently debated how best to penetrate the S5 ventilation shafts.

Master Chief Halgren said, "We can blast through the steel bars with our shaped charges but the racket will reverberate through the pipe. Probably sound like thunder inside S5."

"Maybe we can muffle the blast," offered CPO Murphy.

"Doubtful. That shaft is a perfect sound conductor." Halgren fingered the stubble on his chin. "We don't have any choice, Murph. We have to use thermite."

"I hate working with that stuff."

"I read you." Halgren engaged Yuri. "What's your take?"

"Thermite is probably our best approach but controlling the discharge will be the challenge. We might be able to construct a tray that hangs under the bars to catch the debris."

"A tray made out of what?" Halgren asked.

Yuri started to respond when Jeff Chang finally jumped in. "Maybe we don't need to get inside S5 after all."

That captured Halgren's instant attention. "What do you mean?"

"Half an hour ago, we spotted the officer in charge of S5 in the parking lot. Captain Zhou Jun. Runs the entire network."

"Snatch him?" Halgren asked.

"We could but the real prize is the woman he was with." He pulled up the Nikon and displayed a digital photograph. "This is Dr. Meng Park. She's a research professor at the the University of Science and Technology of China. She's the brains behind the S5 ASW system."

"She's young," Yuri offered. "How'd she pull that off?"

"You're right. She's only thirty-four. He passed the camera to Halgren. "She's what we call a Sea Turtle."

"And what's that?" Wild Bill Halgren asked as he viewed the digital photo of Meng Park.

"You know the story. Tens of thousands of baby turtles are hatched on a beach. They waddle into the ocean while birds and other critters pick 'em off left and right. Anyway, the turtles spend years at sea before finally returning to their ancestral shores to lay eggs and repeat the entire process.

Halgren handed the camera to Murphy.

Jeff continued the story, "Our little turtle here was born in Beijing. Received her undergraduate degree in electrical engineering. Moved to the USA where she earned a PhD—at MIT no less. Specialized in robotics. Had a postdoc at CAL Berkeley working on unmanned underwater vehicles for oceanographic research. She then went to work for a Bay Area R & D robotics company. That's where we think she finally fulfilled her mission."

"A spy?" Yuri asked.

"More of an obligation to the motherland. We think she managed to get access to another researcher's work, classified stuff for the U.S. Air Force on drones. Something to do with controlling swarms of drones based on natural systems like flocks of birds and schools of fish."

"Let me guess, Yuri said. "She got what she was looking for and took it home with her."

"Correct. Returned after years in the States, bearing a precious gift for the homeland."

"Let's snatch her, too!" Malibu Murph offered.

Chapter 54

Day 35—Tuesday

Master Chief Halgren had the mid watch—midnight to four o'clock. It was 1:25 A.M. The others were asleep, bedded down around the perimeter of the observation post.

After contacting *Colorado* and reporting the issues related to breaching the S5 air shafts and the unintended observation of Dr. Meng, the team was placed on hold. Lieutenant Commander Andrews needed to run Chang's proposed change of mission plan up the chain of command. The men welcomed the downtime.

Standing behind foliage, Halgren peered down the hillside. Like the previous evening, the Fleet Logistics building was sparsely lit. The carrier pier, however, radiated enough light to rival an NFL stadium on game night. Supplementing the pole mounted deck floodlights was an army of new portable lighting. Vehicles rushed across the 900,000 square foot deck, delivering equipment and supplies. Workmen scurried about the *Shandong*.

Three of the feared sea drones also showed up. The cabin-less runabouts were each thirty-three feet long. Equipped with a bow-mounted machine gun turret, torpedo and depth bomb launchers, and a tall mast populated with video cameras, dual radar domes, GPS unit, and multiple secure radio comms, the autonomous surface vessels—ASVs—mimicked similar robotic systems deployed by the U.S. Navy.

The unmanned boats patrolled the harbor. Nav lights and the deep throated snarl of turbo diesels marked the watercraft as they plied the waters near the *Shandong*.

Halgren returned to his collection of gear stashed a couple of meters away from where Murphy slept. He slipped on his helmet with its night vision device. He next grabbed a trenching tool and the precious roll of toilet paper he'd squirreled away in his backpack. He needed to relieve himself—the first time since departing the *Colorado*.

Wild Bill lowered the NVD visor and proceeded upslope. He left his M4 behind, relying on the Heckler & Koch Mark 23 pistol strapped to his right thigh.

Halgren found a suitable location twenty yards from the OP. He excavated a shallow pit. After finishing his business, he pulled up his trousers and reached for the shovel. His right hand had just gripped the handle when a blistering sting erupted in his wrist. "Dammit!" he cried out.

Halgren searched the ground with his NVD. Whatever bit him had already retreated into the undergrowth. He held up his wrist. A pair of punctures, each with a dribble of blood, marked the attack site. He touched the wounds and cursed again. His wrist was on fire.

What shit luck this is!

Halgren collected his gear and started downhill. By the time he reached the encampment, his wrist had noticeably swollen, and blood still flowed from the punctures.

* * * *

Yuri woke, aroused by the chatter of the SEALs.

"It looks nasty, Bill," Murphy said. Both men huddled near the satellite phone antenna. Murphy used a shielded flashlight to examine the wound.

"Hurts like hell."

"Did you see it?"

"No. I'd just taken a dump and was reaching for the shovel when the bitch got me. Never saw it."

"A double puncture...has to be a snake."

"No kidding."

Yuri joined the SEALs, dropping to his knees. "May I see the bite mark?"

Murphy handed him the flashlight. Yuri examined Halgren's right wrist. He returned the light. "I think it might have been a pit viper. Blood from the wound isn't coagulating, which suggests a hemotoxin. We were warned about them on the Yulin mission."

"I concur," Murphy said.

"Besides clotting problems, hemotoxins will kill blood cells, causing the skin and tissue around the punctures to die."

Halgren swore yet again.

Yuri looked at the wounded SEAL. "Master chief, you need immediate medical aid."

"That's right," Murphy added. "I'm calling *Colorado* with a sitrep."

Halgren knew where that action would lead. "No. Don't do that Murph. I can tough it out."

"No way, man. With that shit in you, if it's not treated right you could end up losing your arm or worse. We need to get back to the sub ASAP."

The talk finally woke Jeff Chang. He joined the group. "What's going on?" he asked.

Malibu Murph answered, aiming the flashlight at Halgren's wrist. "Snake bite. Bad one. He needs to be evacuated now. The mission's over."

* * * *

It took half an hour to reestablish comms with the *Colorado*. Wearing a headset, Murphy briefed Andrews on the situation. "Sir, Bill's stable but he's in a hell of a lot of pain."

"Is he mobile?" asked the lieutenant commander.

"He can walk but he's miserable. His entire forearm has swollen up and the punctures are still bleeding."

"Can he get to the Mark 11?"

"We'll get him to the beach. When can you get it in position?"

"I need to confer with the captain. I'll get back to you."

"I'd step on it if you can. I think Bill has a shit load of venom inside him. He's needs help ASAP. The anti-venom we have in our med kits hasn't done anything."

"Understand, Chief. Put Chang on please."

"Hang on."

Murph and Jeff exchanged the headset.

"Chang here."

"I ran your idea up the flagpole. Washington's interested." Earlier in the evening Jeff had briefed Andrews on the Dr. Meng Park issue. Andrews said, "Is there any real chance you can get to her—the secrets she must know."

"If she comes back here, maybe. But she could also be spending time in Sanya at that maritime center or worse, on her way back to her lab on the mainland."

"Jeff, I can't go into details now but S5 went active yesterday. Took out a Russian sub in the South China Sea near Luzon Island. We heard it all from here. COMSUBPAC is conferring with his chain of command on our next steps."

"So, our mission is still on?" Chang asked.

"Yes, it's even more important than before."

"Will Murphy be coming back?"

"Yes. And I'll be joining him as Halgren's replacement."

"Got it."

"Tell Murph I'll be calling back soon with an update on the Mark 11's ETA."

"Roger that."

After Andrews signed off, Jeff checked Halgren. Stretched out on a ground cloth, Wild Bill gritted his teeth.

Jeff turned toward Murphy. Despite the darkness, he made eye contact. "Andrews is checking on the arrival time of the Mark 11. He'll be calling back soon."

"Okay, great."

Jeff glanced Yuri's way. "I guess you heard part of the conversation. The mission is still on and Andrews seemed really interested in our Sea Turtle. I expect we'll be getting a mission update soon as well."

Before Yuri could respond, Murphy said, "So, we're not bugging out?"

"No. In fact, Andrews said he was coming back with you after transferring Bill to the *Colorado*."

Murphy nodded and returned to Halgren's side.

Yuri addressed the CIA officer. "Something else has happened, hasn't it?" Like Murphy had earlier speculated, Yuri also expected the mission to be cancelled—too many unknowns to proceed.

Jeff lowered his voice. "Andrews said S5 just went active. It took out a sub...a Russian boat."

"*Govnó!*"

Chapter 55

The *Heilong* was 365 meters—about 1,200 feet—below the surface cruising northwestward at five knots. Avacha Bay was fourteen nautical miles ahead. The Russian port city of Petropavlovsk-Kamchatskiy lay on the north shore of the bay just beyond its entrance from the North Pacific Ocean.

Commander Yang Yu sat in his captain's chair inside the submarine's attack center. The tension in the compartment had heightened. The sixteen officers and sailors manning the consoles and work stations inside the control room were all aware that the *Heilong* was approaching the enemy's lair. The ship had visited these waters earlier in the year on a recon patrol. Its current mission called for hostile action.

"Maneuvering, all stop," ordered Yang.

The officer of the deck repeated Yang's order and implemented the command.

"Helm, hover in place," Yang said next.

"Hover in place, aye."

Yang turned to address the sonar technician who manned a nearby console. "Sonar, report."

The CPO swiveled in his chair. "Captain, we continue to track Warship One-Six. Range thirteen kilometers, course two seven three, speed twenty knots. Also tracking Commercial contact Eight-Nine. Range sixty-seven kilometers, course two seven zero, speed twelve knots. No other traffic on our screens."

"Very well. Report any new activity."

Heilong's executive officer approached Yang. "Looks like One-Six is heading home."

"That's to be expected. There aren't any other port facilities this far north."

Heilong detected the Russian guided missile destroyer ten hours earlier. The warship cruised northward, following the Kamchatskiy Peninsula's eastern coastline.

Lieutenant Commander Zheng Qin checked his wristwatch. "Captain, we've got three hours before deployment. With your permission, I'd like to have Weapons run another complete systems check on the *Shing Long*. If anomalies come up, that will provide time to remedy the problem."

"All right, you may proceed. But if anything negative does show up, I want to know about it immediately."

"Understood, Captain."

After XO Zheng departed for the Weapons compartment, Yang relocated to the adjacent plot table. The horizontal flat-panel screen displayed an electronic chart of the waters offshore of Petropavlovsk-Kamchatskiy. A red submarine icon exhibited the *Heilong's* position, located just beyond Russia's territorial waters as directed by Beijing. The Russian destroyer approaching Avacha Bay was marked with a fluorescent orange warship symbol. A canary yellow icon identified the commercial vessel approaching from the south. The South Korean break bulk cargo ship from Pusan would pass near the submarine's position in approximately three hours. The *Shing Long* would be waiting.

When the Korean ship cruised by overhead, the autonomous underwater vehicle would ascend from the deep and take up position just aft of the freighter's propeller. Racket generated from the whirling prop and the ship's noisy diesel engine would mask the *Shing Long's* already minuscule acoustic signature.

Commander Yang worked the plot table's keyboard, replacing the chart with a high resolution satellite photo of the Rybachiy submarine base. Superimposed on the photo was a bright red line that marked the pre-planned course of the autonomous underwater vehicle in Avacha Bay. The Central Military Commission specified the target location, identified with a red star.

Once inside Avacha Bay, the *Shing Long* would break away from the freighter and transport the nuclear bomb to the exact coordinates specified by the CMC. After flooding its ballast tanks, the autonomous underwater vehicle would settle onto the mud bottom and wait for further orders.

* * * *

The fifteen-foot-long "spybot" swam out of a torpedo tube and proceeded northward. Tethered to its host with a fiber-optic cable, the remotely operated vehicle carried a high definition video camera along with acoustic and laser-based sensors. The data collected was transmitted by the cable to the *Mississippi's* control room.

Chapter 56

Yuri stood at the water's edge with Jeff Chang. They had the remote beach to themselves—no drunken teenagers to worry about this night.

The sea was calm, just tiny wavelets brushing the broad sandy beach. The three-quarter full moon hung over the distant horizon, abating the darkness. Both men perspired profusely. A breeze would have been welcome to mitigate the stagnant tepid heat.

Murphy and Halgren were chest deep in the water about eighty feet from shore, both geared up for the dive including rucksacks and weapons. Murphy dropped below the surface where he slipped fins onto Halgren's rubber booties. It was a task impossible for the master chief to undertake himself; his injured arm useless. Murphy surfaced. He peered landward and raised his right hand with the thumb pointed down.

"There's the signal," Yuri whispered.

The SEALs submerged.

"I don't know about this," Chang offered. "Halgren's going downhill fast."

"He's tough. He'll make it."

Yuri and Jeff turned around and headed upland.

* * * *

Murphy kept a close watch on his partner, using a portable dive light. Halgren appeared stable. They were inside the passenger compartment of the SEAL Delivery Vehicle. They had switched from their rebreathers to the SDV's onboard compressed air system. Murphy wore a full face mask while Halgren used a standard scuba regulator. Wild Bill waved off Murphy when he tried to strap a full face mask on him.

Nearly an hour earlier the two men swam aboard the wet minisub. Driller and Runner had guided the Mark 11 close to shore to minimize Halgren's swim.

"How's he doing," copilot Chief Dillon asked over the intercom.

"Good," Murphy said. "Right, Bill?"

Halgren signaled he was okay with his working hand. The earphone in his dive hood piped in the cross talk. Lacking a full face mask, he could not speak.

"We're fifteen minutes from rendezvousing with *Colorado*."

"Roger that," Murphy said.

Eight minutes away from the sub, Halgren struggled with the mouthpiece to his regulator.

Murphy shifted closer, unsure of what had happened. That's when he noticed Halgren had spat out his mouthpiece. Murphy reached for one of the backup regulators plumbed to the Mark 11's onboard air tank. He shoved the emergency breathing device toward his partner just as a torrent of white fluid erupted from Halgren's mouth.

Oh shit!

After vomiting and involuntary inhaling seawater, Halgren convulsed. His body thrashed inside the confines of the passenger compartment.

"Bill's in trouble," Murphy shouted into his dive mask microphone. "Surface—SURFACE NOW!"

* * * *

The SDV bobbed on the moonlit sea.

"How's Bill?" Runner asked over the intercom system. Senior Chief Aaron Baker piloted the Mark 11.

"He's unconscious," CPO Ryan Murphy reported from the passenger compartment. He held Wild Bill's head above the water.

"Is he still breathing?" Runner asked.

"I think so but we've got to get him aboard the sub now or we're going to lose him."

"Don's sending *Colorado* a sitrep right now."

"Tell 'em to hustle. He doesn't have much time left."

* * * *

The *Colorado* emerged from the deep a hundred yards east of the Mark 11. The submarine was in a partial surfaced configuration with only five feet of freeboard between the top of the sail and the sea surface.

Within five minutes the SDV was twenty feet away from the sub. An inflatable rubber raft stored in an exterior sail locker was in the water next to the hull. After inflating Halgren's horse collar buoyancy compensator, Murph extracted Wild Bill from the passenger compartment and towed him to the raft. Sailors manning the inflatable hauled the unconscious SEAL aboard.

Once inside the raft, another team inside the sail's bridge cockpit assisted with the transfer of Halgren onto the *Colorado's* bridge. Finally, he was lowered down the sail's tunnel to the pressure casing and rushed to sickbay.

All total, it took eight minutes after surfacing for the *Colorado* to reclaim the injured SEAL. SSN 788 promptly submerged followed by the Mark 11 SDV with Murph aboard. It was eight minutes of exposure that *Colorado's* captain dreaded.

* * * *

"Captain, the Mark 11 is secure in the shelter. All divers are locked-in." *Colorado's* executive officer reported from a compartment aft of the sail. Commander Jenae Mauk had remotely managed the retrieval operation of the SDV. Besides the SEALs, three sailors trained as divers from the *Colorado* assisted in returning the minisub to the dry deck shelter.

"What's the status of our injured SEAL?"

"I'm on my way to sickbay now."

"When you finish, I need you back here ASAP."

"Understood, skipper."

Commander Bowman returned the microphone to its receptacle by the control room workstation. He addressed the officer of the deck. "Proceed with the exit plan, Mr. Marshall."

"Aye aye, Captain." The lieutenant began issuing a series of commands to the pilot and copilot, following Bowman's previously issued procedures to exit hostile waters.

While on the surface, *Colorado* was "painted" with a search radar emanating from the Yulin Naval Base. Only five nautical miles away, the newly installed radar unit was in direct response to the e-bomb attack. Bowman prayed that the operator manning the radar would interpret the reflection from the sail's minimal above water exposure as nothing more than a fishing vessel.

But he couldn't take that risk. Expecting a possible response, he cancelled the Mark 11's return trip to shore and ordered its retrieval. It was time for *Colorado* to disappear.

"Captain, I've got high speed propellers."

"From where?"

Petty Officer Anderson studied the sonar waterfall display on his console while listening with a set of Bose headphones. "Not sure yet. Appears to be a vessel coming out of the Yulin Naval Base."

"Patrol craft?" Bowman said, now at Anderson's side.

"Maybe, it's noisy. Sounds like twin diesels. It could be—no, wait, I've got another one. Similar signature. This one's coming from Shendao."

Bowman barked new orders, "Officer of the deck, full ahead on current course. Make turns for thirty knots. Do not cavitate."

The OOD repeated the order and *Colorado* began speeding ahead.

Chapter 57

Three thousand miles northeast of the South China Sea, the *Heilong* prepared to execute the final element of its mission. The attack center's apprehension index reached supercharged status.

Commander Yang Yu and executive officer Zheng Qin gawked at the electronic chart. "What are they doing?" asked Lieutenant Commander Zheng.

"Must be delaying for the pilot."

The yellow icon on the digital display marked the position of the Korean cargo ship from Pusan. It was half a mile east of the *Heilong*. The ship had slowed to a crawl. The *Heilong* matched the freighter's speed; earlier it had ascended to one hundred meters depth.

"Why do they need a pilot for such a small port?"

"Must be its size. I don't think many hundred and sixty meter ships call at Petropavlovsk."

"Captain, new contact," called out the sonar tech. "Range twenty-four kilometers, course one two two, speed twenty-five knots."

Yang stepped to the sonar section. "What is it?"

"Twin engine, diesels, probably less than twenty meters. Projected course intercepts the Korean ship. Ah captain, this might be the pilot boat."

"Very well. Continue to monitor."

The executive officer cracked a grin. "So, we start deployment now?"

"Yes, proceed."

* * * *

Twenty meters above the *Heilong's* aft deck, the probe from the USS *Mississippi* spied on the undersea warship. The spybot was connected to SSN 782 with a fiberoptic cable; the probe pumped a steady stream of data to the Virginia class submarine that lurked two miles away. Included in the digital flow were infrared images of the Chinese sub's hull.

The sensor operator aboard the *Mississippi* focused on the appendage jutting from the Type 095's hull aft of the sail. The hemispherical door at the aft end of the external chamber opened. Half a minute later an AUV swam out.

The *Shing Long* rose ten meters above its transport pod. It hovered for half a minute before proceeding eastward toward the Korean freighter.

On command from the *Mississippi,* the spybot's computer brain switched operational modes from ROV (remotely operated vehicle) to AUV (autonomous underwater vehicle). The probe severed the cable and began following the *Shing Long.*

Chapter 58

Yuri Kirov and Jeff Chang crouched by the SATCOM radio. They had returned to the hillside observation post two hours earlier at sunrise. Yuri listened as the CIA officer attempted to reestablish contact with the *Colorado*.

After half a dozen attempts, Jeff turned toward Yuri. "Still no response. Something's wrong."

"They may have had to go offline for a while. Let's give it a rest. We'll try again in an hour."

"Okay." Jeff yawned while stretching his arms.

"Take a nap. I'll keep watch."

"Thanks."

Yuri peered through an opening in the brush. Downslope he spotted another vehicle as it pulled into the parking lot of the Fleet Logistics building. Yuri suspected a shift change. Beyond the building, workers scurried about the massive warship moored to the pier. Around the clock repairs to the *Shandong* were underway.

Yuri took a swig from his canteen. It was nearly empty. The team was low on supplies. Chief Murphy accompanied by Lieutenant Commander Andrews were tasked with resupplying the OP with extra water and MREs. Until they returned, Jeff and Yuri would ration the remaining supplies. Thankfully, Murphy and Halgren left their extra water and MREs behind.

Yuri and Jeff had hidden in the brush above the beach, waiting for the SEALs to emerge from the water. But they were a no show. Just before sunup, they had hoofed it back to the OP.

Something's wrong.

The missed rendezvous with the returning SEALs worried Yuri—and Jeff. *I hope Halgren made it.*

Yuri suspected the SEAL's injury delayed Murphy and Andrews's return trip to Hainan Island.

They'll be back tonight.

Maybe, maybe not.

After starting the mission, Yuri had managed to repress his negative thoughts. But they now resurfaced.

Maybe something happened to the Colorado.

What if Murph and Andrews don't come back?

How the hell will we get out of here?

Jeff's Chinese and speaks Mandarin. He's got a chance. But me—no way!

Yuri closed his eyes and commenced a series of breathing exercises, his attempt to flush demon thoughts. After a couple of minutes, he opened his eyes. The wave of dread had dissipated.

Another vehicle pulled into the parking lot. He watched as the passenger exited from a rear door of the taxicab. Yuri pulled up a pair of field glasses and trained them on the female in the red dress.

Meng Park's face snapped into focus.

* * * *

"Anything new on the contact?" asked Dr. Meng. She had just joined Captain Zhou, returning to S5 via taxi. Zhou left her hotel room two hours earlier, driving his BMW to the base.

"No. None of our hydrophones have picked up anything. Same for the drones."

Meng Park and Zhou Jun were in Zhou's S5 underground office. She sat in a chair beside his desk. Park wore a crimson pencil skirt cut two inches above her knees. "Maybe it was a false reading."

"I don't think so. I reviewed the radar recording—it was real. Tracked it for eight minutes before it went off the screen. Disappeared like a ghost."

"A partially surfaced sub with just the fin exposed?"

"Yes, that's my assessment."

Park crossed her legs. "Americans?"

"I'm sure of it. Probably one of their new boats or maybe a Seawolf."

"What would they be doing?"

"Reconnaissance."

"That's bold of them—coming inside our territorial waters."

Zhou raised his hands. "S5 was designed to detect intruders like this long before they ever enter our waters. But it failed to track this one."

Meng cast an encouraging smile. "Jun, we know the system works. It tracked the Russian boat."

"Yes, but it's the Americans that are the worry. They patrol the South China Sea with impunity. Right now, I have no idea what they're up to. S5 was supposed to take care of it."

Meng considered her lover's dilemma. "Maybe the hydrophones are spaced too far apart. Adding more bottom units might fill in the coverage gaps."

"We're considering that but I'm worried it won't be enough."

"Why's that?"

"I'm beginning to think the Americans know where all of our hydrophones are located."

That possibility had not occurred to Meng. "If that's true, the entire S5 network including Serpent could be compromised."

"Exactly."

* * * *

"How's he doing?" asked *Colorado's* commanding officer. He was in his cabin, seated at the compact desk. Executive officer Jenae Mauk stood in the open doorway.

"Still unconscious but finally stable." Mauk returned from another visit to sickbay. "He inhaled a lot of water. Doc thinks both lungs are damaged, which happens with near drownings."

"What about the snakebite?"

"His right arm is in terrible shape. Forearm from wrist to elbow is swollen and it's started to turn black around the punctures. Looks awful."

"Prognosis?"

"Doc says he's at the limit of his abilities. In order to save the chief's arm, he needs to be hospitalized immediately. So, I guess that means we'll be heading to the Philippines."

Bowman signaled for Mauk to step inside and close the door.

"Jenae, I didn't want to discuss this in front of the control room crew." He gestured to the computer monitor sitting on the desk. "We can't get the chief to shore yet. New orders from COMSUBPAC. I just decrypted the message." Bowman turned the Dell toward Mauk.

She stepped forward and leaned over. It took a minute to speed-read the directive from Pearl Harbor. "Wow, that's a tall order, skipper. They expect us to do all of it by ourselves?"

"For now, yes. We don't have any other boats in the area."

"Well, after that encounter with those drones, the Chinese know we're in their backyard."

"I'm sure they have raised their defense posture but it's unlikely they ID'd us specifically. Just a fraction of the sail was exposed."

For nearly two hours, autonomous surface vessels from Yulin and Shendao had probed the waters offshore of Hainan Island with active sonar. High powered pings from the unmanned patrol boats saturated the water column across a five-mile radius centered on the radar coordinates of *Colorado's* sail when it surfaced to rescue Halgren.

Even with the ASVs' coordinated search, SSN 788 evaded discovery thanks to Commander Bowman's skill and the sound absorbing rubberlike tiles that covered *Colorado's* hull.

Commander Mauk processed the new orders. "What about the guys still on Hainan. How are they going to get out?"

"They're on their own for the time being. We're not heading back to pick them up."

Taken aback, Mauk arched her eyebrows. "Okay, so I gather the entire Shendao op is suspended?"

"Correct."

"Do they know yet?"

"No." Bowman checked his wristwatch. "I'm going to brief Andrews next. He can tell them."

"So, I assume you want me to start preparing target packages."

"Affirmative. "

* * * *

"He's still unconscious but stable." SEAL team leader Andrews called from the *Colorado*. He reestablished secure comms with the shore team half a minute earlier. It was late morning.

"How's his arm?" asked Jeff Chang.

"Still swollen. The ship's medic is pumping meds through IVs. Antibiotics, anti-inflammatories, and other stuff."

"Antivenom?"

"Yes, but it's the same drug Murph administered."

"He needs to be in a hospital."

"Agreed. We're working towards that but we have another task here to take care of that's going to require us to bugout for a while."

"You're leaving...what about us?"

"Not my call. Can't provide any details but the op has been suspended. You two will need to sit tight."

"We're kind of low on supplies."

"Conserve what you've got. I'll know more soon. Plan for a call from me at 1300 hours."

"But we have some new—"

Andrews cut Chang off. "Sorry, they're telling me I've got to end the call. Talk to you at 1300." The line went dead.

Jeff returned the handset to the satphone console and muttered a curse. He turned to Yuri. "I guess you got the gist of that call."

Gist was not a word in Yuri's vocabulary nevertheless he figured it out. "We're marooned."

"Right, that about sums it up."

* * * *

As scheduled, Lieutenant Commander Andrews checked in with the shore team. He reported Halgren was stable. Andrews also notified Jeff Chang and Yuri that it might be a week before the *Colorado* could return to retrieve them. He offered no explanation other than that the submarine was on a new mission that took priority. And when Jeff reported that Meng Park had returned to S5, Andrews wasn't interested. COMSUBPAC cancelled the mission.

"Something big must have happened to pull the sub off our op," Jeff offered.

While peering downslope at the *Shandong* Yuri replied, "With all the new troops, something obviously spooked the Chinese."

About an hour earlier, a couple of military trucks drove onto the pier and discharged two dozen armed soldiers, doubling the existing contingent of sentries.

"Not a good sign," Jeff said.

Yuri turned back. "I'm now wondering if the minisub or the *Colorado* were spotted. That might explain the increase in security on the pier."

Chang considered Yuri's revelation. "Andrews didn't mention anything about that possibility."

"If the Mark 11 or the sub passed near a bottom sensor, they likely would not know they'd been detected. The PLAN, however, would be alerted to a possible intruder."

Jeff's brow creased. "If that's the case, the Chinese might start searching up here, looking for the likes of us."

"After what happened at the Yulin base, I'm sure the PLAN is paranoid about another potential attack on their facilities."

Jeff said, "And here we are, sitting on our butts in the backyard of one of their most important antisubmarine warfare units."

"Exactly."

"It's time to get out of Dodge."

Yuri cocked his head, not familiar with the American idiom.

Jeff said, "We need to get out of here."

"Didn't Andrews order us to wait here?"

"I don't work for the Navy." Jeff winked.

Yuri puckered his brow. "Okay...but where can we go?"

"Sanya. We have a safehouse there."

Chapter 59

Day 36—Wednesday

Yuri Kirov and Jeff Chang vacated the observation post at zero dark thirty—half past midnight. As they cautiously made their way down the hillside, Jeff used his portable night vision scope to scout the path ahead. Yuri followed. Both kept an extra eye out for snakes and other nocturnal creepy crawlers.

After an eighteen minute trek, they reached the edge of the brush line next to the parking lot. The asphalt surface served the Shendao Fleet Logistics and Support Center building—and S5. The lot contained just seven vehicles; all had arrived several hours earlier before the shift change at 10:00 P.M. From previous observations, Yuri and Jeff knew the night crew would not be relieved until 6:00 A.M.

"How about the Audi?" Jeff said, pointing to a four door sedan parked fifty feet away. The lot was poorly lit from its own pole lights but glare from the adjacent pier complex and the moored *Shandong* overflowed into the parking facility.

"Can you start it?"

"Of course, grand theft auto is one of the skillsets you get at the Farm."

Once again, Jeff's slang flew right over Yuri's head. Nevertheless, he deciphered it. "Okay, let's go."

* * * *

Jeff drove; Yuri slinked low in the backseat. They had been on the go for twenty minutes, following the road that skirted the bay for several miles before turning inland.

"We're coming up on a freeway," Jeff said. "Better cover up now."

"All right." Yuri pulled out a jacket from his rucksack and used it to cover his head and torso. The worry was surveillance cameras. China had millions of them. Jeff Chang wouldn't draw attention, at least not yet. But a Caucasian driving around in the wee hours of the morning would. Although Sanya was a tourist mecca, it mainly served the indigenous population. Foreign tourists visited Hainan Island, but not yet in droves.

"Where are we now?" Yuri asked from the backseat. They had travelled another fifteen minutes.

"We're close, maybe five minutes."

As part of Jeff's mission gear, he carried a Chinese manufactured smartphone with the latest maps. Once they turned onto the G224, he switched off the phone and had Yuri remove its battery. Jeff didn't want to risk leaving the phone active for fear of tracking by the MSS. Besides, he didn't need it, having memorized the rest of the route.

It took seven minutes. Jeff exited the Audi and punched in the code on the keypad by the garage. The panel door rolled up. He climbed back in and drove the car inside. He turned to address Yuri. "Stay put while I shut the door."

"Okay."

* * * *

"What is this place?" Yuri asked. He was inside a posh living room that overlooked a darkened harbor area and Sanya Bay in the background.

"Its owner is officially registered as an Australian businessman. Has an import export business run out of Melbourne. Supplies a lot of Aussie beef and luxury foodstuffs to the resorts here and elsewhere on Hainan Island."

"So, who really owns it?"

Jeff smirked. "We do...the Company does."

"Why am I not surprised."

"The guy from Melbourne does stay here on occasion. His business is strictly legitimate and I might add, quite lucrative. We have an arrangement with him through ASIS—Australian Secret Intelligence Service."

"Five Eyes asset?" Yuri asked, referring to an intelligence alliance consisting of the United Kingdom, Canada, Australia, New Zealand and the United States.

"Yes, it's a shared resource. Lately, we've been coordinating with the ASIS."

"They're an impressive group."

"Definitely, and they're just as concerned with Beijing's adventurism as we are. Plus they're a lot closer to China."

Yuri again glanced out the window. "What're those?" He pointed to a collection of high-rise towers in the distance. Perimeter lighting from the twenty-eight story tall buildings dominated the dim skyline. Shaped like billowing spinnaker sails, the five towers appeared to rise from the sea itself.

"Phoenix Island Resort. Quite the tourist attraction. The buildings are covered with a zillion LED lights that are computer controlled. From what I understand, they broadcast an amazing lightshow every evening."

"Really?"

"Yeah. The Chinese are masters at outdoor lighting."

Yuri turned back to Jeff. "So, how did you know the place was vacant?"

"Contingency planning by Langley. If the mission fell apart, I had orders to get to the Sanya safehouse. We have others on the island but this is particularly attractive because it's a single unit, no nosey neighbors in the same building, and it has a garage."

That triggered another concern for Yuri. "What about the car? When the owner gets off duty and discovers it missing, he's going to be pissed."

"I'm going to deal with that now."

"How?"

"I spotted a shopping area a couple of miles away. That's where I'm going to dump it—and wipe it clean. I want it found quickly. Make it look like a joyride so the MSS doesn't get involved, just the local cops." Jeff yawned. "The freeway we took to get here has lots of cameras and Sanya's loaded with 'em too. The quicker the car is found, the less likely the authorities will pursue the investigation by pulling videos and tracking our movements. To our knowledge, police surveillance cameras are not yet located in this neighborhood."

"So, you're walking back?"

"Yep. I'll use side streets. And I have ID that will hold up if I'm stopped."

"I'll go with you—"

"No thanks!" Jeff interrupted. "A big white guy like you hanging around me at oh dark hundred…that for sure would generate a cop stop."

Yuri grinned. "Got it."

Chapter 60

Captain Zhou Jun sipped tea at the kitchen table in his apartment. He wore his uniform. It was a few minutes after eight o'clock in the morning. The television was on, tuned to a news channel. The mid-twenties female newsreader reported on the day's lead story. Another United States warship had violated the People's Republic of China's sovereign territory by passing within twelve nautical miles of an artificial island constructed in the Spratly Island group. Beijing issued a strong rebuke to Washington, warning of severe consequences if such behavior persisted.

Meng Park joined Zhou in the kitchen. No sleek dress today, just blue jeans, long sleeved shirt and sneakers.

Zhou reached for the teapot and poured a fresh cup for Park.

She took a seat at the table beside Zhou. "Thank you," Meng said accepting the porcelain cup. She glanced at the TV. "What's going on?"

"Americans are pushing again. Another one of their so-called freedom of navigation patrols."

"Where."

"In the Nanshas."

She took a sip of tea. "They're persistent."

"Yes, but that's going to change soon, thanks in part to your work."

That sparked an unwelcome reminder from Meng. "Anything about the Russian sub?"

"Nothing…not a word. I'm sure Moscow knows it's missing by now."

The video of the *Novosibirsk's* escape capsule obliterated by her creation played on a looped feedback in Dr. Meng's brain. "The Russians will be suspicious if they spot the *Lian* in the same area."

"Don't worry about it. Your cover's intact."

The *Lian's* official cruise plan called for collecting bottom samples from the submerged peak of the Stewart Seamount near Luzon Island in the Philippines. It was part of an ongoing China Academy of Sciences' geophysical study of the South China Sea. The ship's submersible would dive to the bottom, deploy a soil coring device and collect the samples.

Along with the scientific work, the *Lian* would visit Serpent Station 6. Beijing ordered S5 to reload the ASW weapon system. Six new Viperina canisters were scheduled to arrive in Sanya late morning, transported from Hefei Xinqiao International Airport by military transport. Dr. Meng would monitor loading of the units aboard the *Lian* followed up with a series of diagnostic tests to verify each weapon was operational. The following morning, the ship was scheduled to depart Sanya at ten o'clock with Meng aboard. She was tasked with overseeing the installation.

The couple chatted about the deployment for another minute when Zhou's cell announced its presence. He checked the screen and glanced at Park. "Operations, shouldn't take long."

He accepted the call. "Zhou here," he said.

Park poured herself a refill.

"When did this happen?

"He's certain it was locked?

"Yes, let the police know. Maybe they can find it.

"I'll be in soon."

Zhou ended the call. "One of the staff had his car stolen last night."

"From S5?"

"Yes, from the logistics building parking lot."

"That's odd. Who would do such a thing?"

"Who knows. And taking it with all that activity across the road with the *Shangdong*—a foolish thing to do."

"You don't think it's one of the crew?"

"Maybe. They've been restricted to the ship for weeks. Someone may have flipped out. Anyway, we'll let the local police handle it."

Park drained the cup and said, "I'll get my gear."

"Good."

* * * *

Yuri entered the living room. It was 8:35 A.M. local time.

Jeff Chang knelt on the bamboo flooring, rummaging through his backpack when he spotted Yuri. "Good morning," he called out.

"Morning." Yuri stretched out his arms. "How long have you been up?"

"Hour or so."

After taking a shower, Yuri had collapsed onto the bed. He slept five solid hours. "Ditching the car go okay?"

"Yep, no problem."

Yuri caught a whiff of an intoxicating odor. "Is that coffee?"

"It is. I made a pot. Help yourself."

Yuri found the Chinese knockoff of an American brand name coffee brewer in the kitchen. He poured a cup and returned to the living room. "This is great," he said, savoring the taste.

"Sumatra blend. I found an unopened bag stored in the freezer. Great stuff."

"I'll say."

Yuri noticed that the CIA officer had extracted the compact military SATCOM radio from his pack—the top secret device Murph had operated at the OP. Jeff was currently spreading apart the radio's retractable antenna blades. Fully extended, the antenna array was about the size of a basketball.

"Calling home?" Yuri asked.

"That's the plan but I'll have to do it on the roof to connect with satellites."

"How are you going to do that?"

"Ladder access in the utility room."

"Hmmm," Yuri said. He took another sip and wandered to the nearby window wall. The turquoise waters of Sanya Bay dominated the distant vista. But it was the foreground view that captured Yuri's instant attention.

"The vessels moored at the dock—they look military." He'd spotted hull silhouettes when they first arrived at the safehouse but could not make out details due to darkness.

Jeff glanced Yuri's way. "This area of Sanya is a mix of residential and commercial uses. I suppose the Navy or Coast Guard may control some of the docks."

"Can I use your binoculars?" Yuri asked.

"Sure, they're in my backpack someplace."

Yuri homed in on one particular vessel that caught his eye. It was moored to a pier two football fields away. About three hundred feet long, the ship's hull was painted cobalt blue. The superstructure above the main deck was snow-white. The bow and forward superstructure had a distinctive bulbous flare that set itself apart from conventional ships. He focused on the ship's name displayed near the port bow, stenciled in white over the blue hull in Mandarin symbols and English letters.

"I don't believe it?" Yuri uttered.

"What?"

"See the ship with the blue and white colors?" He pointed seaward.

Jeff peered out the window. "Yeah, what about it?"

"It's the *Lian*."

Jeff cast a questioning glare.

"It was in the mission briefing documents. Registered as a Chinese Academy of Sciences vessel but it's really controlled by the PLAN."

Jeff's eyes blossomed. "The one that's been deploying the S5 weapon system?"

"Yes."

"I'll be damned!"

* * * *

"Call me when you're done and I'll pick you up," Captain Zhou said from the driver's seat of his parked BMW.

Meng Park sat in the adjacent passenger seat. "It'll probably be late in the afternoon. And if I run into problems . . ."

"Doesn't matter. I want to see you before the ship departs. It'll be a week or more before you return." Zhou grinned. "That's an eternity."

Park caught the gaze, knowing what he wanted—what she also desired. "We'll have to do something about that, won't we?"

Zhou took a quick look around. He had parked on the pier that moored the *Lian*. It was currently deserted. He leaned across the seat and gently cupped Park's head with his hands. "A down payment on tonight," he offered. He kissed her, a long delicious kiss.

* * * *

Yuri was in the living room trying in vain to find an English-speaking channel on the HD television while Jeff Chang tested the SATCOM radio from the roof. Neither one noticed the BMW when it parked beside the *Lian*. Both men also missed Meng Park when she exited the vehicle, walked along the concrete pier towing a wheeled suitcase, and with an attaché case in hand, sauntered up the aluminum gangway to the ship's main deck.

Chapter 61

"All stop," ordered Commander Tom Bowman.

The officer of the deck repeated the directive and power to the propulsor was switched off. The 7,800 ton vessel slipped through the abyss eight hundred feet below the surface.

After several minutes, the *Colorado's* forward momentum ceased. "Commence hovering," Bowman said, again addressing the OOD.

"Commence hovering, aye."

Bowman turned to address the Weapons Officer. "Mr. Conway, you may proceed."

"Aye, aye, Captain."

Bowman joined *Colorado's* executive officer at the horizontal large screen display. Commander Jenae Mauk had returned to the ship's nerve center a couple minutes earlier. She studied the electronic chart. A blue submarine icon marked *Colorado's* position. Just inches away was a crimson skull and crossbones symbol, which marked the target.

"This one is over twice as deep as the other one," Mauk said, eyeing her boss.

"It is but the probes should be able to handle the pressure."

"Any threats?"

"All quiet."

"Let's hope it stays that way." She pointed to the death's head. "Whatever those things are, we sure don't want to wake 'em up." The sinking of the *Novosibirsk* remained fresh to all aboard the *Colorado.*

SSN 788 was two miles north of Viper Station 2. Located 265 nautical miles southeast of Sanya, the subsea installation was near the summit of Margetts Seamount in 4,400 feet of water. The PRC's military fortress on

Woody Island, part of the Parcel Islands, lay 135 miles north of VS2. China controlled the Parcels but Vietnam and Taiwan also claimed the archipelago.

"Both probes are wet, Captain," announced Weps.

"Very well, proceed."

"Aye, aye, Captain."

Mauk said, "Let's hope this one goes as smooth as the first one."

"I read you."

Twelve hours earlier, the *Colorado* made a similar stealth approach to Viper Station 1, about 170 nautical miles north of VS2. It also launched two self-propelled probes from torpedo tubes, a sea mine and a tethered tracker. Both units swam to the PLAN bottom installation where the sea mine burrowed into the bottom muck beside the canisters housing half a dozen Viperinas. The tracker employed its video camera and floodlight to record the mine's successful deployment and concealment, relaying the images to *Colorado* via the tether. After completing a video survey of all components of Viper Station 1, the ROV returned to the submarine.

Bowman was about to check in with sonar when he recalled another concern. "How's our SEAL?" Commander Mauk had just visited sickbay.

"About the same. Doc has him stabilized." Mauk frowned. "I think he's going to lose his arm if he doesn't get help soon."

"No recovery?"

"No, it's just black as before. The antibiotics haven't done anything."

"You know our orders."

"I know. It's just not fair."

COMSUBPAC's orders were explicit. Neutralize the threat before seeking aid for the SEAL.

"Anything else that we can do to help?" Bowman asked.

"Doc says he's doing everything he can, but the flesh around the punctures is dying."

"Sounds like gangrene."

"It's something like that. The tissue rots, which poisons the rest of the body. Doc says that may be worse than the venom."

"That's awful."

After Mauk left the control room, Bowman stayed behind to catch up on electronic paperwork. His thoughts soon wandered. *There's got to be something else we can do.*

Finally, he remembered. *Gangrene—yes, that just might work.*

* * * *

Jeff Chang peered skyward. He raised his right arm and waved. "Can you see me now?" he asked, speaking into the handset of the military SATCOM radio, which he affectionately referred to as the SEAL phone.

"I have you," replied the recipient of Jeff's call. CIA counterintelligence officer Steve Osberg was on the end of the satellite link in his office in Langley, Virginia. It was 1:35 A.M. his time, twelve hours behind Sanya time. Jeff's boss was summoned an hour earlier at his residence after Chang contacted CIA headquarters. Osberg had returned home after his last meeting with Chang and Yuri in Honolulu.

"Okay, good," Jeff said. "Now pan northward to the waterway opposite my position and you'll see the ship. The superstructure from the bow to the bridge is all white."

"I have it."

The cutting edge optical telescope aboard the three month old orbiting U.S. Air Force spy satellite transmitted razor-sharp real time images of the Chinese research vessel to Langley. This was the new spy bird's first live operations application.

Jeff said, "We think that ship is responsible for deploying the ASW system."

Osberg called up a digital file on his PC, another satellite image recorded a couple of weeks earlier in the South China Sea. "You're right. That's the same ship, the *Lian*. But what does it have to do with getting you and Kirov out of China?"

"About an hour ago, a flatbed truck showed up and offloaded half a dozen metal canisters onto the fantail."

"I see them. What are they?"

"Kirov thinks those canisters might be what we've been after from day one."

"The weapon is inside?"

"It fits with what the Navy told us."

"What's your intention, Jeff?"

"We ended up with zilch at the other location. So, before bugging out, I'd like to get aboard and take a look around. Might be able to find something to help salvage the mission."

"What's Kirov's take on your plan?"

"He thinks I'm nuts."

* * * *

"Terrific idea, Captain. This is really going to help."

"Let's hope so."

Commander Bowman was in sickbay with Independent Duty Corpsman Karl ("Doc") Rawley. With skills similar to a Physician's Assistant, the twenty-eight-year-old Petty Officer First Class was *Colorado's* sole medical professional.

"I wish I'd thought about this earlier," Rawley said, his tone remorseful.

"Don't worry about it. The XO and the SEAL commander knew about it too. And so did I. But it just didn't click for me until a little while ago."

"Thanks, skipper."

Both men squatted next to a two-foot diameter flexible tube constructed of high strength nylon fabric. The portable hyperbaric chamber stretched out eight feet along the deck. Master Chief Petty Officer Halgren lay on his back inside the cylinder, visible through transparent ports at either end of the tube. The chamber was pressurized with compressed air.

The Hyperlite Portable Hyperbaric Chamber was stored in *Colorado's* diving equipment locker adjacent to the SEAL lockout chamber. It served as an emergency recompression chamber. Should a diver operating from the submarine become impaired from decompression sickness aka the bends, the portable system offered rapid lifesaving critical care.

But today the inflatable chamber was put to an alternative use. With the pressure in the tube increased 2.3 times above normal air pressure, Halgren's lungs received more oxygen than when he had been inhaling pure oxygen through a mask at just room pressure. His blood now carried the extra oxygen throughout his body, supercharging his natural healing defenses by releasing stem cells and growth factors. Hyperbaric oxygen therapy was especially helpful in treating gangrene.

Commander Bowman leaned toward the acrylic plastic viewport. Halgren's head rested on a pillow just a couple of feet away. "How are you doing, Master Chief?" he called out.

Wild Bill angled his head back, making eye contact. The oxygen mask covered his mouth and nose. He raised his unencumbered arm with the thumb extended upwards.

* * * *

"I know you're not wild about this but I really need your help."

"What do you have in mind?" Yuri stared at Jeff Chang. They were in the safehouse living room, sitting on opposing sofas. It was late afternoon.

"I need to get aboard the ship and open up one of those canisters."

Yuri rubbed the stubble on his chin. Despite the first-class accommodations, there were no razor blades or even an electric shaver in any of the three bathrooms. "So, you open up one, what then?"

"Langley wants us to steal whatever we can... ideally the CPU, if it's accessible."

Yuri bit his upper lip while taking in Jeff's plan. "That's a real longshot. The thing is designed to operate several thousand feet underwater. Trying to crack the pressure casing to get access to its computer will be a bitch."

"I know but that's where you come in. You know what to look for. Me, I'd just be guessing."

Yuri pondered Jeff's request. All he wanted was to leave China ASAP. He had spent the day coming up with a plausible out. From the safehouse roof he spotted several runabouts with powerful outboards mixed in with the larger and slower vessels moored to the nearby piers. Deliverance was just 150 nautical miles away. Stealing the right boat could deliver Yuri and Jeff to Da Nang, Vietnam in five hours. Despite past bad blood between Washington and Hanoi, relations had improved, sparked in part by Beijing's bullying tactics in the South China Sea.

We should just go! Yuri thought.

Still, Yuri recognized that the CIA officer had a point. The mission was a bust at this point. Whatever intel they could gather before escaping might help the cause.

"All right," Yuri said. "I'll help but it has to be a quick in, quick out. I want to have enough time to find our ride while it's dark."

"Great, we'll get aboard, crack open a canister and take a look-see. Then we'll get the hell out of here."

"Bring your camera. A couple of IR snapshots may be all we get after opening it up."

"I'll have it ready—plus my other toys." Jeff gestured to his backpack on the floor. Earlier, he'd revealed the contents of his spy kit to Yuri.

"Okay." Yuri stood. He motioned toward the windows and the moored ship beyond. "Let's first figure out how we get aboard that thing without being seen."

"Sounds good!"

Chapter 62

Twelve time zones behind Sanya and half a world away, it was early morning in Washington, D.C. The President of the United States was in the Oval Office joined by his national security advisor. The meeting was not scheduled.

President Tyler Magnuson drank coffee from his desk. NSA Peter Brindle had taken a chair fronting the president. Already charged with caffeine from his all-nighter at the Pentagon, he declined a cup.

"So, Pete, what's going on?" POTUS asked.

"Your favorite subjects, Russia and China."

Magnuson groaned but did not comment.

Brindle said, "Moscow has formally acknowledged that one of its submarines has been lost in the South China Sea. The story is hitting the news outlets this morning."

"Did they blame China?" POTUS was briefed the previous day on the *Colorado's* report of the *Novosibirsk's* demise.

"No. The press release only states that the sub is missing and presumed lost."

"What do you expect the Chinese will do?"

"Offer to help search for it."

POTUS smirked. "That's rich."

"Russia and China are gaming each other, feigning their alliance."

"Well, they're joined at the hip in one cause—screw us over however they can."

"Agreed. And that brings me to the next item." Brindle cleared his voice. "One of our subs tracked a Chinese boat to Petropavlovsk-Kamchatskiy.

It released an autonomous underwater vehicle that penetrated the harbor and swam to the Rybachiy submarine base."

"Some kind of a spy device for recording Russian subs?" Magnuson asked.

"That was the original speculation but CIA is backing off, based on input from DIA." Brindle removed an enlarged photograph from a file folder he carried. He slid the print from the Defense Intelligence Agency across the desk.

Magnuson picked up the photo. The black and white image revealed a gray cylinder partially embedded in mud. "What am I looking at?"

"The Chinese probe. Our sub, the *Mississippi*, launched an autonomous underwater vehicle that followed it into the harbor. This is one of the infrared photos recorded before it returned to the *Mississippi*."

"I have the feeling you're going to tell me that it's not a spy gadget."

"I'm afraid so. DIA is of the opinion that it's a weapon."

"What kind?"

"Some type of sea mine but its unlike anything we know about in the Chinese arsenal."

"They want to sink another submarine...this time right at a base?"

"That's possible. But based on what happened at Qingdao, both CIA and DIA now believe, and I concur, that the probe likely contains a nuclear device."

Magnuson slumped in his chair. "Revenge?"

"I'm afraid so."

"When is this nightmare going to end?"

* * * *

Nick Orlov lay on his side in the hotel bed staring at the television. It was a few minutes past five in the morning. He was in Vancouver but his body clock was stuck on Hong Kong time.

Unable to sleep any longer, Nick had turned on the television. The top of the hour news summary was underway. A thirty something perky blonde recited the newsflash: "Breaking news this morning from Vladivostok, Russia. The Russian Pacific Fleet reports that one of its submarines is missing and presumed to have sunk. The submarine *Novosibirsk* was based in Vladivostok. It was on patrol in the South China Sea near the Philippines but contact was lost two days ago. The Russian Navy is mounting a search but no trace of the 120 meter submarine has been detected so far. Ninety men were aboard. The *Novosibirsk* was..."

Nick focused on the television screen. A file image of a submarine filled the screen. *That's the sub Yuri was on!*

Nick knew Yuri was aboard the *Novosibirsk* during its spy missions in Yulin and Qingdao but had no details on his ops.

This is too much to be a coincidence.

SVR director Borya Smirnov pressured Nick for an update on Yuri Kirov's whereabouts. After Nick completed his assignment in Hong Kong, he had expected to return to Moscow. Instead, Smirnov sent him back to Vancouver.

Laura Newman did not respond to his texts or leave a response on the Gmail account they shared.

I've got to get her attention—somehow. Russia's still not done with Yuri!

* * * *

"So, what's next?" asked Chen Wu Mei.

President Chen Shen keyed 'mute' on the TV remote. Facing his wife, he said, "We continue as planned."

The couple were in the entertainment room of their Zhongnanhai residence. They had just watched the evening news broadcast, which featured the loss of the Russian submarine *Novosibirsk*. Wu Mei sat on a futon across from her husband. She wore a casual floral frock that displayed her comely legs. President Chen was stretched out in his favorite La-Z-Boy Recliner; he wore a robe. Blossom leaned against the chair. Chen massaged the golden retriever's ears with a hand.

"Do you still plan to warn the Americans?" Wu Mei asked.

"On Monday, the Foreign Ministry will issue a general notice, announcing the new policy regarding navigation and air routes within the Cows Tongue. All vessels and aircraft must seek advance permission to pass."

"No advance notice to Washington…regarding submarines?"

"It's no longer necessary."

"The *Novosibirsk*?"

"Yes."

Wu Mei processed the news, elated at the success of the Serpent program and her husband's decision to expel the U.S. Navy from China's home waters. China was rising, soon to take its rightful place as the world's dominant superpower. Still, the national lesion festered. "What about Qingdao?" she asked. "Sinking one of their submarines doesn't atone for what they did."

"That is to be determined."

"You must act soon; the people will demand revenge."

Chen Shen nodded as he triggered the remote, restoring the TV audio. The newsreader was in the middle of the sports segment.

Irritated, Wu Mei snatched a fashion magazine from a side table and began paging through it.

President Chen pretended interest in the latest soccer scores but his thoughts were elsewhere. *What should I do?*

The nuclear weapon sitting on the bottom of the Russian harbor listened for the acoustic command signal. The Politburo Standing Committee deferred to Chen. Admiral Soo at the Central Military Commission was ready to execute upon receiving Chen's orders. An MSS spy at the Rybachiy sub base stood by, ready to deploy a hydrophone into the harbor waters.

Lebedev is a sneaky rat. He does not fear us like the Americans do.

The Qingdao response option favored by the PSC was the invasion of Siberia and the confiscation of its vast mineral, oil and gas resources.

The Kremlin would never tolerate the loss of Russian soil.

Remembering Hitler's failed invasion of the USSR in World War Two, Chen put the kibosh on invasion talk.

But how will Lebedev respond to losing his submarine base? Risk all out nuclear war with us—or will he accept that consequence?

President Chen banked on Lebedev's reluctance to escalate, accepting the *quid pro quo*: Rybachiy for Qingdao.

But what if I'm wrong?

Russia's titanic nuclear arsenal could send China back to the aftermath of the Mongol's annihilation of the Jin and Song dynasties, the Dali Kingdom and Western Xia.

Everything we've built for the past seventy years could be lost. We'd have to start over.

Chen dismissed the negative thoughts, falling back on the grand plan.

China's secret scheme to retain its rightful place as the supreme world power commenced in 1949 with the founding of the People's Republic of China. The undisclosed strategy called for China to achieve world dominance by the PRC's hundredth anniversary. Through a series of long-term measured phases that employed deception, obfuscation and manipulation, the PRC's goal was to surpass the United States in all key superpower factors: economic, cultural and military.

With implementation of Serpent the final goal might be obtained decades earlier than planned.

Serpent is the key to everything. Once we evict the Americans from our home waters, the final elements of the plan will fall into place!

President Chen engaged the recliner's side lever and stood.

Wu Mei looked up. "Where are you going?"

"You know."

China's first lady rolled her eyes.

"Come on Blossom, let's go."

After a short walk, Chen was in the garden behind the residence. He lit up his fourteenth Marlboro for the day while Blossom made her rounds, sniffing plants and inspecting stone tiles. As President Chen took in a deep drag, he decided—sort of.

There's no hurry. Soo says it can stay on the bottom for months...I can even recall the underwater machine that has the bomb, allowing it to sink onto the ocean floor far from Russian territory. Lebedev would never know.

* * * *

"Oh, dear Lord," Laura Newman said as she stared at the television in the kitchen. It was half past seven in the morning. She had just returned from working out in the condominium building's gym. She was in her sweats, sipping a glass of orange juice beside a counter. Amanda was in Maddy's room, dressing her for the day.

The network news broadcast announced the loss of a Russian submarine in the South China Sea.

"Novosibirsk! That's the boat Yuri was on." Yuri had told Laura bits and pieces of his last mission.

Unexpectedly chilled with dread, Laura's thoughts leapfrogged. *Where are you? What do they have you doing? When are you coming home?*

Chapter 63

Day 37—Thursday

With rucksacks strapped to their backs, Yuri Kirov and Jeff Chang were on the move at 12:25 A.M. The sticky night air hovered around ninety degrees Fahrenheit. Across the navigation channel to the north, the Phoenix Island Resort towers glistened. The beat of live rock and roll with Mandarin lyrics—Chengdu Rock—flowed across the waterway. A cruise ship from Shanghai had docked at the Phoenix Island terminal in the late afternoon. An outdoor shipboard party was underway on the aft deck.

As expected, the pier mooring the *Lian* was not approachable from the shore. Its squad of pole mounted floodlights lit up the pier deck. The main pier ran parallel to the shore for 620 feet. Two trestles, each about 230 feet long, were located near the east and west ends of the main pier. The trestles provided access from the shore to the main pier.

Yuri located a work float tied up to a bulkhead east of the pier. The eight-foot-wide by twenty-foot-long raft had a timber deck and frame. Foam filled plastic pontoons supported the deck.

Yuri and Jeff kneeled on the float with Yuri at the lead. Each held an eight foot stick of lumber swiped from a pile on the uplands. About the size of a standard two-by-four, they used the boards as paddles. Once under the eastern trestle, they had worked their way seaward between the clusters of steel pipe pilings that supported the concrete superstructure. The tide was low, which provided just enough room to pass under the trestle's lateral reinforced concrete beams—pile caps—that rested on top of piles.

Light from the pier's floodlights spilled under the dock, allowing Yuri and Jeff to see. After paddling the length of the trestle, they traveled westward under the main pier. When they neared the middle of the pier, Yuri turned around and said, "I think we're close." He spoke with a whisper. "Are you ready?"

Jeff tapped the Taser riding in a holster on his right hip—part of his spy gear. "Yep, all set." Canary yellow and about the size of a pistol, the electroshock stun weapon was a standard police issue. Jeff also carried a Beretta in a shoulder holster that he'd been issued, as did Yuri. But gunfire was a last resort. Their immediate mission was a quick in and out. The Taser was their first line of defense.

Yuri set his paddle on the float deck. Jeff followed. Yuri pushed against a pile, propelling the raft from under the overhead pier. The float drifted next to the stern of the *Lian*. After standing, Yuri cautiously peered over the ship's transom. The Viperina canisters were thirty feet away.

* * * *

The BMW drove onto the pier and parked adjacent to a gangway. The aluminum ramp provided pedestrian access to the *Lian*. While still in the front passenger seat, Meng Park embraced Captain Zhou Jun—one last time. "Thank you for a wonderful evening," she said.

"My pleasure."

They had just driven from Zhou's apartment. After a late dinner out, they had returned to the naval captain's quarters for a nightcap and sex.

Park opened her door and slipped a leg out. Just before exiting, Zhou said, "Good luck with your mission, and please keep me posted on your progress."

"Thank you, and I will."

Meng Park exited and the BMW drove forward, leaving the pier via the west trestle. Before heading up the gangway, Park took time to scan the *Lian's* aft deck. The Viperina canisters were as she remembered, stored under the A-frame hoist.

Where's the guard? she wondered.

Meng eventually located the sentry. He was on an upper deck that overlooked the stern. The PLAN sentry wore civilian attire but he carried an assault rifle. Park waved; the sailor returned the greeting.

Dr. Meng boarded the ship, bound for her cabin. Jun had wanted her to stay until morning, reminding Park that most of the crew also avoided the ship. Homeported in Sanya, the *Lian's* twenty-two person military crew all lived in or near the city. Just three elected to spend their last night of shore leave aboard the ship—all bachelors. Park chose not to push her luck. So far, she had managed to conceal her affair with the S5 commander. She could only imagine the shipboard gossip should their secret be exposed.

Sated from drink and sex, all Park sought now was a hot shower and sleep.

* * * *

"Damn!" whispered Jeff Chang as he watched Meng Park board the ship. "It's her."

Yuri muttered a Russian expletive. He and the CIA officer squatted beside an eight foot high stainless steel cannister. When the BMW drove onto the pier, the sentry they'd been watching walked to the port side of the ship to investigate. That's when Yuri and Jeff scurried over the transom and made their way to the collection of steel drums.

Jeff Chang surveyed their surroundings. The sentry leaned against a bulkhead in the shadows. He had just lit up. The tip of the cigarette glowed as he inhaled, marking his position.

Jeff whispered to Yuri. "We need to take out the guard first and then snatch her, like we talked about with the SEALs."

"No way. We're not ready to deal with her. We should stick to the plan. Knock out the guard and crack open one of these things." Yuri pointed to the nearest barrel. "Photograph the guts, take what we can, and get out."

Jeff ignored Yuri. He crawled forward along the steel deck, using the Viperina canisters as cover. Exasperated, Yuri followed.

* * * *

The sentry was blindsided. One moment he was strolling on the upper deck and then he found himself flat on his face, his teeth clutched vise tight and his body on electric fire from a 1,200 volt jolt.

Jeff Chang handed the Taser gun to Yuri and rushed forward. He injected the incapacitated sailor with a knockout drug. The dose of ketamine would render the twenty-four-year-old comatose for several hours.

After binding the sentry's wrists behind his back, Jeff and Yuri dragged the sailor down a companionway to the aft deck. They hauled the guard into a cargo container box, dumping him behind boxes of spare parts.

"Let's go find Meng now," Jeff said.

"No, not yet," Yuri ordered. He held the sentry's rifle. "We open one of those damn drums first. Get what we can, and then…only if we haven't been compromised, we try to find her."

Jeff Chang reluctantly agreed.

Chapter 64

"Doctor Meng, please open the door." The *Lian's* engineering officer rapped his right hand knuckles on the cabin door. He repeated his request, but louder.

"Who's there?"

"I'm the ship's chief engineer. There's an emergency call for you on the bridge."

Meng Park cracked open the door. Her damp hair was wrapped with a towel; a white cotton bathrobe concealed her torso. "Who's calling me?"

Yuri Kirov yanked the engineer back into the passageway as Jeff Chang jammed his right foot in the door opening while simultaneously grasping for Meng Park's arm.

Meng lurched backward, screaming. Jeff managed to snag the robe. They ended up on the bunk with Jeff on top. During the ensuing struggle, Meng's robe tore open, exposing her breasts. With his legs locked around her hips, Jeff held a dive knife to Dr. Meng's throat. "Stop struggling," he ordered in Mandarin.

* * * *

The *Lian's* chief engineer ambled into the cabin, the barrel of a nine-millimeter pistol pressed against the back of his skull. Yuri followed, glued to his captive.

"You okay?" Yuri asked.

Entangled with Meng Park, Jeff Chang ignored Yuri, addressing the PLAN scientist instead. "Don't move," he commanded, again using

Mandarin. He withdrew the knife and unraveled himself from his captive. He slipped the blade into its scabbard on his belt.

Jeff faced Yuri. Switching to English, he said, "I'm all right. She fought me like a banshee." He reached up to caress his left cheek.

That's when Yuri noticed the parallel welts from Meng's fingernails.

"We need to get going." Yuri shoved the engineer forward, signaling him to sit on the bed beside Meng. They had captured the PLAN officer in the galley raiding a refrigerator for a snack.

Meng managed to close her robe. She homed in on Yuri and in flawless English said, "Who are you?" During the initial encounter, she had feared rape but now suspected something worse.

Jeff responded. "Dr. Meng, you're wanted back home for espionage."

"You're Americans!" Park shouted, stunned—terrified.

"That's right and you're coming with us."

* * * *

Jeff and Yuri were inside the *Lian's* bridge, both leaning against the chart table. Dr. Meng was in a corner with knees bent and wrists bound behind her back with plastic cable ties—another goodie from Jeff Chang's spy kit. She wore a white cotton blouse, jeans and sneakers. The ship's engineer was perched on the captain's pedestal chair next to the helm, his hands similarly lashed behind his back. Lighting inside the compartment was set for night conditions—scarlet. A minuscule tremor vibrated in the deck, transmitted by the ship's idling diesels.

Yuri pointed to the chart of Sanya harbor and the adjacent South China Sea. "We depart here. We'll have a direct route to Da Nang."

"How far away?"

"About 150 nautical miles."

Jeff ran the math. "That's still a long time. Once they figure out what's going on, they'll be all over us."

"I know. That's why we need to go now so we have time to prepare."

"Okay, let's do it."

* * * *

Meng Park studied the thugs. The muscular Caucasian with short dark hair and a developing beard obviously knew his way around ships. He had just taken command. Back in her cabin, the skinny Asian with the scraggly beard was in charge.

The engineer—what a jellyfish, thought Ming.

Jeff Chang had interrogated the *Lian's* engineer in Meng's cabin. With the threat of the knife tip probing his groin, the mid thirties, pig nosed and broomstick thin lieutenant commander revealed everything—the number of personnel aboard and their location, the ship's scheduled sailing time, required time for off duty crew to return to the ship, the ship's maximum speed, procedures to start the engines and a host of critical shipboard operations.

Meng had remained bound and gagged in her cabin while the two intruders, accompanied by the submissive engineer, secured the ship. The Asian-American subsequently collected Meng, forcing her to walk to the bridge.

Meng had not seen the other two crew members who slept aboard or the guard. She feared the Americans had murdered the men.

They're after the Vipers—and me!

She'd heard them talking.

Vietnam—no way is that going to happen!

When the first crew members showed up at the dock around six o'clock in the morning, less than four hours away, the alarm would be issued.

Jun will come looking for me.

Knowing the *Lian's* maximum speed of eighteen knots, Meng estimated PLAN helicopters would intercept the ship several hours before it could reach Da Nang.

Jun will make the scum pay—with their lives.

* * * *

"Change of plans, boss," Jeff Chang said, speaking into the handset of the SEAL satphone. He was outside on the port bridge wing. It was his first opportunity to call since boarding the *Lian*.

"What change?" Steve Osberg asked from his office at CIA headquarters in Langley.

"We're on the ship and guess who we found aboard?"

"What are you talking about?"

"Dr. Meng Park, we have her."

Stunned, Osberg said, "Jeff, this changes everything."

Chapter 65

"All lines are released," Yuri announced as he reentered the *Lian's* bridge from an aft passageway. He had spent the past ten minutes jettisoning the ship's mooring lines, allowing the hawsers to dangle from the pier's bollards and cleats.

"Great," Jeff Chang said. He had stayed behind to monitor radio traffic and keep an eye on Meng Park and the *Lian's* engineer.

"Hear anything?" Yuri asked.

"Just some chatter between what sounded like a couple of fishing boats working offshore."

"Okay, time for us to go."

Yuri, Jeff and the ship's engineer assembled beside the *Lian's* maneuvering console, which was adjacent to the helm.

Yuri pointed to a dial like knob control on the panel. There was no nameplate under the knob. "I don't trust this guy. Ask him to again verify that this really is the bow thruster. Impress him with what will happen if he's lying."

Jeff withdrew the knife from his belt scabbard and placed the tip of the blade under the engineer's chin. He applied pressure. The engineer stood on the tips of his toes.

Jeff repeated Yuri's question in Mandarin. The engineer responded, his voice stressed.

With the knife still in place, Jeff said, "He claims it's the bow thruster."

"We'll see if he's lying." Yuri rotated the dial a quarter turn. There was no response at first but after half a minute the bow began to pivot away from the pier.

"It's working," Yuri said.

Jeff withdrew the knife. The engineer let out an audible sigh.

"Put him back in the chair," Yuri said.

"Got it."

Yuri set the dual throttles to ten percent and dialed in a course on the autopilot control.

At 2:55 A.M., the *Lian* eased away from the pier and headed toward the open waters of the South China Sea.

While Yuri steered the ship, Jeff Chang grabbed his rucksack. He needed to provide Langley with an update. Just as he pulled back the sliding door to the port bridge wing, he spotted a pickup truck drive onto the pier. The ship was only a hundred feet away from the dock.

Jeff watched as the passenger door flew open and a male raced to the edge of the pier, waving his hands wildly. He could hear the man's shrill voice over the shipboard noise.

"Oh shit!" Jeff muttered.

Jeff Chang rejoined Yuri on the bridge. He whispered to Yuri, "An early arrival just showed up on the dock, one of the crew yelled for the boat to come back and pick him up."

Yuri glanced at the engineer, still planted in the captain's chair. "He said they wouldn't show up until six. That bastard lied to us."

"I know but what's done is done. If we're lucky, there'll be some confusion for half an hour or so before they figure it out."

"Damn! All we needed was a couple hours head start."

"That's gone now."

"What do you want to do?"

"Let me think."

* * * *

"We're on our way," Jeff Chang said, speaking into the handset of the satphone from the port bridge wing.

"Where are you now?" Steve Osberg asked. After Jeff's first call, Osberg had transferred to the CIA's National Clandestine Service's operations center in Langley. He used a speakerphone to take the call. A dozen other CIA officers and analysts supported Osberg in one of the center's super-secret ops rooms; they all listened to Osberg's conversation with their colleague in China. Multiple flat-panel screens filled the wall at the front of the room. The screens depicted maps, charts and aerial photos of Hainan Island, Sanya and the South China Sea.

"We left the dock a few minutes ago. Heading southwest."

Osberg gestured to a nearby technician. The woman raised both hands, presenting ten digits. "We're ten minutes away from having live satellite video coverage. How many are aboard?"

"Besides the two of us, we've got Meng, the ship's engineer, and two crew plus a guard."

"What are you doing with them?"

"Meng and the engineer are on the bridge with us, secure. The others are locked up in a shipping container near the stern."

"What about the weapon system? Can you get access to it?"

"We opened one of the drums. Looks like a giant snake coiled up inside. Thing's about a foot in diameter. Kirov said it will take major surgery to get inside it. Has some kind of flexible exterior armor."

"We need you to try your best to get the control module."

"I did take photos and I'll upload them to you."

"Jeff, the photos are welcome but we need hardware."

"I read you, boss. Kirov said he's going to give it a try after he works on our new out."

"What new out?'"

"We were spotted just as we pulled away from the dock. Kirov thinks they'll be on us within an hour."

"Dammit, Jeff! Can't you switch to the RIB right now and make a run for it?"

The original escape plan called for using the *Lian* to clear the harbor. Once in the open sea the ship's autopilot would be set on a false heading. While the *Lian* charged southeastward toward the Philippines at flank, Yuri and Jeff with Dr. Meng would make a speed run to Da Nang aboard the ship's tender. At thirty knots, the twenty-four foot rigid-hulled inflatable boat could complete the crossing in just under five hours.

"The RIB's still a possibility but Kirov thinks we'd be too vulnerable, even with its speed. The PLA will throw everything it has to get Meng back."

"Aircraft?"

"Right, they won't bother to send patrol boats or ships."

Osberg understood the threat. The PLA airbase at Fenghuang near Sanya had a squadron of fighters and helicopters. The PLA-Navy airbase at Lingshui on southern Hainan Island served as the headquarters for a fleet of naval patrol craft.

Chang said, "Without the head start, Kirov says there won't be enough time in the RIB to make it to shore. A chopper or jet will find us first. That's why he's opting for Plan B, and I agree with him."

"Plan B—explain."

Jeff spent the next few minutes doing so.

* * * *

Once again, Meng Park had observed the pirates' ruthlessness. Terrorizing the engineer and gaining control of the ship was bad enough. But it was the equipment the Asian accessed that now horrified Meng.

They know what they're doing.

After the ship was underway, the Asian brute relocated to a bridge wing, hauling his backpack. The other thug stayed behind, monitoring the ship's progress. Through a tempered glass panel in the bridge door, Meng watched the Asian remove the compact portable satellite phone. After deploying the antenna, he aimed it skyward and dialed the handset.

The communications device was far more sophisticated than the run of the mill commercially produced satphone.

They must be military!

Meng Park closed her eyes and bowed her head. She prayed to the Buddhist divinity *Guanyin*—the goddess of mercy. Twenty miles west of the *Lian's* position, along Hainan Island's southern shore, a spectacular 354 foot tall statue of the idol overlooked the South China Sea.

Park pleaded for rescue by Zhou Jun before the devils could complete their criminal work.

Chapter 66

Yuri Kirov was in the pilot's seat inside the six foot diameter transparent sphere. He was more than impressed with the submersible. The *Xiu Shan's* construction was top notch and it appeared to be equipped with the latest navigation, sonar and communications equipment. His principle concern centered on the gauges and instruments; all of the cockpit nameplates were marked with Mandarin characters. The actual numerical readouts, however, were in standard English digital format. So far, he had identified the depth and speed gauges as well as the air supply and battery life readouts. He currently searched for the ballast controls but no joy yet.

Yuri checked his watch: 3:35 A.M. He decided to deal with the controls when Chang was available to translate.

Yuri exited the acrylic pressure hull through the top hatch and climbed down to the *Lian's* deck. The submersible was parked inside a hangar located forward of the stern deck. The hangar was large enough to house two minisubs but the *Xiu Shan* was alone. It rested on its launching cradle over the starboard set of tracks. Earlier, Yuri had spotted the sub through the open hangar door.

Yuri examined the parallel tracks that extended aft to the ship's stern. Steel wheels from the *Xiu Shan's* cradle rode atop twin recessed rails.

It took a minute to locate the hangar control panel. After a brief trial and error process, Yuri found the right controls to the cradle's electric drive system. He backed the submersible out of the hangar, stopping the *Xiu Shan* next to the Viperina canisters. Yuri looked up, studying the overhead A-frame hoist system.

Okay, now how do I get this thing in the water?

* * * *

After planting a mine at its third target, the *Colorado* was on its way to the next subsea Viper station when the radio room received a bell ringer ELF (extremely low frequency) radio message. The submarine ascended to a shallower depth where it deployed a floating wire antenna that intercepted a VLF (very low frequency) radio message from Pearl Harbor.

The orders were delivered to Commander Bowman. He was in the wardroom with executive officer Jenae Mauk. They were alone.

After speeding through a printed copy of the dispatch from COMSUBPAC, Bowman turned toward the XO. "We need to return to Hainan at best possible speed."

Commander Mauk cast a questioning gaze.

Bowman said, "The two 'guests' we left behind have been busy."

"Doing what?"

"Sounds like they jumped into the proverbial briar patch. And now they need us to pull 'em out."

* * * *

"What do you mean it's gone?" demanded Captain Zhou from his apartment bedroom. He was in bed with his cell phone pasted to an ear, irritated at the unexpected wake-up call from the S5 duty officer.

"One of the crew arrived at the pier an hour ago. He said he wanted to board early. But the boat was sailing away with all of the mooring lines left hanging from the dock."

Zhou checked the clock of the stand next to the bed: 3:55 A.M. "The ship isn't supposed to depart until ten hundred."

"I understand, sir. The crewman thought he had the departure time wrong. He ended up calling his supervisor who was still at his home, like most of the crew. That's when they knew something was wrong. Eventually, the supervisor called the ship's captain. He called the Shendao base where his call was finally routed to me."

"They left the mooring lines?" Normal procedure called for the lines to be hauled aboard and stowed on the ship.

"Affirmative, dangling from the dock."

"Call Fenghuang. I want a helo on the pad fully crewed, fueled and armed, ready to go in thirty minutes."

"Aye, aye, Captain."

As Zhou walked to the bathroom for a quick shower, one thought dominated. *It's the Americans—they're after Serpent.*

And then a new horror struck. *Park!*

Chapter 67

Yuri and Jeff were on the *Lian's* aft deck adjacent to the Viperina canisters. The ship tracked southward at eighteen knots. After engaging the autopilot and checking radar for vessel traffic, Yuri accessed the ship's master electrical panel. He switched off all exterior and interior lighting, including navigation lights. Yuri and Jeff relied on flashlights discovered in a bridge locker.

Yuri turned and peered over the stern. Sanya glowed in the distance. "We don't have much time left. They'll be coming soon."

CIA officer Chang trained his light on the nearest canister. "I've got to at least try to get a piece of the damn thing."

"Five minutes and that's it."

"Okay, let's do it."

Using a portable aluminum ladder found earlier inside the submersible hangar, Yuri and Jeff climbed onto the lids of the eight-foot-tall canisters. The closely spaced twin parallel rows of steel drums housed Vipers 1 to 6. Yuri carried a canvas bag stuffed with tools liberated from the ship's workshop.

The lid from one of the containers was already open from their first inspection. They knelt on the unopened drums next to it. Jeff reached inside and grabbed the exposed end of Viper 2 with both hands. He extracted several feet of the one-foot diameter tube.

Yuri aimed his flashlight at the exposed section—the first coil of the eighty-two-foot-long weapon. He noted what appeared to be a cover plate within the first foot. "Looks like that might be an access panel."

"Right, this end probably has the computer in it."

Yuri reached forward and touched the main tube beyond the head. The exterior surface consisted of a transparent waterproof membrane that covered the cylindrical pressure casing. The casing consisted of inner connected metallic rings, each about two inches long. "Incredible," Yuri said. "It's metal but all of those joints make it flexible."

Jeff took a closer look. "Are the rings made of steel?"

"Maybe. But if I had to guess, I'd say titanium. Stronger than steel but lighter. And titanium is less magnetic than steel, which makes it harder to detect."

Jeff rotated the tube exposing the underside. "What do you think this is for?" he said gesturing to a two inch wide by one inch high bulge that appeared to run the length of the tube.

Yuri homed in on the appendage, noting the continuous rows of metallic spikes laying flush inside the housing, like talons from a bird of prey. "Clever," he said. "I think it's a retractable grapple device. The tube wraps itself around a target and those spikes extend outward and grab hold."

"The gouges in the *Tucson's* sail!"

"Exactly."

"Wicked," Jeff said.

Yuri pointed his light into the interior of the five foot diameter barrel. The coils extended to the bottom. He looked back at Jeff. "I don't see any indication of where the explosive charges are located."

"They must be inside the thing."

"That's my assessment and that's a problem for us."

"Why?"

"Because if we're going to take a sample and we happen to cut the explosive by accident that could be very bad."

"I see your point, but Langley still needs a sample."

Yuri massaged the stubble on his chin. "Just the head only."

"Works for me."

Yuri reached into the tool bag and pulled out a hacksaw.

* * * *

Meng Park sat on the diamond plated steel deck. Her spine was propped against the shipping cradle that housed the replacement module for Viper Station 6.

The *Lian* pulsed with energy. Moving at flank speed, the deck vibrated under Park's buttocks with the frenzy of a washing machine on the spin cycle. The drone of the engines racing at peak output deep inside the hull masked sea sounds and the chatter between her captors. The two Americans were on top of the canisters, just above Meng.

What are those devils doing now? she wondered.

Dr. Meng's wrists remained cabled behind her back. The Asian had also hobbled her ankles. And to prevent her from bunny hopping across the deck and leaping overboard in a suicide escape, the Asian-American had looped a rope around her waist and one of the cradle's steel beams. He'd cinched it tight—too tight.

She'd protested, cursing him in Mandarin. He slapped duct tape across her mouth.

Resting on the deck ten feet away was the Asian's backpack. Half of her life was inside. Before vacating her cabin, the two Americans turned it upside down. They found her laptop and cell phone, placing both inside the pack. Thankfully each device was passcode protected and all critical files encrypted.

The devils also emptied the entire contents of Meng's attaché case into the rucksack including a hard copy of a draft report she was editing on the implementation plan for Phase 2 of Serpent. She preferred working with paper when editing, which violated the security protocol she was mandated to follow regarding Serpent.

Once that turncoat reads the report, he'll know everything.

Before securing Meng to the cradle, she had observed the other barbarian march the ship's engineer into a nearby shipping container. After a couple of minutes, the Caucasian thug emerged from the steel box and locked the door.

Did he murder the engineer?

Furious at the brazenness of the kidnappers, another worry haunted Park. The submersible was in the hangar when she boarded the ship but now it was on the deck next to the replacement Viperinas.

Why did they move the Xiu Shan?

Park's thoughts were interrupted by a new distraction, metal grating on metal. She looked upward. That's when she spotted a partial coil from one of the Viperinas. It extended half a foot beyond the canister's rim.

I've got to stop them—somehow!

* * * *

Atop an unopened barrel, Yuri and Jeff examined a two-foot segment of Viper 2. Yuri held a two-inch diameter by three-inch-long plastic cylinder in his hands, extracted from the severed head.

"What's that?" asked Jeff Chang.

"It's a miniature hydrophone—omnidirectional."

"This thing is incredible," Chang said.

Yuri had already extracted the next hydrophone from the open end of the tube. "These units are linked together by a cable that connects with the CPU, very much like the towed sonar arrays used on subs."

Severing the tube was a messy proposition. Yuri needed four hacksaw blades to cut around the armored circumference. In that process, he nicked one of the hydraulic hoses that ran the length of the tube, releasing a spray of oil. When pressurized, the fluid activated the hydraulic actuators that created body oscillations. The sinuous movements propelled the weapon, mimicking the serpentine motion of a real sea snake.

The system that powered the Viperina consisted of a three inch diameter tube that ran the length of the weapon. Yuri speculated it was a lithium-ion battery configured in a flexible linear array.

"Should we grab one of the charges?" Jeff asked, pointing to the main body of Viper 2. The wedge of plastic explosive was visible a few inches inside the opening, just above the battery.

"No way. Not touching it. Your people will have to rely on photos only." Yuri checked his watch. He was three minutes over his planned autopsy. "We've got to go now."

"Okay."

Chapter 68

Yuri stood on a portable aluminum ladder beside the access hatch to the submersible's six-foot diameter acrylic sphere. He lowered a canvas bag through the opening. The bag contained the severed brain of Viper 2.

"Got it," Jeff Chang said as he grabbed the bag. He was seated in the pilot's station at the aft end of the sphere. Meng Park was in the forward starboard passenger seat. Jeff lowered the bag onto the port seat, setting it next to his backpack.

Yuri leaned through the opening. "You can go ahead and shut the hatch."

Jeff pointed to a switch on the pilot's console and looked up at Yuri.

"That's the one." Yuri started to back away when he glanced down at Meng. "Keep a close eye on her, Jeff. She's big trouble."

"Will do."

The hatch with its thick rubber seals rotated shut, ensuring a watertight fit.

Jeff eyed his captive in the starboard seat. Her torso slumped to the side, deflated.

Meng Park was indeed 'big trouble'. She'd fought vigorously when he and Yuri had struggled to lower her into the sphere, twisting and contorting her body with the verve of a python. Despite the gag, she'd uttered a litany of curses.

But when she tried to smash the control panel with her bound feet, Jeff had had enough. He injected her with the last dose of the ketamine and cabled her forearms to the seat's armrests.

Jeff watched as Yuri climbed down to the *Lian's* deck where he pulled the ladder away and set it aside. The ship was adrift; Yuri had idled the diesels ten minutes earlier.

Yuri pointed to the A-frame control station some twenty feet away. Jeff waved back.

A minute later, the A-frame's hoist cable tightened. Secured to the submersible's lifting tab, the steel cable raised the *Xiu Shan* from its cradle.

The submersible swayed as Yuri pivoted the A-frame assembly toward the stern.

Jeff peered down through the bottom of the transparent sphere. The minisub was now suspended ten feet over the placid sea surface.

Jeff rehearsed his next moves, instructed by Yuri. *Once in the water, turn on the exterior floodlights. Engage the horizontal thrusters. Reverse until fifty feet away from the ship and . . .*

* * * *

Yuri lowered the rigid-hulled inflatable boat, using a hydraulic crane designed to launch and retrieve the tender. The RIB plopped into the water near the *Lian's* stern. He retrieved the assault rifle commandeered from the guard and pointed the barrel overboard. Selecting the burst mode, he emptied the thirty-round magazine with ten trigger pulls, shredding the inflatable bladder and peppering the fiberglass hull.

As the RIB sank, Yuri sprinted forward.

* * * *

Commanders Bowman and Mauk stood beside the horizontal large screen display in the *Colorado's* control room. An electronic chart of the waters offshore of Hainan Island's southern shore filled the touch screen.

"It's shallow for quite a distance from Sanya," Jenae Mauk commented. "We'll have to be careful, especially during any daylight ops."

Colorado's commanding officer nodded his agreement. "We'll maintain at least three hundred feet of water over us."

Water clarity in the South China Sea was currently exceptional due to calm weather conditions and a pause in water column biological activity. *Colorado's* dark hull would contrast sharply with the white sandy bottom offshore of Sanya, allowing patrol aircraft to observe the submarine.

"Hopefully, we can make the pickup at night," Mauk offered.

"Amen to that."

The *Colorado* was a thousand feet deep, running northwest at thirty-two knots. The submarine was on a rescue mission—a mission that it had never trained for and bordered on the impossible.

Chapter 69

Buffeted by whirling rotors, Captain Zhou Jun climbed into the military helicopter. It was 4:35 A.M. He moved forward to the cockpit's center console. With a raised voice he spoke to both pilots. "The *Lian* is ninety-four meters long. It departed around zero three hundred, heading south. That's all we know at this time."

"What's the ship's maximum speed, sir?" asked the pilot, a PLAN lieutenant.

"Eighteen knots."

"Can you tell us what we might be up against...weapons, hostiles?"

"We don't know what happened. Just that the ship left abruptly seven hours ahead of its scheduled departure and with only a handful of crew aboard."

"Thanks, Captain. Please buckle up. We'll be airborne in thirty seconds.

* * * *

Yuri checked the autopilot, verifying the ship's new course. He took one last look around the darkened bridge. The only illumination came from the instrument panels and consoles.

Yuri dialed the ship's throttle, rotating the knob from idle to flank.

The deck under his feet shuddered as the diesel engines throttled up.

Time to go!

Yuri switched on his flashlight and trod briskly to an aft passageway.

By the time Yuri passed through the submersible hangar and hurried onto the aft deck, the ship was moving at thirteen knots and accelerating.

He ran past the cradle housing the replacement Viperinas. Stopping at the ship's stern he looked seaward, searching.

Where are you?

He spotted the glowing glasslike dome; it retreated as the ship surged southwestward.

Yuri took a mental fix on the submersible and checked the life jacket he'd liberated from a bridge locker. Satisfied, he leaped overboard.

* * * *

Jeff Chang's feet rested on the pilot's seat. His head and shoulders protruded from the transparent orb's hatchway. The submersible's exterior lights radiated an eerie luminous glow into the surrounding tropical waters.

Although the *Lian* was blacked out, Jeff could see the ship's silhouette in the reflected moonlight as it sped away. A boil of churning white water marked the ship's stern. The din of racing diesels penetrated the still night air.

He peered into the darkness, searching. *Okay, Yuri, where are you?*

Two minutes went by. Still no Yuri. Jeff looked down at the starboard seat. Dr. Meng had slumped to the side, still sedated.

Jeff again peered into the darkness, searching. It wasn't long before he heard the rush of water.

What's that?

Within an eyeblink, wake wash from the *Lian* raced up the sphere's smooth exterior and soaked Jeff. Several gallons of seawater spilled through the hatchway.

Jeff cussed his carelessness. Yuri had instructed him to keep the hatch shut until he arrived. Jeff closed the hatch and retreated to the interior trying to assess damage. Most of the water pooled in the pilot's seat. But he worried about the electronics. The submersible was chock-full of electrically powered equipment.

Jeff used clothing from his backpack to soak up the water when he heard a rapping sound. He turned to the source.

Yuri bobbed in the water next to the hatch. The palm of his right hand pounded on the twelve-inch-thick acrylic sphere.

* * * *

Airborne for eighteen minutes, the Z-9D Dauphin raced southwestward two hundred meters above the South China Sea. The PLAN helicopter's radar had a solid lock on the *Lian.*

The pilot keyed the intercom mike. "Captain, we should have a visual on the target in about a minute."

"Very well," Zhou Jun said. He wore a helmet with built-in comms, allowing him to hear and speak with the flight crew over the roar of the helicopter's powerplant and rotating rotors.

Zhou peered out the windscreen through a gap between the pilots. The waters were ink black. Sunrise was an hour and a half away. *Where is it*? he wondered.

On cue, the copilot called out. "I have the target."

"Copy that," the pilot said.

It took several seconds before Captain Zhou could see the ship.

"Captain," the pilot said, "I don't see nav lights or any lights at all. The ship is blacked out."

"Bring it down lower and get closer. I want to check the bridge."

"Roger that."

Matching the *Lian's* pace, the Dauphin descended to bridge deck level. Like the rest of the ship, the pilothouse was dark.

"I can't see inside," Zhou said. "Use your light."

The fifty million candlepower searchlight lit up the bridge deck.

"No one inside," Zhou announced, stunned.

"Must be on autopilot," offered the pilot.

"Orbit around the entire ship with the light on."

When the spotlight illuminated the stern deck, Zhou noticed the change. One of the lids for the replacement Vipers was missing. *What's going on?*

The helicopter completed the 360-degree scan of *Lian's* external decks. "Sorry, Captain," the pilot reported, "but we don't see anyone outside. They must be inside one of the compartments."

"What's the projected course?"

The copilot responded. "I'll enter the course into our nav computer."

Zhou waited.

"Captain, the ship is on a direct course to Da Nang."

"Bastards! I need to get aboard it now."

The pilot answered. "The ship doesn't have a heliport."

"Lower me down."

"We don't have a hoist aboard sir. We're not SAR equipped." The pilot referred to search and rescue.

Shit!

Zhou schemed for a quarter minute. "The Coast Guard cutter, does it have a helo deck?"

"Yes, I believe it does."

"Where is it now?"

"I'll check." The pilot pivoted the helicopter, allowing the radar to probe the waters to the west. The cutter was conducting a fisheries patrol in the southern Tonkin Gulf when diverted. "I have it, Captain. It's on an intercept course…should close on the *Lian* in about an hour."

* * * *

Yuri piloted the *Xiu Shan*. For the past fifty-five minutes, the submersible hugged the seabed, running full out at seven knots.

Jeff Chang sat in the forward passenger seat on the port side. The unconscious Meng Park occupied the adjacent bucket seat, her wrists still bound to the armrests.

Jeff stared downward at the sandy bottom, mesmerized by the passing flora and fauna. Yuri had switched on the low power floods to help him navigate. He was not yet comfortable with the sub's controls and needed a visual reference to avoid colliding with the bottom.

Jeff looked over his shoulder at Yuri. "This is frigging incredible. I've never seen anything like this before."

Yuri did not respond. After a minute of silence, Jeff asked, "How deep are we now?"

Yuri checked the control panel. "Ninety-eight meters."

"How deep can this thing go?"

"I don't know for sure. The depth gauge has a red line at two thousand meters so that's probably the limit."

Jeff settled back into the bucket seat, once again watching the seafloor pass by.

Yuri worked the joystick, slowly gaining confidence with the controls. Still waterlogged from his swim and forced to endure the soaked pilot's station seat, he coped. What worried Yuri was the high-pitched whine that permeated the acrylic sphere. The submersible's horizontal thrusters were maxed out. Not only was the din annoying but it was hazardous. The right kind of sonar could detect the racket. Yuri's goal was to speed to deep water. By dipping below the thermocline—a rapid change in seawater temperature identified by a warm layer above and cold water below—the difference in water temperature would help shield the noisy sub from surface sonars.

Yuri pulled up the chart he'd liberated from the *Lian*. *Dammit, it's just too far to risk it at this speed!*

Yuri throttled back, reducing the undersea vessel's speed to four knots. The annoying racket diminished to a mellow hum.

"What's going on?" Jeff asked.

"This thing makes too much noise at max speed. Could give us away."

"So, it's going to take us longer."

"Yes, a lot longer."

Chapter 70

"It's starting to get light outside," Jeff said as he peered upward through the plastic sphere. The solid black water column had evolved into hazy tones of turquoise.

"Sun's coming up," Yuri noted. An hour had elapsed since he throttled back the minisub.

Amazed by the dive, Jeff said, "The water… it's so beautiful."

Yuri ignored Jeff's enchantment. "Check Meng's bindings. She could wake up anytime now."

"Okay boss."

Once Yuri took command of the *Lian* and the submersible, Jeff started addressing him as boss.

"Everything's cool," Jeff reported.

"Thanks."

"Are we any deeper yet?"

Yuri shifted in his seat, uncomfortable in his damp trousers. "Not much. It's just a hundred meters or so deep here."

"This is going to take forever."

"According to the chart, the bottom is flat in this area. It'll be another hour before we see much of a change. But even after that, we'll still have twenty miles to go before we reach the real drop off."

"And we're sitting ducks the entire time."

Yuri instantly deciphered Jeff's latest idiom. "The reduced speed helps but until we dip below the thermocline, we're naked."

* * * *

With eyes sealed and slumped to the side of the seat, Meng Park eavesdropped on the crosstalk between the barbarians. She'd regained consciousness several minutes before the Asian tugged on the bindings that anchored her wrists to the armrests.

The Asian's English was flawless. From her years as a college student in the U.S., Meng determined that he was American born. She was not certain about the other thug. Although he was fluent in English, she detected a slight accent, which she couldn't place.

Meng took a peek, her third since the knockout drug wore off.

Good, it's getting lighter!

She again prayed to *Guanyin.*

Send Jun to rescue me—and to dispose of these vermin.

* * * *

Captain Zhou Jun and the officer in charge of the China Coast Guard security detail were inside the *Lian's* bridge alongside the windscreen. The sun had emerged twenty minutes earlier. The research ship's engines idled. The sixty-four-meter cutter from CCG Hainan's Second Flotilla loitered two hundred meters to the south. China's Coast Guard was part of the People's Armed Police Force. The PAP, in turn, was controlled by the Central Military Commission, which allowed Zhou to assume operational control of the cutter.

After the PLAN helicopter landed on the cutter and Zhou transferred to the ship, he ordered the Z-9D Dauphin pilots to return to the *Lian* and wait until the Coast Guard cutter caught up. Low on fuel, the helo returned to shore after Zhou boarded the *Lian.*

Captain Zhou scanned the horizon to the southwest with a pair of binoculars. Finding nothing of interest he lowered the glasses. Discouraged, he muttered, "Where are they?"

"Could they have returned to Sanya?" asked the CCG lieutenant.

"That would make no sense at all," Zhou said, frustrated. "Call your helicopter again." He referred to another version of the Z-9 Dauphine deployed from the Coast Guard base at Sanya.

The lieutenant used a portable radio he carried to contact the helo. The crew reported no sign of *Lian's* runabout. The CCG Dauphine had flown on a heading for Da Nang at an altitude of two hundred meters. It exceeded the RIB's maximum possible range by fifty kilometers.

When Zhou had boarded the *Lian* after the Coast Guard assault team secured the ship, he noticed that the RIB was missing. Stored on the ship's stern deck near the A-frame control station, the twenty-four-foot inflatable served as the ship's tender and was also used to support the deployment of scientific equipment. With its thirty-knot speed, the RIB also made an ideal getaway platform.

Zhou stepped to the navigator's station; the Coast Guard officer followed. Zhou studied the digital chart before facing his subordinate. "They're tricky bastards. They set the ship on a course to Da Nang to throw us off. The RIB isn't headed there…it's going to rendezvous with another boat."

The lieutenant caught on straight away. "We need to expand the search!"

"Exactly, you call your flotilla commander and tell him I want every air asset he has available launched immediately plus all of his floaters. If we have to, we're going to search every ship, boat and skiff within a hundred twenty-kilometer radius of our position."

"Aye, aye, Captain."

Zhou entered the *Lian's* radio room. He needed to update S5.

Just hang on Park. We're on the way now.

Another hour would pass before Zhou discovered he had erred.

Chapter 71

Dr. Meng Park couldn't stand it any longer. Her legs cramped and her lumbar spine ached. Besides, the barbarians had stopped talking fifteen minutes earlier. The Asian sitting in the adjacent passenger seat fell asleep; she heard him snoring.

Park faked a cough and stirred in the bucket seat, shifting her hips.

The brute occupying the pilot's station noticed. He called out to his companion, "Jeff, wake up. She's back with us."

Park turned to her side. The bare chested Asian awoke instantly. He smiled while stretching out his arms. "Hi there," he said.

Chang had shed his T-shirt twenty minutes earlier. The temperature inside the submersible was eighty-five degrees Fahrenheit. With three radiating bodies, no air conditioning and surrounding tropical waters, the *Xiu Shan's* closed atmosphere had warmed.

She tried to talk but the gag mumbled her words. The Asian peeled away the strip of tape, taking care not to injure her skin.

"Where are you taking me?" Park demanded.

"You'll know soon enough."

"Why are you doing this to me?"

"You know why, Dr. Meng."

"You stinking pigs!" Park screamed in Mandarin as she arched her spine upwards from the bucket seat. She leveraged her body mass, trying to break free of the cable ties that bound her wrists to the armrests. After two additional attempts, she gave up and settled back into the seat. Red welts erupted on her skin under the plastic ties.

Defeated, she eventually asked, "May I have some water?"

* * * *

Captain Zhou and the CCG Lieutenant relocated to the *Lian's* submersible hanger. Ten minutes earlier, the assault team discovered the engineer and other detained crew members gagged, bound and locked inside the shipping container near the hanger.

"You're certain it was aboard and not transferred to shore for maintenance?" Zhou asked the engineer, stunned at the turn of the events.

"Yes, Captain. I saw it yesterday afternoon when I was in the hangar. No question about it, the *Xiu Shan* was in its cradle."

Zhou stared at the parallel tracks that ran aft through the open hangar door to the A-frame crane at the stern. The cradle was parked at the end of the tracks under the hoist—minus the submersible. Zhou cursed.

"Captain," the China Coast Guard officer said, "do you think they escaped in the submersible instead of the tender?"

"That just doesn't make any sense. The submersible is slow compared to the RIB. Why would they?" Zhou's voice faded as a new horror flashed into focus. "We've been deceived. An American submarine must be nearby. That's where they're going with the *Xiu Shan*."

* * * *

Half a world away in Langley, Virginia, CIA officer Steve Osberg monitored the events taking place offshore of Sanya. He currently had control of several NRO minisatellites. Each spy bird was about the size of a shopping cart basket and was equipped with a high resolution video camera. The medium orbit constellation provided sporadic real time monitoring of the South China Sea.

Osberg was seated at a workstation in the Ops Center. He eyeballed a Dell monitor. Displayed on the flat panel wide-screen was a bird's-eye view of the *Lian*. The ship sailed southward at eight knots. The sun was up, allowing direct satellite observation without the need for infrared optics.

Osberg massaged the back of his neck. *So far, so good,* he thought. During Chang's last call from the *Lian*, Osberg learned of Kirov's seat of the pants Plan B. Da Nang was out; they'd never make it in time with the RIB. Besides, they had a prisoner. Should China unravel the charade, removing Dr. Meng from Vietnam would be a diplomatic nightmare.

Using the RIB as a decoy—brilliant plan!

By monitoring comms from the China Coast Guard cutter and other local Sanya maritime radio traffic, the National Security Agency and Naval Intelligence ascertained that the Chinese had yet to discover the real escape avenue.

What incredible balls Kirov has!

Osberg marveled at Yuri's mettle. Earlier, he had watched Yuri when he jumped overboard as the *Lian* accelerated from a deadstart.

Too bad our birds can't see underwater.

Once the submersible descended, Osberg lost contact with his operatives. Chang had provided the rendezvous coordinates during his last transmission. Osberg checked his wristwatch. In roughly fourteen hours, the minisub was scheduled to surface at the designated earth coordinates.

I just hope Colorado *arrives in time.*

Chapter 72

"Are we getting close?" Jeff Chang asked. He had pulled on his T-shirt twenty minutes earlier. The *Xiu Shan* cooled as it descended into the deeper and cooler waters.

Yuri checked the *Xiu Shan's* control panel. The water depth gauge displayed 191 meters—627 feet. The digital clock showed: 12:25 PM. He did the math. "We've got about five nautical miles to go before we hit the steep part of the bottom slope. That will take another hour and a quarter."

"They must be looking for us by now."

"I know. Hopefully, we'll get below the thermocline before we're spotted."

* * * *

Still restrained in the starboard bucket seat, Dr. Meng Park stared through the acrylic sphere. The submersible cruised just above the seabed. Sunlight penetrated to the *Xiu Shan's* depth but its intensity gradually lessened as the water depth increased.

Dipping below the thermocline—so that's his plan.

Schooled in submarine evasion tactics as part of her work on Serpent, Dr. Meng understood how effective the thermocline could be for a hiding a submarine. Once below the layer of rapidly changing water temperature, a submarine could hide from sonar. The thermocline (aka the "layer") acts as a barrier to acoustic energy, shielding a sub from surface sonars deployed by ships and aircraft.

Jun must be looking for me by now. Somehow, I've got to let him know where we are before it's too late.

* * * *

Captain Zhou Jun took command of the *Lian* and the overall search operation. He also drafted the China Coast Guard officer who had accompanied him from the cutter to serve as the search coordinator. The taskforce had ballooned to six aircraft and five additional Coast Guard vessels beyond the *Lian* and the cutter.

Zhou and the lieutenant hovered over the chart table. The *Lian's* current position was marked by a cobalt blue ship icon as forty-four nautical miles south of Sanya. Nineteen miles to the north was a solid red dot. It represented the assumed dive location of the submersible, which was determined by reconstructing the *Lian's* path from the ship's GPS log. After departing Sanya, the research ship had loitered for nearly half an hour some twenty-five miles south of Hainan Island.

Centered on the red spot was a red circle with a radius of 178 kilometers—ninety-six nautical miles. Zhou was privy to the *Xiu Shan's* basic operational parameters from his deep-sea excursion with Meng Park. The submersible had enough power for twenty-four hours at four knots, which he used to establish the maximum possible search ring. Higher submersible speeds would dramatically cut battery power life, reducing the range.

Captain Zhou pointed to the southeast quadrant of the circle. "I want at least sixty percent of our assets in this sector. It's deep there. That's where the sub will be lurking."

"Understood, sir. How about the northeast sector, should we task additional assets there, too?" The autonomous patrol boats guarding Yulin and Shendao searched the nearshore waters but were useless elsewhere. The drones were configured for shallow water ASW ops only.

"Maybe later, if we can get anything running from Yulin."

To Zhou's dismay, none of the antisubmarine warfare combatants moored at the Yulin Naval Base were operational due to the EMP attack. The only ASW warship immediately available to Zhou was a destroyer from the Shendao Naval Base. Moored at a pier in an inlet north of the aircraft carrier pier and S5, the *Nanchang* had arrived a week earlier. It was on loan from the North Sea Fleet.

To further muddy the tactical situation, none of the CCG helicopters currently in the air were ASW equipped. However, three PLA-Navy antisubmarine warfare helos and two fixed wing ASW airplanes at Lingshui were presently being prepped for subsea combat.

Captain Zhou pointed to the southwest quadrant of the circle. "Keep two vessels and two helicopters here. Even though the submersible doesn't have the range to make it all the way to Da Nang underwater, the hijackers may have a backup plan to rendezvous with a boat and then make a highspeed run to shore."

"They'd probably try that at night."

"Exactly. It's unlikely but we need to be prepared just in case."

"If that does occur and they make it into the territorial waters of Vietnam, should our people continue the pursuit?"

"Absolutely. They are not to land on Vietnamese soil."

"Understood."

The lieutenant noted another ship icon on the electronic chart near the center of the southeast search quadrant. He pointed to the chart. "How soon will the *Nanchang* start its search?"

"It's making a passive run to reestablish background conditions. It shouldn't be long before it goes active. That's when it will get really interesting."

"The American submarine?"

"Yes, if one of their subs is hiding anywhere near here and expects to sneak in for a quick rescue, that's not going to happen."

"The destroyer will attack it."

"Yes, with depth charges and torpedoes."

The lieutenant nodded ardently. "What about the submersible."

"When the *Xiu Shan* runs out of power, they'll have no choice but to surface."

"And we'll be waiting," the lieutenant said smirking.

"That's my plan."

Chapter 73

"It sounds like it's getting closer," Jeff Chang said, his voice strained.

"They haven't found us. We're well below the layer now." Yuri checked the depth gauge: 373 meters—1,224 feet. He piloted the submersible ten feet above the sterile mud bottom. Blackness surrounded the transparent dome even though it was 2:10 P.M. topside. To conserve power, Yuri had cut the floods to just one light.

Another distant muffled "ping" reverberated through the deep, its tone muted by the thermocline. The PLAN destroyer patrolled several miles away, executing a grid search with its bow mounted active sonar. The hunt had started fifty minutes earlier.

Although they were able to reach deeper water without detection, Yuri's worry factor had skyrocketed. If the ship hunting them also had variable depth sonar capability, hiding under the water temperature gradient would not shield the submersible from detection. A VDS or Variable Depth Sonar towed body equipped with active and passive sonars could be lowered below the thermocline by the vessel that stalked the minisub. That would allow the waters below the 'layer' to be searched uninhibited.

Battery life was Yuri's other concern. The initial seven knot sprint had consumed power at a prodigious rate, a mistake Yuri now realized. The submersible's current power supply was marginal—just 32 percent charge. Half an hour earlier, Yuri reduced speed from four to three knots and shut off all noncritical systems.

Yuri had to reserve enough juice to keep the submersible hidden until it could rendezvous with the *Colorado*. Although the *Xiu Shan* could ascend without propulsion by jettisoning ballast, electrical power was required for navigation and life support systems.

Fortunately, oxygen was not a worry. The submersible had a reserve supply of sixty hours of air. CO_2 toxicity, however, was a huge concern. The minisub employed electric powered fans to pump air into the scrubber system, which removed excess carbon dioxide by a chemical filtration process. Without removal of the exhaled carbon dioxide from the three occupants, the atmosphere inside the acrylic dome would turn toxic in minutes.

Yuri adjusted a vertical thruster to maintain ten foot bottom clearance when Meng Park looked over her shoulder at Yuri. "I'm cold." Still restrained, she visibly shivered. "Please turn on the heater."

"Can't do that. We're all cold. You'll just have to deal with it."

Meng sneered and turned back.

Jeff Chang glanced at Yuri, rolling his eyes.

Once the submersible had dipped under the thermocline, the chilled outside water temperature began to seep into the sphere. The current water temperature was 13.3 degrees Celsius—56 degrees Fahrenheit. Earlier, Jeff had put on his T-shirt and donned a jacket from his rucksack. Yuri's own jacket draped Meng's shoulders. He endured the chilly atmosphere in his now dried out long sleeved shirt and pants.

* * * *

"What is it?" asked Commander Bowman. He stood beside the sonar supervisor in the *Colorado's* control room.

"Ah Captain, we're close enough now for a tentative ID. The hull's acoustic output is consistent with one of their new platforms, probably a Type 055." Petty officer Anderson had swiveled his chair away from the sonar console to speak with *Colorado's* commanding officer.

Anderson's report raised the hackles on the back of Bowman's neck. The 055 was China's latest guided missile destroyer. At nearly six hundred feet in length, the ship was actually in the 'cruiser' class. Bristling with sensors and weapons, the 055's main role was to serve as an escort for China's aircraft carriers, providing air defense and protection from submarines. The Type 055's leading edge sonar systems and arsenal of ASW weapons were designed to seek out and destroy hostile subs like the *Colorado*.

"What's the range?"

"Best guess at this point is two convergence zones, say sixty nautical miles."

"So, it's still offshore of Sanya."

"Yes, mowing the lawn. They're obviously looking for something."

"Very well. Let me know ASAP if you think they've got a target."

"Aye, aye, Captain."

The *Colorado's* sensors detected the active sonar about three hours earlier. Bowman ordered the ship's speed reduced from thirty-two knots to sixteen knots to lessen the chance of detection. The high-powered sonar pings at that time were emitted by the Type 055's hull-mounted transducer.

But twenty minutes earlier, *Colorado* detected a new active sonar. The destroyer's variable depth towed sonar fish sank below the thermocline and began a new round of pinging.

The submersible was a tiny target and if it went deep, as Commander Bowman expected, locating it was akin to finding the proverbial needle in the haystack. But that also applied to *Colorado*. How would the sub find and rescue the mini with the Type 055 looming overhead?

Chapter 74

"I understand, Admiral. I'll implement your orders immediately." Captain Zhou Jun returned the telephone handset to the desk stand. He was alone inside the *Lian's* radio room, sitting at the military-grade satellite phone console.

Zhou's conversation with the commander of the South Sea Fleet did not go well. The admiral requested an update on the search for Dr. Meng and the missing submersible. It was 5:53 P.M. Sunset was half an hour away and there still was no sign of the *Xiu Shan*. The PLAN destroyer probed the depths with its VDS sonar but had not yet detected the minisub.

The Xiu Shan *must be hiding on the bottom—but for how long?*

The one positive finding so far was the absence of hostile submarine activity in or near the search zone. Besides the *Nanchang* and its two helicopters, three shore based ASW helicopters with dipping sonars and two antisubmarine patrol planes from Lingshui Airbase had joined the hunt. Sonobuoys parachuted from the planes and choppers saturated the ocean with acoustic sensors above and below the thermocline. Magnetic sensors in the tails of both four-engine propeller-driven airplanes also sniffed for the presence of steel hulls.

Maybe I have this all wrong! What if they jettisoned the submersible to throw us off but really escaped in the RIB?

That revelation dumbfounded Zhou but it was soon dismissed.

No. We covered that possibility.

The swarm of China Coast Guard patrol boats, helicopters and planes assigned to the northwest and southwest search quadrants checked every ship, fishing boat, skiff and runabout within the range of the *Lian's* rigid-hull inflatable boat. One CCG vessel even stopped a Da Nang based boat a mile inside Vietnam's twelve mile territorial boundary. The RIB was loaded with tourists on a scuba diving excursion. The incident generated a harsh diplomatic rebuke by Hanoi.

Captain Zhou had no choice—the admiral's orders were direct: "End this situation now!"

Zhou returned to the bridge. The *Lian's* captain hovered over the navigation table. The PLAN officer and the rest of the crew stranded in Sanya were ferried to the ship hours earlier by a CCG patrol boat. Zhou transferred command back to the captain but he retained overall control of the search taskforce.

"We have orders from Fleet," Zhou announced as he approached the chart table.

The Navy commander made eye contact with his superior. "Yes sir."

"We need to prep the Serpent units for immediate deployment."

"For the *Xiu Shan?*"

"Yes. We can't delay any longer. Assemble the Serpent team and prepare for deployment.

"Aye, aye, Captain."

Zhou peered through the windscreen. It was an exquisite afternoon, the turquoise sea tranquil and the azure sky vibrant with golden hues from the sinking sun.

Zhou was immune to the setting. He dreaded what was to come.

Please forgive me, Park.

Chapter 75

"How long do we stay put?" Jeff Chang asked.

"At least a couple more hours," Yuri said. Fearing detection by the *Nanchang*'s VDS sonar, Yuri had bottomed out the submersible two hours earlier as the destroyer maneuvered nearby.

It was 7:48 P.M. The *Xiu Shan* rested on the silty bottom in pitch black 2,945 feet below the surface. The only light inside the six-foot diameter orb radiated from the control panel of the pilot's station. Battery life had declined to just 12 percent. Despite the depth, the temperature inside the minisub stabilized at fifty-four degrees Fahrenheit. Chilly but tolerable.

Meng Park dozed as Yuri and Jeff chatted.

"What do you think they're doing now?" Jeff said.

"I'm sure they're still listening."

The sonar pings ceased forty minutes earlier, which was a huge relief to Yuri and Jeff. Without the persistent acoustic pulses probing the depths, quietude returned to the submersible. Other than the occasional refrain from a distant whale or the prattle from other local biologics, the principal background sound inside the minisub was the soft purr from the CO_2 scrubber fans.

"The *Colorado* must be close by now, don't you think," Jeff said, his tone optimistic.

"Right." But Yuri was not confident the U.S. Navy supersub was anywhere near the *Xiu Shan*. The scheduled rendezvous time with the *Colorado* was 2200—10:00 P.M. However, the aggressive sonar search by the destroyer and other PLAN assets were enough to give pause to any sub skipper about venturing into such troubled waters.

Yuri watched as Jeff switched on a flashlight and rifled through the backpack parked at the base of his seat.

"What are you looking for?" Yuri asked.

"I want to check the satphone to make sure its batteries are up to snuff."

The submersible was equipped with a marine VHF radio for communication with the *Lian* while it operated on the surface. But Jeff and Yuri couldn't risk an open-air radio link to the *Colorado*. Instead, the plan called for Jeff to employ the SEAL phone once they surfaced. The encrypted call to Langley would be relayed back to the submarine. It was an awkward procedure but one that ensured privacy.

As Jeff inspected the portable satellite phone, Meng Park stirred. Yuri noticed. She turned toward Chang, drawn by the flashlight's illumination. After a few seconds, she began to squirm in the bucket seat, her wrists still anchored to the armrests. Finally, she announced, "I can't stand this anymore. I have to pee."

They'd had this discussion before. Several hours earlier, Yuri had informed Meng she needed to hold her water, just like he and Jeff.

Meng's latest request was not unreasonable. She had boarded the *Xiu Shan* over fifteen hours beforehand. The submersible was equipped with a compact portable toilet but it was stored under the pilot's seat. Access required rotating the seat forward between the passenger seats. That was a procedure not possible while Yuri maneuvered the minisub. But now, parked on the bottom, it was doable. All three would welcome the relief.

Yuri said, "All right. We can give it a try now." He switched on an interior light.

Meng uttered an audible sigh. Jeff glanced at Yuri. She missed his smirk.

After returning the satphone to his backpack, Jeff used a pocketknife to cut the plastic cable ties that bound Meng's wrists to the armrests.

Yuri shifted to the narrow space between the pilot's seat and the port side of the sphere, arching his spine against the curvature of the hull. He rotated the pilot's seat forward, exposing the portable toilet.

"Okay," he said glancing Meng's way, "climb over your seat."

Meng complied. After she crouched beside the receptacle, she stared at Yuri, "Are you going to watch me, too?"

"Don't touch anything." Yuri signaled for Jeff to relocate to Meng's seat. Yuri next stepped over the seat back and sat down in Jeff's vacated seat.

Meng went about her business. They could hear everything. When she finished, she pulled up her jeans.

Yuri turned and peered aft. He was about to direct Meng's return to her passenger seat when she made her move.

Meng reached for the minisub's search sonar control panel located beside the right side of the pilot's station. She flipped the trigger guard covering the transmit switch and pressed the button.

Yuri lunged forward, wrenching Meng's torso away from the panel. But he was too late.

An audible metallic ping broadcast into the deep.

"What happened?" Jeff asked.

"You bitch!" Yuri bellowed.

Meng snickered.

Chapter 76

"Do you think they heard it, as far down as we are?" Jeff Chang asked.

"We're deep and the sonar unit isn't all that powerful," Yuri said. "But yes, one of the platforms topside no doubt heard it."

Five minutes had passed since Meng had pulled her stunt. Yuri reoccupied the pilot's station. Meng was back in the starboard passenger seat, her wrists again bound to the armrests and one of Jeff's smelly socks from his rucksack stuffed in her mouth. She had once more mocked her captors; Jeff had had enough—again.

Jeff said, "How deep are we going?"

"To at least 1,100 meters. That destroyer most likely has torpedoes. The typical depth limit for a torpedo is 800 to 1,000 meters."

"Typical limit?"

"I don't know what the Chinese have pitted against us. But most of their torpedoes are based on Russian design."

"Okay, got it." Jeff recalled another worry. "How much power have we got left?"

"Not enough."

* * * *

The sonar detail aboard the *Nanchang* noticed the errant sonar ping. Passive hydrophones on the VDS towed body some three hundred meters below the surface detected the acoustic pulse from the *Xiu Shan*. The destroyer's captain, however, did not order a torpedo strike. The computed depth of the target exceeded the pressure rating of the weapons aboard his warship. But even if the target were within range, he was not authorized to attack. His ship was re-tasked to monitoring only.

Captain Zhou took command of the assault from the *Lian*, deploying a new weapon system unknown to the *Nanchang's* CO.

* * * *

The two pairs of Viperinas hunted in a coordinated pattern, centered on the isolated sonar ping originating from the deep. Vipers 3 and 4 approached from the north. Vipers 5 and 6 swam westward. Viper 1, the mate to the dissected Viper 2, remained aboard the *Lian* as a reserve.

V-3 and V-4 detected the minuscule whine of the *Xiu Shan's* horizontal thrusters as it scurried along the bottom.

* * * *

"What's that?" Jeff Chang said, pointing forward.

Yuri squinted, peering through the plastic bubble. At the edge of the floodlight's radiance he also spotted the bottom debris. Yuri cut power to the thrusters; the minisub settled onto the bottom. He checked the depth gauge: 3,022 feet.

The fragments of torn metal a dozen feet away from the submersible appeared alien in the otherwise sterile seascape. Yuri had observed similar seabed deposits before. "This looks like a debris field…there might be a wreck ahead."

Yuri was tempted to use the onboard sonar to check the route but couldn't risk the acoustic noise. Just before engaging the thrusters, Jeff called out, "Whoa, did you see that?" Jeff rotated his head back and stared at the peak of the dome. Meng Park did the same, her eyes ballooning. Yuri focused on her obvious terror.

"What did you see?" Yuri asked.

Searching the overhead, Jeff said, "Something big just went by. Looked like a—" He froze for an instant. "My god, it was one of those snake things."

Astonished, Yuri prepared to engage the thrusters when Meng shook her head vigorously while mumbling through her gag. Yuri backed off the throttle. He reached forward and extracted the sock.

"Don't use the thrusters," she whispered. "They'll hear it. And keep your voices down, too."

"What is it?" Yuri asked
"What you kidnapped me for."
"Govnó!"

* * * *

Viper 3 lost acoustic lock on the submersible when the *Xiu Shan* cut power and settled onto the seabed. V-3's passive sensors relied on acoustic energy from its prey for long distance hunting. When close to its target, V-3 activated its low-powered search sonar to close in for the kill.

Viper 3 was in terminal search mode. Designed to prey on large nuclear-powered submarines, the *Xiu Shan's* minuscule size appeared to be nothing more than a bump on the otherwise gently sloping bottom when V-3 passed by. But just ahead, another target materialized.

The hulk of the World War II warship jutted over ten meters above the bottom. The *Shonan*, a frigate in the Imperial Japanese Navy, was sent to the bottom by a U. S. Navy submarine on February 25, 1945.

The bulk of the wreckage fit within the V-3's target profile. It beamed the finding via optical laser to its partner and closed in for the kill.

Chapter 77

The underwater shockwave careened the *Xiu Shan* across the seafloor at 8:17 P.M. The submersible ended up on its starboard side, tossing its occupants pell-mell. Jeff Chang found himself tangled with Meng Park. Yuri smashed his forehead against a control panel. Blood oozed from the gash.

"What the hell was that?" Jeff yelled.

"That thing must have blown up."

Yuri pressed a palm against his brow. He frantically scanned the plastic globe, praying the foot thick acrylic pressure hull escaped damage. "Thank God," he murmured in Russian. No cracks.

Yuri pulled himself up to check the master control panel. *Ten percent power left. No choice now.*

Yuri engaged a thruster and righted the minisub.

Resettled in the pilot's station, Yuri announced, "We can't sit down here anymore. We're going up now."

"About time," Jeff said.

Still in shock from the blast, Meng said nothing.

Yuri reached under the console and disconnected the safety latch that secured a red lever. He pulled the lever back, jettisoning the emergency ballast. A muffled metallic clang rang out inside the sphere as two hundred kilos of lead shot plummeted to the bottom.

* * * *

Viper 4 swam over the wreckage, using its sonar and laser scanner to search for a secondary target. It started to turn around for a second pass when one of its hydrophones detected the metallic clang of ballast release.

* * * *

The minisub was about a hundred feet above the bottom, ascending from buoyancy only. Yuri shut down almost everything to conserve power. Jeff used a flashlight for interior illumination.

"What did it attack?" Jeff asked.

"Must have been a wreck. Thankfully, that snake thing went after it instead of us."

"So, we should be okay now."

Yuri started to answer when Meng interrupted. "They hunt in pairs. I only heard one detonation."

Jeff aimed the flashlight outward. "Another one of those damn things is out there?"

"I don't know, maybe," Meng Park offered, dumbfounded at the turn of events.

No Serpent bottom stations were located this close to Sanya. The only Vipers were those aboard the *Lian*—replacements for Viper Station 6. And only Captain Zhou Jun had the authority to re-task the weapons for local use.

He knows I'm down here...damn him!

Betrayal cut deep yet she remained loyal to the cause. But that was about to change.

* * * *

Viper 4 scanned the target ahead. Its sonar detected a doppler shift, which identified movement. The target ascended at an unhurried pace of eight meters per minute.

Like Viper 3, the minuscule target profile did not match the hull configuration of a hostile submarine. Yet the target's size was consistent with a large AUV underway. V-4 decided to investigate.

* * * *

"There's one of 'em!" Jeff Chang said, his voice quavering. The flashlight beam illuminated the sensor laden end of Viper 4. It hovered ten feet away from the *Xiu Shan*.

Meng whipped her head toward Yuri. "Find my cell phone, or we're all going to die."

"Why?"

"I have a shutdown code recorded on it."

"Jeff?" Yuri said.

"On it." Jeff began rummaging through his backpack. He found the Huawei, switched the power on and held it up. "What's the code to open your phone?" Meng's arms were still bound to the armrests.

She recited the numerical passcode and Jeff keyed up the homepage. "Where's the recording?"

Meng supplied the information.

"Okay, now what?" Jeff asked.

"You need to use the *Xiu Shan's* underwater radio to send the message. Adjust the cell's speakerphone to maximum volume."

Jeff set it up and handed the cell to Yuri. "Just press the arrow to play it."

Holding the cell phone, Yuri scanned the underwater radio control panel when Jeff sounded a new alarm. "It's moving again."

Viper 4 began to wrap its foot thick body around the submersible's transparent dome. Its claws deployed, digging into the outer layers of plastic. The ensuing screech rivaled fingernails dragged across a blackboard.

"There's no time for the radio," Meng yelled. "Play the recording now—next to the sensors." She peered upward, focusing on the top of the dome.

Yuri held the cell phone against the twelve-inch-thick acrylic sphere beside V-4's coiled head. He activated the recording, releasing a seven second burst of obscure digital tones.

"Do it again," Meng shrieked.

* * * *

Viper 4 was in terminal countdown, about to execute its mission, when its sonar receiver detected the muffled abort signal. V-4's CPU deactivated the detonation circuit to all fifty-two charges and depowered the grapple system.

* * * *

Yuri, Jeff and Meng Park watched in silence as Viper 4 released its death grip on the *Xiu Shan*. Jeff trained the flashlight beam on the dead machine as it slithered toward the bottom.

Chapter 78

Captain Zhou Jun was inside the Serpent control room deep inside the bowels of the *Lian*. The chief Viper technician and his assistant worked at side by side consoles that fronted an array of bulkhead mounted flat panel widescreen displays. It was 8:28 P.M. A digital navigation chart of the waters offshore of Sanya filled the center screen; it displayed the real time GPS locations of all ships and aircraft searching for the hijacked submersible. Another screen displayed the video image of the *Nanchang's* commanding officer who was inside the Type 055 destroyer's combat information center.

Standing behind the assistant tech, Captain Zhou watched the video doppelgänger of the warship commander. Both Zhou and the destroyer's CO wore headsets with voice activated microphones. Zhou had just requested confirmation of the kill.

"That's affirmative, Captain. We also have positive confirmation regarding the target coordinates. Our sensors detected a significant explosion near the bottom." He and Zhou spoke over a secure ship to ship radio link.

"Very well. I will assume the threat has been neutralized."

"Ah, Captain, I'm really curious about the system you deployed. We detected nothing at all from here. Can you provide me with some background?"

"Soon, Commander but not just yet." Zhou shifted gears. "You may return to Shendao now. We're wrapping up here. Thanks for your assistance."

"Very good, sir. I'm pleased we were able to help."

Zhou terminated the video link. He next addressed the senior technician. "Any response to the recall signal?"

"No, sir. We've heard nothing from our sonar sensors."

"Repeat the signal."

"Aye, aye, Captain."

Dr. Meng Park had warned Zhou about the recall issue. Once in attack mode, the Vipers were designed to ignore acoustic based countermeasures, which sometimes also included the recall signal. The Serpent operational code needed refinement to eliminate the glitch.

What are they doing? he wondered.

Three of the four Vipers were unaccounted for. The energy released by the underwater blast was consistent with just one unit.

Park would know what to do . . .

Zhou backed away from the technicians. Thankfully, the compact control room had minimal lighting, which enhanced viewing of the wide-screen displays. A solitary tear cascaded down his right cheek.

Sweet Park—I had no choice.

Zhou's remorse was short-circuited by the chief Viper tech. "Wow, what was that?" he called out, removing his pair of headphones.

Zhou returned to the CPO's side. "What have you got?"

"Another explosion, Captain, near the *Nanchang* but a hundred meters deep. It's been reeling in the VDS towed body."

"One of the Vipers attacked it?"

"I think so."

"Dammit. We need to warn *Nanchang* now."

* * * *

"Captain, sonar reports a submerged explosion four hundred meters from the stern."

Everyone inside the *Nanchang* felt the underwater blast. The shockwave slapped the hull ten seconds earlier.

The destroyer's commanding officer was about to request clarification when the CIC watch officer relayed another incoming report. "Captain, the deck winch crew reports zero tension on the VDS cable."

"Bring the ship to general quarters, man battle stations."

The lieutenant repeated the order and set about implementing it. Seconds later, the comms officer issued a new report. "Captain, the *Lian* is calling again. Captain Zhou needs to speak with you. Says it's urgent."

"Put him on the screen."

Zhou's video image materialized on the secure display. "Commander," Zhou said, "your ship is in imminent danger of attack. Shut down your propulsion system and execute quiet ship conditions."

"Aye, aye, Captain."

The *Nanchang*'s CO repeated Zhou's orders to the CIC watch officer. He turned back to address the video image of his boss. "Sir, what's going on?"

"Some of the weapons we deployed may have gone rogue. They're designed to—"

The transmission from the *Lian* was interrupted by a ferocious tremor that catapulted all seated CIC personnel from their chairs. Those standing were knocked to the deck, some with their lower leg bones snapping.

* * * *

"Captain, we just picked up another explosion. Similar magnitude but close to the Type 055."

"How close?" asked *Colorado's* commanding officer. Tom Bowman stood beside the sonar supervisor in the control room.

"Real close, possibly on the hull itself," the sonar tech reported from his console. A pair of Bose headphones were draped around his neck.

"Very well, keep monitoring. Try to assess damage conditions."

"Aye, sir."

What the hell is going on? questioned Bowman.

The USS *Colorado* was sixteen nautical miles southeast of the PLAN destroyer. For the past hour, the submarine had hovered six hundred feet below the surface. It listened to everything going on in the water column.

Colorado's executive officer was at Bowman's side. "That makes three detonations. Something's not right."

"I know."

"Misfire?"

"Maybe." Bowman turned back to question the sonar supervisor. "Richey," he called out.

Sonar supervisor Anderson swiveled in his chair, pulling his headphones down. "Sir."

"Did you hear anything to indicate that the Type 055 was deploying weapons...torpedoes, depth charges, AUVs?"

"Negative, sir. Nothing but the VDS array."

XO Mauk processed the tactical condition. "Skipper," she said. "Maybe the research ship deployed some of those specials."

"Hmmm."

Bowman and Mauk stepped to the command workstation at the center of the control room. Bowman called up one of the satellite photos supplied by the CIA. The digital image of the *Lian* snapped into focus. He pointed to the deck near the stern. "They had six of those canisters aboard." He turned to face Mauk. "I think you're right, XO. They deployed the damn things."

"They're designed to operate deep. The first explosion—could it have targeted the submersible?"

Bowman scowled. "That must have been what happened."

* * * *

Two hours had elapsed since the attack on the *Nanchang*. The *Lian* accompanied the destroyer as it limped back to Hainan Island. The Shendao Naval Base was five miles away. Captain Zhou Jun shut down the taskforce and ordered all surface craft to avoid the attack area. One of the Viperinas was unaccounted for; Zhou would delay commencing the search for the rogue weapon until its battery ran out of juice.

Chapter 79

Day 38—Friday

It was a quarter past midnight. The *Xiu Shan* surfaced two hours earlier. With the jettisoning of the emergency ballast, the plastic sphere rode about a foot higher out of the water than when it had launched the previous morning. The extra freeboard allowed the hatch to be opened without the worry of flooding. A breeze from the north kicked up whitecaps atop the long and slow swells that rolled in from the southwest.

Without the ballast, the submersible bobbed in response to the wave chop. Yuri was immune; Jeff tolerated the gyrations, just thankful to be alive. Meng Park suffered, heaving her guts out. Still bound to the starboard passenger seat, an open tool box rested in her lap. Yuri found the container behind the pilot's seat. He removed the tools before providing Meng the makeshift barf-bucket.

Ten minutes earlier, after dumping Meng's latest upchuck overboard, Yuri had checked the surrounding waters from the open hatchway. They were alone in this corner of the South China Sea. The ships, helicopters and planes that had hounded the trio were nowhere in sight.

Despite the lingering odor of vomit, Yuri and Jeff waited patiently, both currently seated inside the blacked-out pressure hull. The submersible's batteries had flatlined twenty minutes after reaching the surface.

Yuri peered upward through the transparent orb. The nearly full moon floated overhead, the cloudless sky blossomed starry bright. Caressed by the sea rhythm, he settled into the seat; the adrenaline rush long gone, his weary body needed recharging.

Yuri started to snooze when Chang broke the silence. "What's taking them so long?"

Yuri yawned as he stretched out his arms. "Relax, Jeff. They'll get here when they can."

"What happens if the sun comes up before they arrive. We're sitting ducks out here. Someone will see us for sure."

"Try to nap."

Upon surfacing, Jeff had set up the SEAL satphone and called Langley. It took fifteen minutes to finally hookup with Steve Osberg at the Ops Center. Yuri managed to obtain a GPS fix from the *Xiu Shan's* navigation module before the mini's batteries petered out. Osberg promised he'd relay their location to *Colorado* but was not able to provide a rendezvous time.

Jeff ignored Yuri's suggestion. "I think we should call Langley again."

"You heard Osberg. They want us to stay off the air. Even though the PLAN can't decrypt the call, that Signals unit at Lingshui might detect the transmission and get interested. There's no other radio traffic out here now. We don't want them coming back here to investigate."

"Yeah, you're right," Jeff muttered.

After a twenty minute catnap, Yuri woke. He checked the others. Jeff snored; Meng Park brooded. Yuri was about to stand and take a quick look topside when a familiar voice called out from above. "How're you guys doing?"

Yuri looked upward.

Malibu Murph, outfitted in an ink-black wetsuit stared down from the open hatchway, a cheery grin breaking out across his bearded face. "Ready to go home?" he asked.

"Yes, Chief, we sure are."

Chapter 80

Half a day behind China time, it was late afternoon at the White House. President Tyler Magnuson was in the Oval Office at his desk catching up on correspondence when his chief of staff opened the door. While standing in the threshold, he said, "Sorry to disturb you Mr. President, but Pete Brindle needs a couple of minutes of your time to brief you on the China operation."

"He's here?"

"In the reception."

"Show him in, please."

National Security Advisor Peter Brindle claimed a chair fronting POTUS. "Just heard from Langley," he offered. "*Colorado* plucked our two wayward agents out of the South China Sea several hours ago."

The President chortled, energized by the news. "Fantastic—are they okay?"

"Just fine." Brindle beamed. "They had Dr. Meng with them, too, plus a treasure trove of data and actual hardware for the Serpent system."

"That's terrific." The President stroked his temple, taking in the news. "Do we now have what's needed to neutralize the threat?"

"With Meng, we have the crown jewels."

The President leaned back in his chair, still processing the turn of events. "So, what do the Chinese know about all of this?"

"From radio traffic intercepts, Langley is of the opinion that Beijing believes their naval forces destroyed the submersible with all aboard." Still astounded by the CIA briefing, Brindle continued the rundown. "Apparently, the PLAN actually deployed the Serpent system to attack the minisub."

"They must have been desperate."

"Indeed." The National Security Advisor retrieved his handwritten notes from his discussion with the Director of the Central Intelligence Agency. He spent the next ten minutes providing POTUS with a summary of the recent events in the South China Sea.

President Magnuson digested Brindle's report. He focused on the last revelation. "Sinking the submersible and blowing it up on the seabed, what a clever idea."

"It was. When the Chinese investigate, which they most certainly will, just as we would, they'll find the minisub obliterated on the bottom. That should provide the closure they'll need to believe they dodged a bullet."

"What about bodies?"

"That sphere imploding at three thousand feet would shred human tissue into fish food."

Magnuson sighed, relieved that he might not have to confront Beijing over the incident. President Chen Shen would have no proof to pursue a claim of espionage by the U.S. "Whose idea was it to blow up the submersible?" he asked.

"Our Russian asset, Yuri Kirov."

"Once again he saves our bacon."

"Definitely." That provided an opportunity for Brindle to address a loose end. "Sir, about the device the Chinese planted at the Russian sub base in Petropavlovsk-Kamchatskiy, the CIA believes that the timing might be right to . . ."

Chapter 81

Yuri Kirov and Jeff Chang had the *Colorado's* radio room to themselves. Commander Tom Bowman ordered the communications officer and the on-duty technician to vacate the compartment—perhaps the most secure section of the ship. Bowman's orders came directly from the White House, bypassing the normal chain of command. Jeff stood while Yuri sat at the satellite telephone console. It was 8:42 A.M. local time. They had been aboard the submarine for over seven hours. The ship hovered at periscope depth 164 nautical miles east of Sanya. The comms mast pierced the sea surface.

"Just give her the number," Jeff said. "She'll take care of it." Jeff wore a pair of headphones that were wired into the encrypted satphone circuit orchestrated by Langley. Steve Osberg directed Jeff to listen in on the call. A Russian speaking CIA officer in the Ops Center was linked in too. Her job was to place the call and interpret in real time for Chang and Osberg.

"Okay," Yuri said, "but I don't know if this is a working number anymore. He moves around a lot." Yuri checked the contact list on his personal cell phone. The recipient's name and number were listed under the company name of one of Northwest Subsea Dynamics' real clients. The individual's name was legitimate but the cell number wasn't. The subterfuge was designed to throw off the FBI if they decided to recheck Yuri's phone.

Yuri held the handset to his right ear. He provided the number and soon heard a ring tone. The ringing persisted. Yuri's forehead furrowed. He was about to hang up when he heard *"Allo"*—Hello in Russian.

"Hi Nick, it's Yuri." He also spoke in their native tongue.

Jeff Chang winked at Yuri, acknowledging the secure linkup.

"Where are you?" Nick Orlov asked.

"I'm in Alaska. You know, the oil spill project."

"Oh, yeah. How's that going?"

"Still a mess but better each day." Before Nick could probe the lie, Yuri said, "So where are you these days?"

"Vancouver."

"Permanent posting?"

"Not sure. But I'll be here at least for the next couple of months."

"That's great. Maybe we can come up to visit you—discreetly, of course."

"I'd like that."

"Nick, the reason I'm calling is that before heading north I came across some intel that really bothered me. It concerns payback from China for an op the Kremlin ordered."

"What?"

"The Chinese have planted some type of device on the bottom at the Rybachiy sub base."

"Petropavlovsk-Kamchatskiy?"

"Yes."

"What kind of device?"

"Possibly a nuke. Supposedly tit for tat for what happened at Qingdao."

"Qingdao—what do you mean?"

"The bomb. Moscow sanctioned it."

Nick cursed. "How'd you get this?"

"I can't reveal the source other than I judge it as highly reliable."

Nick processed Yuri's convoluted tale. "What else can you tell me?"

"I have coordinates. The bottom should be checked immediately to evaluate the threat."

"Coordinates! How could you—"

"Don't ask," interrupted Yuri. "I can't give you that information. You just need to take it on faith that I'm trying to watch out for the homeland. The threat is real. You're my only link to Russia now. I've burnt all of my other bridges."

"Read me the coordinates."

Yuri complied. He subsequently said, "Nick, whoever you report this call to, let 'em know that I offered this information as a goodwill measure. All I want is to be left alone."

"I will."

After a few departing remarks, Yuri ended the call. He looked up at Chang,

"Perfect," Jeff said.

* * * *

Nick set his cell phone on the desk. It was a few minutes before six o'clock. Most staff had already left. He stared at the window wall of his office—the same office that Elena had used. The landscaped park setting was still visible in the fading light.

Mesmerized by Yuri's call, Nick rehashed their conversation

What's he been doing?

One of Nick's principal assignments at the Vancouver Trade Mission was to assess the damage resulting from Yuri's rejection of the homeland. There was a price Yuri would have to pay to the USA for obtaining political amnesty; the Kremlin was desperate to know that cost.

Nick had failed to learn anything new about Yuri's interaction with the American government. He struck out with Laura Newman; she refused all of Nick's inquires. Even more troubling, deep cover SVR operatives in the Seattle area had not observed Yuri for several weeks.

He used a secure line! Nick thought.

Nick recognized the washed-out tone of Yuri's voice and the minuscule time delay in his responses, both indicators of a relayed encrypted circuit.

Yuri lied about Alaska.

Nick had dispatched an SVR officer to Alaska to check up on Northwest Subsea Dynamics's work on the oil spill cleanup operation. The agent was still in Barrow. Yuri was a no show.

We set off the bomb in Qingdao?

Yuri's revelation stunned Nick at first but as he considered what had transpired in recent months, it clicked for him.

It's our retribution!

Nick was aware of China's scheme to pit Russia against the USA. And now China was about to escalate its treachery.

How could Yuri know such a thing?

The warning about a bomb at the Petropavlovsk-Kamchatskiy sub base puzzled Nick and then a new thought materialized.

He must have been there!

The revelation snapped into focus.

Yuri's an underwater expert, operated out of Petro. That's it. The American's sent him to spy on Rybachiy and he found the Chinese bomb.

Nick checked his wristwatch and made the mental calculation for Moscow time.

He's going to be pissed but I have to act on this now.

Nick headed to the Trade Mission's code room.

* * * *

The director of the SVR was alone in the study of the lavish Kremlin apartment. It was 6:58 A.M. More than annoyed by Orlov's urgent telephone call three hours earlier, Borya Smirnov had reluctantly phoned the chief of staff, requesting an immediate audience. President Pyotr Lebedev was an early riser but not that early. The one-on-one was set for seven o'clock.

Despite the telephone security measures in place at the Kremlin, Smirnov wanted facetime with Lebedev. Other than the president and Smirnov, the details of the subject matter were known to less than a dozen scattered between the FSB and SVR, the Kremlin and the Ministry of Defense.

At first, Smirnov didn't believe Nick Orlov's report on Kirov's warning. But after making himself a cup of tea and sitting in the living room of his Moscow residence, he rehashed the events that started nearly two years earlier.

China sabotaged our oil well in the Chukchi Sea and destroyed the Sakhalin oil port, all while playing us off against the Americans.

Russia retaliated with the EMP attack on the Yulin Naval Base and escalated with the Qingdao bomb. Employing China's deception tactic, Russia left evidence blaming the USA for the China attacks. To further obscure matters, Russia set up Beijing as the fall guy for the Pearl Harbor nuke.

The bastards sank one of our subs, even murdering the men who had managed to escape.

The sinking of the *Novosibirsk* traumatized the Russian military. The Navy was clueless as to the technology China had used to destroy Russia's newest attack submarine.

And now they've gone too far...a nuclear weapon sitting on the bottom in Petropavlovsk-Kamchatskiy. If true, that cannot stand—will not stand.

The plan had been in the making for several months—the definitive solution to the China problem. The asset was already in place, standing by for the president's order.

It's time. That son of a bitch deserves it!

The door to the study opened and the President of the Russian Federation strolled in. He wore a bathrobe and was still dressed in pajamas. Slippers covered his feet.

"Well, Borya," President Lebedev said as he took the chair behind his desk, "what's so important for you to be here at this hour?"

"It's China, sir. More disturbing news."

Chapter 82

"Permission to enter?" Yuri Kirov asked.

The single occupant nursing a coffee mug looked up from the mess table. "Come on in."

Yuri entered the *Colorado's* Goat Locker. The compartment was reserved for chief petty officers only. Not even the captain could come in without requesting permission.

Yuri claimed a chair opposite the master chief. Yuri and Jeff Chang had been aboard the submarine for thirty-four hours. "You look a whole lot better than the last time I saw you."

"Thanks," Bill Halgren said. "Believe me, I feel a lot better, too."

Murphy and the other SEALs had already filled Yuri in on Wild Bill's condition. Once he started hyperbaric oxygen therapy, the infection subsided. A sterile dressing covered his forearm but the limb was no longer grossly swollen.

"Do you have much residual pain?"

"Some but I manage…don't need painkillers anymore, just ibuprofen."

"That's great news, Master Chief."

Yuri and Halgren spent the next few minutes catching up on the mission. SEAL team leader Lieutenant Commander Andrews had briefed Halgren and his teammates about Yuri and Jeff's exploits.

"Me and the boys are duly impressed with what you guys pulled off. A real coup!"

"We were lucky."

"No doubt, but hijacking that ship and using the minisub to get away in. That was ballsy as hell man. My cover's off to you."

"Thanks."

Halgren pumped Yuri for mission details, especially the encounter with the Viperinas. Eventually the discussion focused on Meng Park.

"I hear she's the brains behind Serpent," Halgren offered.

"That's my understanding, too."

"So, what's going to happen to her?"

"All I know is that Jeff's in the process of debriefing her right now."

The CIA officer was with Dr. Meng Park in the makeshift brig. Located aft of the Engine Room, the compartment was used for storage. Because of Meng's technical skills and her temperament, *Colorado's* CO ordered the brig guarded around the clock.

"What's she like?" Halgren asked.

"At first, she was mad as hell. But I think reality is starting to seep in." Yuri had sat in on Jeff's first interrogation session.

"Well, if she doesn't cooperate, they ought to send her to Gitmo. That place will change her attitude real quick."

"I suspect she already fears that possibility."

Halgren unconsciously ran his good hand over the bandage. "I hope she spills her guts. From the little I know about those snake things, we've got to figure out a way to get rid of them for good."

"I agree, Master Chief. Anyway, Jeff's got the next couple of days to convince her to see it our way."

"Good."

The *Colorado* was headed back to Yokosuka on orders from COMSUBPAC; transport of Dr. Meng and the Viperina hardware recovered from the *Lian* took priority.

The USS *Hawaii* sailed into the South China Sea the prior day. Provided with the Meng's acoustic signal to disable attacking Vipers, *Hawaii* was tasked with planting sea mines at the remaining Viper bottom stations in both the north and south basins of the SCS. When complete, a pair of P-8 Poseidons would discreetly drop disposable probes over each Viper station. The acoustic signal broadcast by the descending probes would trigger a countdown, leading to the simultaneous detonation of the mines at all Viper stations.

Chapter 83

Day 41—Monday

The machine emerged from the placid sea and silently scampered up the sandy beach slope. It was half past three in the morning on the northern shore of the Bohai Sea. About the size of a fat laptop computer and shaped similar to the shell of a leatherback sea turtle, the crawlerbot propelled itself with two sets of articulated legs, five on each side of its six-inch high hull.

An autonomous underwater vehicle delivered the crawlerbot to its launch point, a hundred yards offshore of the target beach. Two weeks earlier, a Russian freighter from Vladivostok had released the AUV prior to calling at the Nampo seaport on North Korea's western coast. The ship's cargo holds were filled with spare parts for Russian military equipment purchased by Pyongyang.

After transiting the Yellow Sea, the AUV had parked itself on the bottom of the Bohai Sea fifteen miles from the target. At midnight of each day, the robotic submersible would ascend to the surface, extend its radio antenna and listen for orders. Tonight, those orders came—issued from the Kremlin.

The crawlerbot crested the beach berm and stopped inside a patch of dune grass; it was a hundred feet from the water's edge. For the next minute, its electronic sensors probed the still night air for threats. Detecting none, its onboard GPS unit took a fix on the overhead constellation of Russian navigation satellites. Verifying it was within the specified limits of the objective's coordinates, the robotic amphibian commenced the next phase of its self-diagnostic testing program.

The watertight seal over the cargo compartment opened, the lid on its outer shell rotating upward. A microdrone emerged from the opening. About the size of a golf ball, the drone hovered several feet over the crawlerbot. Its whirling propellers scarcely generated a whisper. For the next minute, the autonomous aerial machine with its payload of death verified that its onboard systems were functional.

After completing the tests, the drone returned to its cradle. The cargo lid closed and the amphibian buried itself in the sand, using its legs to dig. Left behind on the surface was an acoustic monitor released from the hull; it mimicked a clump of dune grass. A wire connected the microphone to the crawlerbot's AI brain. During daylight hours, the computer would listen for a particular sound—the bark of a golden retriever.

Chapter 84

Day 43—Wednesday

Yuri Kirov was in the Alaska Airlines departure lounge at Honolulu International, sitting in a chair. It was late morning. He arrived at Joint Base Pearl-Hickam about two hours earlier aboard a C-17 Globemaster from Yokota Air Force Base. He could have delayed until the evening for another military flight bound for Joint Base Lewis-McChord in Washington State but punted instead.

Yuri splurged, paying a premium for an upgrade to a first-class seat aboard the Boeing 737. Absent for nearly three weeks, all he wanted was to get home ASAP.

The *Colorado* arrived at Yokosuka Naval Base 18 hours earlier. After a U.S. Navy helicopter flight to Yokota, Jeff Chang offered Yuri a seat aboard the CIA Gulfstream bound for Joint Base Andrews in Maryland. Yuri declined, deciding to take the C-17 flight.

Having observed several interview sessions conducted by Jeff, Yuri was done with Dr. Meng Park and Serpent. Jeff along with a cadre of CIA, FBI and U.S. Navy technical experts could continue the debriefing without Yuri's input.

Yuri pulled out his iPhone from a jacket pocket. He located the mobile number from his contact list—the same number he'd used while aboard the *Colorado*. He selected text mode and keyed in one word: NEVA. He fingered the send icon. "Delivered," appeared nearly instantaneously on the screen.

Yuri smiled as he thought about Nick Orlov's reaction when he followed the trail. Yuri's message was already in the draft folder of the Gmail account they shared.

It was the concluding element of Yuri's exit plan, one final concession to the homeland. The draft email contained the twenty-four digit passcode to the encrypted video file from Yuri's last spy mission for Russia—China's subterranean ballistic missile submarine base at Yulin.

Yuri checked the time: 11:31 A.M. He had planned to hold off until he landed at Sea-Tac International but he couldn't delay any longer. He hit the speed dial on his phone. Yuri called her cell, bypassing the receptionist.

Laura Newman answered on the third ring. "Yuri!" she called out, reacting to her iPhone's caller ID display.

"Hi sweetie."

"Are you okay?"

"I'm fine."

"Where are you?"

"Honolulu, about to board an Alaska Air jet for home."

Yuri expected a cheerful response but heard weeping instead. "What's wrong?"

"I've been so worried. It's been two weeks and not a word. I just knew they had you doing something dangerous."

"I'm sorry but it was impossible for me to contact you."

"I know, but everything we've been through...I couldn't help myself."

"I'm fine, honey. You can stop worrying."

"But they still have you under their thumb. What will they have you doing next?"

"I'm working all that out. It's going to be okay."

I don't know."

Yuri changed subjects. "How's Maddy?"

"Great, she's doing great. She's missed you, too."

"I can't wait to see her."

"When's your flight get in? We'll pick you up."

"Eight oh five. I'll just take Uber home."

"No way, we're coming!"

"Okay, that would be wonderful."

Laura said, "I do have some good news, about the company."

"What's that?"

"The merger looks like it's really going to happen. The closing is set for next Tuesday."

"Wow, that's terrific. I'm so happy for you." Yuri heard the boarding call for his flight over the gate intercom system. "It's time for me to board now. I want to hear all the details when I see you this evening."

"Okay. Have a safe flight. I love you."

"I love you."

Yuri picked up his overnight bag and walked toward the jetway, grateful to be heading home. All he wanted was to live a long boring and happy life with Laura and Maddy.

Yuri was done with his life as a spy but nothing yet had been settled with the FBI and CIA nor with Russia. And the China threat still loomed.

As Yuri settled into the luxurious leather seat in the first-class cabin of the Boeing, he shoved the negative thoughts into a corner of his brain. He removed his wallet from a pocket and stared at the snapshot of his lover and her child.

Yuri smiled. *It's going to be great to finally be home!*

ACKNOWLEDGMENTS

Thanks to Joe Scott for reviewing the manuscript. Joe's insights and suggestions are greatly appreciated.

I wish to express my continuing gratitude to Michaela Hamilton, executive editor at Kensington Books, for her expert advice and inspiration regarding the Yuri Kirov series. Michaela is a pleasure to work with.

Lastly, I'd like to thank my family, friends, and fans for continuing to encourage me with my writing career.

The Good Spy

Did you miss the first book in the Yuri Kirov thriller series? Not to worry! Here's a sample excerpt from *The Good Spy* to whet your appetite.

All the Yuri Kirov thrillers by Jeffrey Layton are available from Kensington Publishing Corp., www.kensingtonbooks.com.

Chapter 1

Kirov plowed into the gloom. The firestorm deep inside his right shoulder raged but he hung on. He'd lost all sensation below the left knee—it was just dead meat. If the unfeeling crept into his other limbs he was doomed for sure.

He focused on the captain's orders: "Get to shore. Call for help and then coordinate the rescue. Don't get caught!"

He was the crew's only hope. If he failed, they would all perish.

The diver propulsion vehicle surged against the aggressive tidal current. As he gripped the DPV's control handles with both gloved hands, his body trailed prone on the sea surface. Hours earlier he'd exhausted the mixed gas supply, which forced him topside where he used a snorkel to breathe.

The chilled seawater defeated his synthetic rubber armor. His teeth chattered against the snorkel's mouthpiece. He clamped his jaws to maintain the watertight seal.

Shore lights shimmered through his face mask but he remained miles from his destination. The DPV's battery gauge kissed the warning range. When it eventually petered out, he would have to transit the passage on his own, somehow swimming the expanse in the dark while combating the current.

Two grueling hours passed. He abandoned the spent DPV, opening the flood valve and allowing it to sink. He butted the tidal flow until it turned. The flooding current carried him northward.

He swam facedown while still breathing through the snorkel. As he pumped his lower limbs, his good leg overpowered its anesthetized twin, forcing him off course. He soon learned to compensate with his left arm, synchronizing its strokes with his right leg.

The joint pain expanded to include both shoulders and elbows. The frigid sea sapped his vigor to near exhaustion.

While staring downward into the pitch-black abyss, he tried not to dwell on his injuries or his weariness—or the absolute isolation, knowing he could do nothing to mitigate them. Instead, his thoughts converged on the mission. *They're counting on me. Don't give up. I can do this; just keep moving.*

He continued swimming, monitoring his course with the compass strapped to his right wrist. An evolving mantle of fog doused the shore lights he'd been using as a homing beacon. For all he knew, the current could be shoving him into deeper waters.

Maybe at dawn he would be able to get his bearings. Until then, he would plod along.

I wonder where the blackfish are now.

During a rest with fins down and a fresh bubble of air in his buoyancy compensator, he heard dozens of watery eruptions breach the night air as a pod of Orcinus orcas made its approach. Sounding like a chorus of steam engines, the mammals cleared blowholes and sucked air into their mammoth lungs. The sea beasts ghosted by at ten knots. Their slick coal-black hulls spotted with white smears passed just a few meters away from his stationary position.

The killer whales ignored him. They had a mission of their own: pursuing the plump inbound silver and chum salmon that loitered near the tip of the approaching peninsula. At first light, the orcas would gorge themselves.

There was no time to be afraid; instead, he marveled at the close encounter. Oddly, the whales' brief presence calmed him. He was not alone in these alien waters after all.

Time for another check.

He stopped kicking and raised his head. He peered forward.

Dammit!

Still no lights and the fog bank oozed even closer.

Where is it?

He allowed his legs to sink as he mulled his options. His right fin struck something.

He swam ahead for half a minute and repeated the sounding.

I made it!

Chapter 2

Laura Newman sat on the tile floor with her long chocolate legs bent sharply at the knees and her spine propped against a cabinet. She wore only a plain white T-shirt.

Laura cradled her abdomen with both hands; her stomach broiled. "Oh Lord," she moaned. "What's wrong with me?"

It was 6:18 A.M. Jolted awake, she'd just made it to the bathroom before the first purge.

Ten minutes elapsed. Feeling better, Laura stood and walked back into the bedroom. She slipped on a bathrobe. Knowing further sleep would be impossible, she decided to brew a cup of tea. If her stomach settled down, she'd jog along the beach after sunup.

This was the third morning her unsettled tummy had roused her. She suspected stress. The demands from work never ceased, but she'd learned to live with it.

Laura opened the bedroom door and walked down the second-floor hallway of the rented beach house. She flipped on a light switch, illuminating the stairway. When she reached the base of the stairs, her bare feet stepped into a pool of water that covered oak flooring. *What's this?* Laura wondered.

She took a few more steps on her way to the kitchen.

Laura stood opposite a doorway that opened onto a concrete walkway; it led to the beach. Although the side door remained closed, the door frame's splintered molding by the lock had not been that way when she went to bed.

Laura's muscles locked; her heart galloped.

Oh God, no! He's found me already.

Laura recovered enough to sidestep her dread. *I've got to get out of here.*

Laura was reaching for the side door's handle, when she heard movement from behind. She started to turn when a damp, gloved hand clutched her mouth. An arm ensnared her waist.

Laura shrieked but her muffled cries went nowhere.

Chapter 3

"Stop struggling or I'll cut you!"

Pinned by the intruder's bulk on the hardwood flooring, Laura complied when she felt the knife tip on her throat.

He sensed her capitulation and withdrew the blade. He rolled off Laura onto his knees but kept his eyes on her. He stood. The blade remained in his right hand.

"Get up," he ordered, offering his free hand as an assist.

* * * *

Sunlight poured through the waterside windows. Laura sat in the dining room chair, still wearing the bathrobe. Gray duct tape anchored her wrists and ankles to the chair. The intruder was in the adjoining living room. He'd just built a fire in the stone fireplace. The cedar kindling crackled to life.

Laura observed her captor. Standing at least an inch over six feet, he had a muscular build, slate-gray eyes, and dense jet-black hair cut short. His angular face sprouted several days' worth of black stubble. She guessed his age around her own—early thirties.

Laura watched as he shed the diving apparel. He piled the gear onto the hardwood floor next to a window. He wore cobalt-blue coveralls under his neoprene dry suit.

Obviously injured, he favored his left leg as he moved about. He hobbled into the dining room.

That's when Laura decided to confront him.

"What do you want?" she demanded.

"Just stay quiet."

"Who are you?"

"No one."

"Where did you come from?"

"Stop asking questions."

"Why were you in diving gear?"

* * * *

More tape secured a dishcloth he'd stuffed inside Laura's mouth. It encircled her head in two orbits, restraining her shoulder-length auburn hair. If she turned too far, hair at the nape of her neck pulled viciously. She had to sit statue-stiff, peering at a blank wall.

But she could still see him—out of the corner of her left eye.

Laura's captor was about twenty feet away on the sofa by the fireplace. After a thirty-minute catnap, he sat upright and stretched his arms. He picked up her smartphone from the coffee table. He must have discovered it on the nightstand in her bedroom. There were no other working telephones in the rental.

He keyed the phone, studying the screen. Laura guessed he was running a search. A couple of minutes later, he dialed.

"I'd like to speak with the security officer," he said.

There was a trace accent but Laura couldn't place it.

He was mute for a minute before responding, "Yes, I want to report an accident."

The call lasted ten minutes. None of what he said made any sense to Laura. Some doctor had been in an automobile accident and was in a Seattle hospital. And he'd asked for a "security officer." What was that about?

The intruder nodded off again, his head slumping forward.

What is this jerk up to?

* * * *

It was almost noon. Laura's spine ached and her limbs cramped, but her bladder demanded relief. She couldn't hold it much longer.

"Heyyyy!" she blurted in spite of the gag.

His eyes blinked open.

She called out again, louder.

He stood and shuffled toward her.

"What is it?" he asked. Now his accent sounded Eastern European. Laura mumbled.

He leaned forward and pulled down a section of tape covering her mouth.

She spat out the dishcloth and met his eyes. "Please—I need to use the bathroom." Her frail voice transmitted a palpable quaver.

"Bathroom?"

She gestured with her head, ripping half a dozen strands of hair anchored by tape.

He spotted the open door near the base of the stairs. "Oh, you need to use the toilet."

"Yes, please."

He replaced the gag and then limped to the bathroom. After inspecting its interior, he returned to Laura where he withdrew his dive knife from a scabbard lying on the nearby coffee table. He sliced the tape that anchored her arms and legs to the chair. She stood as quickly as her cramped muscles would allow.

With the knife still in his right hand he said, "You can use it but the door stays open. And don't touch the window."

Laura nodded her understanding and made a beeline for the bathroom. He followed.

She walked inside, immune to the embarrassment. Laura was thankful to be alive.

Chapter 4

"Aloha," he said, speaking into the cell phone. "I'd like Laura Newman's room.

"That's right, Laura Newman. From Redmond . . . Washington State.

"Hmm, she's not registered . . . you know, she might be using her maiden name, Laura Lynn Wilson. Could you check that for me?"

Half a minute passed. "No luck there, either. Well, I guess I got some bum info. Thanks."

Ken Newman had already called fourteen hotel and condominium resorts on Kauai, and as on his last call, he'd failed. There were nearly twenty more to go.

He'd searched the Web for an hour, compiling a list of candidates. He concentrated on four- and five-star establishments; he knew his wife's preferences. He would check the remaining resorts but didn't expect the effort to yield anything.

Ken called from his Spartan studio apartment in Bellevue, sitting at the kitchen table. Dirty dishes overfilled the sink, sports magazines and newspapers littered the coffee table, and a two-foot-high pile of soiled clothing occupied a corner by the window. They'd been living apart for four months. The previous morning a King County sheriff's deputy had served him with the breakup papers and a temporary restraining order.

But Ken wasn't done.

Laura had changed cell phones so he'd called her secretary this morning, ignoring the no contact order. Ken learned that Laura had flown to Kauai for a two-week vacation. He had no reason to doubt the secretary's storyline but remained suspicious.

Ken retrieved a coffee mug from the table. As he sipped, he planned.

Tonight he would drive to Sea-Tac and cruise the huge parking garage's aisles. If Laura had parked her silver BMW 7 Series at the airport, he'd know that she'd fled. If he didn't find it, she might still be around.

* * * *

"Why are you doing this to me?" Laura asked.

"Just cooperate and you'll be fine."

Laura again sat in the dining room chair, her wrists and ankles re-taped to the chair's mahogany armrests and legs. An eight-place black marble table occupied the room. The view of the beach and the water's edge—just steps away—was dazzling.

Sweat beaded across Laura's brow. Her captor stood at her side, a half-full water glass in hand. She leaned forward and took another gulp, draining the glass.

Her thirst satisfied, she said, "Thank you."

He was about to reseal her mouth when Laura turned her head to the side. "Please, don't gag me. My stomach's bothering me; I might vomit."

"All right, for now I won't but keep quiet. I need to rest."

"I will—I promise."

Laura watched as he made his way back to the connecting living room; his limp had worsened. He lay down on the sofa facing the fireplace. Searing heat radiated from the fresh charge of fuel.

He'd turned up the home's gas furnace to maximum, too, roasting Laura. *What's wrong with him?*

* * * *

He hobbled onto the timber deck, dragging his useless lower left leg. The mid-afternoon sky was cloudless, allowing the sun to bathe his body; it had been weeks since he'd last felt its touch.

Water lapped at the rock revetment fronting the home. In the distance, a mammoth ship steamed northward, its decks overflowing with hundreds of shipping containers.

Although no longer chilled to his marrow, he remained unpleasantly cool. A wool blanket from a bedroom encased his shoulders and upper torso. He also shed the jumpsuit, replacing it with the civilian clothing he'd carried during the ascent. The waterproof bag leaked, soaking the blue jeans, black long sleeve shirt, running shoes, and other gear. He discovered the home's laundry room, where he washed and dried the garments.

He unconsciously shook his head, still amazed that he had survived. It could have been much worse. The bends could have just as easily killed him, or he could have succumbed to hypothermia.

Why had God spared him?

His mother had sparked his early belief, but her guidance ceased after his twelfth birthday and his faith withered. Nevertheless, his impermeable armor of disregard now had a couple of chinks in it. Surviving the sinking came first. His solo escape followed.

He again wondered why he was alive when so many others were not.

His thoughts dissolved as something caught his eye far in the distance. The floatplane cruised northward up the inland sea, about two hundred meters above the water. He couldn't help but think that it probably passed right over the *Neva*.

* * * *

Seven nautical miles to the southeast and over seven hundred feet below the surface, the Neva's crew was oblivious to the Kenmore Air charter. The beat of the Beaver's propeller penetrated the water but never reached the stranded submarine.

Underwater sounds rarely travel in a straight line. Instead, they refract or bend due to varying temperature, salinity, and pressure. On this afternoon, the only sounds that the *Neva's* passive sonar sensors registered were biologics.

The thirty-four-year-old slightly balding and fleshy engineering officer left the central command post and entered the sonar room. Catapulted to acting-captain status nearly forty hours earlier, he hoped for good news.

"Anything new?" he asked the sole inhabitant of the compartment. Packed with electronic gear from the deck to the overhead, the space contained three consoles.

"No, Captain," said the technician, a man in his early twenties sitting in the center console.

They spoke in their native tongue—Russian.

The tech removed his earphones and flipped a switch on his console, activating a bulkhead speaker. The sound of bacon sizzling on a grill broadcast throughout the compartment. "Still the same biologic we've had all day long—fornicating shrimp."

"Anything else?"

"I did pick up a ship's propeller. Merchantmen most likely headed to Vancouver."

"How about small vessels?"

"No, sir, nothing like that. In our degraded condition, they would need to be close by for our remaining sensors to register."

The commanding officer nodded. He'd anticipated something more encouraging. The diver should have made it to the shore by now. Still, it was early.

"Captain, how's the scrubber repair going?"

"It's working again. CO-two is stabilized."

"Good . . . that's good." The sonar tech scratched the stubble on his chin. "And the reactors?"

"We're still bailing out muck. We might be able to test a heat exchanger in a few hours. Once circulation is reestablished, we should be able to restart Unit Two."

"That will help a lot."

"Yes, it will."

Neither man wanted to ask the ultimate "what if" question: What if they couldn't restart the reactor?

Programmed to prevent a core meltdown, the computer controlling the reactor would automatically squash the chain reaction if the coolant system were not adequate. Without the heat generated by the fission process, there would be no steam. Without steam, the generator would not turn. Without the generator, there would be no electrical current to run the ship's oxygen maker. And without fresh oxygen, they would all die.

About the Author

Photo by Michael D. McCarter

Jeffrey Layton launched his Yuri Kirov spy thriller series with *The Good Spy* and continued it with *The Forever Spy*, and *The Faithful Spy*. He is also the author of the acclaimed novels *Vortex One*, *Warhead*, and *Blowout*. Jeff is a professional engineer who specializes in coastal engineering. He uses his knowledge of diving, yachting, offshore engineering, and underwater warfare in the novels he writes. He lives in the Pacific Northwest.

Please visit him at www.jeffreylayton.com.

ed in the United States
aker & Taylor Publisher Services

Prin
by B